# REVOLUTIONARY TALES

African American Women's Short Stories,
from the First Story to the Present

### Edited by Bill Mullen

A LAUREL BOOK

Published by
Dell Publishing
a division of
Bantam Doubleday Dell Publishing Group, Inc.
1540 Broadway
New York, New York 10036

Copyright © 1995 by Bill Mullen

ISBN: 0-440-22082-3

Printed in the United States of America

Published simultaneously in Canada

December 1995

10 9 8 7 6 5 4 3 2 1

OPM

# GREAT STORIES, GREAT WRITERS—
# A NATIONAL TREASURE TOO LONG
# IGNORED . . .

### "Emmy" (1913–1914) by Jessie Fauset
An editor of the NAACP magazine *The Crisis,* which helped make short story writing by African American women a crucial element of the Harlem Renaissance, Jessie Fauset herself created this moving tale of interracial relationships and the psychological effects of "passing."

### "The Typewriter" (1926) by Dorothy West
In a story now seventy years old, the author of the highly acclaimed 1995 novel *The Wedding,* and the last surviving member of the Harlem Renaissance, portrays with her incandescent realism economic hardship, a city apartment, and the brief rekindling of a man's lost dreams.

### "Has Anyone Seen Miss Dora Dean?" (1958)
### by Ann Petry
From the most famous African American female fiction writer of the mid-twentieth century, this haunting story from the pages of *The New Yorker* about the mysterious suicide of a dapper middle-aged servant must still be recognized for what it is—a complex and witty masterpiece of American literature.

### "Ma'Dear" (1987) by Terry McMillan
The storytelling talents of this popular writer extend far beyond her bestselling novels like *Waiting to Exhale,* as seen in this vivid portrait of an elderly woman who refuses to give in to the blues—or government rules and regulations —all told in McMillan's wonderfully humorous voice.

### . . . AND OVER THREE DOZEN MORE

# PERMISSIONS

The following stories are in the public domain:

"Drenched in Light." First published in *Opportunity* (1924). Reprinted in *Spunk*.

"Mrs. Adis." Sheila Kaye-Smith. First published in *The Century Magazine,* vol. 103, no. 3 (Jan. 1922).

"Sanctuary." Nella Larsen. First published in *Forum* 83 (Jan. 1930). Reprinted in Kanwar, Knopf, and Hamer.

"All That Hair." Melissa Linn. First published in *Negro Story* (Apr.–May 1946).

"Aunt Lindy: A Story Founded on Real Life." Victoria Earle Matthews. First published in *Aunt Lindy: A Story Founded on Real Life.* New York: J.J. Little & Co., 1893. Reprinted in Kanwar and Hamer.

"The Taming of a Modern Shrew." Ruth D. Todd. First published in *Colored American Magazine* 7 (Mar. 1904). Reprinted in Ammons.

"Justice Wears Dark Glasses." Grace Tompkins. First published in *Negro Story* (July–Aug. 1944).

"The Typewriter." Dorothy West. First published in *Opportunity* (July 1926). Reprinted in Kanwar and Knopf.

To John and Lynn Mullen
and
In Memory of Lucille Wetmore,
Mina Mullen

Storytellers

# ACKNOWLEDGMENTS

Several people have helped in the preparation of this book. Robert Jakubovic, Theresa Hewitt, Nicholas Veauthier, and David Mularchik have all provided valuable research assistance. The staff at the Schomburg Center for Research in Black Culture was helpful one September tracking down and copying materials for publication in this book. Rane Arroyo, Sherry Linkon, and Liz Petrasovic have offered valuable insight on the introduction. The editor also thanks the Youngstown State University Research Council, and Barbara Brothers, for supporting this book. Elizabeth Kaplan has been an ardent supporter of this project from the start. Trish Todd's editorial guidance and support has been generous. Cherise Davis has helped bring this project to fruition.

# Contents

# A NOTE ON THE TEXT

These stories have been chosen to represent the diversity of African American lives within American history. Their chronological arrangement is meant to reveal both the development and change of those lives over time, and the maturation and success of black women writers in that time. They are not presented as the "best" short stories by black women. Instead, they represent the widest possible range of styles, experiences, moods, and subjects that black women's short story writing yields.

The headnotes to the stories are signposts for readers as they enter into the stories. They tell where the stories come from and provide food for thought.

Biographical notes on each author are provided at the end of the book. These may be especially useful to readers new to black women's writing. They also provide information on writers unfortunately lost to popular history. These lives, like the stories they tell, need to be more fully recovered.

The bibliography at the end of the text is divided into primary materials (short story collections and anthologies by African Americans) and secondary materials (critical or historical writings by black men and women). It is partial, suggesting only some of the most noteworthy and interesting titles. Readers are encouraged to continue exploration through and beyond these suggested readings.

What's the fate of a black story in a white world of white stories?

—John Edgar Wideman

# INTRODUCTION

You may paint her in poetry or fiction as a frail vine,
clinging to her brother man for support and dying when
deprived of it, and all this may sound well enough to
please the imaginations of schoolgirls, or lovelorn
maidens. But woman—the true woman—if you would
render her happy, it needs more than the mere development of her affectional nature.

Frances Ellen Watkins Harper
"The Two Offers" (1859)

You see, we were putting out a magazine called *Love
Black*. It was a group thing, you know, but it really belonged to all the people. We had learned the secret of
why the folks don't read. C'mon, see do you know? You
jive, they can too read. But nobody ever writes for them
or writes anything they can relate to.

Nikki Giovanni
"A Revolutionary Tale" (1970)

Narrative is radical, creating us at the very moment it is
being created.

Toni Morrison
*The Nobel Lecture in Literature,* 1994

Storytelling is the seed of culture. "Once upon a time," says
Toni Morrison, is the oldest sentence in the world.[1] For
African Americans, storytelling is something even more.
African American folk culture, John Edgar Wideman has
written, "preserves and expresses an identity, a history, a
self-evaluation apart from those destructive, incarcerating
images proliferated by the mainline culture."[2] For African
American women in particular, storytelling is what Paule
Marshall has called metaphorically the "kitchen" of every-
day experience. The stories that black mothers tell black

daughters, black daughters tell black sisters, and black sisters tell black friends are improvised moments of sorority and community in a world otherwise without tongues or ears for black women's experience. In 1937 the writer and anthropologist Zora Neale Hurston captured the opportunity in this unique dilemma for black women in her novel *Their Eyes Were Watching God*. Janie Starks, Hurston's protagonist, shares the most intimate details of her life with her friend Phoeby, granting her the right to pass her story on to others. "You can tell 'em what Ah say if you wants to," says Janie. "Dats just de same as me 'cause mah tongue is in mah friend's mouf." Or as Alice Walker, Hurston's spiritual and literary heir, describes this storytelling friend: "She is the woman you trust with your story *as it is happening to you;* she is the woman from whom you hide nothing. She is on your side."[3]

This anthology of short stories by African American women is first and foremost a tribute to black women writers who for centuries have survived in America by telling, listening, and staying "on each other's side." It is also indirectly a tribute to the *real* lives of the black women, and black men, who have inspired their stories. Frequently overlooked and forgotten in the recent rush to acclaim black women's writing is the complex relationship between that writing, its deep historical roots, and the diversity of lives within the African American experience that, more than three centuries after its inception, refuses easy categorization or description.

Indeed, as the epigraphs to this introduction suggest, African American women's storytelling and short story writing have taken place in as many different times, places, and voices as have African American lives. Frances Ellen Watkins Harper, born to free parents in Baltimore in 1825, never suffered slavery but devoted much of her life to abolitionism and the Underground Railroad that carried slaves north to freedom. Her 1859 story "The Two Offers," the first ever published by an African American writer, describes the plight of a white woman who virtuously forgoes marriage to devote her life to the abolition of slavery. Her desire to cross racial lines and deny social convention is also a desire to escape the restrictive power of the "cult of true womanhood" that idealized white females in Victorian America, while marginalizing or erasing from public view—even within Harper's own short story—black women conscripted into slavery. Harper's simple story is thus a subversive parable of gender and race in antebellum America. Like so much African American writing, the story "signifies" on or challenges accepted cultural truths, subtly revealing how much black women have to tell us about the capacity of storytelling to, in Morrison's words, "create" images of self.

Hence the title of this collection, *Revolutionary Tales,* evokes the long, empowering tradition of storytelling and short story writing by black women. It refers to the tasks of self and cultural production that the literary critic Hortense Spillers has identified as essential for black women writers, whose "symbol-making" is done against and out of a history of racism, sexism, and class oppression that would seem to make this task impossible.[4] Like the quilt at the center of Alice Walker's most famous short story, "Everyday Use," the title also suggests a patchwork weave of many threads. These threads are represented by the 42 stories, 36 writers, and almost 150 years of history embedded in these pages. Yet to understand the full beauty and intricacy of any patchwork, it is necessary first to unravel its history, to trace its threads to their beginnings.

Black women's writing in America has taken place in the face of a calculated conspiracy to silence their voices. Phillis Wheatley, who was the first African American to have a book published, composed her poems by the rare fortune of an employer who broke the convention of keeping slaves illiterate and tutored her in reading and writing. Mastering English in four years, Wheatley published *Poems on Various Subjects, Religious and Moral* in 1773, destroying an official censorship of black lives upon which slavery's systematic barbarism depended. Ironically, not only slavery but the debate between proslavery and abolitionist forces in nineteenth-century America both made possible and seriously restricted the realm in which African Americans could write. Black authors were encouraged only to write autobiographies or "slave narratives," which were in turn often published and promoted by white abolitionists. In 1850, for example, the black female abolitionist and feminist Sojourner Truth published her ghostwritten autobiography, *Narrative of Sojourner Truth, Northern Slave, Emancipated from Bodily Servitude by the State of New York, in 1828.* The book presented the life of its illiterate subject as a case study in support of abolishing slavery, complementing the publication of similar better-known works by African American male slaves like Frederick Douglass.

These slave narratives became the most typical and nearly exclusive vehicle by which black Americans could write themselves into American literature and culture. White dominance of commercial and literary markets, magazines, and journals restricted opportunities for black poets, short story writers, and essayists. With the exception of Harper, history records *no publication* of short stories by black women before 1895, a period during which the short story genre was the common province of well-known white male writers like Mark Twain and lesser-known white women like Sarah Orne Jewett, Kate Chopin, and Rebecca Harding Davis.

Yet the post–Civil War era did represent an advance in the fortunes of African American writers. With emancipation came more opportunities for education, and for the privileged few a newfound power to speak. In 1892, Anna Julia Haywood Cooper, the daughter of a North Carolina slave and graduate of Oberlin College, published the essay collection *A Voice from the South: By a Black Woman of the South.* The book included the essay "The Higher Education of Women," a plea for black and white women to enroll in school. Cooper also shocked readers by calling herself a "black woman" in an era when the term *Negro* was in vogue.[5] Cooper's openly feminist, antiracist stance arguably launched a revolution in language and self-definition for black women. The popular press compared her to the English novelist George Eliot, and along with Frances Ellen Watkins Harper she became a leading lecturer on black women's civil rights. In 1899 Cooper shared the rostrum of the historic Pan-African Conference in London with W.E.B. Du Bois, the most powerful black male spokesperson for black civil and social rights in the world.[6] A black female literary star had been born.

By the turn of the century, the works of Sojourner Truth, Cooper, Du Bois, Harper, Douglass, and others had underscored the need for African American men and women to define in writing the circumstances of their own lives. Not coincidentally, this period saw the beginning of official recognition of black women's short story writing and publishing. As Henry Louis Gates, Jr., has noted, more works of fiction by black women were published between 1890 and 1910 than black men had published in a previous half-century.[7] Perhaps most important among them was Alice Dunbar-Nelson, wife of the poet Paul Laurence Dunbar, who in 1895 published under her birth name *Violets and Other Tales,* a collection of sketches, poems, and stories. Four years later the successful commercial publisher Dodd, Mead and Company published Dunbar-Nelson's *The Goodness of St. Rocque,* the first collection of short stories by a black woman.

Publication of Dunbar-Nelson's work by a successful commercial press opened a literal and figurative door through which African American women's writing and storytelling could now pass. Short story writing, more than any other genre, depends upon control of and access to the literary marketplace. Dunbar-Nelson's success made clear the need for black women to enter that marketplace as writers, editors, and owners of their own work. These complex tasks were first realized by Pauline Hopkins, whose career nearly single-handedly ushered in the modern revolution in black women's publishing and short story writing. In 1900 Hopkins published her novel *Contending Forces—A Romance Illustrative of Negro Life North and South* with the small Colored Co-operative Publishing Company of Boston, in which Hopkins was a shareholder.

In the same year the Co-operative brought forth the monthly illustrated *Colored American Magazine,* whose premier issue featured Hopkins's first short story "The Mystery Within Us." In 1903, Hopkins became literary editor of the magazine and began a crusade to discover and publish short fiction, journalism, and essays by black women. Both Frances Ellen Watkins Harper and Angelina Weld Grimké, whose stories are included in this collection, appeared in *Colored American* along with many other unheralded black women.

In 1910, partly inspired by the success of *Colored American Magazine,* Du Bois, founder and leader of the new National Association for the Advancement of Colored People, established the NAACP magazine *The Crisis.* Continuing the practice begun by Hopkins, *Crisis* published black women in unprecedented numbers. One of the first was the brilliant young writer Jessie Redmon Fauset, a graduate of Cornell whose short fiction and "Looking Glass" column appeared regularly in the magazine in its early years. In 1919, Fauset resigned her position as a high school teacher to become the literary editor of *The Crisis.* She immediately inaugurated a short story contest, which helped fuel competition with the other leading black journal of the day, Charles S. Johnson's *Opportunity,* published by the National Urban League. During the 1920s, *The Crisis* and *Opportunity* made short story writing by black women a crucial aspect of the Harlem Renaissance and in turn launched the careers of some of the most important writers of the twentieth century. Zora Neale Hurston, Dorothy West, and Gwendolyn Bennett, all featured in this collection, now took up short story writing in part as a way of capitalizing on the sudden flourishing of a black literary marketplace. Revolutionary in form and intent, the stories began to peel away the stereotypes of black women as matrons, slaves, and slatterns that slavery and the post-Reconstruction era had fostered in an effort to stigmatize black women in the minds of white Americans. This overtly feminist goal made the stories worthy of the avant-garde aims of literary Harlem, black America's new bohemia and intellectual capital.

The Harlem Renaissance symbolized not just a flowering of black arts but a move toward wide variation and autonomy in black women's writing and publishing. Between 1920 and 1935 small black magazines around the country appeared to spread the Renaissance nationwide. Inspired by the literary success of magazines like *The Crisis,* black newspapers like the *Baltimore Afro-American* began publishing short stories by black male and female writers. By the 1930s, success in the short story genre by Fauset, Hurston, and West encouraged young women writers like Marion Cuthbert, Octavia Wynbush, and Hazel Campbell to write and publish stories documenting the response of African Americans to the pressing issues of their day: rapes, lynchings, urban riots, and the Depression. The short story had become not just an acceptable genre in which black women writers could advance their literary careers but a vehicle for social protest and the demand for self-definition.

This growing revolution climaxed during World War II, when Chicago short story writers Alice C. Browning and Fern Gayden launched the first-ever magazine devoted to short story writing by or about African Americans. Between 1944 and 1946 *Negro Story Magazine* published dozens of stories by professional and novice black writers emphasizing the plight of black lives during wartime. These included tales about the newly created black WACs (Women's Army Corps) and about black women thrust into the workplace due to the "manpower" shortage at home. These wartime black writers, literary Rosie the Riveters, included two unheralded women featured in this anthology: Grace Tompkins and Melissa Linn. And though their magazine lasted but two years, Gayden and Browning's leadership of *Negro Story* and their eagerness to publish new black women writers foretold the dazzling chorus of black women's voices in short story writing that emerged in the postwar period.

How many African American stories have you ever seen in *The New Yorker? The Atlantic Monthly? Grand*

*Street*? *Q*? *Redbook*? And even many of the prestigious
literary quarterlies?

Terry McMillan[8]

African American literature since World War II has enjoyed a critical and popular renaissance reflective of the
hardwon cultural and political advances initiated by black
religious, intellectual, and political leaders. African American women writers have been at the forefront of this literary renaissance, and the short story might be called its hub.
Well before the astounding critical and commercial success
of novels like Alice Walker's *The Color Purple,* Toni Morrison's *Beloved,* and Terry McMillan's *Mama,* contemporary
black women writers were experimenting and succeeding in
the short story form. In fact, virtually all of the black
women writers well-known for their novels, poetry, and
plays today began their careers or enjoyed early success as
short story writers. Ann Petry, best known to most for her
novel *The Street,* first gained critical acclaim for her 1945
short story "Like a Winding Sheet," a powerful tale about a
black couple's wartime struggle. Petry's contemporary Alice Childress, though better known for her novel for ado-
lescents *A Hero Ain't Nothing But a Sandwich,* also broke
new ground in black women's short story writing in her
1956 book *Like One of the Family: Conversations from a
Domestic's Life,* a pointed series of vignettes showcasing
the distinctive voice of an unsinkably shrewd black domestic.

Together, Petry and Childress kindled the flame that became a black fire in the world of black women's short story
writing after 1960. Inspired in part by the Black Arts Movement of the 1960s, which wedded many black artists to the
civil rights and black nationalist movements, black women
exploded onto the short fiction scene as correspondents for
a black *women's* revolution. Toni Cade Bambara, Alice
Walker, Gayl Jones, Paule Marshall, Ann Allen Shockley,
Julia Fields, Anita Cornwell, Diane Oliver, and Nikki Giovanni all published their first important short stories during
the decade. Their work began to appear in magazines and

journals carrying the message of black struggle across America: *Ebony, Callaloo, Negro Digest,* and others. Much more than during the Harlem Renaissance, black women writers were now reaching and creating a new class of readers, writers, and intellectuals eager to refute years of stereotypical representation of black women. Their stories sought to counter the tendency of white American magazines to publish minority stories that, in John Edgar Wideman's words, "appear at best as exotic slices of life and local color, at worst as ghettoized irrelevancies."[9] Black women storytellers of the 1960s replaced images of themselves as maternal, domesticated, sexually promiscuous, and helpless with empowering portraits of black women as warriors in the struggle for racial and sexual emancipation. While Aretha Franklin demanded "Respect" for black women, Alice Walker began to warn readers that *You Can't Keep a Good Woman Down.* Literary Rosie the Riveters had become pen-wielding Rosa Parkses. Post–civil rights era writers imagined black women struggling against school desegregation, neighborhood harassment, and institutional racism, while exposing black men and white men as frequent oppressors often unconscious of their own sexism, racism, and hypocrisy.

By the early 1970s, these incendiary stories were gathered into collections published by a white-dominated literary culture jolted by the Black Arts and black nationalist movements into long-overdue recognition of black writing. Ironically, the crossover signaled what black women writers had long known: that their revolution was now official. Toni Cade Bambara's *Black Women: An Anthology* (1970) and her own short story collection *Gorilla, My Love* (1972); Alice Walker's *In Love & Trouble* (1973); Gayl Jones's *White Rat* (1977), coupled with the publication of Toni Morrison's novel *The Bluest Eye* (1970) and the works of Maya Angelou, marked the 1970s as the decade of the popular emergence of black women writers.

By the 1980s, this emergence had deepened and broadened to include an astonishing diversity within black women's short story writing. Crucial to this was the emergence of writing by or about black lesbians. Following the lead of the pioneering Anita Cornwell, black women writers began to affirm their own sexual difference and to challenge the norms of heterosexual literary culture. Important to this second-wave revolution was Ann Allen Shockley's 1980 short story collection *The Black and White of It,* from which comes "Play It, But Don't Say It" in this anthology, a dramatic story of a black political candidate's struggle to "pass" sexually. In 1983 Becky Birtha's *For Nights Like This One: Stories of Loving Women* produced the short story "Babies" (included here), a sensitive exploration of a lesbian couple's contemplation of childbearing. These works, published by small independent publishers like Florida's Naiad Press and San Francisco's Frog in the Well, marked yet another successful step in the revolutionary tale of black women's storytelling. Culminating the sexual and political diversity in black women's writing fostered by small journals like *Azaleas* and *Salsa Soul Gayzette,* the independent Kitchen Table Press, a black women's cooperative, brought forth its landmark *Home Girls: A Black Feminist Anthology* (1983), presenting fiction, essays, and poetry by black feminists, womynists, womanists, and lesbian writers. Now more than ever, sisters were doing it for themselves.

Recent years have seen an even more marked accelerataion in the quality, diversity, and acceptance of black women's short story writing. In the last decade U.S. Poet Laureate Rita Dove, experimental California writer Wanda Coleman, groundbreaking bestseller Terry McMillan, and the inventive Colleen McElroy have brought forward new collections of short stories or anthologies of black fiction representing the best of black women's short story writing. Maxine Clair's dazzling collection *Rattlebone* (1994), from which this anthology's "The Last Day of School" is taken, is only the most recent sign that black women's short story writing is still going strong. The short story has in fact moved from back burner to center stage in the literary revolution of black women's writing, keeping the flame of Frances Ellen Watkins Harper, Pauline Hopkins, and Zora Neale Hurston—the genre's pioneers—very much alive. Indeed in her landmark essay collection *In Search of Our Mothers' Gardens,* Alice Walker describes the task of the black woman writer as the constant turning over of literary soil broken years before by black women at work in the everyday fields of self-exploration and creativity, themselves tilling their own "mothers' gardens." Those gardens have for some 150 years now produced exquisite riches, a handful of which are on display here for those sensitive to the color purple and other hues.

## Notes

1. Toni Morrison, *The Nobel Lecture in Literature* (New York: Alfred A. Knopf, 1994), p. 7.

2. Preface to *Breaking Ice: An Anthology of African American Fiction,* ed. Terry McMillan (New York: Penguin, 1990), p. vi.

3. Foreword to J. California Cooper, *A Piece of Mine* (Navarro, CA: Wild Trees Press, 1984), p. viii.

4. As quoted in Henry Louis Gates, Jr.'s, foreword to *The Works of Alice Dunbar-Nelson,* vol. 1, ed. Gloria T. Hull (New York: Oxford University Press, 1988), p. xi.

5. Ann Allen Shockley, *Afro-American Women Writers 1746–1933: An Anthology and Critical Guide.* (Boston: G.K. Hall & Co., 1988), p. 206.

6. *Ibid.,* p. 207.

7. See Hull, foreword, p. xvi.

8. As quoted in McMillan, *Breaking Ice,* p. xxii.

9. *Ibid.,* p. vi.

# The Two Offers

### FRANCES ELLEN WATKINS HARPER

The first short story published by an African American writer, "The Two Offers" originally appeared in the short-lived *Anglo-African Magazine* in 1859. The story combines several nineteenth-century themes in American and African American women's writing, juxtaposing the fate of a woman of means fallen into the "cult of true womanhood" with that of another of modest origins who eschews marriage and social convention to devote her life to social justice. Though on its surface sentimental and affected by Victorian-style purple prose, the story ironically encodes a feminist and antiracist message typical of the work of this groundbreaking journalist and author.

"WHAT IS THE MATTER with you, Laura, this morning? I have been watching you this hour, and in that time you have commenced a half-dozen letters and torn them all up. What matter of such grave moment is puzzling your dear little head, that you do not know how to decide?"

"Well, it is an important matter; I have two offers for marriage, and I do not know which to choose.

"I should accept neither, or to say the least, not at present."

"Why not?"

"Because I think a woman who is undecided between two offers has not love enough for either to make a choice; and in that very hesitation, indecision, she has a reason to pause and seriously reflect, lest her marriage, instead of being an affinity of souls or a union of hearts, should only be a mere matter of bargain and sale, or an affair of convenience and selfish interest."

"But I consider them both very good offers, just such as many a girl would gladly receive. But to tell you the truth, I do not think that I regard either as a woman should the man she chooses for her husband. But then if I refuse, there is the risk of being an old maid, and that is not to be thought of."

"Well, suppose there is? Is that the most dreadful fate that can befall a woman? Is there not more intense wretchedness in an ill-assorted marriage, more utter loneliness in a loveless home, than in the lot of the old maid who accepts her earthly mission as a gift from God and strives to walk the path of life with earnest and unfaltering steps?"

"Oh! what a little preacher you are. I really believe that you were cut out for an old maid—that when nature formed you, she put in a double portion of intellect to make up for a deficiency of love; and yet you are kind and affectionate. But I do not think that you know anything of the grand, overmastering passion, or the deep necessity of woman's heart for loving."

"Do you think so?" resumed the first speaker, and bending over her work, she quietly applied herself to the knitting that had lain neglected by her side during this brief conversation. But as she did so, a shadow flitted over her pale and intellectual brow, a mist gathered in her eyes, and a slight quivering of the lips revealed a depth of feeling to which her companion was a stranger.

But before I proceed with my story, let me give you a slight history of the speakers. They were cousins who had met life under different auspices. Laura Lagrange was the only daughter of rich and indulgent parents who had spared no pains to make her an accomplished lady. Her cousin, Janette Alston, was the child of parents rich only in goodness and affection. Her father had been unfortunate in business and, dying before he could retrieve his fortunes, left his business in an embarrassed state. His widow was unacquainted with his business affairs, and when the estate was settled, hungry creditors had brought their claims, and the lawyers had received their fees, she found herself homeless and almost penniless, and she, who had been sheltered in the warm clasp of loving arms, found them too powerless to shield her from the pitiless pelting storms of adversity. Year after year she struggled with poverty and wrestled with want, till her toilworn hands became too feeble to hold the shattered chords of existence, and her tear-dimmed eyes grew heavy with the slumber of death.

Her daughter had watched over her with untiring devotion, had closed her eyes in death and gone out into the busy, restless world, missing a precious tone from the voices of earth, a beloved step from the paths of life. Too self-reliant to depend on the charity of relations, she endeavored to support herself by her own exertions, and she had succeeded. Her path for a while was marked with struggle and trial, but instead of uselessly repining, she met them bravely, and her life became a thing not of ease and indulgence, but of conquest, victory, and accomplishments.

At the time when this conversation took place, the deep trials of her life had passed away. The achievements of her genius had won her a position in the literary world, where she shone as one of its bright particular stars. And with her fame came a competence of worldly means, which gave her leisure for improvement and the riper development of her rare talents. And she, that pale intellectual woman, whose genius gave life and vivacity to the social circle and whose presence threw a halo of beauty and grace around the charmed atmosphere in which she moved, had at one period of her life known the mystic and solemn strength of an all-absorbing love. Years faded into the misty past had seen the kindling of her eye, the quick flushing of her cheek, and the wild throbbing of her heart at tones of a voice long since hushed to the stillness of death. Deeply, wildly, passionately, she had loved. . . . This love quickened her talents, inspired her genius, and threw over her life a tender and spiritual earnestness.

And then came a fearful shock, a mournful waking from that "dream of beauty and delight." A shadow fell around her path; it came between her and the object of her heart's worship. First a few cold words, estrangement, and then a painful separation: the old story of woman's pride. . . . And thus faded out from that young heart her bright, brief, and saddened dream of life. Faint and spirit-broken, she turned from the scenes associated with the memory of the loved and lost. She tried to break the chain of sad associations that bound her to the mournful past; and so . . . her genius gathered strength from suffering, and wondrous power and brilliancy from the agony she hid within the desolate chambers of her soul . . . and turning, with an earnest and shattered spirit, to life's duties and trials, she found a calmness and strength that she had only imagined in her dreams of poetry and song.

We will now pass over a period of ten years, and the cousins have met again. In that calm and lovely woman, in whose eyes is a depth of tenderness tempering the flashes of her genius, whose looks and tones are full of sympathy and love, we recognize the once smitten and stricken Janette Alston. The bloom of her girlhood had given way to a higher type of spiritual beauty, as if some unseen hand had been polishing and refining the temple in which her lovely spirit found its habitation. . . .

Never in the early flush of womanhood, when an absorbing love had lit up her eyes and glowed in her life, had she appeared so interesting as when, with a countenance which seemed overshadowed with a spiritual light, she bent over the deathbed of a young woman just lingering at the shadowy gates of the unseen land.

"Has he come?" faintly but eagerly exclaimed the dying woman. "Oh! how I have longed for his coming, and even in death he forgets me."

"Oh, do not say so, dear Laura. Some accident may have detained him," said Janette to her cousin; for on that bed, from whence she will never rise, lies the once beautiful and lighthearted Laura Lagrange, the brightness of whose eyes had long since been dimmed with tears, and whose voice had become like a harp whose every chord is tuned to sadness—whose faintest thrill and loudest vibrations are but the variations of agony. A heavy hand was laid upon her once warm and bounding heart, and a voice came whispering through her soul that she must die. But to her the tidings was a message of deliverance—a voice hushing her wild sorrows to the calmness of resignation and hope.

Life had grown so weary upon her head—the future looked so hopeless—she had no wish to tread again the track where thorns had pierced her feet and clouds overcast her sky, and she hailed the coming of death's angel as the footsteps of a welcome friend. And yet, earth had one object so very dear to her weary heart. It was her absent and recreant husband; for, since that conversation [ten years earlier], she had accepted one of her offers and become a wife. But before she married she learned that great lesson of human experience and woman's life—to love the man who bowed at her shrine, a willing worshipper.

He had a pleasing address, raven hair, flashing eyes, a voice of thrilling sweetness, and lips of persuasive eloquence; and being well versed in the ways of the world, he won his way to her heart and she became his bride, and he was proud of his prize. Vain and superficial in his character, he looked upon marriage not as a divine sacrament for the soul's development and human progression, but as the title deed that gave him possession of the woman he thought he loved. But alas for her, the laxity of his principles had rendered him unworthy of the deep and undying devotion of a pure-hearted woman. But, for a while, he hid from her his true character, and she blindly loved him, and for a short period was happy in the consciousness of being beloved. Though sometimes a vague unrest would fill her soul, when, overflowing with a sense of the good, the beautiful, and the true, she would turn to him but find no response to the deep yearnings of her soul—no appreciation of life's highest realities, its solemn grandeur and significant importance. Their souls never met, and soon she found a void in her bosom that his earthborn love could not fill. He did not satisfy the wants of her mental and moral nature: between him and her there was no affinity of minds, no intercommunion of souls.

Talk as you will of woman's deep capacity for loving—of the strength of her affectional nature. I do not deny it. But will the mere possession of any human love fully satisfy all the demands of her whole being? You may paint her in poetry or fiction as a frail vine, clinging to her brother man for support and dying when deprived of it, and all this may sound well enough to please the imaginations of school-girls, or lovelorn maidens. But woman—the true woman—if you would render her happy, it needs more than the mere development of her affectional nature. Her conscience should be enlightened, her faith in the true and right established, and scope given to her heaven-endowed and God-given faculties. The true aim of female education should be, a development of not one or two but all the faculties of the human soul, because no perfect womanhood is developed by imperfect culture. Intense love is often akin to intense suffering, and to trust the whole wealth of woman's nature on the frail bark of human love may often be like trusting a cargo of gold and precious gems to a bark that has never battled with the storm or buffeted the waves. Is it any wonder, then, that so many life-barks . . . are stranded on the shoals of existence, mournful beacons and solemn warnings for the thoughtless, to whom marriage is a careless and hasty rushing together of the affections? Alas, that an institution so fraught with good for humanity should be so perverted, and that state of life which should be filled with happiness become so replete with misery. And this was the fate of Laura Lagrange.

For a brief period after her marriage her life seemed like a bright and beautiful dream, full of hope and radiant with joy. And then there came a change: he found other attractions that lay beyond the pale of home influences. The gambling saloon had power to win him from her side; he had lived in an element of unhealthy and unhallowed excitements, and the society of a loving wife, the pleasures of a well-regulated home, were enjoyments too tame for one who had vitiated his tastes by the pleasures of sin. There were charmed houses of vice built upon dead men's loves, where, amid a flow of song, laughter, wine, and careless mirth, he would spend hour after hour, forgetting the cheek that was paling through his neglect, heedless of the tear-dimmed eyes peering anxiously into the darkness, waiting or watching his return.

The influence of old associations was upon him. In early life, home had been to him a place of ceilings and walls, not a true home built upon goodness, love, and truth. It was a place where velvet carpets hushed his tread, where images of loveliness and beauty, invoked into being by painter's art and sculptor's skill, pleased the eye and gratified the taste, where magnificence surrounded his way and costly clothing adorned his person; but it was not the place for the true culture and right development of his soul. His father had been too much engrossed in making money and his mother in spending it, in striving to maintain a fashionable position in society and shining in the eyes of the world, to give the proper direction to the character of their wayward and impulsive son. His mother put beautiful robes upon his body but left ugly scars upon his soul; she pampered his appetite but starved his spirit. . . .

That parental authority which should have been preserved as a string of precious pearls, unbroken and unscattered, was simply the administration of chance. At one time obedience was enforced by authority, at another time by flattery and promises, and just as often it was not enforced. . . . His early associations were formed as chance directed, and from his want of home training, his character received a bias, his life a shade, which ran through every avenue of his existence and darkened all his future hours. . . .

Before a year of his married life had waned, his young wife had learned to wait and mourn his frequent and uncalled-for absence. More than once had she seen him come home from his midnight haunts, the bright intelligence of his eye displaced by the drunkard's stare, and his manly gait changed to the inebriate's stagger; and she was beginning to know the bitter agony that is compressed in the mournful words

"drunkard's wife."

And then there came a bright but brief episode in her experience. The angel of life gave to her existence a deeper meaning and loftier significance: she sheltered in the warm clasp of her loving arms a dear babe, a precious child whose love filled every chamber of her heart. . . . How many lonely hours were beguiled by its winsome ways, its answering smiles and fond caresses! How exquisite and solemn was the feeling that thrilled her heart when she clasped the tiny hands together and taught her dear child to call God "Our Father"!

What a blessing was that child! The father paused in his headlong career, awed by the strange beauty and precocious intellect of his child; and the mother's life had a better expression through her ministrations of love. And then there came hours of bitter anguish, shading the sunlight of her home and hushing the music of her heart. The angel of death bent over the couch of her child and beckoned it away. Closer and closer the mother strained her child to her wildly heaving breast and struggled with the heavy hand that lay upon its heart. Love and agony contended with death. . . .

But death was stronger than love and mightier than agony and won the child for the land of crystal founts and deathless flowers, and the poor stricken mother sat down beneath the shadow of her mighty grief, feeling as if a great light had gone out from her soul and that the sunshine had suddenly faded around her path. She turned in her deep anguish to the father of her child, the loved and cherished dead. For a while his words were kind and tender, his heart seemed subdued, and his tenderness fell upon her worn and weary heart like rain on perishing flowers, or cooling waters to lips all parched with thirst and scorched with fever. But the change was evanescent; the influence of unhallowed associations and evil habits had vitiated and poisoned the springs of his existence. They had bound him in their meshes, and he lacked the moral strength to break his fetters and stand erect in all the strength and dignity of a true manhood, making life's highest excellence his ideal and striving to gain it.

And yet moments of deep contrition would sweep over him, when he would resolve to abandon the wine cup forever, when he was ready to forswear the handling of another card, and he would try to break away from the associations that he felt were working his ruin. But when the hour of temptation came, his strength was weakness, his earnest purposes were cobwebs, his well-meant resolutions ropes of sand—and thus passed year after year of the married life of Laura Lagrange. She tried to hide her agony from the public gaze, to smile when her heart was almost breaking. But year after year her voice grew fainter and sadder, her once light and bounding step grew slower and faltering.

Year after year she wrestled with agony and strove with despair, till the quick eyes of her brother read, in the paling of her cheek and the dimming eyes the secret anguish of her worn and weary spirit. On that wan, sad face he saw the death tokens, and he knew the dark wing of the mystic angel swept cold around her path.

"Laura," said her brother to her one day, "you are not well, and I think you need our mother's tender care and nursing. You are daily losing strength, and if you will go, I will accompany you."

At first she hesitated; she shrank almost instinctively from presenting that pale, sad face to the loved ones at home. . . . But then a deep yearning for home sympathy woke within her a passionate longing for love's kind words, for tenderness and heart support, and she resolved to seek the home of her childhood and lay her weary head upon her mother's bosom, to be folded again in her loving arms, to lay that poor, bruised and aching heart where it might beat and throb closely to the loved ones at home.

A kind welcome awaited her. All that love and tenderness could devise was done to bring the bloom to her cheek and the light to her eye. But it was all in vain; hers was a disease that no medicine could cure, no earthly balm would heal. It was a slow wasting of the vital forces, the sickness of the soul. The unkindness and neglect of her husband lay like a leaden weight upon her heart. . . .

And where was he that had won her love and then cast it aside as a useless thing, who rifled her heart of its wealth and spread bitter ashes upon its broken altars? He was lingering away from her when the death damps were gathering on her brow, when his name was trembling on her lips! Lingering away! when she was watching his coming, though the death films were gathering before her eyes and earthly things were fading from her vision.

"I think I hear him now," said the dying woman, "surely that is his step," but the sound died away in the distance.

Again she started from an uneasy slumber: "That is his voice! I am so glad he has come."

Tears gathered in the eyes of the sad watchers by that dying bed, for they knew that she was deceived. He had not returned. For her sake they wished his coming. Slowly the hours waned away, and then came the sad, soul-sickening thought that she was forgotten, forgotten in the last hour of human need, forgotten when the spirit, about to be dissolved, paused for the last time on the threshold of existence, a weary watcher at the gates of death.

"He has forgotten me," again she faintly murmured, and the last tears she would ever shed on earth sprang to her mournful eyes, and . . . a few broken sentences issued from her pale and quivering lips. They were prayers for strength, and earnest pleading for him who had desolated her young life by turning its sunshine to shadows, its smiles to tears.

"He has forgotten me," she murmured again, "but I can bear it; the bitterness of death is passed, and soon I hope to exchange the shadows of death for the brightness of eternity, the rugged paths of life for the golden streets of glory, and the care and turmoils of earth for the peace and rest of heaven."

Her voice grew fainter and fainter; they saw the shadows that never deceive flit over her pale and faded face and knew that the death angel waited to soothe their weary one to rest, to calm the throbbing of her bosom and cool the fever of her brain. And amid the silent hush of their grief, the freed spirit, refined through suffering and brought into divine harmony through the spirit of the living Christ, passed over the dark waters of death as on a bridge of light, over whose radiant arches hovering angels bent. They parted the dark locks from her marble brow, closed the waxen lids over the once bright and laughing eye, and left her to the dreamless slumber of the grave.

Her cousin turned from that deathbed a sadder and wiser woman. She resolved more earnestly than ever to make the world better by her example, gladder by her presence, and to kindle the fires of her genius on the altars of universal love and truth. She had a higher and better object in all her writings than the mere acquistion of gold or acquirement of fame. She felt that she had a high and holy mission on the battlefield of existence—that life was not given her to be frittered away in nonsense or wasted away in trifling pursuits. She would willingly espouse an unpopular cause, but not an unrighteous one.

In her the downtrodden slave found an earnest advocate; the flying fugitive remembered her kindness as he stepped cautiously through our Republic to gain his freedom in a monarchial land, having broken the chains on which the rust of centuries had gathered. Little children learned to name her with affection; the poor called her blessed as she broke her bread to the pale lips of hunger.

Her life was like a beautiful story, only it was clothed with the dignity of reality and invested with the sublimity of truth. True, she was an old maid; no husband brightened her life with his love or shaded it with his neglect. No children nestling lovingly in her arms called her mother. No one appended Mrs. to her name.

She was indeed an old maid, not vainly striving to keep up an appearance of girlishness when "departed" was written on her youth, not vainly pining at her loneliness and isolation. The world was full of warm, loving hearts, and her own beat in unison with them. Neither was she always sentimentally sighing for something to love; objects of affection were all around her, and the world was not so wealthy in love that it had no use for hers. In blessing others she made a life and benediction, and as old age descended peacefully and gently upon her, she had learned one of life's most precious lessons: that true happiness consists not so much in the fruition of our wishes as in the regulation of desires and the full development and right culture of our whole natures.

# Aunt Lindy: A Story Founded on Real Life

## Victoria Earle Matthews

A fascinating curio in African American women's literary history, this story was originally published as a book in 1893. Republication for the first time in Ann Allen Shockley's *Afro-American Women Writers 1746–1933* has helped restore its place in the short story tradition. Like Charles Chesnutt's better known tales in *The Conjure Woman*, the story is a reminiscence on slavery years after its end. Its melodramatic plotting is a vehicle for a powerful, recurring theme in African American literature: slavery's traumatic effects on the family. It also suggests forgiveness as an antidote to racism.

IN THE ANNALS of Fort Valley, Georgia, few events will last longer in the minds of her slow, easygoing dwellers than the memory of a great conflagration that left more than half the town a complete waste. 'Twas generally conceded to be the most disastrous fire that even her oldest residents had ever witnessed. It was caused, as far as could be ascertained, by someone who, while passing through the sampling room of the Cotton Exchange, had thoughtlessly tossed aside a burning match; this, embedding itself in the soft fleecy cotton, burned its way silently, without smoke, through the heart of a great bale to the flooring beneath, before it was discovered.

Although the watchman made his regular rounds an hour or so after the building closed for the night, yet he saw nothing to indicate the treacherous flame which was then, like a serpent, stealing its way through the soft snowy cotton. But now a red glare, a terrified cry of "Fire! Fire!" echoing on the still night air, had aroused the unconscious sleepers and summoned quickly strong, brave-hearted men from every direction, who, as though with one accord, fell to fighting the fire-fiend (modern invention was unknown in this out-of-the-way settlement); even the women flocked to the scene, not knowing how soon a helping hand would be needed.

Great volumes of black smoke arose from the fated building, blinding and choking the stout fellows who had arranged themselves in small squads on the roofs of adjacent dwellings to check, if possible, the progress of the fire, while others in line passed water to them.

As the night wore on, a rising wind fanned the fiery tongue into a fateful blaze; and, as higher rose the wind, fiercer grew the flame; from every window and doorway poured great tongues of fire, casting a lurid glare all over the valley, with its shuddering groups of mute, frightened white faces, and its shrieking, prayerful, terror-stricken ne-groes, whose religion, being of a highly emotional charac-ter, was easily rendered devotional by any unusual excite-ment: their agonized " 'Mi'ty Gawd! he'p us pore sinners," chanted in doleful tones, as only the emotional Southern negro can chant or moan, but added to the weird, wild scene. Men and women with blanched faces looked anx-iously at each other; piercing screams rent the air, as some child, relative, or loved one was missed, for like a curse, the consuming fire passed from house to house, leaving noth-ing in its track but the blackened and charred remains of what had been, but a few short hours before, "home."

All through the night the fire raged, wasting its force as the early morning light gradually penetrated the smoky haze, revealing to the well-nigh frantic people a sad, sad scene of desolation. When home has been devastated, hearts may only feel and know the extent of the void; no pen or phrase can estimate it.

As the day advanced, sickening details of the night's hor-ror were brought to light. Magruder's Tavern, the only ho-tel the quaint little town could boast of, served as a death

trap; several perished in the flames; many were hurt by
falling beams; some jumped from windows and lay maimed
for life; others stood in shuddering groups, homeless, but
thankful withal that their lives had been spared: as the distressed were found, neighbors who had escaped the
scourge threw wide their doors and bestirred themselves to
give relief to the sufferers and temporary shelter to those
who had lost all. Ah! let unbelievers cavil and contend, yet
such a time as this proves that there is a mystic vein running through humanity that is not deduced from the mechanical laws of nature.

A silver-haired man, a stranger in the town, had been
taken to a humble cot where many children in innocent
forgetfulness passed noisily to and fro, unconscious that
quiet meant life to the aged sufferer. Old Dr. Bronson, with
his great heart and gentle, childlike manner, stood doubly
thoughtful as he numbered the throbbing pulse. "His brain
won't—can't bear it unless he's nursed and has perfect
quiet," he murmured as he quitted the house. Acting upon
a sudden thought, he sprang into his buggy and quickly
drove through the shady lanes, by the redolent orchards, to
a lone cabin on the outskirts of the town, situated at the
entrance to the great sighing pine-woods.

Seeing a man weeding a small garden plot, he called,
without alighting, "Hi there, Joel: where's Aunt Lindy?"

"Right dar, in de cabin, doctor; jes wait a minnit," as he
disappeared through the doorway.

"Good day, Aunt Lindy," as a tall, ancient-looking negro
dame hurried from the cabin to the gate. Well accustomed
was she to these sudden calls of Dr. Bronson, for her fame
as a nurse was known far beyond the limits of Fort Valley.

"Mawning, doctor; Miss Martha and de chil'en was not
teched by de fi'er?" she inquired anxiously.

"Oh, no; the fire was not our way. Lindy, I have a bad
case, and nowhere to take him. Mrs. Bronson has her
hands full of distressed, suffering children. No one to nurse
him, so I want to bring him here—a victim of the great
fire."

"De Lawd, doctor, yo kin, yo kno' yo kin; de cabin is

pore, but Joel ner me ain't heathins; fetch him right along, my han's ain't afeered of wuk when trubble comes."

Tenderly they lifted him, and bore him from the cottage resounding with childish prattle and glee, to the quiet, cleanly cabin of the lonely couple, Lindy and Joel, who years before had seen babes torn from their breasts and sold—powerless to utter a complaint or appeal, whipped for the tears they shed, knowing their children would return to them not again till the graves gave up their dead. But in the busy life that freedom gave them, oft, when work was done and the night of life threw its waning shadows around them, their tears would fall for the scattered voices —they would mourn o'er their past oppression. Yet they hid their grief from an unsympathizing generation, and the memory of their oppressors awoke but to the call of fitful retrospection.

"Joel, does yo 'member what de scriptur' ses about de stranger widin dy gates?" asked Aunt Lindy, as she hurriedly made ready for the "victim of the great fire."

"Ole 'oman, I gits mo' forgitful each day I lib, but it 'pears to me dat it says su'thin 'bout 'Heal de sick an' lead the blind,'" the old man said, as he stood with a look of deep concern settling on his aged face; "yes, ole 'oman," brightening up, "yes, dat's hit, kase I 'member de words de bressed Marster say to dem lis'ning souls geddered 'roun him, 'If yo hab dun it to de least ob dese my brudderin, yo hab dun it onto me.'"

"Yas, yas, I 'members now," Aunt Lindy murmured, as she moved the bed that the stranger was to rest upon out in the middle of the small room, the headboard near the window almost covered with climbing honeysuckle, all in sweet bloom.

"It am won'erful," she continued, meditatively, "how de Marster 'ranges t'ings to suit His work and will. I'se kep dis bed fixed fur yeahs, 'maginin' dat somehow, in de prov'dence ob Gawd, one ob de chil'en mou't chance dis away wid no place to lay his hed—de law me! Joel, mak' hast' an' fetch in dat shuck bed, de sun hab made it as sweet as de flowers, 'fore de dew falls offen dem, an' reck-olec I wants a hole passel of mullen leaves; dey's powerful good fur laying fever, an' as yo's gwine dat way yo mou't jes as well get er han'ful ob mounting mint, sweet balsam—an' cam'ile," she called after him, "ef yo pass enny."

About candle-light Dr. Bronson arrived with his patient, while his two assistants placed him on the bed prepared for him; the doctor explained the critical condition of the sick man to the trusty old nurse and directed as to the medicine. "Do not disturb him for an hour at least, Aunt Lindy; let him sleep, for he needs all the strength he can rally—he has but one slim chance out of ten."

"Pore sole, I'll look arter him same's ef he war my own chile."

"I know that, Aunt Lindy; I will stop in on my way back from the ridge in about a couple of hours."

"All rite, sah."

Uncle Joel, with the desired herbs, returned shortly afterward. "Is he cum yit, old 'oman?"

"Shsh! sure nuff," she whispered, with a warning motion of her head toward the partitioned room where the sick man lay. Heeding the warning, Uncle Joel whispered back:

"If dar's nuffin I kin do jes now to he'p yo, I'll jes step ober to Brer An'erson's; I heah dere's a new brudder who's gwine to lead de meetin', as Brer Wilson is ailin'."

"Go 'long, Joel, dere's nuffin yo kin do jes now."

"Well den, s'long, ole 'oman," the old man said, as he stepped noiselessly out into the sweet perfume-laden air.

For a long time Aunt Lindy sat dozing by the smothered fire; so lightly, though, that almost the rustling of the wind through the leaves would have awakened her.

The moonlight streamed in the doorway; now and then sounds issuing from the "pra'r meetin'," a few doors away, could be heard on the still evening air. After a while the nurse rose, lighted a candle, and went to make sure the sick man was comfortable. Entering softly, she stepped to the bedside and looked at the face of the sleeper; suddenly she grew dizzy, breathless, amazed, as though her eyes had deceived her; she placed the candle close by his face and peered wildly at this bruised, bandaged, silver-haired stranger in a fascinated sort of way, as though she were powerless to speak. At last:

"Great Gawd! it's Marse Jeems!"

The quick, vengeful flame leaped in her eyes, as her mind, made keen by years of secret suffering and toil, traveled through time and space; she saw wrongs which no tongue can enumerate; demoniac gleams of exultation and bitter hatred settled upon her now grim features; a pitiless smile wreathed her set lips, as she gazed with glaring eyeballs at this helpless, homeless "victim of the great fire," as though surrounded by demons; a dozen wicked impulses rushed through her mind—a life for a life—no mortal eye was near, an intercepted breath, a gasp, and—

"Lindy, Lindy, don't tell Miss Cynthia," the sick man weakly murmured: in the confused state of his brain, it required but this familiar black face to conduct his disordered thoughts to the palmiest period of his existence. He again reveled in opulence, saw again the cotton fields—a waving tract of bursting snowballs—the magnolia, the oleander—

"Whar's my chil'en?" Nurse Lindy fairly shrieked in his face. "To de fo' win's ob de ear'fh, yo ole debbil, yo." He heard her not now, for white and unconscious he lay, while the long pent-up passion found vent. Her blood was afire, her tall form swayed, her long, bony hands trembled like an animal at bay; she stepped back as if to spring upon him, with clutching fingers extended; breathless she paused; the shouts of the worshippers broke upon the evening air—the oldentime melody seemed to pervade the cabin; she listened, turned, and fled—out through the open doorway,—out into the white moonlight, down the shadowed lane, as if impelled by unseen force. She unconsciously approached the prayer-meeting door. "Vengeance is mine, ses de Lawd," came from within; her anger died away; quickly her steps she retraced. "Mi'ty Gawd, stren'fin my arm, and pur'fy my heart," was all she said.

* * *

Soon from the portals of death she brought him, for untiringly she labored, unceasingly she prayed in her poor broken way; nor was it in vain, for before the frost fell the crisis passed, the light of reason beamed upon the silver-haired stranger, and revealed in mystic characters the service rendered by a former slave—Aunt Lindy. He marveled at the patient faithfulness of these people. He saw but the gold—did not dream of the dross burned away by the great Refiner's fire. From that time Aunt Lindy and Uncle Joel never knew a sorrow, secret or otherwise; for not only was the roof above their heads secured to them, but the new "brudder" who came to "lead de meetin' in Brer Wilson's place," was proved beyond a doubt, through the efforts of the silver-haired stranger, to be their first-born. The rest were "sleeping until the morning," and not to the "fo' win's ob de ear'fh," as was so greatly feared by Aunt Lindy.

# Black Is, As Black Does (A Dream)

## ANGELINA WELD GRIMKÉ

Christianity has historically played a complex role in African American life, providing hope and communion while also being used to justify racial atrocities like slavery. Grimké, who published this story at the age of twenty, here uses the dream story to examine the conscience of Christian morality as it pertains to the treatment of blacks and whites in America. The story's biblical cadences and ethereal allegory are part of Grimké's effort to seduce turn-of-the-century readers into contemplation of their own unexamined ideas and emotions about racial injustice. The story first appeared in 1900 in *Colored American Magazine*.

IT CAME TO ME one dark, rainy morning as I was half awake and half asleep. The wind was blowing drearily, and I listened to the swish of the rain upon the glass and the dripping from the eaves. As I lay listening I thought many things, and my thoughts grew hazier and hazier, and I fell into deep slumber.

Then methought a great feeling of peace came upon me and that all my cares were falling from me and rolling away —away into infinity. As I lay with my eyes closed, this great feeling of peace increased, and my heart was glad within me. Then someone touched me lightly upon the shoulder and eyes, causing my heart to give a great bound, for I was not prepared for the loveliness of the scene which now burst upon my sight. Stretched all around was a wide, green, grassy plain. Each little blade of grass sang in the gentle wind, and here and there massive trees spread their branches. The leaves and the birds made music, while the river passing through the meadow sparkled and sang as it sped on its way. Listening, I heard no discord, for all the voices blended with each other, mingling, and swelling, and making one grand sweet song. I longed to sing too, and I lifted up my voice, but no song came, so that I wondered. Then a voice at my side answered: "Thou art not one of us yet." The voice was sweeter than the babbling brook, more tender than the voice of a mother to her erring child, lower than the beating of the restless surf on the shore. Then I turned to see whence this voice came. As I looked I fell upon my face weeping.

For there stood before me a figure clad in white. As she moved she seemed like a snowy-white cloud, which sails o'er the sky in summertime. A soft light shone above, around, behind, illuminating her. It was not for this I fell to weeping. I had looked upon the face, and the truth which shone forth from the mild eyes, the sweetness which smiled around the mouth, and all the pity, the mercy, the kindness, expressed in that divine countenance, revealed to me how wicked I was, and had been. But she took me by the hand, bidding me arise, and kissed me on the brow. Between my sobs I asked: "Where am I?" The low voice answered: "This is heaven." I said: "Who art thou?" She answered: "One of the lovers of God." And as she spoke that name, the heavens brightened, the grass sang sweeter, as did the leaves and the birds, also the silvery river. Looking up, I saw that she was no longer by my side, but was moving o'er the plain, and turning, she beckoned to me. I followed without knowing why.

Thus we passed silently over the velvety grass, o'er hill and dale, by laughing brooks and swift-flowing rivers. Often turning, she smiled upon me, but on and on we went; now and then other bright spirits passed us, all smiling kindly upon me as they went their way. Some came and kissed my forehead and said they were glad to see me, and I was happy, *so* happy. Then methought we came to a city, but ah! so unlike our cities: no hurrying this and that way, no deafening roar of passing wagons, no shrieking hucksters, no loud talking, no anxious, worried faces. All was peace.

And as we passed up the noiseless streets, many spirits clad in spotless white, and gleaming with that ineffable light, passed, and all smiled and greeted me tenderly as they went their shining way.

Then we came to a great hall. The doors thereby were three and opened wide, and I saw many people going in through the first door, but they were not clad in snowy white, and I could see no light illuminating their bodies. I asked: "Pray tell me who are these?" And the spirit said: "These are those, like you, who have just come from earth." And as she spoke, I saw some passing forth from the second door, clad in white, but I saw no light, and I said perplexed: "Pray who are these, and why does no light illuminate them?" She answered: "These are they whom our *Father* has blessed of those who have just come from earth, and they will have the light when they have been with us a long time, when they have done some service which has particularly gratified *'our Father.'*" She had scarcely ceased speaking when I saw several ragged ones, with looks downcast, coming through the third door; and I asked: "Pray who are these?" As she answered, her voice trembled, and gazing upon her, I saw a tear glide down her cheek as she answered, simply: "The lost." And, groaning within me I said: "Pray what is this place?" And solemnly she answered: "This is where God weeds out the wicked from the good." And as she ceased speaking, she glided to the first door and beckoned me.

We came within a hall, large and gloomy, and we passed down one end, and looking up, I saw a great, dazzling light, that was all; for I fell upon the floor, overcome. I had looked upon *God*! As I lay I heard His voice now low and tender beyond expression, now stern and mighty, like the roll of thunder. When I took courage I gazed around, but I dared not look upon *His* face again.

I saw a vast multitude of those lately come from earth, waiting to stand before the bar of judgment; also those who had been tried, passing out through the doors. Looking at my companion, I saw that she was gazing upon *God,* and His brightness shone upon her face, and I was dazzled and looked down. When I glanced upon the throng of the lately dead, I saw one pass to the bar and fall with a loud cry for mercy. I heard him weeping and confessing all his sins, excusing himself in nothing, and I saw that his skin was black; looking closer, I saw that he was lame, torn, and bleeding, and quite unrecognizable, for most of his features were gone. I saw him waving his poor stumps of arms, begging for mercy. By these tokens I knew that he came from my country, and that he was one of an oppressed race; for in America, alas! it makes a difference whether a man's *skin* be black or white. Nothing was said, but I perceived that he had been foully murdered.

I heard *God's* voice speaking to him, and I was lost in its sweetness. It seemed to me I was floating down a stream of loveliness, and I was so happy. When He ceased, I thought I had gently come to some bank, and all was peace and rest. And I saw the man pass from the bar, and that he was clad in pure white. Beautiful spirits came and tended his wounds, and lo! he stood forth glorified, a dim light shining round him. I looked at my companion and she smiled, and then I understood. And behold another stood before the *Judgment-seat.* I did not hear *him* beg for mercy, but I heard him telling all the good he had done, and I heard a sound as of distant mutterings of thunder, and I felt the angry flashings above the *Judgment-seat.* And I saw the man waiting calmly in his own conceit. And I heard the muffled thunder of God's voice asking: "And didst thou treat all my children justly?" And I heard the man say: "Yea, yea, O Lord!" And I heard God again: "Whether their skin was black or white?" And the man answered: "Yea, yea, Lord," and laughed.

Then I heard the thunder of God's voice saying: "I know thee, who thou art; it wast thou who didst murder yon man, one of my faithful servants; it wast thou who didst hate and torture him, and who trampled upon and crushed him; but in-as-much as thou didst this wrong unto him, thou didst it unto me. Begone!" And I saw him who was condemned stagger from the bar, and that his hands and his clothes were covered with blood, and that he left behind him footprints tracked in blood; and as I looked at him more closely, I saw that his skin was white, but that his *soul* was black. For it makes a difference in heaven whether a man's *soul* be black or white!

And I beheld the man with the black skin creep up to the *Judgment-seat* and sob, brokenly: "Forgive, oh, forgive my brother, for he knew not what he did." And I felt my heart beating and tumbling against my side,—and I awoke. The wind was moaning drearily, the rain was still sobbing against the glass, and I lay there and wept.

# The Stones of the Village

### ALICE DUNBAR-NELSON

This story belongs to both the "tragic mulatto" and passing
tale traditions typical of African American writing. Victor
Grabért, a mixed-race Creole, attempts to cast off impover-
ished origins and the color caste of his New Orleans boyhood to
assimilate into the world of legal, professional white power in
turn-of-the-century America. Dunbar-Nelson's treatment of
Grabért's inner conflict at concealing his racial identity is an
explicit handling of a theme that later African American writers like Jessie Fauset would handle with more subtlety, if not
more insight. The story is an excellent example of Dunbar-
Nelson's talents as a regional local-colorist set to explore the
mixed-racial and ethnic world of New Orleans, the site of
much of her best short fiction. It was originally intended for
publication in the book *Stories of Women and Men*, which
Dunbar-Nelson composed between 1900 and 1910 and which
remained unpublished until Oxford University Press's three-
volume *The Works of Alice Dunbar-Nelson* (1988).

VICTOR GRABERT STRODE down the one, wide, tree-
shaded street of the village, his heart throbbing with a bitterness and anger that seemed too great to bear. So often
had he gone home in the same spirit, however, that it had
grown nearly second nature to him—this dull, sullen resentment, flaming out now and then into almost murderous
vindictiveness. Behind him there floated derisive laughs
and shouts, the taunts of little brutes, boys of his own age.
  He reached the tumbledown cottage at the farther end of

the street and flung himself on the battered step. Grandmère Grabért sat rocking herself to and fro, crooning a bit of song brought over from the West Indies years ago; but when the boy sat silent, his head bowed in his hands, she paused in the midst of a line and regarded him with keen, piercing eyes.

"Eh, Victor?" she asked. That was all, but he understood. He raised his head and waved a hand angrily down the street toward the lighted square that marked the village center.

"Dose boy," he gulped.

Grandmère Grabért laid a sympathetic hand on his black curls, but withdrew it the next instant.

"*Bien,*" she said angrily. "Fo' what you go by dem, eh? W'y not keep to yo'self? Dey don' want you, dey don' care fo' you. H'ain' you got no sense?"

"Oh, but Grandmère," he wailed piteously, "I wan' fo' to play."

The old woman stood up in the doorway, her tall, spare form towering menacingly over him.

"You wan' fo' to play, eh? Fo' w'y? You don' need no play. Dose boy"—she swept a magnificent gesture down the street—"dey fools!"

"Eef I could play wid—" began Victor, but his grandmother caught him by the wrist and held him as in a vise.

"Hush," she cried. "You mus' be goin' crazy." And still holding him by the wrist, she pulled him indoors.

It was a two-room house, bare and poor and miserable, but never had it seemed so meager before to Victor as it did this night. The supper was frugal almost to the starvation point. They ate in silence, and afterward Victor threw himself on his cot in the corner of the kitchen and closed his eyes. Grandmère Grabért thought him asleep and closed the door noiselessly as she went into her own room. But he was awake, and his mind was like a shifting kaleidoscope of miserable incidents and heartaches. He had lived fourteen years, and he could remember most of them as years of misery. He had never known a mother's love, for his mother had died, so he was told, when he was but a few months old. No one ever spoke to him of a father, and Grandmère Grabért had been all to him. She was kind, after a stern, unloving fashion, and she provided for him as best she could. He had picked up some sort of an education at the parish school. It was a good one after its way, but his life there had been such a succession of miseries that he rebelled one day and refused to go anymore.

His earliest memories were clustered about this poor little cottage. He could see himself toddling about its broken steps, playing alone with a few broken pieces of china which his fancy magnified into glorious toys. He remembered his first whipping too. Tired one day of the loneliness which even the broken china could not mitigate, he had toddled out the side gate after a merry group of little black and yellow boys of his own age. When Grandmère Grabért, missing him from his accustomed garden corner, came to look for him, she found him sitting contentedly in the center of the group in the dusty street, all of them gravely scooping up handfuls of the gravelly dirt and trickling it down their chubby bare legs. Grandmère snatched at him fiercely, and he whimpered, for he was learning for the first time what fear was.

"What you mean?" she hissed at him. "What you mean playin' in de strit wid dose niggers?" And she struck at him wildly with her open hand.

He looked up into her brown face surmounted by a wealth of curly black hair faintly streaked with gray, but he was too frightened to question.

It had been loneliness ever since. For the parents of the little black and yellow boys, resenting the insult Grandmère had offered their offspring, sternly bade them have nothing more to do with Victor. Then when he toddled after some other little boys, whose faces were white like his own, they ran him away with derisive hoots of "Nigger! Nigger!" And again, he could not understand.

Hardest of all, though, was when Grandmère sternly bade him cease speaking the soft Creole patois that they chattered together and forced him to learn English. The result was a confused jumble which was no language at all;

that when he spoke it in the streets or in the school, all the boys, white and black and yellow, hooted at him and called him "White nigger! White nigger!"

He writhed on his cot that night and lived over all the anguish of his years until hot tears scalded their way down a burning face, and he fell into a troubled sleep wherein he sobbed over some dreamland miseries.

The next morning, Grandmère eyed his heavy swollen eyes sharply, and a momentary thrill of compassion passed over her and found expression in a new tenderness of manner toward him as she served his breakfast. She, too, had thought over the matter in the night, and it bore fruit in an unexpected way.

Some few weeks after, Victor found himself timidly ringing the doorbell of a house on Hospital Street in New Orleans. His heart throbbed in painful unison to the jangle of the bell. How was he to know that old Madame Guichard, Grandmère's one friend in the city, to whom she had confided him, would be kind? He had walked from the river landing to the house, timidly inquiring the way of busy pedestrians. He was hungry and frightened. Never in all his life had he seen so many people before, and in all the busy streets there was not one eye which would light up with recognition when it met his own. Moreover, it had been a weary journey down the Red River, thence into the Mississippi, and finally here. Perhaps it had not been devoid of interest, after its fashion, but Victor did not know. He was too heartsick at leaving home.

However, Madame Guichard was kind. She welcomed him with a volubility and overflow of tenderness that acted like balm to the boy's sore spirit. Thence they were firm friends, even confidants.

Victor must find work to do. Grandmère Grabért's idea in sending him to New Orleans was that he might "mek one man of himse'f," as she phrased it. And Victor, grown suddenly old in the sense that he had a responsibility to bear, set about his search valiantly.

It chanced one day that he saw a sign in an old bookstore on Royal Street that stated in both French and English the need of a boy. Almost before he knew it, he had entered the shop and was gasping out some choked words to the little old man who sat behind the counter.

The old man looked keenly over his glasses at the boy and rubbed his bald head reflectively. In order to do this, he had to take off an old black silk cap, which he looked at with apparent regret.

"Eh, what you say?" he asked sharply, when Victor had finished.

"I—I—want a place to work," stammered the boy again.

"Eh, you do? Well, can you read?"

"Yes sir," replied Victor.

The old man got down from his stool, came from behind the counter, and putting his finger under the boy's chin, stared hard into his eyes. They met his own unflinchingly, though there was the suspicion of pathos and timidity in their brown depths.

"Do you know where you live, eh?"

"On Hospital Street," said Victor. It did not occur to him to give the number, and the old man did not ask.

*"Très bien,"* grunted the book-seller, and his interest relaxed. He gave a few curt directions about the manner of work Victor was to do and settled himself again upon his stool, poring into his dingy book with renewed ardor.

Thus began Victor's commercial life. It was an easy one. At seven, he opened the shutters of the little shop and swept and dusted. At eight, the book-seller came down stairs and passed out to get his coffee at the restaurant across the street. At eight in the evening, the shop was closed again. That was all.

Occasionally, there came a customer, but not often, for there were only odd books and rare ones in the shop, and those who came were usually old, yellow, querulous bookworms, who nosed about for hours and went away leaving many bank notes behind them. Sometimes there was an errand to do, and sometimes there came a customer when the proprietor was out. It was an easy matter to wait on them. He had but to point to the shelves and say, "Monsieur will be in directly," and all was settled, for those who came here to buy had plenty of leisure and did not mind waiting.

So a year went by, then two and three, and the stream of Victor's life flowed smoothly on its uneventful way. He had grown tall and thin, and often Madame Guichard would look at him and chuckle to herself, "Ha, he is lak one bean-pole, yaas, *mais—*" and there would be a world of unfinished reflection in that last word.

Victor had grown pale from much reading. Like a shadow of the old book-seller he sat day after day poring into some dusty yellow-paged book, and his mind was a queer jumble of ideas. History and philosophy and old-fashioned social economy were tangled with French romance and classic mythology and astrology and mysticism. He had made few friends, for his experience in the village had made him chary of strangers. Every week, he wrote to Grandmère Grabért and sent her part of his earnings. In his way he was happy, and if he was lonely, he had ceased to care about it, for his world was peopled with images of his own fancying.

Then all at once, the world he had built about him tumbled down, and he was left, staring helplessly at its ruins. The little book-seller died one day, and his shop and its books were sold by an unscrupulous nephew who cared not for bindings nor precious yellowed pages, but only for the grossly material things that money can buy. Victor ground his teeth as the auctioneer's strident voice sounded through the shop where all once had been hushed quiet, and wept as he saw some of his favorite books carried away by men and women who he was sure could not appreciate their value.

He dried his tears, however, the next day, when a grave-faced lawyer came to the little house on Hospital Street and informed him that he had been left a sum of money by the book-seller.

Victor sat staring at him helplessly. Money meant little to him. He never needed it, never used it. After he had sent Grandmère her sum each week, Madame Guichard kept the rest and doled it out to him as he needed it for carfare and clothes.

"The interest of the money," continued the lawyer clearing his throat, "is sufficient to keep you very handsomely without touching the principal. It was my client's wish that you should enter Tulane College and there fit yourself for your profession. He had great confidence in your ability."

"Tulane College!" cried Victor. "Why—why—why—" Then he stopped suddenly, and the hot blood mounted to his face. He glanced furtively about the room. Madame Guichard was not near; the lawyer had seen no one but him. Then why tell him? His heart leaped wildly at the thought. Well, Grandmère would have willed it so.

The lawyer was waiting politely for him to finish his sentence.

"Why—why—I should have to study in order to enter there," finished Victor lamely.

"Exactly so," said Mr. Buckley, "and as I have, in a way, been appointed your guardian, I will see to that."

Victor found himself murmuring confused thanks and good-byes to Mr. Buckley. After he had gone, the boy sat down and gazed blankly at the wall. Then he wrote a long letter to Grandmère.

A week later, he changed boarding places at Mr. Buckley's advice and entered a preparatory school for Tulane. And still, Madame Guichard and Mr. Buckley had not met.

It was a handsomely furnished office on Carondelet Street in which Lawyer Grabért sat some years later. His day's work done, he was leaning back in his chair and smiling pleasantly out of the window. Within was warmth and light and cheer; without, the wind howled and gusty rains beat against the window pane. Lawyer Grabért smiled again as he looked about at the comfort and found himself half pitying those without who were forced to buffet the storm afoot. He rose finally and, donning his overcoat, called a cab and was driven to his rooms in the most fashionable part of the city. There he found his old-time college friend, awaiting him with some impatience.

"Thought you never were coming, old man," was his greeting.

Grabért smiled pleasantly, "Well, I was a bit tired, you know," he answered, "and I have been sitting idle for an hour or more, just relaxing, as it were."

Vannier laid his hand affectionately on the other's shoulder. "That was a mighty effort you made today," he said earnestly. "I, for one, am proud of you."

"Thank you," replied Grabért simply, and the two sat silent for a minute.

"Going to the Charles' dance tonight?" asked Vannier finally.

"I don't believe I am. I am tired and lazy."

"It will do you good. Come on."

"No, I want to read and ruminate."

"Ruminate over your good fortune of today?"

"If you will have it so, y⸺

But it must not simply ove⸜ his good fortune of that day over which Grabért pondered. It was over the good fortune of the past fifteen years. From school to college, and from college to law school he had gone, and thence into practice, and he was now accredited a successful young lawyer. His small fortune, which Mr. Buckley, with generous kindness, had invested wisely, had almost doubled, and his school career, while not of the brilliant, meteoric kind, had been pleasant and profitable. He had made friends, at first, with the boys he met, and they in turn had taken him into their homes. Now and then, the Buckleys asked him to dinner, and he was seen occasionally in their box at the opera. He was rapidly becoming a social favorite, and girls vied with each other to dance with him. No one had asked any questions, and he had volunteered no information concerning himself. Vannier, who had known him in preparatory school days, had said that he was a young country fellow with some money, no connections, and a ward of Mr. Buckley's, and somehow, contrary to the usual social custom of the South, this meager account had passed muster. But Vannier's family had been a social arbiter for many years, and Grabért's personality was pleasing without being aggressive, so he had passed through the portals of the social world and was in the inner circle.

One year, when he and Vannier were in Switzerland, pretending to climb impossible mountains and in reality smoking many cigars a day on hotel porches, a letter came to Grabért from the priest of his old-time town, telling him that Grandmère Grabért had been laid away in the parish churchyard. There was no more to tell. The little old hut had been sold to pay funeral expenses.

"Poor Grandmère," sighed Victor. "She did care for me after her fashion. I'll go take a look at her grave when I go back."

But he did not go, for when he returned to Louisiana, he was too busy, then he decided that it would be useless, sentimental folly. Moreover, he had no love for the old village. Its very name suggested things that made him turn and look about him nervously. He had long since eliminated Madame Guichard from his list of acquaintances.

And yet, as he sat there in his cozy study that night and smiled as he went over in his mind triumph after triumph which he had made since the old bookstore days in Royal Street, he was conscious of a subtle undercurrent of annoyance; a sort of mental reservation that placed itself on every pleasant memory.

"I wonder what's the matter with me?" he asked himself as he rose and paced the floor impatiently. Then he tried to recall his other triumph, the one of the day. The case of Tate vs. Tate, a famous will contest, had been dragging through the courts for seven years, and his speech had decided it that day. He could hear the applause of the courtroom as he sat down, but it rang hollow in his ears, for he remembered another scene. The day before he had been in another court and found himself interested in the prisoner before the bar. The offense was a slight one, a mere technicality. Grabért was conscious of a something pleasant in the man's face; a scrupulous neatness in his dress, an unostentatious conforming to the prevailing style. The Recorder, however, was short and brusque.

"Wilson—Wilson—" he growled. "Oh, yes, I know you,

always kicking up some sort of a row about theater seats and cars. Hum-um. What do you mean by coming before me with a flower in your buttonhole?"

The prisoner looked down indifferently at the bud on his coat and made no reply.

"Hey?" growled the Recorder. "You niggers are putting yourselves up too much for me."

At the forbidden word, the blood rushed to Grabért's face, and he started from his seat angrily. The next instant, he had recovered himself and buried his face in a paper. After Wilson had paid his fine, Grabért looked at him furtively as he passed out. His face was perfectly impassive, but his eyes flashed defiantly. The lawyer was tingling with rage and indignation, although the affront had not been given him.

"If Recorder Grant had any reason to think that I was in any way like Wilson, I would stand no better show," he mused bitterly.

However, as he thought it over tonight, he decided that he was a sentimental fool. "What have I to do with them?" he asked himself. "I must be careful."

The next week, he discharged the man who cared for his office. He was a Negro, and Grabért had no fault to find with him generally, but he found himself with a growing sympathy toward the man, and since the episode in the courtroom, he was morbidly nervous lest a something in his manner would betray him. Thereafter, a round-eyed Irish boy cared for his rooms.

The Vanniers were wont to smile indulgently at his every move. Elise Vannier particularly was more than interested in his work. He had a way of dropping in of evenings and talking over his cases and speeches with her in a cozy corner of the library. She had a gracious sympathetic manner that was soothing and a cheery fund of repartee to whet her conversation. Victor found himself drifting into sentimental bits of talk now and then. He found himself carrying around in his pocketbook a faded rose which she had once worn, and when he laughed at it one day and started to throw it in the wastebasket, he suddenly kissed it instead and replaced it in the pocketbook. That Elise was not indifferent to him he could easily see. She had not learned yet how to veil her eyes and mask her face under a cool assumption of superiority. She would give him her hand, when they met, with a girlish impulsiveness, and her color came and went under his gaze. Sometimes, when he held her hand a bit longer than necessary, he could feel it flutter in his own, and she would sigh a quick little gasp that made his heart leap and choked his utterance.

They were tucked away in their usual cozy corner one evening, and the conversation had drifted to the problem of where they would spend the summer.

"Papa wants to go to the country house," pouted Elise, "and Mama and I don't want to go. It isn't fair, of course, because when we go so far away, Papa can be with us only for a few weeks when he can get away from his office, while if we go to the country place, he can run up every few days. But it is so dull there, don't you think so?"

Victor recalled some pleasant vacation days at the plantation home and laughed. "Not if you are there."

"Yes, but you see, I can't take myself for a companion. Now if you'll promise to come up sometimes, it will be better."

"If I may, I shall be delighted to come."

Elise laughed intimately. "If you may—" she replied. "As if such a word had to enter into our plans. Oh, but Victor, haven't you some sort of plantation somewhere? It seems to me that I heard Steven years ago speak of your home in the country, and I wondered sometimes that you never spoke of it or ever mentioned having visited it."

The girl's artless words were bringing cold sweat to Victor's brow, his tongue felt heavy and useless, but he managed to answer quietly, "I have no home in the country."

"Well, didn't you ever own one, or your family?"

"It was old quite a good many years ago," he replied, and a vision of the little old hut with its tumbledown steps and weed-grown garden came into his mind.

"Where was it?" pursued Elise innocently.

"Oh, away up in St. Landry parish, too far away from civilization to mention." He tried to laugh, but it was a hollow forced attempt that rang false. But Elise was too absorbed in her own thoughts of the summer to notice.

"And you haven't a relative living?" she continued.

"Not one."

"How strange. Why, it seems to me if I did not have a half a hundred cousins and uncles and aunts that I should feel somehow out of touch with the world."

He did not reply, and she chattered away on another topic.

When he was alone in his room that night, he paced the floor again, chewing wildly at a cigar that he had forgotten to light.

"What did she mean? What did she mean?" he asked himself over and over. Could she have heard or suspected anything that she was trying to find out about? Could any action, any unguarded expression of his, have set the family thinking? But he soon dismissed the thought as unworthy of him. Elise was too frank and transparent a girl to stoop to subterfuge. If she wished to know anything, she was wont to ask out at once, and if she had once thought anyone was sailing under false colors, she would say so frankly and dismiss them from her presence.

Well, he must be prepared to answer questions if he were going to marry her. The family would want to know all about him, and Elise, herself, would be curious for more than her brother Steve Vannier's meager account. But was he going to marry Elise? That was the question.

He sat down and buried his head in his hands. Would it be right for him to take a wife, especially such a woman as Elise, and from such a family as the Vanniers? Would it be fair? Would it be just? If they knew and were willing, it would be different. But they did not know, and they would not consent if they did. In fancy, he saw the dainty girl whom he loved shrinking from him as he told her of Grandmère Grabért and the village boys. This last thought made him set his teeth hard, and the hot blood rushed to his face.

Well, why not, after all, why not? What was the difference between him and the hosts of other suitors who hovered about Elise? They had money; so had he. They had education, polite training, culture, social position; so had he. But they had family traditions, and he had none. Most of them could point to a long line of family portraits with justifiable pride; while if he had had a picture of Grandmère Grabért, he would have destroyed it fearfully, lest it fall into the hands of some too curious person. This was the subtle barrier that separated them. He recalled with a sting how often he had had to sit silent and constrained when the conversation turned to ancestors and family traditions. He might be one with his companions and friends in everything but this. He must ever be on the outside, hovering at the gates, as it were. Into the inner life of his social world, he might never enter. The charming impoliteness of an intercourse begun by their fathers and grandfathers was not for him. There must always be a certain formality with him, even though they were his most intimate friends. He had not fifty cousins, therefore, as Elise phrased it, he was "out of touch with the world."

"If ever I have a son or a daughter," he found himself saying unconsciously, "I would try to save him from this."

Then he laughed bitterly as he realized the irony of the thought. Well, anyway, Elise loved him. There was a sweet consolation in that. He had but to look into her frank eyes and read her soul. Perhaps she wondered why he had not spoken. Should he speak? There he was back at the old question again.   •

"According to the standard of the world," he mused reflectively, "my blood is tainted in two ways. Who knows it? No one but myself, and I shall not tell. Otherwise, I am quite as good as the rest, and Elise loves me."

But even this thought failed of its sweetness in a moment. Elise loved him because she did not know. He found a sickening anger and disgust rising in himself at a people whose prejudices made him live a life of deception. He would cater to their traditions no longer; he would be honest. Then he found himself shrinking from the alternative with a dread that made him wonder. It was the old problem of his life in the village; and the boys, both white and black and yellow, stood as before, with stones in their hands to hurl at him.

He went to bed worn out with the struggle, but still with no definite idea what to do. Sleep was impossible. He rolled and tossed miserably and cursed the fate that had thrown him in such a position. He had never thought very seriously over the subject before. He had rather drifted with the tide and accepted what came to him as a sort of recompense the world owed him for his unhappy childhood. He had known fear, yes, and qualms now and then, and a hot resentment occasionally when the outsideness of his situation was inborne to him; but that was all. Elise had awakened a disagreeable conscientiousness within him, which he decided was as unpleasant as it was unnecessary.

He could not sleep, so he arose, and dressing, walked out and stood on the banquette. The low hum of the city came to him like the droning of some sleepy insect, and ever and anon, the quick flash and fire of the gas houses like a huge winking fiery eye lit up the south of the city. It was inexpressingly soothing to Victor; the great unknowing city, teeming with life and with lives whose sadness mocked his own teacup tempest. He smiled and shook himself as a dog shakes off the water from his coat.

"I think a walk will help me out," he said absently, and presently he was striding down St. Charles Avenue, around Lee Circle and down to Canal Street, where the lights and glare absorbed him for a while. He walked out the wide boulevard toward Claiborne Street, hardly thinking, hardly realizing that he was walking. When he was thoroughly worn out, he retraced his steps and dropped wearily into a restaurant near Bourbon Street.

"Hullo!" said a familiar voice from a table as he entered. Victor turned and recognized Frank Ward, a little oculist, whose office was in the same building as his own.

"Another night owl besides myself," laughed Ward, making room for him at his table. "Can't you sleep too, old fellow?"

"Not very well," said Victor, taking the proferred seat. "I believe I'm getting nerves. Think I need toning up."

"Well, you'd have been toned up if you had been in here a few minutes ago. Why—why—" and Ward went off into peals of laughter at the memory of the scene.

"What was it?" asked Victor.

"Why—a fellow came in here, nice sort of fellow, apparently, and wanted to have supper. Well, would you believe it, when they wouldn't serve him, he wanted to fight everything in sight. It was positively exciting for a time."

"Why wouldn't the waiter serve him?" Victor tried to make his tone indifferent, but he felt the quaver in his voice.

"Why? Why, he was a darkey, you know."

"Well, what of it?" demanded Grabért fiercely. "Wasn't he quiet, well-dressed, polite? Didn't he have money?"

"My dear fellow," began Ward mockingly. "Upon my word, I believe you are losing your mind. You do need toning up or something. Would you—could you—?"

"Oh, pshaw," broke in Grabért. "I—I—believe I am losing my mind. Really, Ward, I need something to make me sleep. My head aches."

Ward was at once all sympathy and advice, and chiding to the waiter for his slowness in filling their order. Victor toyed with his food and made an excuse to leave the restaurant as soon as he could decently.

"Good heavens," he said when he was alone. "What will I do next?" His outburst of indignation at Ward's narrative had come from his lips almost before he knew it, and he was frightened, frightened at his own unguardedness. He did not know what had come over him.

"I must be careful, I must be careful," he muttered to himself. "I must go to the other extreme, if necessary." He was pacing his rooms again, and suddenly, he faced the mirror.

"You wouldn't fare any better than the rest, if they knew," he told the reflection. "You poor wretch, what are you?"

When he thought of Elise, he smiled. He loved her, but

he hated the traditions which she represented. He was conscious of a blind fury which bade him wreak vengeance on those traditions, and of a cowardly fear which cried out to him to retain his position in the world's and Elise's eyes at any cost.

Mrs. Grabért was delighted to have visiting her her old school friend from Virginia, and the two spent hours laughing over their girlish escapades, and comparing notes about their little ones. Each was confident that her darling had said the cutest things, and their polite deference to each other's opinions on the matter was a sham through which each saw without resentment.

"But Elise," remonstrated Mrs. Allen, "I think it so strange you don't have a mammy for Baby Vannier. He would be so much better cared for than by that harum-scarum young white girl you have."

"I think so too, Adelaide," sighed Mrs. Grabért. "It seems strange for me not to have a darkey maid about, but Victor can't bear them. I cried and cried for my old mammy, but he was stern. He doesn't like darkies, you know, and he says old mammies just frighten children and ruin their childhood. I don't see how he could say that, do you?" She looked wistfully to Mrs. Allen for sympathy.

"I don't know," mused that lady. "We were all looked after by our mammies, and I think they are the best kind of nurses."

"And Victor won't have any kind of darkey servant either here or at the office. He says they're shiftless and worthless and generally no-account. Of course, he knows, he's had lots of experience with them in his business."

Mrs. Allen folded her hands behind her head and stared hard at the ceiling. "Oh, well, men don't know everything," she said, "and Victor may come around to our way of thinking after all."

It was late that evening when the lawyer came in for dinner. His eyes had acquired a habit of veiling themselves under their lashes as if they were constantly concealing something which they feared might be wrenched from them by a stare. He was nervous and restless, with a habit of glancing about him furtively, and a twitching compressing of his lips when he had finished a sentence, which somehow reminded you of a kindhearted judge who is forced to give a death sentence.

Elise met him at the door as was her wont, and she knew from the first glance into his eyes that something had disturbed him more than usual that day, but she forbore asking questions, for she knew he would tell her when the time had come.

They were in their room that night when the rest of the household lay in slumber. He sat for a long while gazing at the open fire, then he passed his hand over his forehead wearily.

"I have had a rather unpleasant experience today," he began.

"Yes."

"Pavageau, again."

His wife was brushing her hair before the mirror. At the name she turned hastily with the brush in her uplifted hand.

"I can't understand, Victor, why you must have dealings with that man. He is constantly irritating you. I simply wouldn't associate with him."

"I don't," and he laughed at her feminine argument. "It isn't a question of association, *chérie,* it's a purely business and unsocial relation, if relation it may be called, that throws us together."

She threw down the brush petulantly and came to his side. "Victor," she began hesitatingly, her arms about his neck, her face close to his, "won't you—won't you give up politics for me? It was ever so much nicer when you were just a lawyer and wanted only to be the best lawyer in the state, without all this worry about corruption and votes and such things. You've changed, oh, Victor, you've changed so. Baby and I won't know you after a while."

He put her gently on his knee. "You musn't blame the poor politics, darling. Don't you think, perhaps, it's the inevitable hardening and embittering that must come to us all as we grow older?''

"No, I don't," she replied emphatically. "Why do you go into this struggle, anyhow? You have nothing to gain but an empty honor. It won't bring you more money, or make you more loved or respected. Why must you be mixed up with such—such—awful people?''

"I don't know," he said wearily.

And in truth, he did not know. He had gone on after his marriage with Elise making one success after another. It seemed that a beneficent Providence had singled him out as the one man in the state upon whom to heap the most lavish attentions. He was popular after the fashion of those who are high in the esteem of the world; and this very fact made him tremble the more, for he feared that should some disclosure come, he could not stand the shock of public opinion that must overwhelm him.

"What disclosure?" he would say impatiently when such a thought would come to him. "Where could it come from, and then, what is there to disclose?''

Thus he would deceive himself for as much as a month at a time.

He was surprised to find awaiting him in his office one day the man Wilson, whom he remembered in the courtroom before Recorder Grant. He was surprised and annoyed. Why had the man come to his office? Had he seen the telltale flush on his face that day?

But it was soon evident that Wilson did not even remember having seen him before.

"I came to see if I could retain you in a case of mine," he began, after the usual formalities of greeting were over.

"I am afraid, my good man," said Grabért brusquely, "that you have mistaken the office."

Wilson's face flushed at the appellation, but he went on bravely. "I have not mistaken the office. I know you are the best civil lawyer in the city, and I want your services."

"An impossible thing."

"Why? Are you too busy? My case is a simple thing, a

mere point in law, but I want the best authority and the best opinion brought to bear on it."

"I could not give you any help—and—I fear, we do not understand each other—I do not wish to." He turned to his desk abruptly.

"What could he have meant by coming to me?" he questioned himself fearfully, as Wilson left the office. "Do I look like a man likely to take up his impossible contentions?"

He did not look like it, nor was he. When it came to a question involving the Negro, Victor Grabért was noted for his stern, unrelenting attitude; it was simply impossible to convince him that there was anything but sheerest incapacity in that race. For him, no good could come out of this Nazareth. He was liked and respected by men of his political belief, because, even when he was a candidate for a judgeship, neither money nor the possible chance of a deluge of votes from the First and Fourth Wards could cause him to swerve one hair's breadth from his opinion of the black inhabitants of those wards.

Pavageau, however, was his *bête noir*. Pavageau was a lawyer, a coolheaded, calculating man with steely eyes set in a grim brown face. They had first met in the courtroom in a case which involved the question whether a man may set aside the will of his father who, disregarding the legal offspring of another race than himself, chooses to leave his property to educational institutions which would not have granted admission to that son. Pavageau represented the son. He lost, of course. The judge, the jury, the people, and Grabért were against him; but he fought his fight with a grim determination which commanded Victor's admiration and respect.

"Fools," he said between his teeth to himself, when they were crowding about him with congratulations. "Fools, can't they see who is the abler man of the two?"

He wanted to go up to Pavageau and give him his hand; to tell him that he was proud of him and that he had really won the case, but public opinion was against him; but he dared not. Another one of his colleagues might; but he was afraid. Pavageau and the world might misunderstand, or would it be understanding?

Thereafter they met often. Either by some freak of nature, or because there was a shrewd sense of the possibilities in his position, Pavageau was of the same political side of the fence as Grabért. Secretly, he admired the man; he respected him; he liked him, and because of this he was always ready with sneer and invective for him. He fought him bitterly when there was no occasion for fighting, and Pavageau became his enemy, and his name a very synonym of horror to Elise, who learned to trace her husband's fits of moodiness and depression to the one source.

Meanwhile, Vannier Grabért was growing up, a handsome lad, with his father's and mother's physical beauty, and a strength and force of character that belonged to neither. In him, Grabért saw the reparation of all his childhood's wrongs and sufferings. The boy realized all his own longings. He had family traditions, and a social position which was his from birth and an inalienable right to hold up his head without an unknown fear gripping at his heart. Grabért felt that he could forgive all; the village boys of long ago, and the imaginary village boys of today when he looked at his son. He had bought and paid for Vannier's freedom and happiness. The coins may have been each a drop of his heart's blood, but he had reckoned the cost before he had given it.

It was a source of great pride for him to take the boy to court with him,* and one Saturday morning when he was starting out, Vannier asked if he might go.

"There is nothing that would interest you today, *mon fils,*" he said tenderly, "but you may go."

In fact, there was nothing interesting that day; merely a troublesome old woman, who instead of taking her fair-skinned grandchild out of the school, where it had been found it did not belong, had preferred to bring the matter to court. She was represented by Pavageau. Of course, there was not the ghost of a show for her. Pavageau had

---

* Editor's note: Grabért is now a judge.

told her that. The law was very explicit about the matter. The only question lay in proving the child's affinity to the Negro race, which was not such a difficult matter to do, so the case was quickly settled, since the child's grandmother accompanied him. The judge, however, was irritated. It was a hot day, and he was provoked that such a trivial matter should have taken up his time. He lost his temper as he looked at his watch.

"I don't see why these people want to force their children into the white schools," he declared. "There should be a rigid inspection to prevent it, and all the suspected children put out and made to go where they belong."

Pavageau, too, was irritated that day. He looked up from some papers which he was folding, and his gaze met Grabért's with a keen, cold, penetrating flash.

"Perhaps Your Honor would like to set the example by taking your son from the schools."

There was an instant silence in the courtroom, a hush intense and eager. Every eye turned upon the judge, who sat still, a figure carved in stone with livid face and fear-stricken eyes. After the first flash of his eyes, Pavageau had gone on cooly sorting the papers.

The courtroom waited, waited, for the judge to rise and thunder forth a fine against the daring Negro lawyer for contempt. A minute passed, which seemed like an hour. Why did not Grabért speak? Pavageau's implied accusation was too absurd for denial; but he should be punished. Was His Honor ill, or did he merely hold the man in too much contempt to notice him or his remark?

Finally Grabért spoke; he moistened his lips, for they were dry and parched, and his voice was weak and sounded far away in his own ears. "My son—does—not—attend the public schools."

Someone in the rear of the room laughed, and the atmosphere lightened at once. Plainly Pavageau was an idiot, and His Honor too far above him; too much of a gentleman to notice him. Grabért continued calmly: "The gentleman" —there was an unmistakable sneer in this word, habit if nothing else, and not even fear could restrain him—"the gentleman doubtless intended a little pleasantry, but I shall have to fine him for contempt of court."

"As you will," replied Pavageau, and he flashed another look at Grabért. It was a look of insolent triumph and derision. His Honor's eyes dropped beneath it.

"What did that man mean, Father, by saying you should take me out of school?" asked Vannier on his way home.

"He was provoked, my son, because he had lost his case, and when a man is provoked, he is likely to say silly things. By the way, Vannier, I hope you won't say anything to your mother about the incident. It would only annoy her."

For the public, the incident was forgotten as soon as it had closed, but for Grabért, it was indelibly stamped on his memory; a scene that shrieked in his mind and stood out before him at every footstep he took. Again and again as he tossed on a sleepless bed did he see the cold flash of Pavageau's eyes, and hear his quiet accusation. How did he know? Where had he gotten his information? For he spoke, not as one who makes a random shot in anger; but as one who knows, who has known a long while, and who is betrayed by irritation into playing his trump card too early in the game.

He passed a wretched week, wherein it seemed that his every footstep was dogged, his every gesture watched and recorded. He fancied that Elise, even, was suspecting him. When he took his judicial seat each morning, it seemed that every eye in the courtroom was fastened upon him in derision; everyone who spoke, it seemed, were but biding their time to shout the old village street refrain which had haunted him all his life, "Nigger!—Nigger!—White nigger!"

Finally, he could stand it no longer, and with leaden feet and furtive glances to the right and left for fear he might be seen, he went up a flight of dusty stairs in an Exchange Alley building, which led to Pavageau's office.

The latter was frankly surprised to see him. He made a polite attempt to conceal it, however. It was the first time in his legal life that Grabért had ever sought out a Negro; the first time that he had ever voluntarily opened conversation with one.

He mopped his forehead nervously as he took the chair Pavageau offered him; he stared about the room for an instant; then with a sudden, almost brutal directness, he turned on the lawyer.

"See here, what did you mean by that remark you made in court the other day?"

"I meant just what I said," was the cool reply.

Grabért paused, "Why did you say it?" he asked slowly.

"Because I was a fool. I should have kept my mouth shut until another time, should I not?"

"Pavageau," said Grabért softly, "let's not fence. Where did you get your information?"

Pavageau paused for an instant. He put his fingertips together and closed his eyes as one who meditates. Then he said with provoking calmness,

"You seem anxious—well, I don't mind letting you know. It doesn't really matter."

"Yes, yes," broke in Grabért impatiently.

"Did you ever hear of a Madame Guichard of Hospital Street?"

The sweat broke out on the judge's brow as he replied weakly, "Yes."

"Well, I am her nephew."

"And she?"

"Is dead. She told me about you once—with pride, let me say. No one else knows."

Grabért sat dazed. He had forgotten about Madame Guichard. She had never entered into his calculations at all. Pavageau turned to his desk with a sigh as if he wished the interview were ended. Grabért rose.

"If—if—this were known—to—to—my—my wife," he said thickly, "it would hurt her very much."

His head was swimming. He had had to appeal to this man, and to appeal in his wife's name. His wife, whose name he scarcely spoke to men whom he considered his social equals.

Pavageau looked up quickly. "It happens that I often

have cases in your court," he spoke deliberately. "I am willing, if I lose fairly, to give up; but I do not like to have a decision made against me because my opponent is of a different complexion from mine, or because the decision against me would please a certain class of people. I only ask what I have never had from you—fair play."

"I understand," said Grabért.

He admired Pavageau more than ever as he went out of his office, yet this admiration was tempered by the knowledge that this man was the only person in the whole world who possessed positive knowledge of his secret. He groveled in a self-abasement at his position; and yet he could not but feel a certain relief that the vague formless fear which had hitherto dogged his life and haunted it had taken on a definite shape. He knew where it was now; he could lay his hands on it and fight it.

But with what weapons? There were none offered him save a substantial backing down from his position on certain questions; the position that had been his for so long that he was almost known by it. For in the quiet deliberate sentence of Pavageau's, he read that he must cease all the oppression, all the little injustices which he had offered Pavageau's clientele. He must act now as his convictions and secret sympathies and affiliations had bidden him act; not as prudence and fear and cowardice had made him act.

Then what would be the result? he asked himself. Would not the suspicions of the people be aroused by this sudden change in his manner? Would not they begin to question and to wonder? Would not someone remember Pavageau's remark that morning and, putting two and two together, start some rumor flying? His heart sickened again at the thought.

There was a banquet that night. It was in his honor, and he was to speak, and the thought was distasteful to him beyond measure. He knew how it all would be. He would be hailed with shouts and acclamations, as the finest flower of civilization. He would be listened to deferentially, and younger men would go away holding him in their hearts as a truly worthy model. When all the while—

He threw back his head and laughed. Oh, what a glorious revenge he had on those little white village boys! How he had made a race atone for Wilson's insult in the courtroom; for the man in the restaurant at whom Ward had laughed so uproariously; for all the affronts seen and unseen given these people of his own whom he had denied. He had taken a diploma from their most exclusive college; he had broken down the barriers of their social world; he had taken the highest possible position among them; and aping their own ways, had shown them that he too could despise this inferior race they despised. Nay, he had taken for his wife the best woman among them all, and she had borne him a son. Ha, ha! What a joke on them all!

And he had not forgotten the black and yellow boys either. They had stoned him too, and he had lived to spurn them; to look down upon them, and to crush them at every possible turn from his seat on the bench. Truly, his life had not been wasted.

He had lived forty-nine years now, and the zenith of his power was not yet reached. There was much more to do, much more, and he was going to do it. He owed it to Elise and the boy. For their sake he must go on and on and keep his tongue still, and truckle to Pavageau and suffer alone. Someday, perhaps, he would have a grandson, who would point with pride to "my grandfather, the famous Judge Grabért!" Ah, that in itself was a reward. To have founded a dynasty; to bequeath to others that which he had never possessed himself, and the lack of which had made his life a misery.

It was a banquet with a political significance; one that meant a virtual triumph for Judge Grabért in the next contest for the District Judge. He smiled around at the eager faces which were turned up to his as he arose to speak. The tumult of applause which had greeted his rising had died away, and an expectant hush fell on the room.

"What a sensation I could make now," he thought. He had but to open his mouth and cry out, "Fools! Fools! I whom you are honoring, I am one of the despised ones. Yes, I'm a nigger—do you hear, a nigger!" What a temptation it was to end the whole miserable farce. If he were alone in the world, if it were not for Elise and the boy, he would, just to see their horror and wonder. How they would shrink from him! But what could they do? They could take away his office; but his wealth, and his former successes, and his learning, they could not touch. Well, he must speak, and he must remember Elise and the boy.

Every eye was fastened on him in eager expectancy. Judge Grabért's speech was expected to outline the policy of their faction in the coming campaign. He turned to the chairman at the head of the table.

"Mr. Chairman," he began, and paused again. How peculiar it was that in the place of the chairman there sat Grandmère Grabért as she had been wont to sit on the steps of the tumbledown cottage in the village. She was looking at him sternly and bidding him give an account of his life since she had kissed him good-bye ere he had sailed down the river to New Orleans. He was surprised, and not a little annoyed. He had expected to address the chairman, not Grandmère Grabért. He cleared his throat and frowned.

"Mr. Chairman," he said again. Well, what was the use of addressing her that way? She would not understand him. He would call her Grandmère, of course. Were they not alone again on the cottage steps at twilight with the cries of the little brutish boys ringing derisively from the distant village square?

"Grandmère," he said softly, "you don't understand—" and then he was sitting down in his seat pointing one finger angrily at her because the other words would not come. They stuck in his throat, and he choked and beat the air with his hands. When the men crowded around him with water and hastily improvised fans, he fought them away wildly and desperately with furious curses that came from his blackened lips. For were they not all boys with stones to pelt him because he wanted to play with them? He would run away to Grandmère, who would soothe him and comfort him. So he arose and, stumbling, shrieking, and beating them back from him, ran the length of the hall and fell across the threshold of the door.

The secret died with him, for Pavageau's lips were ever sealed.

# "As the Lord Lives, He Is One of Our Mother's Children"

## Pauline E. Hopkins

Lynching was common in America in the first half of the twentieth century, though seldom a subject of fiction. Hopkins's story, first published in *Colored American Magazine* in 1903, is one of the first by an African American writer to examine mob rule, black fear, and the complicated role of the Christian church in small American communities gripped by racial hatred. Hopkins weaves a melodramatic morality tale from these materials and creates a vivid picture of racial hostility in the American West, at a time when some blacks fled there to escape prejudice in other parts of the country.

IT WAS SATURDAY AFTERNOON in a large Western town, and the Rev. Septimus Stevens sat in his study writing down the headings for his Sunday sermon. It was slow work; somehow the words would not flow with their usual ease, although his brain was teeming with ideas. He had written for his heading at the top of the sheet these words for a text: "As I live, he is one of our mother's children." It was to be a great effort on the Negro question, and the reverend gentleman, with his New England training, was in full sympathy with his subject. He had jotted down a few headings under it, when he came to a full stop; his mind simply refused to work. Finally, with a sigh, he opened the compartment in his desk where his sermons were packed and began turning over those old creations in search of something suitable for the morrow.

Suddenly the whistles in all directions began to blow

wildly. The Rev. Septimus hurried to the window, threw it open, and leaned out, anxious to learn the cause of the wild clamor. Could it be another of the terrible "cave-ins" that were the terror of every mining district? Men were pouring out of the mines as fast as they could come up. The crowds which surged through the streets night and day were rushing to meet them. Hundreds of policemen were about; each corner was guarded by a squad commanded by a sergeant. The police and the mob were evidently working together. Tramp, tramp, on they rushed; down the serpentine boulevard for nearly two miles they went swelling like an angry torrent. In front of the open window where stood the white-faced clergyman, they paused. A man mounted the empty barrel and harangued the crowd: "I am from Dover City, gentlemen, and I have come here today to assist you in teaching the blacks a lesson. I have killed a nigger before," he yelled, "and in revenge of the wrong wrought upon you and yours, I am willing to kill again. The only way you can teach these niggers a lesson is to go to the jail and lynch these men as an object lesson. String them up! That is the only thing to do. Kill them, string them up, lynch them! I will lead you. On to the prison and lynch Jones and Wilson, the black fiends!" With a hoarse shout, in which were mingled cries like the screams of enraged hyenas and the snarls of tigers, they rushed on.

Nora, the cook, burst open the study door, pale as a sheet, and dropped at the minister's feet. "Mother of God!" she cried. "And is it the end of the wurruld?"

On the maddened men rushed from north, south, east, and west, armed with everything from a brick to a horse-pistol. In the melee a man was shot down. Somebody planted a long knife in the body of a little black newsboy for no apparent reason. Every now and then a Negro would be overwhelmed somewhere on the outskirts of the crowd and left beaten to a pulp. Then they reached the jail and battered in the door.

The solitary watcher at the window tried to move, but could not; terror had stricken his very soul, and his white lips moved in articulate prayer. The crowd surged back. In the midst was only one man; for some reason, the other was missing. A rope was knotted about his neck—charged with murder, himself about to be murdered. The hands which drew the rope were too swift, and half-strangled, the victim fell. The crowd halted, lifted him up, loosened the rope, and let the wretch breathe.

He was a grand man—physically—black as ebony, tall, straight, deep-chested, every fiber full of that life so soon to be quenched. Lucifer, just about to be cast out of heaven, could not have thrown around a glance of more scornful pride. What might not such a man have been, if—but it was too late. "Run fair, boys," said the prisoner, calmly, "run fair! You keep up your end of the rope, and I'll keep up mine."

The crowd moved a little more slowly, and the minister saw the tall form "keeping up" its end without a tremor of hesitation. As they neared the telegraph pole, with its outstretched arm, the watcher summoned up his lost strength, grasped the curtain, and pulled it down to shut out the dreadful sight. Then came a moment of ominous silence. The man of God sank upon his knees to pray for the passing soul. A thousand-voiced cry of brutal triumph arose in cheers for the work that had been done, and curses and imprecations, and they who had hunted a man out of life hurried off to hunt for gold.

To and fro on the white curtain swung the black silhouette of what had been a man.

For months the minister heard in the silence of the night phantom echoes of those frightful voices, and awoke, shuddering, from some dream whose vista was closed by that black figure swinging in the air.

About a month after this happening, the rector was returning from a miner's cabin in the mountains where a child lay dying. The child haunted him; he thought of his own motherless boy, and a fountain of pity overflowed in his heart. He had dismounted and was walking along the road to the ford at the creek which just here cut the path fairly in two.

The storm of the previous night had refreshed all nature

and had brought out the rugged beauty of the landscape in all its grandeur. The sun had withdrawn his last dazzling rays from the eastern highlands upon which the lone traveler gazed, and now they were fast veiling themselves in purple night shadows that rendered them momentarily more grand and mysterious. The man of God stood a moment with uncovered head repeating aloud some lines from a great Russian poet:

> "O Thou eternal One! whose presence bright
> All space doth occupy, all motion guide;
> Unchanged through time's all devastating flight;
> Thou only God! There is no God beside
> Being above all beings, Mighty One!
> Whom none can comprehend and none explore."

Another moment passed in silent reverence of the All-Wonderful, before he turned to remount his horse and enter the waters of the creek. The creek was very much swollen, and he found it hard to keep the ford. Just as he was midway the stream, he saw something lying half in the water on the other bank. Approaching nearer, he discovered it to be a man, apparently unconscious. Again dismounting, he tied his horse to a sapling and went up to the inert figure, ready, like the Samaritan of old, to succor the wayside fallen. The man opened his deep-set eyes and looked at him keenly. He was gaunt, haggard, and despairing, and soaking wet.

"Well, my man, what is the matter?" Rev. Mr. Stevens had a very direct way of going at things.

"Nothing," was the sullen response.

"Can't I help you? You seem ill. Why are you lying in the water?"

"I must have fainted and fallen in the creek," replied the man, answering the last question first. "I've tramped from Colorado hunting for work. I'm penniless, have no home, haven't had much to eat for a week, and now I've got a touch of your d——— mountain fever." He shivered as if with a chill and smiled faintly.

The man, from his speech, was well educated and, in spite of his pitiful situation, had an air of good breeding, barring his profanity.

"What's your name?" asked Stevens, glancing him over sharply as he knelt beside the man and deftly felt his pulse and laid a cool hand on the fevered brow.

"Stone—George Stone."

Stevens got up. "Well, Stone, try to get on my horse, and I'll take you to the rectory. My housekeeper and I together will manage to make you more comfortable."

So it happened that George Stone became a guest at the parsonage and, later, sexton of the church. In that gold-mining region, where new people came and went constantly and new excitements were things of everyday occurrence, and new faces as plenty as old ones, nobody asked or cared where the new sexton came from. He did his work quietly and thoroughly and quite won Nora's heart by his handy ways about the house. He had a room under the eaves and seemed thankful and content. Little Flip, the rector's son, took a special liking to him, and he, on his side, worshipped the golden-haired child and was never tired of playing with him and inventing things for his amusement.

"The reverend sets a heap by the boy," he said to Nora one day in reply to her accusation that he spoiled the boy and there was no living with him since Stone's advent. "He won't let me thank him for what he's done for me, but he can't keep me from loving the child."

One day in September, while passing along the street, Rev. Stevens had his attention called to a flaming poster on the side of a fence by the remarks of a crowd of men near him. He turned and read it:

#### $1,500 REWARD!

The above reward will be paid for information leading to the arrest of "Gentleman Jim," charged with complicity in the murder of Jerry Mason. This nigger is six feet, three inches tall, weight one hundred and sixty pounds. He escaped from jail when his pal was lynched two months ago by a citizens' committee. It is thought that he is in the mountains, etc. He is well educated, and might be taken for a white man. Wore, when last seen, blue jumper and overalls and cowhide boots.

He read it the second time, and he was dimly conscious of seeing, like a vision in the brain, a man playing about the parsonage with little Flip.

"I knowed him. I worked a spell with him over in Lone Tree Gulch before he got down on his luck," spoke a man at his side who was reading the poster with him. "Jones and him was two of the smartest and peaceablest niggers I ever seed. But Jerry Mason kinder sot on 'em both; never could tell why, only some white men can't 'bide a nigger eny mo' than a dog can a cat; it's a natural antiperthy. I'm free to say the niggers seemed harmless, but you can't tell what a man'll do when his blood's up."

He turned to the speaker. "What will happen if they catch him?"

"Lynch him sure; there's been a lot of trouble over there lately. I wouldn't give a toss-up for him if they get their hands on him once more."

Rev. Stevens pushed his way through the crowd and went slowly down the street to the church. He found Stone there sweeping and dusting. Saying that he wanted to speak with him, he led the way to the study. Facing around upon him suddenly, Stevens said, gravely: "I want you to tell me the truth. Is your real name Stone, and are you a Negro?"

A shudder passed over Stone's strong frame, then he answered, while his eyes never left the troubled face before him, "I am a Negro, and my name is not Stone."

"You said that you had tramped from Colorado."

"I hadn't. I was hiding in the woods; I had been there a month ago. I lied to you."

"Is it all a lie?"

Stone hesitated, and then said: "I was meaning to tell you the first night, but somehow I couldn't. I was afraid you'd turn me out; and I was sick and miserable—"

"Tell me the truth now."

"I will; I'll tell you the God's truth."

He leaned his hand on the back of a chair to steady himself; he was trembling violently. "I came out West from Wilmington, North Carolina, Jones and I together. We were both college men and chums from childhood. All our savings were in the business we had at home, when the leading men of the town conceived the idea of driving the Negroes out, and the Wilmington tragedy began. Jones was unmarried, but I lost wife and children that night—burned to death when the mob fired our home. When we got out here, we took up claims in the mountains. They were a rough crowd after we struck pay dirt, but Jones and I kept to ourselves and got along all right until Mason joined the crowd. He was from Wilmington; knew us, and took delight in tormenting us. He was a fighting man, but we wouldn't let him push us into trouble."

"You didn't quarrel with him, then?"

The minister gazed at Stone keenly. He seemed a man to trust. "Yes, I did. We didn't want trouble, but we couldn't let Mason rob us. We three had hot words before a big crowd; that was all there was to it that night. In the morning, Mason lay dead upon our claim. He'd been shot by someone. My partner and I were arrested, brought to this city, and lodged in the jail over there. Jones was lynched! God, can I ever forget that hooting, yelling crowd, and the terrible fight to get away! Somehow I did it—you know the rest."

"Stone, there's a reward for you, and a description of you as you were the night I found you."

Gentleman Jim's face was ashy. "I'll never be taken alive. They'll kill me for what I never did!"

"Not unless I speak. I am in sore doubt what course to take. If I give you up, the vigilantes will hang you."

"I'm a lost man," said the Negro helplessly, "but I'll never be taken alive."

Stevens walked up and down the room once or twice. It was a human life in his hands. If left to the law to decide, even then in this particular case the Negro stood no chance. It was an awful question to decide. One more turn up and down the little room and suddenly stopping, he flung himself upon his knees in the middle of the room and, raising his clasped hands, cried aloud for heavenly guidance. Such a prayer as followed, the startled listener had never before heard anywhere. There was nothing of rhetorical phrases, nothing of careful thought in the construction of sentences; it was the outpouring of a pure soul asking for help from its Heavenly Father with all the trustfulness of a little child. It came in a torrent, a flood; it wrestled mightily for the blessing it sought. Rising to his feet when his prayer was finished, Rev. Stevens said, "Stone,—you are to remain Stone, you know—it is best to leave things as they are. Go back to work."

The man raised his bowed head.

"You mean you're not going to give me up?"

"Stay here till the danger is past; then leave for other parts."

Stone's face turned red, then pale; his voice trembled, and tears were in the gray eyes. "I can't thank you, Mr. Stevens, but if ever I get the chance you'll find me grateful."

"All right, Stone, all right," and the minister went back to his writing.

That fall the Rev. Septimus Stevens went to visit his old New England home—he and Flip. He was returning home the day before Thanksgiving, with his widowed mother, who had elected to leave old associations and take charge of her son's home. It was a dim-colored day.

Engineers were laying out a new road near a place of swamps and oozy ground and dead, wet grass, overarched by leafless, desolate boughs. They were eating their lunch now, seated about on the trunks of fallen trees. The jokes were few, scarcely a pun seasoned the meal. The day was a dampener; that the morrow was a holiday did not kindle merriment.

Stone sat a little apart from the rest. He had left Rev. Stevens when he got this job in another state. They had voted him moody and unsociable long ago—a man who broods forever upon his wrongs is not a comfortable companion; he never gave anyone a key to his moods. He shut himself up in his haunted room—haunted by memory—and no one interfered with him.

The afternoon brought a change in the weather. There was a strange hush, as if Nature were holding her breath. But it was as a wild beast holds its breath before a spring. Suddenly a little chattering wind ran along the ground. It was too weak to lift the sodden leaves, yet it made itself heard in some way and grew stronger. It seemed dizzy and ran about in a circle. There was a pale light over all, a brassy, yellow light, that gave all things a wild look. The chief of the party took an observation and said: "We'd better get home."

Stone lingered. He was paler, older.

The wind had grown vigorous now and began to tear angrily at the trees, twisting the saplings about with invisible hands. There was a rush and a roar that seemed to spread about in every direction. A tree was furiously uprooted and fell directly in front of him; Stone noticed the storm for the first time.

He looked about him in a dazed way and muttered, "He's coming on this train, he and the kid!"

The brassy light deepened into darkness. Stone went upon the railroad track and stumbled over something that lay directly over it. It was a huge tree that the wind had lifted in its great strength and whirled over there like thistledown. He raised himself slowly, a little confused by the fall. He took hold of the tree mechanically, but the huge bulk would not yield an inch.

He looked about in the gathering darkness; it was five miles to the station where he might get help. His companions were too far on their way to recall, and there lay a huge mass, directly in the way of the coming train. He had no watch, but he knew it must be nearly six. Soon—very soon—upon the iron pathway, a great train, freighted with life, would dash around the curve to wreck and ruin! Again he muttered, "Coming on this train, he and the kid!" He pictured the faces of his benefactor and the little child, so like his own lost one, cold in death; the life crushed out by the cruel wheels. What was it that seemed to strike across the storm and all its whirl of sound—a child's laugh? Nay, something fainter still—the memory of a child's laugh. It was like a breath of spring flowers in the desolate winter—a touch of heart music amid the revel of the storm. A vision of other fathers with children climbing upon their knees, a soft babble of baby voices assailed him.

"God help me to save them!" he cried.

Again and again he tugged at the tree. It would not move. Then he hastened and got an iron bar from among the tools. Again he strove—once—twice—thrice. With a groan the nearest end gave way. Eureka! If only his strength would hold out. He felt it ebbing slowly from him, something seemed to clutch at his heart; his head swam. Again and yet again he exerted all his strength. There came a prolonged shriek that awoke the echoes. The train was coming. The tree was moving! It was almost off the other rail. The leafless trees seemed to enfold him—to hold him with skeleton arms. "Oh, God save them!" he gasped. "Our times are in Thy hand!"

Something struck him a terrible blow. The agony was ended. Stone was dead.

Rev. Stevens closed his eyes, with a deadly faintness creeping over him, when he saw how near the trainload of people had been to destruction. Only God had saved them at the eleventh hour through the heroism of Stone, who lay dead upon the track, the life crushed out of him by the engine. An inarticulate thanksgiving rose to his lips as soft and clear came the sound of distant church bells, calling to weekly prayer, like "horns of Elfland softly blowing."

Sunday, a week later, Rev. Septimus Stevens preached the greatest sermon of his life. They had found the true murderer of Jerry Mason, and Jones and Gentleman Jim were publicly exonerated by a repentant community.

On this Sunday Rev. Stevens preached the funeral ser-mon of Gentleman Jim. The church was packed to suffocation by a motley assemblage of men in all stages of dress and undress, but there was sincerity in their hearts as they listened to the preacher's burning words: "As the Lord lives, he is one of our mother's children."

# The Taming of a Modern Shrew

## Ruth D. Todd

Few early black writers could afford the luxury of writing comedy in the novel or short fiction. This rare piece of whimsical social satire is an exception. Playing off the plot and theme of Shakespeare's *The Taming of the Shrew*, Ruth Todd sketches the brief courtship of Edward Reynolds and Jennie Leigh as a contemporary black romance, lightly encumbered by the romantic conventions of the time. Todd's career was brief and undistinguished, but her story is important for revealing a desire among early black women writers to write in and against the dominant Western tradition of letters of which they are a part. Pauline Hopkins chose this story for publication in *Colored American Magazine* in 1904.

THAT EDWARD REYNOLDS was the most daring young fellow in Liston was quite a settled fact. There was no mischief, no diabolical trick that could frighten him off. As a boy he was the terror of the town, for Liston was only a small town in southern Arkansas, where the major number of the inhabitants were Negroes.

Once, when he was quite a small lad, his companions had dared him to jump from the high town bridge into the stream below, and he had dared to do so with very fatal results.

That his neck hadn't been broken years before he arrived at manhood was no fault of his; however, he had come out of it all unscathed; a tall, perfectly built young man, as handsome as a god. His complexion was a reddish brown, his hair coarse, black, and as straight as an Indian's, and his eyes, which were the most striking feature about him, were large, fearless eyes, as black as night and sparkling with mischief, but a greater amount of daring.

Still, he was even-tempered, although his voice had a firm and commanding ring. He was certainly the most popular young fellow about town, and any one of the girls would have been proud to call him her "young man." But this youth, although not vain or egotistical, would have none of them, that is, excepting a certain beautiful damsel named Jennie Leigh, who, it seemed, would have none of him.

Jennie was the acknowledged belle of Liston. Her complexion was a trifle darker than Edward's, but she had soft, curly black hair, as fine and as glossy as silk, and large, bewitching black eyes; in fact, many of the young men had been wont to declare that "Jennie Leigh's eyes always made a fellow feel deuced uncomfortable." She was fashionable, clever, witty, very charming, and possessed a temper that was, unlike Ed's, very uneven. In fact, when once aroused, she was a veritable shrew, though when things pleased her, there was not a young lady in Liston whose temper was so sweet or whose manner was gentler.

Edward was exceedingly fond of Jennie, in fact, had loved her when they were tots; and as schoolmates, he had carried no other girl's books but Jennie's to and from the village school; and after both had graduated from the high school, the intimacy had never decreased. So it was quite evident that they would someday marry, despite the fact that they were forever "scrapping" with each other.

It was quite amusing to see them together, for Ed's temper was so even, and his vein of humor so tantalizing, that he always managed to arouse Jennie's ire. He had often asked her to marry him, a thing which any other young man would not dare to even think of, and Jennie had flatly refused Ed's every proposal.

But this fearless young man's courage never deserted him; his will was indomitable, and he inwardly avowed that Jennie Leigh should wed none save him. That he would win her or devote his whole life to the attempt, he was determined. One day when they were attending a certain afternoon garden party, Jennie had looked so lovely in a beautiful gown of some pale blue, soft material that Ed had blurted out in his abrupt fashion: "Oh, Jennie, won't you be mine?"

"Ed Reynolds, you are the silliest person I know. Every blessed time you see me, you ask me to 'marry you,' or 'be yours,' or something equally as stupid! You must think that I am going about looking for a husband, don't you?" she exclaimed impatiently.

"No, I did not think that, or I would have asked you nothing, because I'd have taken it for granted that I was your future spouse and led you to the minister's years ago," answered Ed, gazing admiringly at her beautiful face and exquisite gown.

"Oh, you are just horrid, and sometimes I think I hate you," cried Jennie, angrily.

But Ed was so used to these angry outbursts of Jennie's that it would have seemed very unnatural if she had acted otherwise. They were seated on a little rustic seat quite out of "earshot," and Ed answered her, paying no attention whatever to her angry words:

"Gee, but that's a lovely dress you have on, Jennie. You look awfully sweet in it, Jen. I wish you belonged to me. Won't you tell me you will wed me, dear? Oh, please say yes, Jennie!" and he caught one of her soft little hands in his.

"Oh, Ed, don't be stupid; people are looking at us!" she cried, trying in vain to draw her hand away.

"Who cares?" answered he. "You know as well as they that I love you, Jen, have loved you all my life, and there isn't another girl that I'd even waste a thought on. I'm quite serious now, and if you send me away from you again, I'll do something desperate, I swear I will!"

"What will you do—commit suicide?" she asked, glancing mischievously up at him, for he had arisen now and with a slight frown upon his handsome face, and both hands thrust into his trousers pockets, he stood looking down upon her.

"Certainly not! Do you think I'm some darned idiot!" he exclaimed, indignantly.

"Men who are violently in love always commit suicide when the lady of their choice persistently refuses them."

"Let them, they're quite welcome, I'm sure. If they haven't got sense enough to bear up, they ought to die! What I'm going to do is to live and marry you."

"Oh, you are, are you? I'd like to see you without my consent."

"Oh, you'll consent all right."

"You are a conceited prig!" she cried, scornfully. "I'll show you whether I'll consent or not by accepting James Wilson the next time he asks me to marry him."

"What, that puppet! Has he asked you to marry him?"

"Why, of course he has. You are not the only person worthy of existence as yet," she exclaimed, indignantly.

"Why, confound him, if he even dares look at you again, I'll punch his head!" cried Ed, vehemently.

"Why, Ed Reynolds, you wouldn't dare. I'd hate you forever if you did such an ungentlemanly thing."

"I'd dare do anything for you. Oh, Jennie, dear Jennie, please say that you will be my own, my very own."

"You are absolutely incorrigible, Ed; do give me some rest."

"I will, when you promise to marry me, dear. Please say yes. Honest, I—I worship you. I don't know how on earth I can give you up. But I swear I'll leave town and never visit these parts again if you do not promise to marry me. I'm dead earnest this time. I know I've sworn to do all sorts of things time and again, but I'll—oh, Jennie, how can you be so cruel?"

"Cruel! Why I think I am extremely kind to you. There is not another person that I would allow to talk to me as you do, Ed Reynolds, but now I'll tell you what I will do."

"What will you do?"

"I'll marry you on one condition."

"Oh, name it! name it!" cried Ed, gladly.

"If you will write a novel or compose some poems worthy of notice, and have them published, I'll marry you—let's see—Easter."

"That's worse than cruel, Jennie. You know quite well that I'm not a literary chap, that I know nothing whatever of literature, and, er—you can't care anything for me if you ask me to do what you know is an impossibility."

"I never said I did care for you, did I?"

"But you do, don't you, Jen?"

"Do as I ask you to, and you will hear something that you have waited long to hear."

"Confound it, I'll try it, if I win or lose; I'd do anything to win you, dear Jennie."

And so it was announced that Jennie and Ed were to be married at Easter.

That was in September, and the last of March was drawing near before Ed was sure of winning his prize.

He knew that he would be very unsuccessful if he attempted such a serious thing as a novel, so he had tried his hand at poetry, but I'm afraid with very sad results. The following are specimens of his works:

> It was a nice bright day in May,
> The birds were warbling out their lay,
> When everybody on that day
> Would stare at my girl named May.

This terminated quite abruptly, as though the writer was disgusted with such rubbish.

Then another:

### Pathos

> "My darling, I love you," the young man cried,
> As he whispered these words to the maid at his side,
> "If you will only say that you love me true,
> I'll worship, adore you, my only dear Sue."

In fact this daring young man wasted a small fortune in stationery, with the most disgusting results, when it suddenly occurred to him to try his hand at nonsense poems, or stories in modern slang. So he wrote this:

### To Jennie

There was once a young chap called Bennie,
Who loved a sweet maiden named Jennie,
  Implored the lad, "Don't refuse me."
  Cried the maid, "You confuse me,
For I don't know my mind, if I've any."

Said she, "I can't quite discover,
Why you are such a persistent young lover,
  If you love me, dear Ben,
  Win fame with the pen,
And I'll wed you instead of another."

"No, no!" cried the lad with a shiver,
That shook him and stirred up his liver,
  "A pen I detest,
  Ask me anything else,
For I'd rather jump into the river."

Then the maid oped her eyes wide in surprise,
"For a lover," said she, "you're unwise,
  If you refuse my plan
  You're a nutty young man,
And for a dunce you'd take the first prize."

The lad thought the maiden was joking,
But instead with anger she was choking,
  "To the river," she said,
  "For you've such a thick head,
That I'm sure it needs a good soaking."

Then the lad left the maiden quite sadly,
Said he, "I want you so badly,
  That I'll try at the pen,
  If I'm successful, why then,
Will you have me?" cried the maiden, "Oh, gladly!"

This lad's brain was as thick as fog,
It was even as thick as a log,
   For he thought that dear Jen,
   When she mentioned the pen,
Could mean nothing excepting the hog.

So this bug-housed young man named Ben
Built him an enormous big pen,
   And then he spent
   Every blessed red cent
Invested in hogs, he told Jen.

Then Jennie thought sure he was broke,
And she thought this a freak of a joke.
   "He's quite crazy," she said,
   "He's off of his head,"
And she laughed till she thought she would choke.

But Ben made a big pile of money,
And Jen said, "It's just too funny,
   But wed you I must,
   Or with laughter I'll bust."
And she kissed him, and called him her honey.

Then Ed wrote a story in modern slang, as follows:

### To Jennie

Once upon a time there was a girl whose first name
was Jennie. She was the swellest girl among the whole
bunch with which she traveled. And there wasn't a chap
in the whole neighborhood who wasn't dead gone on
her. She wore such towering pompadours and such swell
dresses she called gowns, and looked so much like a
gorgeous queen, that all the other girls turned green
with envy and the annoying disease called jealousy. And
you can bet your life that this dusky damsel of the
dreamy eyes was the only pebble on the beach. And as
far as hot air was concerned, she could give more of that
in ten minutes than any other girl could in fourteen hun-

dred and ninety-eight hours. And she was quicker than lightning at spitting fire when a guy rubbed her the wrong way. She had no favorite guy that she doted on unless it was a swell-looking guy who lived near her, and who so persistently dogged this baby's cute little foot-steps that she was forced to chew the taffy he gave her. This guy wore big-legged trousers and thought he looked wise and smart in rimless eye-glasses, which he donned after the maiden bade him do some intellectual stunts ere she would wed him.

It was a settled fact that this guy would win, so the other chaps all gave him a wide berth, but he failed to do these intellectual stunts and was about to give the whole business up as a bad job, when it rushed through his noggin that all girls liked loads of presents and a plenty of dough, and when these were rushed in upon her, she told him 'twas up to him to get the license, and she'd make the angel food with which to cholerize all of the guests, and the thing was completed in a swell church around the corner. Moral—Dough and a plenty of it is always the winning card.

He had no trouble to get Edson, the one and only colored editor in Liston, to promise to publish a nonsense poem or story in modern slang each week in his paper, and Ed hastened to the residence of his lady-love to tell her of his success.

"Oh, Ed, I think they are horrid!" cried Jennie, after she had read both poem and story.

"They are horrid, all right, but that's the only sort of literature now-a-days that makes a hit," answered Ed.

"I hope you are not going to have them published?" she asked anxiously.

"Of course I am. Do you suppose I'd give it up after seven long—almost intolerably long—months?"

"But surely you don't call this poetry or anything decent to read, even?"

"Sure—sure it is! It will make a hit all right."

"But why did you dedicate such horrid stuff to me? Oh, I

think you are awful—just awful, and I hate you, Ed Reynolds!"

"You'll have to marry me, though," replied Ed, smiling triumphantly.

"I wouldn't marry you if there wasn't another man left," cried she, vehemently.

"You'll have to now. There's your promise that you'd wed me if I became successful, and I've leased a nonsense column in Edson's paper every week as long as I like to deal in literature," said Ed, quite complacently.

"Literature nothing. Why you know you wouldn't dare have such rubbish published, not if you cared anything for me."

"That's just why I'm going to have it published, because I think so much of you, I want the whole world to know. I shall sign my own name, Edward Benjamin Reynolds, in capital letters instead of a non-de-plume."

"Oh, you can't be serious, Ed."

"Never was more serious before in my life."

"Oh, Ed, please don't have it published, for my sake! The girls will all make the greatest joke of me. Oh, Ed, please don't!" she pleaded.

But Edward knew that he held the winning card in his hand, and he thought that now was the best time to get Jennie's consent to wed him in two weeks' time, so he firmly avowed that he'd have them published—that, in fact, Edson already had a type-written copy of them in his possession.

Then Jennie—the untamable, high-spirited Jennie Leigh —became quite meek and gentle, telling Ed that she would wed him on the morrow or whenever he wished if he would only promise her that he would not publish that awful stuff.

"But I won't marry you if you hate me, Jen," said Ed.

"You know that I love you, Ed, have always loved you and could never live without you, dear, and if you loved me, you would tear that paper up and throw it in the grate."

"Do you really love me, Jennie? Oh, Jennie, if I thought you cared enough to marry me Easter, I'd be the happiest man in Liston."

"And you wouldn't have them published?"

"Certainly not, darling."

"Then I am yours!" she cried, and Ed drew her to him, etc. etc.

On Easter morn, 'neath an arch of lilies and surrounded by huge exotic plants in "St. James' Mission," Edward B. Reynolds and Jennie Leigh were happily wedded.

# Emmy

## Jessie Fauset

"Emmy" addresses the social stigmatization of interracial relationships through a psychological study of the effects of "passing" on a pair of young lovers, Archie and Emmy. Like "The Stones of the Village," the story makes clear the conflict between social aspiration and personal integrity that plagued the mulatto, yet with a decidedly more optimistic and hopeful twist. The story also delineates the double-bind of the black female beholden both to masculine social privilege and to contemporary racism. The story was first published in successive issues of *The Crisis* in 1913 and 1914.

## I

"THERE ARE FIVE RACES," said Emmy confidently. "The white or Caucasian, the yellow or Mongolian, the red or Indian, the brown or Malay, and the black or Negro."

"Correct," nodded Miss Wenzel mechanically. "Now to which of the five do you belong?" And then immediately Miss Wenzel reddened.

Emmy hesitated. Not because hers was the only dark face in the crowded schoolroom, but because she was visualizing the pictures with which the geography had illustrated its information. She was not white, she knew that—nor had she almond eyes like the Chinese, nor the feathers which the Indian wore in his hair and which, of course, were to Emmy a racial characteristic. She regarded the color of her slim brown hands with interest—she had never thought of it before. The Malay was a horrid, ugly-looking thing with a ring in his nose. But he was brown, so she was, she supposed, really a Malay.

And yet the Hottentot, chosen with careful nicety to represent the entire Negro race, had on the whole a better appearance.

"I belong," she began tentatively, "to the black or Negro race."

"Yes," said Miss Wenzel with a sigh of relief, for if Emmy had chosen to ally herself with any other race except, of course, the white, how could she, teacher though she was, set her straight without embarrassment? The recess bell rang, and she dismissed them with a brief but thankful "You may pass."

Emmy uttered a sigh of relief, too, as she entered the schoolyard. She had been terribly near failing.

"I was so scared," she breathed to little towheaded Mary Holborn. "Did you see what a long time I was answering? Guess Eunice Lecks thought for sure I'd fail and she'd get my place."

"Yes, I guess she did," agreed Mary. "I'm so glad you didn't fail—but, oh, Emmy, didn't you mind?"

Emmy looked up in astonishment from the orange she was peeling.

"Mind what? Here, you can have the biggest half. I don't like oranges anyway—sort of remind me of niter. Mind what, Mary?"

"Why, saying you were black and"—she hesitated, her little freckled face getting pinker and pinker—"a Negro, and all that before the class." And then mistaking the look on Emmy's face, she hastened on. "Everybody in Plainville says all the time that you're too nice and smart to be a—er —I mean, to be colored. And your dresses are so pretty, and your hair isn't all funny either." She seized one of Emmy's hands—an exquisite member, all bronze outside, and within a soft pinky white.

"Oh, Emmy, don't you think if you scrubbed real hard you could get some of the brown off?"

"But I don't want to," protested Emmy. "I guess my hands are as nice as yours, Mary Holborn. We're just the same, only you're white and I'm brown. But I don't see any difference. Eunice Lecks's eyes are green and yours are blue, but you can both see."

"Oh, well," said Mary Holborn, "if you don't mind—"

If she didn't mind—but why should she mind?

"Why should I mind, Archie?" she asked that faithful squire as they walked home in the afternoon through the pleasant "main" street. Archie had brought her home from school ever since she could remember. He was two years older than she; tall, strong, and beautiful, and her final arbiter.

Archie stopped to watch a spider.

"See how he does it, Emmy! See him bring that thread over! Gee, if I could swing a bridge across the pond as easy as that! What d'you say? Why should you mind? Oh, I don't guess there's anything for us to mind about. It's white people, they're always minding—I don't know why. If any of the boys in your class say anything to you, you let me know. I licked Bill Jennings the other day for calling me a 'guiney.' Wish I were a good, sure-enough brown like you, and then everybody'd know just what I am."

Archie's clear olive skin and aquiline features made his Negro ancestry difficult of belief.

"But," persisted Emmy, "what difference does it make?"

"Oh, I'll tell you some other time," he returned vaguely. "Can't you ask questions though? Look, it's going to rain. That means uncle won't need me in the field this afternoon. See here, Emmy, bet I can let you run ahead while I count fifteen, and then beat you to your house. Want to try?"

They reached the house none too soon, for the soft spring drizzle soon turned into gusty torrents. Archie was happy—he loved Emmy's house with the long, high rooms and the books and the queer foreign pictures. And Emmy had so many sensible playthings. Of course, a great big fellow of thirteen doesn't care for locomotives and blocks in the ordinary way, but when one is trying to work out how a bridge must be built over a lopsided ravine, such things are by no means to be despised. When Mrs. Carrel, Emmy's mother, sent Céleste to tell the children to come to dinner, they raised such a protest that the kindly French woman finally set them a table in the sitting room and left them to their own devices.

"Don't you love little fresh green peas?" said Emmy ecstatically. "Oh, Archie, won't you tell me now what difference it makes whether you are white or colored?" She peered into the vegetable dish. "Do you suppose Céleste would give us some more peas? There's only about a spoonful left."

"I don't believe she would," returned the boy, evading the important part of her question. "There were lots of them to start with, you know. Look, if you take up each pea separately on your fork—like that—they'll last longer. It's hard to do, too. Bet I can do it better than you."

And in the exciting contest that followed both children forgot all about the "problem."

## II

Miss Wenzel sent for Emmy the next day. Gently but insistently, and altogether from a mistaken sense of duty, she tried to make the child see wherein her lot differed from that of her white schoolmates. She felt herself that she hadn't succeeded very well. Emmy, immaculate in a white frock, her bronze elfin face framed in its thick curling black hair, alert with interest, had listened very attentively. She had made no comments till toward the end.

"Then because I'm brown," she had said, "I'm not as good as you." Emmy was at all times severely logical.

"Well, I wouldn't—quite say that," stammered Miss Wenzel miserably. "You're really very nice, you know, especially nice for a colored girl, but—well, you're different."

Emmy listened patiently. "I wish you'd tell me how, Miss Wenzel," she began. "Archie Ferrers is different, too, isn't he? And yet he's lots nicer than almost any of the boys in Plainville. And he's smart, you know. I guess he's pretty poor—I shouldn't like to be that—but my mother isn't poor, and she's handsome. I heard Céleste say so, and she has beautiful clothes. I think, Miss Wenzel, it must be rather nice to be different."

It was at this point that Miss Wenzel had desisted and, tucking a little tissue-wrapped oblong into Emmy's hands, had sent her home.

"I don't think I did any good," she told her sister wonderingly. "I couldn't make her see what being colored meant."

"I don't see why you didn't leave her alone," said Hannah Wenzel testily. "I don't guess she'll meet with much prejudice if she stays here in central Pennsylvania. And if she goes away, she'll meet plenty of people who'll make it their business to see that she understands what being colored means. Those things adjust themselves."

"Not always," retorted Miss Wenzel, "and anyway, that child ought to know. She's got to have some of the wind taken out of her sails, someday, anyhow. Look how her mother dresses her. I suppose she does make pretty good money—I've heard that translating pays well. Seems so funny for a colored woman to be able to speak and write a foreign language." She returned to her former complaint.

"Of course it doesn't cost much to live here, but Emmy's clothes! White frocks all last winter, and a long red coat—broadcloth it was, Hannah. And big bows on her hair—she has got pretty hair, I must say."

"Oh, well," said Miss Hannah, "I suppose Céleste makes her clothes. I guess colored people want to look nice just as much as anybody else. I heard Mr. Holborn say Mrs. Carrel used to live in France; I suppose that's where she got all her stylish ways."

"Yes, just think of that," resumed Miss Wenzel vigorously, "a colored woman with a French maid. Though if it weren't for her skin, you'd never tell by her actions what she was. It's the same way with that Archie Ferrers, too, looking for all the world like some foreigner. I must say I like colored people to look and act like what they are."

She spoke the more bitterly because of her keen sense of failure. What she had meant to do was to show Emmy kindly—oh, very kindly—her proper place, and then, using the object in the little tissue-wrapped parcel as a sort of text, to preach a sermon on humility without aspiration.

The tissue-wrapped oblong proved to Emmy's interested eyes to contain a motto of Robert Louis Stevenson, entitled: "A Task"—the phrases picked out in red and blue and gold, under glass and framed in passepartout. Everybody nowadays has one or more of such mottoes in his house, but the idea was new then to Plainville. The child read it through carefully as she passed by the lilac-scented "front yards." She read well for her age, albeit a trifle uncomprehendingly.

"To be honest, to be kind, to earn a little and to spend a little less;"—"there," thought Emmy, "is a semicolon—let's see—the semicolon shows that the thought"—and she went on through the definition Miss Wenzel had given her, and returned happily to her motto:

"To make upon the whole a family happier for his presence"—thus far the lettering was in blue. "To renounce when that shall be necessary and not be embittered"—this phrase was in gold. Then the rest went on in red: "To keep a few friends, but these without capitulation; above all, on the same given condition to keep friends with himself— here is a task for all that a man has of fortitude and delicacy."

"It's all about some man," she thought with a child's literalness. "Wonder why Miss Wenzel gave it to me? That big word, cap-it-u-la-tion"—she divided it off into syllables, doubtfully—"must mean to spell with capitals I guess. I'll say it to Archie sometime."

But she thought it very kind of Miss Wenzel. And after she had shown it to her mother, she hung it up in the bay window of her little white room, where the sun struck it every morning.

## III

Afterward Emmy always connected the motto with the beginning of her own realization of what color might mean. It took her quite a while to find it out, but by the time she was ready to graduate from the high school, she had come to recognize that the occasional impasse which she met now and then might generally be traced to color. This knowledge, however, far from embittering her, simply gave to her life keener zest. Of course she never met with any of the grosser forms of prejudice, and her personality was the kind to win her at least the respect and sometimes the wondering admiration of her schoolmates. For unconsciously she made them see that she was perfectly satisfied with being colored. She could never understand why anyone should think she would want to be white.

One day a girl—Elise Carter—asked her to let her copy her French verbs in the test they were to have later in the day. Emmy, who was both by nature and by necessity independent, refused bluntly.

"Oh, don't be so mean, Emmy," Elise had wailed. She hesitated. "If you'll let me copy them—I'll—I tell you what I'll do, I'll see that you get invited to our club spread Friday afternoon."

"Well, I guess you won't," Emmy had retorted. "I'll probably be asked anyway. 'Most everybody else has been invited already."

Elise jeered. "And did you think as a matter of course that we'd ask you? Well, you have got something to learn."

There was no mistaking the "you."

Emmy took the blow pretty calmly for all its unexpectedness. "You mean," she said slowly, the blood showing darkly under the thin brown of her skin, "because I'm colored?"

Elise hedged—she was a little frightened at such directness.

"Oh, well, Emmy, you know colored folks can't expect to have everything we have, or if they do they must pay extra for it."

"I—I see," said Emmy, stammering a little, as she always did when she was angry. "I begin to see for the first time why you think it's so awful to be colored. It's because you think we are willing to be mean and sneaky and"—with a sudden drop to schoolgirl vernacular—"soup-y. Why, Elise Carter, I wouldn't be in your old club with girls like you for worlds." There was no mistaking her sincerity.

"That was the day," she confided to Archie a long time afterward, "that I learned the meaning of making friends 'without capitulation.' Do you remember Miss Wenzel's motto, Archie?"

He assured her he did. "And of course you know, Emmy, you were an awful brick to answer that Carter girl like that. Didn't you really want to go to the spread?"

"Not one bit," she told him vigorously, "after I found out why I hadn't been asked. And look, Archie, isn't it funny, just as soon as she wanted something, she didn't care whether I was colored or not."

Archie nodded. "They're all that way," he told her briefly.

"And if I'd gone, she'd have believed that all colored people were sort of—well, you know, 'meachin'—just like me. It's so odd the ignorant way in which they draw their conclusions. Why, I remember reading the most interesting article in a magazine—the *Atlantic Monthly* I think it was. A woman had written it, and at this point she was condemning universal suffrage. And all of a sudden, without any warning, she spoke of that 'fierce, silly, amiable creature, the uneducated Negro,' and—think of it, Archie—of 'his baser and sillier female.' It made me so angry. I've never forgotten it."

Archie whistled. "That was pretty tough," he acknowledged. "I suppose the truth is," he went on smiling at her earnestness, "she has a colored cook who drinks."

"That's just it," she returned emphatically. "She probably has. But, Archie, just think of all the colored people we've both seen here and over in Newtown, too; some of them just as poor and ignorant as they can be. But not one of them is fierce or base or silly enough for that to be considered his chief characteristic. I'll wager that woman never spoke to fifty colored people in her life. No, thank you, if that's what it means to belong to the 'superior race,' I'll come back, just as I am, to the fiftieth reincarnation."

Archie sighed. "Oh, well, life is very simple for you. You see, you've never been up against it like I've been. After all, you've had all you wanted practically—those girls even came around finally in the high school and asked you into their clubs and things. While I—" He colored sensitively.

"You see, this plagued—er—complexion of mine doesn't tell anybody what I am. At first—and all along, too, if I let them—fellows take me for a foreigner of some kind—Spanish or something, and they take me up hail-fellow-well-met. And then, if I let them know—I hate to feel I'm taking them in, you know, and besides that I can't help being curious to know what's going to happen—"

"What does happen?" interrupted Emmy, all interest.

"Well, all sorts of things. You take that first summer just before I entered preparatory school. You remember I was working at that camp in Cottage City. All the waiters were fellows just like me, working to go to some college or other. At first I was just one of them—swam with them, played cards—oh, you know, regularly chummed with them. Well, the cook was a colored man—sure enough, colored you know—and one day one of the boys called him a—of course I couldn't tell you, Emmy, but he swore at him and called him a Nigger. And when I took up for him, the fellow said—he was angry, Emmy, and he said it as the worst insult he could think of—'Anybody would think you had black blood in your veins, too.'

" 'Anybody would think right,' " I told him.

"Well?" asked Emmy.

He shrugged his shoulders. "That was all there was to it. The fellows dropped me completely—left me to the company of the cook, who was all right enough as cooks go, I suppose, but he didn't want me any more than I wanted him. And finally the manager came and told me he was sorry, but he guessed I'd have to go." He smiled grimly as at some unpleasant reminiscence.

"What's the joke?" his listener wondered.

"He also told me that I was the blankest kind of a blank fool—oh, you couldn't dream how he swore, Emmy. He said why didn't I leave well enough alone.

"And don't you know that's the thought I've had ever since—why not leave well enough alone?—and not tell people what I am. I guess you're different from me," he broke off wistfully, noting her look of disapproval; "you're so complete and satisfied in yourself. Just being Emilie Carrel seems to be enough for you. But you just wait until color keeps you from the thing you want the most, and you'll see."

"You needn't be so tragic," she commented succinctly. "Outside of that one time at Cottage City, it doesn't seem to have kept you back."

For Archie's progress had been miraculous. In the seven years in which he had been from home, one marvel after another had come his way. He had found lucrative work each summer, he had got through his preparatory school in three years, he had been graduated number six from one of the best technical schools in the country—and now he had a position. He was to work for one of the biggest engineering concerns in Philadelphia.

This last bit of good fortune had dropped out of a clear sky. A guest at one of the hotels one summer had taken an interest in the handsome, willing bellboy and inquired into his history. Archie had hesitated at first, but finally, his eye alert for the first sign of dislike or superiority, he told the man of his Negro blood.

"If he turns me down," he said to himself boyishly, "I'll never risk it again."

But Mr. Robert Fallon—young, wealthy, and quixotic— had become more interested than ever.

"So it's all a gamble with you, isn't it? By George! How exciting your life must be—now white and now black— standing between ambition and honor, what? Not that I don't think you're doing the right thing—it's nobody's confounded business anyway. Look here, when you get through look me up. I may be able to put you wise to something. Here's my card. And say, mum's the word, and when you've made your pile, you can wake some fine morning and find yourself famous simply by telling what you are. All rot, this beastly prejudice, I say."

And when Archie had graduated, his new friend, true to his word, had gotten for him from his father a letter of introduction to Mr. Nicholas Fields in Philadelphia, and Archie was placed. Young Robert Fallon had gone laughing on his aimless, merry way.

"Be sure you keep your mouth shut, Ferrers," was his only enjoinment.

Archie, who at first had experienced some qualms, had finally completely acquiesced. For the few moments' talk with Mr. Fields had intoxicated him. The vision of work, plenty of it, his own chosen kind—and the opportunity to do it as a man—not an exception, but as a plain ordinary man among other men—was too much for him.

"It was my big chance, Emmy," he told her one day. He was spending his brief vacation in Plainville, and the two, having talked themselves out on other things, had returned to their old absorbing topic. He went on a little pleadingly, for she had protested. "I couldn't resist it. You don't know what it means to me. I don't care about being white in itself any more than you do—but I do care about a white man's chances. Don't let's talk about it anymore though; here it's the first week in September and I have to go the fifteenth. I may not be back till Christmas. I should hate to think that you—you were changed toward me, Emmy."

"I'm not changed, Archie," she assured him gravely, "only somehow it makes me feel that you're different. I can't quite look up to you as I used. I don't like the idea of considering the end justified by the means."

She was silent, watching the falling leaves flutter like golden butterflies against her white dress. As she stood there in the old-fashioned garden, she seemed to the boy's adoring eyes like some beautiful but inflexible bronze goddess.

"I couldn't expect you to look up to me, Emmy, as though I were on a pedestal," he began miserably, "but I do want you to respect me, because—oh, Emmy, don't you see? I love you very much and I hope you will—I want you to—oh, Emmy, couldn't you like me a little? I—I've never thought ever of anyone but you. I didn't mean to tell you all

about this now—I meant to wait until I really was successful, and then come and lay it all at your beautiful feet.
You're so lovely, Emmy. But if you despise me—" he was
very humble.

For once in her calm young life Emmy was completely
surprised. But she had to get to the root of things. "You
mean," she faltered, "you mean you want"—she couldn't
say it.

"I mean I want you to marry me," he said, gaining courage from her confusion. "Oh, have I frightened you, Emmy,
dearest—of course you couldn't like me well enough for
that all in a heap—it's different with me. I've always loved
you, Emmy. But if you'd only think about it."

"Oh," she breathed, "there's Céleste. Oh, Archie, I don't
know, it's all so funny. And we're so young. I couldn't really
tell anything about my feelings anyway—you know, I've
never seen anybody but you." Then as his face clouded—
"Oh, well, I guess even if I had, I wouldn't like him any
better. Yes, Céleste, we're coming in. Archie, mother says
you're to have dinner with us every night you're here, if you
can."

There was no more said about the secret that Archie was
keeping from Mr. Fields. There were too many other things
to talk about—reasons why he had always loved Emmy;
reasons why she couldn't be sure just yet; reasons why, if
she were sure, she couldn't say yes.

Archie hung between high hope and despair, while
Emmy, it must be confessed, enjoyed herself, albeit innocently enough, and grew distractingly pretty. On the last
day as they sat in the sitting room, gaily recounting childish
episodes, Archie suddenly asked her again. He was so grave
and serious that she really became frightened.

"Oh, Archie, I couldn't—I don't really want to. It's so
lovely just being a girl. I think I do like you—of course I
like you lots. But couldn't we just be friends and keep going
on—so?"

"No," he told her harshly, his face set and miserable;
"no, we can't. And, Emmy—I'm not coming back anymore
—I couldn't stand it." His voice broke, he was fighting to

keep back the hot boyish tears. After all he was only twenty-one. "I'm sorry I troubled you," he said proudly.

She looked at him pitifully. "I don't want you to go away forever, Archie," she said tremulously. She made no effort to keep back the tears. "I've been so lonely this last year since I've been out of school—you can't think."

He was down on his knees, his arms around her. "Emmy, Emmy, look up—are you crying for me, dear? Do you want me to come back—you do—you mean it? Emmy, you must love me, you do—a little." He kissed her slim fingers.

"Are you going to marry me? Look at me, Emmy—you are! Oh, Emmy, do you know I'm—I'm going to kiss you."

The stage came lumbering up not long afterward and bore him away to the train—triumphant and absolutely happy.

"My heart," sang Emmy rapturously as she ran up the broad, old-fashioned stairs to her room—"my heart is like a singing bird."


## IV

The year that followed seemed to her perfection. Archie's letters alone would have made it that. Emmy was quite sure that there had never been any other letters like them. She used to read them aloud to her mother.

Not all of them, though, for some were too precious for any eye but her own. She used to pore over them alone in her room at night, planning to answer them with an abandon equal to his own, but always finally evolving the same shy, almost timid epistle, which never failed to awaken in her lover's breast a sense equally of amusement and reverence. Her shyness seemed to him the most exquisite thing in the world—so exquisite, indeed, that he almost wished it would never vanish, were it not that its very disappearance would be the measure of her trust in him. His own letters showed plainly his adoration.

Only once had a letter of his caused a fleeting pang of

misapprehension. He had been speaking of the persistent good fortune which had been his in Philadelphia.

"You can't think how lucky I am anyway," the letter ran on. "The other day I was standing on the corner of Fourth and Chestnut Streets at noon—you ought to see Chestnut Street, at twelve o'clock, Emmy—and someone came up, looked at me and said: 'Well, if it isn't Archie Ferrers!' And guess who it was, Emmy? Do you remember the Higginses who used to live over in Newtown? I don't suppose you ever knew them, only they were so queer looking that you must recall them. They were all sorts of colors from black with 'good' hair to yellow with the red, kinky kind. And then there was Maude, clearly a Higgins, and yet not looking like any of them, you know; perfectly white, with blue eyes and fair hair. Well, this was Maude, and, say, maybe she didn't look good. I couldn't tell you what she had on, but it was all right, and I was glad to take her over to the Reading Terminal and put her on a train to New York.

"I guess you're wondering where my luck is in all this tale, but you wait. Just as we started up the stairs of the depot, whom should we run into but young Peter Fields, my boss's son and heir, you know. Really, I thought I'd faint, and then I remembered that Maude was whiter than he in looks, and that there was nothing to give me away. He wanted to talk to us, but I hurried her off to her train. You know, it's a queer thing, Emmy; some girls are just naturally born stylish. Now there are both you and Maude Higgins, brought up from little things in a tiny inland town, and both of you able to give any of these city girls all sorts of odds in the matter of dressing."

Emmy put the letter down, wondering what had made her grow so cold.

"I wonder," she mused. She turned and looked in the glass to be confronted by a charming vision, slender—and dusky.

"I am black," she thought, "but comely." She laughed to herself happily. "Archie loves you, girl," she said to the face in the glass and put the little fear behind her. It met her insistently now and then, however, until the next week brought a letter begging her to get her mother to bring her to Philadelphia for a week or so.

"I can't get off till Thanksgiving, dearest, and I'm so lonely and disappointed. You know, I had looked forward so to spending the fifteenth of September with you—do you remember that date, sweetheart? I wouldn't have you come now in all this heat—you can't imagine how hot Philadelphia is, Emmy—but it's beautiful here in October. You'll love it, Emmy. It's such a big city—miles and miles of long, narrow streets, rather ugly, too, but all so interesting. You'll like Chestnut and Market Streets, where the big shops are, and South Street, teeming with Jews and colored people, though there are more of these last on Lombard Street. You never dreamed of so many colored people, Emmy Carrel—or such kinds.

"And then there are the parks and the theaters, and music and restaurants. And Broad Street late at night, all silent with gold, electric lights beckoning you on for miles and miles. Do you think your mother will let me take you out by yourself, Emmy? You'd be willing, wouldn't you?"

If Emmy needed more reassurance than that, she received it when Archie, a month later, met her and her mother at Broad Street station in Philadelphia. The boy was radiant. Mrs. Carrel, too, put aside her usual reticence, and the three were in fine spirits by the time they reached the rooms which Archie had procured for them on Christian Street. Once ensconced, the older woman announced her intention of taking advantage of the stores.

"I shall be shopping practically all day," she informed them. "I'll be so tired in the afternoons and evenings, Archie, that I'll have to get you to take my daughter off my hands."

Her daughter was delighted, but not more transparently so than her appointed cavalier. He was overjoyed at the thought of playing host and of showing Emmy the delights of city life.

"By the time I've finished showing you one-fifth of what I've planned, you'll give up the idea of waiting 'way till next October and marry me Christmas. Say, do it anyway,

Emmy, won't you?" He waited tensely, but she only shook her head.

"Oh, I couldn't, Archie, and anyway you must show me first your wonderful city."

They did manage to cover a great deal of ground, though their mutual absorption made its impression on them very doubtful. Some things, though, Emmy never forgot. There was a drive one wonderful, golden October afternoon along the Wissahickon. Emmy, in her perfectly correct gray suit and smart little gray hat, held the reins—in itself a sort of measure of Archie's devotion to her, for he was wild about horses. He sat beside her ecstatic, ringing all the changes from a boy's nonsense to the most mature kind of seriousness. And always he looked at her with his passionate though reverent eyes. They were very happy.

There was some wonderful music, too, at the Academy. That was by accident though. For they had started for the theater—had reached there in fact. The usher was taking the tickets.

"This way, Emmy," said Archie. The usher looked up aimlessly, then, as his eyes traveled from the seeming young foreigner to the colored girl beside him, he flushed a little.

"Is the young lady with you?" he whispered politely enough. But Emmy, engrossed in a dazzling vision in a pink décolleté gown, would not in any event have heard him.

"She is," responded Archie alertly. "What's the trouble, isn't tonight the seventeenth?"

The usher passed over this question with another—who had bought the tickets? Archie of course had, and told him so, frankly puzzled.

"I see. Well, I'm sorry," the man said evenly, "but these seats are already occupied, and the rest of the floor is sold out besides. There's a mistake somewhere. Now if you'll take these tickets back to the office, I can promise you they'll give you the best seats left in the balcony."

"What's the matter?" asked Emmy, tearing her glance from the pink vision at last. "Oh, Archie, you're hurting my arm; don't hold it that tight. Why—why are we going away from the theater? Oh, Archie, are you sick? You're just as white!"

"There was some mistake about the tickets," he got out, trying to keep his voice steady. "And a fellow in the crowd gave me an awful dig just then; guess that's why I'm pale. I'm so sorry, Emmy—I was so stupid, it's all my fault."

"What was the matter with the tickets?" she asked, incuriously. "That's the Bellevue-Stratford over there, isn't it? Then the Academy of Music must be near here. See how fast I'm learning? Let's go there; I've never heard a symphony concert. And, Archie, I've always heard that the best way to hear big music like that is at a distance, so get gallery tickets."

He obeyed her, fearful that if there were any trouble this time, she might hear it. Emmy enjoyed it all thoroughly, wondering a little, however, at his silence. "I guess he's tired," she thought. She would have been amazed to know his thoughts as he sat there staring moodily at the orchestra. "This damnation color business," he kept saying over and over.

That night as they stood in the vestibule of the Christian Street house, Emmy, for the first time, volunteered him a kiss. "Such a nice, tired boy," she said gently. Afterward he stood for a long time bareheaded on the steps looking at the closed door. Nothing he felt could crush him as much as that kiss had lifted him up.

## V

Not even for lovers can a week last forever. Archie had kept till the last day what he considered his choicest bit of exploring. This was to take Emmy down into old Philadelphia and show her how the city had grown up from the waterfront—and by means of what tortuous self-governing streets. It was a sight at once dear and yet painful to his methodical, mathematical mind. They had explored Dock and Beach Streets and had got over into Shackamaxon, where he showed her Penn Treaty Park, and they had sat in the little pavilion overlooking the Delaware.

Not many colored people came through this vicinity, and the striking pair caught many a wondering, as well as admiring, glance. They caught, too, the aimless, wandering eye of Mr. Nicholas Fields as he lounged, comfortably smoking, on the rear of a "Gunner's Run" car, on his way to Shackamaxon Ferry. Something in the young fellow's walk seemed vaguely familiar to him, and he leaned way out toward the sidewalk to see who that he knew could be over in this cheerless, forsaken locality.

"Gad!" he said to himself in surprise, "if it isn't young Ferrers, with a lady, too! Hello, why it's a colored woman! Ain't he a rip? Always thought he seemed too proper. Got her dressed to death, too; so that's how his money goes!" He dismissed the matter with a smile and a shrug of his shoulders.

Perhaps he would never have thought of it again had not Archie, rushing into the office a trifle late the next morning, caromed directly into him.

"Oh, it's you," he said, receiving his clerk's smiling apology. "What d'you mean by knocking into anybody like that?" Mr. Fields was facetious with his favorite employees. "Evidently your Shackamaxon trip upset you a little. Where'd you get your black Venus, my boy? I'll bet you don't have one cent to rub against another at the end of a month. Oh, you needn't get red; boys will be boys, and everyone to his taste. Clarkson," he broke off, crossing to his secretary, "if Mr. Hunter calls me up, hold the 'phone and send over to the bank for me."

He had gone, and Archie, white now and shaken, entered his own little room. He sat down at the desk and sank his head in his hands. It had taken a moment for the insult to Emmy to sink in, but even when it did, the thought of his own false position had held him back. The shame of it bit into him.

"I'm a coward," he said to himself, staring miserably at the familiar wall. "I'm a wretched cad to let him think that of Emmy—Emmy! and she the whitest angel that ever lived, purity incarnate." His cowardice made him sick. "I'll go and tell him," he said, and started for the door.

"If you do," whispered common sense, "you'll lose your job and then what would become of you? After all Emmy need never know."

"But I'll always know I didn't defend her," he answered back silently.

"He's gone out to the bank anyhow," went on the inward opposition. "What's the use of rushing in there and telling him before the whole board of directors?"

"Well, then, when he comes back," he capitulated, but he felt himself weaken.

But Mr. Fields didn't come back. When Mr. Hunter called him up, Clarkson connected him with the bank, with the result that Mr. Fields left for Reading in the course of an hour. He didn't come back for a week.

Meanwhile Archie tasted the depths of self-abasement. "But what am I to do?" he groaned to himself at nights. "If I tell him I'm colored, he'll kick me out, and if I go anywhere else, I'd run the same risk. If I'd only knocked him down! After all she'll never know, and I'll make it up to her. I'll be so good to her—dear little Emmy! But how could I know that he would take that view of it—beastly low mind he must have!" He colored up like a girl at the thought of it.

He passed the week thus, alternately reviling and defending himself. He knew now though that he would never have the courage to tell. The economy of the thing he decided was at least as important as the principle. And always he wrote to Emmy letters of such passionate adoration that the girl for all her natural steadiness was carried off her feet.

"How he loves me," she thought happily. "If mother is willing I believe—yes, I will—I'll marry him Christmas. But I won't tell him till he comes Thanksgiving."

When Mr. Fields came back he sent immediately for his son Peter. The two held some rather stormy consultations, which were renewed for several days. Peter roomed in town, while his father lived out at Chestnut Hill. Eventually Archie was sent for.

"You're not looking very fit, my boy," Mr. Fields greeted him kindly; "working too hard, I suppose, over those specifications. Well, here's a tonic for you. This last week has shown me that I need someone younger than myself to take a hand in the business. I'm getting too old or too tired or something. Anyhow I'm played out.

"I've tried to make this young man here,"—with an angry glance at his son—"see that the mantle ought to fall on him, but he won't hear of it. Says the business can stop for all he cares; he's got enough money anyway. Gad, in my day young men liked to work, instead of dabbling around in this filthy social settlement business—with a lot of old maids."

Peter smiled contentedly. "Sally in our alley, what?" he put in diabolically. The older man glared at him, exasperated.

"Now look here, Ferrers," he went on abruptly. "I've had my eye on you ever since you first came. I don't know a thing about you outside of Mr. Fallon's recommendation, but I can see you've got good stuff in you—and what's more, you're a born engineer. If you had some money, I'd take you into partnership at once, but I believe you told me that all you had was your salary." Archie nodded.

"Well, now, I tell you what I'm going to do. I'm going to take you in as a sort of silent partner, teach you the business end of the concern, and in the course of a few years, place the greater part of the management in your hands. You can see you won't lose by it. Of course I'll still be head, and after I step out, Peter will take my place, though only nominally, I suppose."

He sighed; his son's business defection was a bitter point with him. But that imperturbable young man only nodded.

"The boss guessed right the very first time," he paraphrased cheerfully. "You bet I'll be head in name only. Young Ferrers, there's just the man for the job. What d'you say, Archie?"

The latter tried to collect himself. "Of course I accept it,

Mr. Fields, and I—I don't think you'll ever regret it." He actually stammered. Was there ever such wonderful luck?

"Oh; that's all right," Mr. Fields went on, "you wouldn't be getting this chance if you didn't deserve it. See here, what about your boarding out at Chestnut Hill for a year or two? Then I can lay my hands on you anytime, and you can get hold of things that much sooner. You live on Green Street, don't you? Well, give your landlady a month's notice and quit the first of December. A young man coming on like you ought to be thinking of a home anyway. Can't find some nice girl to marry you, what?"

Archie, flushing a little, acknowledged his engagement.

"Good, that's fine!" Then with sudden recollection— "Oh, so you're reformed. Well, I thought you'd get over that. Can't settle down too soon. A lot of nice little cottages out there at Chestnut Hill. Peter, your mother says she wishes you'd come out to dinner tonight. The youngest Wilton girl is to be there, I believe. Guess that's all for this afternoon, Ferrers."

# VI

Archie walked up Chestnut Street on air. "It's better to be born lucky than rich," he reflected. "But I'll be rich, too— and what a lot I can do for Emmy. Glad I didn't tell Mr. Fields now. Wonder what those 'little cottages' out to Chestnut Hill sell for. Emmy—" He stopped short, struck by a sudden realization.

"Why, I must be stark, staring crazy," he said to himself, standing still right in the middle of Chestnut Street. A stout gentleman whom his sudden stopping had seriously incommoded gave him, as he passed by, a vicious prod with his elbow. It started him on again.

"If I hadn't clean forgotten all about it. Oh, Lord, what am I to do? Of course Emmy can't go out to Chestnut Hill to live—well, that would be a give-away. And he advised me to live out there for a year or two—and he knows I'm engaged, and—now—making more than enough to marry on."

He turned aimlessly down 19th Street and spying Rittenhouse Square, sat down in it. The cutting November wind swirled brown, crackling leaves right into his face, but he never saw one of them.

When he arose again, long after his dinner hour, he had made his decision. After all Emmy was a sensible girl; she knew he had only his salary to depend on. And, of course, he wouldn't have to stay out in Chestnut Hill forever. They could buy, or perhaps—he smiled proudly—even build now, far out in West Philadelphia, as far as possible away from Mr. Fields. He'd just ask her to postpone their marriage—perhaps for two years. He sighed a little, for he was very much in love.

"It seems funny that prosperity should make a fellow put off his happiness," he thought ruefully, swinging himself aboard a North 19th Street car.

He decided to go to Plainville and tell her about it—he could go up Saturday afternoon. "Let's see, I can get an express to Harrisburg, and a sleeper to Plainville, and come back Sunday afternoon. Emmy'll like a surprise like that." He thought of their improvised trip to the Academy and how she had made him buy gallery seats. "Lucky she has that little saving streak in her. She'll see through the whole thing like a brick." His simile made him smile. As soon as he reached home he scribbled her a note:

"I'm coming Sunday," he said briefly, "and I have something awfully important to ask you. I'll be there only from three to seven. 'When Time lets slip one little perfect hour,' that's that Omar thing you're always quoting, isn't it? Well, there'll be four perfect hours this trip."

All the way on the slow poky local from Harrisburg he pictured her surprise. "I guess she won't mind the postponement one bit," he thought with a brief pang. "She never was keen on marrying. Girls certainly are funny. Here she admits she's in love and willing to marry, and yet she's always hung fire about the date." He dozed fitfully.

As a matter of fact Emmy had fixed the date. "Of

course," she said to herself happily, "the 'something important' is that he wants me to marry him right away. Well, I'll tell him that I will, Christmas. Dear old Archie coming all this distance to ask me that. I'll let him beg me two or three times first, and then I'll tell him. Won't he be pleased? I shouldn't be a bit surprised if he went down on his knees again." She flushed a little, thinking of that first wonderful time.

"Being in love is just—dandy," she decided. "I guess I'll wear my red dress."

Afterward the sight of that red dress always caused Emmy a pang of actual physical anguish. She never saw it without seeing, too, every detail of that disastrous Sunday afternoon. Archie had come—she had gone to the door to meet him—they had lingered happily in the hall a few moments, and then she had brought him in to her mother and Céleste.

The old French woman had kissed him on both cheeks. "See, then it's thou, my cherished one!" she cried ecstatically. "How long a time it is since thou art here."

Mrs. Carrel's greeting, though not so demonstrative, was no less sincere, and when the two were left to themselves "the cherished one" was radiant.

"My, but your mother can make a fellow feel welcome, Emmy. She doesn't say much, but what she does, goes."

Emmy smiled a little absently. The gray mist outside in the somber garden, the fire crackling on the hearth and casting ruddy shadows on Archie's hair, the very red of her dress, Archie himself—all this was making for her a picture, which she saw repeated on endless future Sunday afternoons in Philadelphia. She sighed contentedly.

"I've got something to tell you, sweetheart," said Archie.

"It's coming," she thought. "Oh, isn't it lovely! Of all the people in the world—he loves me, loves me!" She almost missed the beginning of his story. For he was telling her of Mr. Fields and his wonderful offer.

When she finally caught the drift of what he was saying, she was vaguely disappointed. He was talking business, in which she was really very little interested. The "saving

streak" which Archie had attributed to her was merely spo-
radic and was due to a nice girl's delicacy at having money
spent on her by a man. But, of course, she listened.

"So you see the future is practically settled—there's only
one immediate drawback," he said earnestly. She shut her
eyes—it was coming after all.

He went on a little puzzled by her silence; "only one
drawback, and that is that, of course, we can't be married
for at least two years yet."

Her eyes flew open. "Not marry for two years! Why—
why ever not?"

Even then he might have saved the situation by telling
her first of his own cruel disappointment, for her loveliness,
as she sat there, all glowing red and bronze in the firelit
dusk, smote him very strongly.

But he only floundered on.

"Why, Emmy, of course, you can see—you're so much
darker than I—anybody can tell at a glance what you—er—
are." He was crude, he knew it, but he couldn't see how to
help himself. "And we'd have to live at Chestnut Hill, at
first, right there near the Fields', and there'd be no way
with you there to keep people from knowing that I—that—
oh, confound it all—Emmy, you must understand! You
don't mind, do you? You know you never were keen on
marrying anyway. If we were both the same color—why,
Emmy, what is it?"

For she had risen and was looking at him as though he
were someone entirely strange. Then she turned and gazed
unseeingly out the window. So that was it—the "something
important"—he was ashamed of her, of her color; he was
always talking about a white man's chances. Why, of
course, how foolish she'd been all along—how could he be
white with her at his side? And she had thought he had
come to urge her to marry him at once—the sting of it sent
her head up higher. She turned and faced him, her beautiful silhouette distinctly outlined against the gray blur of the
window. She wanted to hurt him—she was quite cool now.

"I have something to tell you, too, Archie," she said
evenly. "I've been meaning to tell you for some time. It

seems I've been making a mistake all along. I don't really love you"—she was surprised dully that the words didn't choke her—"so, of course, I can't marry you. I was wondering how I could get out of it—you can't think how tiresome it's all been." She had to stop.

He was standing, frozen, motionless like something carved.

"This seems as good an opportunity as any—oh, here's your ring," she finished, holding it out to him coldly. It was a beautiful diamond, small but flawless—the only thing he'd ever gone into debt for.

The statue came to life. "Emmy, you're crazy," he cried passionately, seizing her by the wrist. "You've got the wrong idea. You think I don't want you to marry me. What a cad you must take me for. I only asked you to postpone it a little while, so we'd be happier afterward. I'm doing it all for you, girl. I never dreamed—it's preposterous, Emmy! And you can't say you don't love me—that's all nonsense!"

But she clung to her lie desperately.

"No, really, Archie, I don't love you one bit; of course I like you awfully—let go my wrist, you can think how strong you are. I should have told you long ago, but I hadn't the heart—and it really was interesting." No grand lady on the stage could have been more detached. He should know, too, how it felt not to be wanted.

He was at her feet now, clutching desperately, as she retreated, at her dress—the red dress she had donned so bravely. He couldn't believe in her heartlessness. "You must love me, Emmy, and even if you don't, you must marry me anyway. Why, you promised—you don't know what it means to me, Emmy—it's my very life—I've never even dreamed of another woman but you! Take it back, Emmy, you can't mean it."

But she convinced him that she could. "I wish you'd stop, Archie," she said wearily; "this is awfully tiresome. And, anyway, I think you'd better go now if you want to catch your train."

He stumbled to his feet, the life all out of him. In the hall he turned around: "You'll say good-bye to your mother for me," he said mechanically. She nodded. He opened the front door. It seemed to close of its own accord behind him.

She came back into the sitting room, wondering why the place had suddenly grown so intolerably hot. She opened a window. From somewhere out of the gray mists came the strains of "Alice, Where Art Thou?" executed with exceeding mournfulness on an organ. The girl listened with a curious detached intentness.

"That must be Willie Holborn," she thought; "no one else could play as wretchedly as that." She crossed heavily to the armchair and flung herself in it. Her mind seemed to go on acting as though it were clockwork and she were watching it.

Once she said: "Now this, I suppose, is what they call a tragedy." And again: "He did get down on his knees."

# VII

There was nothing detached or impersonal in Archie's consideration of his plight. All through the trip home, through the long days that followed and the still longer nights, he was in torment. Again and again he went over the scene.

"She was making a plaything out of me," he chafed bitterly. "All these months she's been only fooling. And yet I wonder if she really meant it, if she didn't just do it to make it easier for me to be white. If that's the case, what an insufferable cad she must take me for. No, she couldn't have cared for me, because if she had, she'd have seen through it all right away."

By the end of ten days he had worked himself almost into a fever. His burning face and shaking hands made him resolve, as he dressed that morning, to 'phone the office that he was too ill to come to work.

"And I'll stay home and write her a letter that she'll have to answer." For although he had sent her one and sometimes two letters every day ever since his return, there had been no reply.

"She must answer that," he said to himself at length, when the late afternoon shadows were creeping in. He had torn up letter after letter—he had been proud and beseeching by turns. But in this last he had laid his very heart bare.

"And if she doesn't answer it"—it seemed to him he couldn't face the possibility. He was at the writing desk where her picture stood in its little silver frame. It had been there all that day. As a rule he kept it locked up, afraid of what it might reveal to his landlady's vigilant eye. He sat there, his head bowed over the picture, wondering dully how he should endure his misery.

Someone touched him on the shoulder.

"Gad, boy," said Mr. Nicholas Fields, "here I thought you were sick in bed, and come here to find you mooning over a picture. What's the matter? Won't the lady have you? Let's see who it is that's been breaking you so up." Archie watched him in fascinated horror, while he picked up the photograph and walked over to the window. As he scanned it, his expression changed.

"Oh," he said, with a little puzzled frown and yet laughing, too, "it's your colored lady friend again. Won't she let you go? That's the way with these black women, once they get hold of a white man—bleed 'em to death. I don't see how you can stand them anyway; it's the Spanish in you, I suppose. Better get rid of her before you get married. Hello—" he broke off.

For Archie was standing menacingly over him. "If you say another word about that girl, I'll break every rotten bone in your body."

"Oh, come," said Mr. Fields, still pleasant, "isn't that going it a little too strong? Why, what can a woman like that mean to you?"

"She can mean," said the other slowly, "everything that the woman who has promised to be my wife ought to mean." The broken engagement meant nothing in a time like this.

Mr. Fields forgot his composure. "To be your wife! Why, you idiot, you—you'd ruin yourself—marry a Negro—have you lost your senses? Oh, I suppose it's some of your crazy foreign notions. In this country white gentlemen don't marry colored women."

Archie had not expected this loophole. He hesitated, then with a shrug he burnt all his bridges behind him. One by one he saw his ambitions flare up and vanish.

"No, you're right," he rejoined. "White gentlemen don't, but colored men do." Then he waited calmly for the avalanche.

It came. "You mean," said Mr. Nicholas Fields, at first with only wonder and then with growing suspicion in his voice, "you mean that you're colored?" Archie nodded and watched him turn into a maniac.

"Why, you low-lived young blackguard, you—" he swore horribly. "And you've let me think all this time—" He broke off again, hunting for something insulting enough to say. "You Nigger!" he hurled at him. He really felt there was nothing worse, so he repeated it again and again with fresh imprecations.

"I think," said Archie, "that that will do. I shouldn't like to forget myself, and I'm in a pretty reckless mood today. You must remember, Mr. Fields, you didn't ask me who I was, and I had no occasion to tell you. Of course I won't come back to the office."

"If you do," said Mr. Fields, white to the lips, "I'll have you locked up if I have to perjure my soul to find a charge against you. I'll show you what a white man can do—you—"

But Archie had taken him by the shoulder and pushed him outside the door.

"And that's all right," he said to himself with a sudden heady sense of liberty. He surveyed himself curiously in the mirror. "Wouldn't anybody think I had changed into some horrible ravening beast. Lord, how that one little word changed him." He ruminated over the injustice—the petty, foolish injustice of the whole thing.

"I don't believe," he said slowly, "it's worthwhile having a white man's chances if one has to be like that. I see what Emmy used to be driving at now." The thought of her sobered him.

"If it should be on account of my chances that you're letting me go," he assured the picture gravely, "it's all quite unnecessary, for I'll never have another opportunity like that."

In which he was quite right. It even looked as though he couldn't get any work at all along his own line. There was no demand for colored engineers.

"If you keep your mouth shut," one man said, "and not let the other clerks know what you are, I might try you for a while." There was nothing for him to do but accept. At the end of two weeks—the day before Thanksgiving—he found out that the men beside him, doing exactly the same kind of work as his own, were receiving for it five dollars more a week. The old injustice based on color had begun to hedge him in. It seemed to him that his unhappiness and humiliation were more than he could stand.

## VIII

But at least his life was occupied. Emmy, on the other hand, saw her own life stretching out through endless vistas of empty, useless days. She grew thin and listless, all the brightness and vividness of living toned down for her into one gray, flat monotony. By Thanksgiving Day the strain showed its effects on her very plainly.

Her mother, who had listened in her usual silence when her daughter told her the cause of the broken engagement, tried to help her.

"Emmy," she said, "you're probably doing Archie an injustice. I don't believe he ever dreamed of being ashamed of you. I think it is your own wilful pride that is at fault. You'd better consider carefully—if you are making a mistake, you'll regret it to the day of your death. The sorrow of it will never leave you."

Emmy was petulant. "Oh, Mother, what can you know about it? Céleste says you married when you were young, even younger than I—married to the man you loved, and you were with him, I suppose, till he died. You couldn't know how I feel." She fell to staring absently out the window. It was a long time before her mother spoke again.

"No, Emmy," she finally began again very gravely, "I wasn't with your father till he died. That is why I'm speaking to you as I am. I had sent him away—we had quarrelled —oh, I was passionate enough when I was your age, Emmy. He was jealous—he was a West Indian—I suppose Céleste has told you—and one day he came past the sitting room— it was just like this one, overlooking the garden. Well, as he glanced in the window, he saw a man, a white man, put his arms around me and kiss me. When he came in through the side door, the man had gone. I was just about to explain— no, tell him—for I didn't know he had seen me when he began." She paused a little, but presently went on in her even, dispassionate voice:

"He was furious, Emmy; oh, he was so angry, and he accused me—oh, my dear! He was almost insane. But it was really because he loved me. And then I became angry and I wouldn't tell him anything. And finally, Emmy, he struck me—you mustn't blame him, child; remember, it was the same spirit showing in both of us, in different ways. I was doing all I could to provoke him by keeping silence, and he merely retaliated in his way. The blow wouldn't have harmed a little bird. But—well, Emmy, I think I must have gone crazy. I ordered him from the house—it had been my mother's—and I told him never, never to let me see him again." She smiled drearily.

"I never did see him again. After he left, Céleste and I packed up our things and came here to America. You were the littlest thing, Emmy. You can't remember living in France at all, can you? Well, when your father found out where I was, he wrote and asked me to forgive him and to let him come back. 'I am on my knees,' the letter said. I wrote and told him yes—I loved him, Emmy; oh, child, you with your talk of color; you don't know what love is. If you really loved Archie, you'd let him marry you and lock you off, away from all the world, just so long as you were with him.

"I was so happy," she resumed. "I hadn't seen him for

two years. Well, he started—he was in Hayti then; he got to New York safely and started here. There was a wreck—just a little one—only five people killed, but he was one of them. He was so badly mangled, they wouldn't even let me see him."

"Oh!" breathed Emmy. "Oh, Mother!" After a long time she ventured a question. "Who was the other man, Mother?"

"The other man? Oh! That was my father; my mother's guardian, protector, everything, but not her husband. She was a slave, you know, in New Orleans, and he helped her to get away. He took her to Hayti first, and then, afterward, sent her over to France, where I was born. He never ceased in his kindness. After my mother's death, I didn't see him for ten years, not till after I was married. That was the time Emile—you were named for your father, you know—saw him kiss me. Mr. Pechegru, my father, was genuinely attached to my mother, I think, and had come after all these years to make some reparation. It was through him I first began translating for the publishers. You know yourself how my work has grown."

She was quite ordinary and matter-of-fact again. Suddenly her manner changed.

"I lost him when I was twenty-two. Emmy—think of it—and my life has been nothing ever since. That's why I want you to think—to consider—" She was weeping passionately now.

Her mother in tears! To Emmy it was as though the world lay in ruins about her feet.

## IX

As it happened, Mrs. Carrel's story only plunged her daughter into deeper gloom.

"It couldn't have happened at all if we hadn't been colored," she told herself moodily. "If grandmother hadn't been colored, she wouldn't have been a slave, and if she hadn't been a slave—That's what it is, color—color—it's wrecked mother's life, and now it's wrecking mine."

She couldn't get away from the thought of it. Archie's words, said so long ago, came back to her: "Just wait till color keeps you from the thing you want the most," he had told her.

"It must be wonderful to be white," she said to herself, staring absently at the Stevenson motto on the wall of her little room. She went up close and surveyed it unseeingly. "If only I weren't colored," she thought. She checked herself angrily, enveloped by a sudden sense of shame. "It doesn't seem as though I could be the same girl."

A thin ray of cold December sunlight picked out from the motto a little gilded phrase: "To renounce when that shall be necessary and not be embittered." She read it over and over and smiled whimsically.

"I've renounced—there's no question about that," she thought, "but no one could expect me not to be bitter."

If she could just get up strength enough, she reflected, as the days passed by, she would try to be cheerful in her mother's presence. But it was so easy to be melancholy.

About a week before Christmas her mother went to New York. She would see her publishers and do some shopping and would be back Christmas Eve. Emmy was really glad to see her go.

"I'll spend that time in getting myself together," she told herself, "and when mother comes back, I'll be all right." Nevertheless, for the first few days she was, if anything, more listless than ever. But Christmas Eve and the prospect of her mother's return gave her a sudden brace.

"Without bitterness," she kept saying to herself, "to renounce without bitterness." Well, she would—she would. When her mother came back, she should be astonished. She would even wear the red dress. But the sight of it made her weak; she couldn't put it on. But she did dress herself very carefully in white, remembering how gay she had been last Christmas Eve. She had put mistletoe in her hair, and Archie had taken it out.

"I don't have to have mistletoe," he had whispered to her proudly.

In the late afternoon she ran out to Holborn's. As she came back 'round the corner, she saw the stage drive away. Her mother, of course, had come. She ran into the sitting room wondering why the door was closed.

"I will be all right," she said to herself, her hand on the knob, and stepped into the room—to walk straight into Archie's arms.

She clung to him as though she could never let him go.

"Oh, Archie, you've come back, you really wanted me."

He strained her closer. "I've never stopped wanting you," he told her, his lips on her hair.

Presently, when they were sitting by the fire, she in the armchair and he at her feet, he began to explain. She would not listen at first, it was all her fault, she said.

"No, indeed," he protested generously, "it was mine. I was so crude; it's a wonder you can care at all about anyone as stupid as I am. And I think I was too ambitious—though in a way it was all for you, Emmy; you must always believe that. But I'm at the bottom rung now, sweetheart; you see, I told Mr. Fields everything and—he put me out."

"Oh, Archie," she praised him, "that was really noble, since you weren't obliged to tell him."

"Well, but in one sense I was obliged to—to keep my self-respect, you know. So there wasn't anything very noble about it after all." He couldn't tell her what had really happened. "I'm genuinely poor now, dearest, but your mother sent for me to come over to New York. She knows some pretty all-right people there—she's a wonderful woman, Emmy—and I'm to go out to the Philippines. Could you—do you think you could come out there, Emmy?"

She could, she assured him, go anywhere. "Only don't let it be too long, Archie—I—"

He was ecstatic. "Emmy—you—you don't mean you would be willing to start out there with me, do you? Why, that's only three months off. When—" He stopped, peering out the window. "Who is that coming up the path?"

"It's Willie Holborn," said Emmy. "I suppose Mary sent him around with my present. Wait, I'll let him in."

But it wasn't Willie Holborn, unless he had been suddenly converted into a small and very grubby special-delivery boy.

"Mr. A. Ferrers," he said laconically, thrusting a book out at her. "Sign here."

She took the letter back into the pleasant room, and A. Ferrers, scanning the postmark, tore it open. "It's from my landlady; she's the only person in Philadelphia who knows where I am. Wonder what's up?" he said incuriously. "I know I didn't forget to pay her my bill. Hello, what's this?" For within was a yellow envelope—a telegram.

Together they tore it open.

"Don't be a blooming idiot," it read; "the governor says come back and receive apologies and accept job. Merry Christmas. Peter Fields."

"Oh," said Emmy, "isn't it lovely? Why does he say 're-ceive apologies,' Archie?"

"Oh, I don't know," he quibbled, reflecting that if Peter hadn't said just that, his return would have been as impossible as ever. "It's just his queer way of talking. He's the funniest chap! Looks as though I wouldn't have to go to the Philippines after all. But that doesn't alter the main question. How soon do you think you can marry me, Emmy?"

His voice was light, but his eyes—

"Well," said Emmy bravely, "what do you think of Christmas?"

# My House and a Glimpse of My Life Therein

JESSIE FAUSET

What are the boundaries of the female imagination? It was a pressing question for early twentieth-century women writers, from Virginia Woolf to Charlotte Perkins Gilman, each searching for real and metaphorical space in which to write—*A Room of One's Own*, as Woolf called it. In her early short fiction, such as this story first published in *The Crisis* in 1914, Fauset ponders female creativity while probing her own talents. "My House and a Glimpse of My Life Therein" is a fanciful but serious meditation on artistic and creative perfection. It is striking for an insouciant spirit Woolf, Fauset's contemporary, would have admired.

FAR AWAY ON THE TOP of a gently sloping hill stands my house. On one side the hill slopes down into a valley, the site of a large country town; on the other it descends into a forest, thick with lofty trees and green, growing things. Here in stately solitude amid such surroundings towers my dwelling; its dull-red brick is barely visible through the thick ivy, but the gleaming tops of its irregular roof and sloping gables catch the day's sunlight and crown it with a crown of gold.

An irregular, rambling building is this house of mine, built on no particular plan, following no order save that of desire and fancy. Peculiarly jutting rooms appear, and unsuspected towers and bay-windows,—the house seems almost to have built itself and to have followed its own will in so doing. If there be any one distinct feature at all, it is that

halls long and very broad traverse the various parts of the
house, separating a special set of rooms here, making another division there. Splendid halls are these, with fire-
places and cozy armchairs, and delightful, dark corners,
and mysterious closets, and broad, shallow stairs. Just the
place in winter for a host of young people to gather before
the fireplace and, with popcorn and chestnuts, stories and
apples, laugh away the speeding hours, while the wind
howls without.

The hall on the ground floor has smaller corridors that
branch off and lead at their extremity into the garden.
Surely, no parterre of the East, perfumed with all the odors
of Araby, and peopled with houris, was ever so fair as my
garden! Surely, nowhere does the snow lie so pure and
smooth and deep, nowhere are the evergreen trees so very
tall and stately as in my garden in winter! Most glorious is it
in late spring and early June. Out on the green, green
sward I sit under the blossoming trees; in sheer delightful
idleness I spend my hours, listening to the blending of
wind-song with the "sweet jargoning" of little birds. If a
shower threatens, I flee across my garden's vast expanse,
past the gorgeous rosebushes and purple lilacs, and safe
within my little summer-house, watch the "straight-falling
rain," and think of other days, and sighing, wish that Kath-
leen and I had not parted in anger that far-off morning.

When the shower ceases, I hasten down the broad path,
under the shelter of lofty trees, until I reach one of my
house's many doors. Once within, but still in idle mood, I
perch myself on a window-seat and look toward the town.
Tall spires and godly church steeples rise before me; high
above all climbs the town clock; farther over in the west,
smoke is curling from the foundries. How busy is the life
beyond my house! Through the length of the long hall to
the window at the opposite side I go and watch the friendly
nodding of tall trees and the tender intercourse of all this
beautiful green life. Suddenly the place becomes transformed—this is an enchanted forest, the Forest Morgraunt
—in and out among the trees pass valiant knights and distressed ladies. Prosper le Gai rides to the rescue of Isoult la

Desirous. Surely, the forest life beyond my house is full of purpose and animation, too.

From the window I roam past the sweet, familiar chambers, to the attic staircase, with its half-hidden angles and crazy old baluster. Up to the top of the house I go, to a dark little store-room under the eaves. I open the trap-door in the middle of the ceiling, haul down a small ladder, mount its deliciously wobbly length, and behold, I am in my chosen domain—a queen come into her very own! If I choose I can convert it into a dread and inaccessible fortress, by drawing up my ladder and showering nutshells and acorns down on the heads of would-be intruders. Safe from all possible invasion, I browse through the store of old, old magazines and quaint books and journals, or wander half-timidly through my infinite unexplored land of mystery, picking my way past heaps of delightful rubbish and strong, secret chests, fancying goblins in the shadowy corners, or watching from the little windows the sunbeams play on the garden, and the gray-blue mist hanging far off over the hollow valley.

From such sights and fancies I descend to my library, there to supplement my flitting ideas with the fixed conception of others. Although I love every brick and little bit of mortar in my dwelling, my library is of all portions the very dearest to me. In this part of the house, more than any-place else, have those irregular rooms been added, to receive my ever-increasing store of books. In the large room, —the library proper,—is a broad, old-fashioned fireplace, and on the rug in front I lie and read, and read again, all the dear simple tales of earlier days, *Mother Goose, Alice in Wonderland, The Arabian Nights;* here, too, I revel in modern stories of impossible adventure. But when a storm rises at night, say, and the rain beats and dashes, and all without is raging, I draw a huge, red armchair before the fire and curl into its hospitable depths.

> And there I sit
> Reading old things,
> Of knights and lorn damsels,

While the wind sings—
Oh, drearily sings!

Off in one of the little side-rooms stands my desk, covered with books that have caught my special fancy and awakened my thoughts. This is my *living*-room, where I spend my moods of bitterness and misunderstanding, and questioning, and joy, too, I think. Often in the midst of a heap of books, the Rubaiyat and a Bible, Walter Pater's essays, and *Robert Elsmere* and *Aurora Leigh,* and books of belief, of insinuation, of open unbelief, I bow my head on my desk in a passion of doubt and ignorance and longing, and ponder, ponder. Here on this desk is a book in which I jot down all the little, beautiful word-wonders, whose meanings are so often unknown to me, but whose very mystery I love. I write, "In Vishnu Land what Avatar?" and "After the red pottage comes the exceedingly bitter cry," and all the other sweet, incomprehensible fragments that haunt my memory so.

High up on many of the shelves in the many rooms are books as yet unread by me, Schopenhauer and Gorky, Petrarch and Sappho, Goethe and Kant and Schelling; much of Ibsen, Plato and Ennius and Firdausi, and Lafcadio Hearn,—a few of these in the original. With such reading in store for me, is not my future rich?

Can such a house as this one of mine be without immediate and vivid impression on its possessor? First and most of all, it imbues me with a strong sense of home; banishment from my house would surely be life's most bitter sorrow. It is so eminently and fixedly mine, my very own, that the mere possession of it,—a house not yours or another's, but mine, to live in as I will,—is very sweet to me. It is absolutely the *chey soi* of my soul's desire. With this sense of ownership, a sense which is deeper than I can express, a sense which is almost a longing for some unknown, unexplainable, entire possession—passionate, spiritual absorption of my dwelling—comes a feeling that is almost terror. Is it right to feel thus, to have this vivid, permeating, and yet wholly intellectual enjoyment of the material loveliness and attractiveness of my house? May this not be perhaps a sensuality of the mind, whose influence may be more insidious, more pernicious, more powerful to unfit me for the real duties of life than are other lower and yet more open forms of enjoyment? Oh, I pray not! My house is inexpressibly dear to me, but the light of the ideal beyond, "the light that never was on sea or land," is dearer still.

This, then, is my house, and this, in measure, is my life in my house. Here, amid my favorite books, and pictures, and fancies, and longings, and sweet mysteries, shall old age come upon me, in fashion most inglorious, but in equal degree most peaceful and happy. *Perhaps*—that is! For after all my house is constructed of dream-fabric, and the place of its building is—*Spain!*

# Drenched in Light

## Zora Neale Hurston

The seeds of Hurston's most famous character and novel lie in this story, her first, published in *Opportunity* in 1924. Isis Watts is an impish girl whose imagination and curiosity make her the bane of her controlling grandmother and the darling of her Florida community, probably the Eatonville of Hurston's own childhood. In *Their Eyes Were Watching God*, Isie Watts grows up to become Janie Starks, whose search for the "horizon" of life is literally prefigured in this story of Isis's short trip down a dusty road. Isis's namesake, the Egyptian goddess of fertility, reflects Hurston's use of anthropological sources for her fiction, begun well before she published her later collections of folklore and folktales. The story announced the start of Hurston's career as a writer. It has been reprinted in *Spunk: The Selected Short Stories of Zora Neale Hurston* (Turtle Island Foundation, 1985).

"YOU ISIE WATTS! Git 'own offen dat gate post an' rake up dis yahd!"

The small brown girl perched upon the gate post looked yearningly up the gleaming shell road that lead to Orlando. After a while, she shrugged her thin shoulders. This only seemed to heap still more kindling on Grandma Potts's already burning ire.

"Lawd a-mussy!" she screamed, enraged—"Heah Joel, gimme dat wash stick. Ah'll show dat limb of Satan she cain't shake herself at *me*. If she ain't down by the time Ah gets dere, Ah'll break huh down in de lines."

"Aw Gran'ma, Ah see Mist' George and Jim Robinson comin' and Ah wanted to wave at 'em," the child said impatiently.

"You jes' wave dat rake at dis heah yahd, madame, else Ah'll take you down a buttonhole lower. Youse too 'oomanish jumpin' up in everybody's face dat pass."

This struck the child sorely, for nothing pleased her so much as to sit atop of the gate post and hail the passing vehicles on their way south to Orlando, or north to Sanford. That white shell road was her great attraction. She raced up and down the stretch of it that lay before her gate, like a round-eyed puppy hailing gleefully all travelers. Everybody in the country, white and colored, knew little Isis Watts, Isis the Joyful. The Robinson brothers, white cattlemen, were particularly fond of her and always extended a stirrup for her to climb up behind one of them for a short ride, or let her try to crack the long bullwhips and *yee whoo* at the cows.

Grandma Potts went inside, and Isis literally waved the rake at the "chaws" of ribbon cane that lay so bountifully about the yard in company with the knots and peelings, with a thick sprinkling of peanut hulls.

The herd of cattle in their envelope of gray dust came alongside, and Isis dashed out to the nearest stirrup and was lifted up.

"Hello theah, Snidlits, I was wonderin' wheah you was," said Jim Robinson as she snuggled down behind him in the saddle. They were almost out of the danger zone when Grandma emerged. "You Isie," she bawled.

The child slid down on the opposite side of the house and executed a flank movement through the corn patch that brought her into the yard from behind the privy.

"You li'l hasion you! Wheah you been?"

"Out in de back yahd," Isis lied and did a cartwheel and a few fancy steps on her way to the front again.

"If you doan git in dat yahd, Ah make a mommuk of you!" Isis observed that Grandma was cutting a fancy assortment of switches from peach, guana, and cherry trees.

She finished the yard by raking everything under the

edge of the porch and began a romp with the dogs, those lean, floppy-eared hounds that all country folks keep. But Grandma vetoed this also.

"Isie, you set on dat porch! Uh great big 'leben yeah ole gal racin' an' rompin' lak dat—set 'own!"

Isis flung herself upon the steps.

"Git up offa dem steps, you aggravatin' limb, 'fore Ah git dem hick'ries tuh you, an' set yo'seff on a cheah."

Isis arose, and then sat down as violently as possible in the chair. She slid down, and down, until she all but sat on her own shoulder blades.

"Now look atcher," Grandma screamed. "Put yo' knees together, an' git up offen yo' backbone! Lawd, you know dis hellion is gwine make me stomp huh insides out."

Isis sat bolt upright as if she wore a ramrod down her back and began to whistle. Now there are certain things that Grandma Potts felt no one of this female persuasion should do—one was to sit with the knees separated, "settin' brazen" she called it; another was whistling, another playing with boys. Finally, a lady must never cross her legs.

Grandma jumped up from her seat to get the switches.

"So youse whistlin' in mah face, huh!" She glared till her eyes were beady and Isis bolted for safety. But the noon hour brought John Watts the widowed father, and this excused the child from sitting for criticism.

Being the only girl in the family, of course she must wash the dishes, which she did in intervals between frolics with the dogs. She even gave Jake, the puppy, a swim in the dishpan by holding him suspended above the water that reeked of "pot likker"—just high enough so that his feet would be immersed. The deluded puppy swam and swam without ever crossing the pan, much to his annoyance. Hearing Grandma, she hurriedly dropped him on the floor, which he tracked-up with feet wet with dishwater.

Grandma took her patching and settled down in the front room to sew. She did this every afternoon and invariably slept in the big red rocker with her head lolled back over the back, the sewing falling from her hand.

Isis had crawled under the center table with its red plush

cover with little round balls for fringe. She was lying on her back imagining herself various personages. She wore trailing robes, golden slippers with blue bottoms. She rode white horses with flaring pink nostrils to the horizon, for she still believed that to be land's end. She was picturing herself gazing over the edge of the world into the abyss when the spool of cotton fell from Grandma's lap and rolled away under the whatnot. Isis drew back from her contemplation of the nothingness at the horizon and glanced up at the sleeping woman. Her head had fallen far back. She breathed with a regular "mark" intake and "poosah" exhaust. But Isis was a visual-minded child. She heard the snores only subconsciously, but she saw the straggling beard on Grandma's chin, trembling a little with every "mark" and "poosah." They were long gray hairs curled every here and there against the dark brown skin. Isis was moved with pity for her mother's mother.

"Poah Gran-ma needs a shave," she murmured, and set about it. Just then Joel, next older than Isis, entered with a can of bait.

"Come on, Isie, les' we all go fishin'. The Perch is bitin' fine in Blue Sink."

"Sh-sh—" cautioned his sister. "Ah got to shave Gran'ma."

"Who say so?" Joel asked, surprised.

"Nobody doan hafta tell me. Look at her chin. No ladies don't weah whiskers if they kin help it. But Gran-ma gittin' ole, an' she doan know how to shave lak *me.*"

The conference adjourned to the back porch lest Grandma wake.

"Aw, Isie, you doan know nothin' 'bout shavin' a-tall— but a *man* lak *me*—"

"Ah do so know."

"You don't not. Ah'm goin' shave her mahseff."

"Naw, you won't neither, Smarty. Ah saw her first an' thought it all up first," Isis declared, and ran to the calico-covered box on the wall above the wash basin and seized her father's razor. Joel was quick and seized the mug and brush.

"Now!" Isis cried defiantly. "Ah got the razor."

"Goody, goody, goody, pussy cat, Ah got th' brush an' you can't shave 'thout lather—see! Ah know mo' than you," Joel retorted.

"Aw, who don't know dat?" Isis pretended to scorn. But seeing her progress blocked from lack of lather, she compromised.

"Ah know! Les' we all shave her. You lather, an' Ah shave."

This was agreeable to Joel. He made mountains of lather and anointed his own chin, and the chin of Isis and the dogs, splashed the wall, and at last was persuaded to lather Grandma's chin. Not that he was loath, but he wanted his new plaything to last as long as possible.

Isis stood on one side of the chair with the razor clutched cleaver fashion. The niceties of razor-handling had passed over her head. The thing with her was to *hold* the razor— sufficient in itself.

Joel splashed on the lather in great gobs, and Grandma awoke.

For one bewildered moment she stared at the grinning boy with the brush and mug, but sensing another presence, she turned to behold the business face of Isis and the razor-clutching hand. Her jaw dropped, and Grandma, forgetting years and rheumatism, bolted from the chair and fled the house, screaming.

"She's gone to tell Papa, Isie. You didn't have no business wid his razor, and he's gonna lick yo' hide," Joel cried, running to replace mug and brush.

"You too, chuckle-head, you too," retorted Isis. "You was playin' wid his brush and put it all over the dogs—Ah seen you put in on Ned an' Beulah." Isis shaved and replaced it in the box. Joel took his bait and pole and hurried to Blue Sink. Isis crawled under the house to brood over the whipping she knew would come. She had meant well.

But sounding brass and tinkling cymbal drew her forth. The local lodge of the Grand United Order of Odd Fellows, led by a braying, thudding band, was marching in full regalia down the road. She had forgotten the barbecue and log-rolling to be held today for the benefit of the new hall.

Music to Isis meant motion. In a minute razor and whipping forgotten, she was doing a fair imitation of a Spanish dancer she had seen in a medicine show sometime before. Isis's feet were gifted—she could dance most anything she saw.

Up, up, went her spirits, her small feet doing all sorts of intricate things and her body in rhythm, hand curving above her head. But the music was growing faint. Grandma was nowhere in sight. Isis stole out of the gate, running and dancing after the band.

Not far down the road, Isis stopped. She realized she couldn't dance at the carnival. Her dress was torn and dirty. She picked a long-stemmed daisy and placed it behind her ear, but her dress remained torn and dirty just the same. Then Isis had an idea. Her thoughts returned to the battered, round-topped trunk back in the bedroom. She raced back to the house; then, happier, she raced down the white dusty road to the picnic grove, gorgeously clad. People laughed good-naturedly at her, the band played, and Isis danced because she couldn't help it. A crowd of children gathered admiringly about her as she wheeled lightly about, hand on hip, flower between her teeth with the red and white fringe of the tablecloth—Grandma's new red tablecloth that she wore in lieu of a Spanish shawl—trailing in the dust. It was too ample for her meager form, but she wore it like a gypsy. Her brown feet twinkled in and out of the fringe. Some grown people joined the children about her. The Grand Exalted Ruler rose to speak; the band was hushed, but Isis danced on, the crowd clapping their hands for her. No one listened to the Exalted one, for little by little the multitude had surrounded the small brown dancer.

An automobile drove up to the Crown and halted. Two white men and a lady got out and pushed into the crowd, suppressing mirth discreetly behind gloved hands. Isis looked up and waved them a magnificent hail and went on dancing until—

Grandma had returned to the house and missed Isis. She straightaway sought her at the festivities, expecting to find her in her soiled dress, shoeless, standing at the far edge of the crowd. What she saw now drove her frantic. Here was her granddaughter dancing before a gaping crowd in her brand-new red tablecloth, and reeking of lemon extract. Isis had added the final touch to her costume. Of course she must also have perfume.

When Isis saw her grandma, she bolted. She heard her grandma cry—"Mah Gawd, mah brand-new tablecloth Ah just bought f'um O'landah!"—as Isis fled through the crowd and on into the woods.

Isis followed the little creek until she came to the ford in a rutty wagon road that led to Apopka and lay down on the cool grass at the roadside. The April sun was quite warm.

Misery, misery and woe, settled down upon her. The child wept. She knew another whipping was in store.

"Oh, Ah wish Ah could die, then Gran'ma an' Papa would be sorry they beat me so much. Ah b'leeve Ah'll run away and never go home no mo'. Ah'm goin' drown mah-seff in th' creek!"

Isis got up and waded into the water. She routed out a tiny 'gator and a huge bullfrog. She splashed and sang. Soon she was enjoying herself immensely. The purr of a motor struck her ear, and she saw a large, powerful car jolting along the rutty road toward her. It stopped at the water's edge.

"Well, I declare, it's our little gypsy," exclaimed the man at the wheel. "What are you doing here, now?"

"Ah'm killin' mahseff," Isis declared dramatically, " 'Cause Gran'ma beats me too much."

There was a hearty burst of laughter from the machine.

"You'll last some time the way you are going about it. Is this the way to Maitland? We want to go to the Park Hotel."

Isis saw no longer any reason to die. She came up out of the water, holding up the dripping fringe of the tablecloth.

"Naw, indeedy. You go to Maitlan' by the shell road—it

goes by mah house—an' turn off at Lake Sebelia to the clay road that takes you right to the do'."

"Well," went on the driver, smiling furtively, "could you quit dying long enough to go with us?"

"Yessuh," she said thoughtfully, "Ah wanta go wid you."

The door of the car swung open. She was invited to a seat beside the driver. She had often dreamed of riding in one of these heavenly chariots but never thought she would, actually.

"Jump in then, Madame Tragedy, and show us. We lost ourselves after we left your barbecue."

During the drive Isis explained to the kind lady who smelt faintly of violets and to the indifferent men that she was really a princess. She told them about her trips to the horizon, about the trailing gowns, the gold shoes with blue bottoms—she insisted on the blue bottoms—the white charger, the time when she was Hercules and had slain numerous dragons and sundry giants. At last the car approached her gate, over which stood the umbrella chinaberry tree. The car was abreast of the gate and had all but passed when Grandma spied her glorious tablecloth lying back against the upholstery of the Packard.

"You Isie-e!" she bawled, "You li'l wretch you! Come heah *dis instant.*"

"That's me," the child confessed, mortified, to the lady on the rear seat.

"Oh Sewell, stop the car. This is where the child lives. I hate to give her up though."

"Do you wanta keep me?" Isis brightened.

"Oh, I wish I could. Wait, I'll try to save you a whipping this time."

She dismounted with the gaudy lemon-flavored culprit and advanced to the gate where Grandma stood glowering, switches in hand.

"You're gointuh ketchit f'um yo' haid to yo' heels, m'lady. Jes' come in heah."

"Why, good afternoon," she accosted the furious grand-parent. "You're not going to whip this poor little thing, are you?" the lady asked in conciliatory tones.

"Yes, ma'am. She's de wustest li'l limb dat ever drawed bref. Jes' look at mah new tablecloth, dat ain't never been washed. She done traipsed all over de woods, uh dancin' an' uh prancin' in it. She done took a razor to me t'day, an' Lawd knows whut mo'."

Isis clung to the stranger's hand fearfully.

"Ah wuzn't gointer hurt Gran'ma, miss—Ah wuz just gointer shave her whiskers fuh huh 'cause she's old an' can't."

The white hand closed tightly over the little brown one that was quite soiled. She could understand a voluntary act of love even though it miscarried.

"Now, Mrs. er—er—I didn't get the name—how much did your tablecloth cost?"

"One whole big silvah dollar down at O'landah—ain't had it a week yit."

"Now here's five dollars to get another one. I want her to go to the hotel and dance for me. I could stand a little light today—"

"Oh, yessum, yessum," Grandma cut in, "everything's alright, sho' she kin go, yessum."

Feeling that Grandma had been somewhat squelched did not detract from Isis's spirit at all. She pranced over to the waiting motor-car and this time seated herself on the rear seat between the sweet-smiling lady and the rather aloof man in gray.

"Ah'm gointer stay wid you all," she said with a great deal of warmth and snuggled up to her benefactress. "Want me tuh sing a song fuh you?"

"There, Helen, you've been adopted," said the man with a short, harsh laugh.

"Oh, I hope so, Harry." She put her arm about the red-draped figure at her side and drew it close until she felt the warm puffs of the child's breath against her side. She looked hungrily ahead of her and spoke into space rather than to anyone in the car. "I would like just a little of her sunshine to soak into my soul. I would like that a lot."

# The Typewriter

## DOROTHY WEST

The famous Harlem literary Renaissance of the 1920s didn't reach everyone, as ironically demonstrated in this classic story by West. The middle-aged janitor at the center of the story represents the "dream deferred" of many post–World War I blacks who came north seeking jobs, opportunity, and a new life. This sad story, which won West a split with Zora Neale Hurston of second prize in *Opportunity*'s short story contest of 1926, also tells of a young girl's dream to write and the economic hardships that complicate that task. This is the best story of West's short, distinguished career.

IT OCCURRED TO HIM, as he eased past the bulging knees of an Irish wash lady and forced an apologetic passage down the aisle of the crowded car, that more than anything in all the world he wanted not to go home. He began to wish passionately that he had never been born, that he had never been married, that he had never been the means of life's coming into the world. He knew quite suddenly that he hated his flat and his family and his friends. And most of all the incessant thing that would "clatter clatter" until every nerve screamed aloud, and the words of the evening paper danced crazily before him, and the insane desire to crush and kill set his fingers twitching.

He shuffled down the street, an abject little man of fifty-odd years, in an ageless overcoat that flapped in the wind. He was cold, and he hated the North, and particularly Boston, and saw suddenly a barefoot pickaninny sitting on a fence in the hot Southern sun with a piece of steaming corn bread and a piece of fried salt pork in either grimy hand.

He was tired, and he wanted his supper, but he didn't want the beans, and frankfurters, and light bread that Net would undoubtedly have. That Net had had every Monday night since that regrettable moment fifteen years before when he had told her—innocently—that such a supper tasted "right nice. Kinda change from what we always has."

He mounted the four brick steps leading to his door and pulled at the bell; but there was no answering ring. It was broken again, and in a mental flash he saw himself with a multitude of tools and a box of matches shivering in the vestibule after supper. He began to pound lustily on the door and wondered vaguely if his hand would bleed if he smashed the glass. He hated the sight of blood. It sickened him.

Someone was running down the stairs. Daisy probably. Millie would be at that infernal thing, pounding, pounding. . . . He entered. The chill of the house swept him. His child was wrapped in a coat. She whispered solemnly, "Poppa, Miz Hicks an' Miz Berry's orful mad. They gointa move if they can't get more heat. The furnace's bin out all day. Mama couldn't fix it." He said hurriedly, "I'll go right down. I'll go right down." He hoped Mrs. Hicks wouldn't pull open her door and glare at him. She was large and domineering, and her husband was a bully. If her husband ever struck him, it would kill him. He hated life, but he didn't want to die. He was afraid of God and in his wildest flights of fancy couldn't imagine himself an angel. He went softly down the stairs.

He began to shake the furnace fiercely. And he shook into it every wrong, mumbling softly under his breath. He began to think back over his uneventful years, and it came to him as rather a shock that he had never sworn in all his life. He wondered uneasily if he dared say "damn." It was taken for granted that a man swore when he tended a stubborn furnace. And his strongest interjection was "Great balls of fire!"

The cellar began to warm, and he took off his inadequate

overcoat that was streaked with dirt. Well, Net would have to clean that. He'd be damned—! It frightened him and thrilled him. He wanted suddenly to rush upstairs and tell Mrs. Hicks if she didn't like the way he was running things, she could get out. But he heaped another shovelful of coal on the fire and sighed. He would never be able to get away from himself and the routine of years.

He thought of that eager Negro lad of seventeen who had come North to seek his fortune. He had walked jauntily down Boylston Street, and even his own kind had laughed at the incongruity of him. But he had thrown up his head and promised himself: "You'll have an office here someday. With plate-glass windows and a real mahogany desk." But, though he didn't know it then, he was not the progressive type. And he became successively, in the years, bellboy, porter, waiter, cook, and finally janitor in a downtown office building.

He had married Net when he was thirty-three and a waiter. He had married her partly because—though he might not have admitted it—there was no one to eat the expensive delicacies the generous cook gave him every night to bring home. And partly because he dared hope there might be a son to fulfill his dreams. But Millie had come, and after her twin girls who had died within two weeks, then Daisy, and it was tacitly understood that Net was done with child-bearing.

Life, though flowing monotonously, had flowed peacefully enough until that sucker of sanity became a sitting-room fixture. Intuitively at the very first he had felt its undesirability. He had suggested hesitatingly that they couldn't afford it. Three dollars the eighth of every month. Three dollars: food and fuel. Times were hard, and the twenty dollars apiece the respective husbands of Miz Hicks and Miz Berry irregularly paid was only five dollars more than the thirty-five a month he paid his own Hebraic landlord. And the Lord knew his salary was little enough. At which point Net spoke her piece, her voice rising shrill. "God knows I never complain 'bout nothin'. Ain't no other woman got less than me. I bin wearin' this same dress here five years, an' I'll wear it another five. But I don't want nothin'. I ain't never wanted nothin'. An' when I does as', it's only for my children. You're a poor sort of father if you can't give that child jes' three dollars a month to rent that typewriter. Ain't 'nother girl in school ain't got one. An' mos' of 'ems bought an' paid for. You know yourself how Millie is. She wouldn't as' me for it till she had to. An' I ain't going to disappoint her. She's goin' to get that type-writer Saturday, mark my words."

On a Monday then it had been installed. And in the months that followed, night after night he listened to the murderous "tack, tack, tack" that was like a vampire slowly drinking his blood. If only he could escape. Bar a door against the sound of it. But tied hand and foot by the eco-nomic fact that "Lord knows we can't afford to have fires burnin' an' lights lit all over the flat. You'all gotta set in one room. An' when y'get tired settin' y'c'n go to bed. Gas bill was somep'n scandalous las' month."

He heaped a final shovelful of coal on the fire and watched the first blue flames. Then, his overcoat under his arm, he mounted the cellar stairs. Mrs. Hicks was standing in her kitchen door, arms akimbo. "It's warmin'," she vol-unteered.

"Yeh"—he was conscious of his grime-streaked face and hands—"it's warmin'. I'm sorry 'bout all day."

She folded her arms across her ample bosom. "Tending a furnace ain't a woman's work. I don't blame your wife none 'tall."

Unsuspecting he was grateful. "Yeh, it's pretty hard for a woman. I always look after it 'fore I goes to work, but some days it jes' ac's up."

"Y'oughta have a janitor, that's what y'ought," she flung at him. "The same cullud man that tends them apartments would be willin'. Mr. Taylor has him. It takes a man to run a furnace, and when the man's away all day—"

"I know," he interrupted, embarrassed and hurt, "I know. Tha's right, Miz Hicks, tha's right. But I ain't in a position to make no improvements. Times is hard."

She surveyed him critically. "Your wife called down 'bout

three times while you was in the cellar. I reckon she wants you for supper."

"Thanks," he mumbled, and escaped up the back stairs.

He hung up his overcoat in the closet, telling himself, a little lamely, that it wouldn't take him more'n a minute to clean it up himself after supper. After all Net was tired and prob'bly worried what with Miz Hicks and all. And he hated men who made slaves of their womenfolk. Good old Net.

He tidied up in the bathroom, washing his face and hands carefully and cleanly so as to leave no—or very little —stain on the roller towel. It was hard enough for Net, God knew.

He entered the kitchen. The last spirals of steam were rising from his supper. One thing about Net, she served a full plate. He smiled appreciatively at her unresponsive back, bent over the kitchen sink. There was no one could bake beans just like Net's. And no one who could find a market with frankfurters quite so fat.

He sank down at his place. "Evenin', hon."

He saw her back stiffen. "If your supper's cold, 'tain't my fault. I called and called."

He said hastily, "It's fine, Net, fine. Piping."

She was the usual tired housewife. "Y'oughta et your supper 'fore you fooled with that furnace. I ain't bothered 'bout them niggers. I got all my dishes washed 'cept yours. An' I hate to mess up my kitchen after I once get it straightened up."

He was humble. "I'll give that old furnace an extra lookin' after in the mornin'. It'll las' all day tomorrow, hon."

"An' on top of that," she continued, unheeding him and giving a final wrench to her dish towel, "that confounded bell don't ring. An'—"

"I'll fix it after supper," he interposed hastily.

She hung up her dish towel and came to stand before him looming large and yellow. "An' that old Miz Berry, she claim she was expectin' comp'ny. An' she knows they must 'a' come an' gone while she was in her kitchen an' couldn't be at her winder to watch for 'em. Old liar," she brushed back a lock of naturally straight hair. "She wasn't expectin' nobody."

"Well, you know how some folks are—"

"Fools! Half the world," was her vehement answer. "I'm goin' in the front room an' set down a spell. I bin on my feet all day. Leave them dishes on the table. God knows I'm tired, but I'll come back an' wash 'em." But they both knew, of course, that he, very clumsily, would.

At precisely quarter past nine when he, strained at last to the breaking point, uttering an inhuman, strangled cry, flung down his paper, clutched at his throat, and sprang to his feet, Millie's surprised young voice, shocking him to normalcy, heralded the first of that series of great moments that every humble little middle-class man eventually experiences.

"What's the matter, Poppa? You sick? I wanted you to help me."

He drew out his handkerchief and wiped his hot hands. "I declare I must 'a' fallen asleep an' had a nightmare. No, I ain't sick. What you want, hon?"

"Dictate me a letter, Poppa. I c'n do sixty words a minute.—You know, like a business letter. You know, like those men in your building dictate to their stenographers. Don't you hear 'em sometimes?"

"Oh, sure, I know, hon. Poppa'll help you. Sure. I hear that Mr. Browning—sure."

Net rose. "Guess I'll put this child to bed. Come on now, Daisy, without no fuss.—Then I'll run up to Pa's. He ain't bin well all week."

When the door closed behind them, he crossed to his daughter, conjured the image of Mr. Browning in the process of dictating, so arranged himself, and coughed importantly.

"Well, Millie—"

"Oh, Poppa, is that what you'd call your stenographer?" she teased. "And anyway pretend I'm really one—and you're really my boss, and this letter's real important."

A light crept into his dull eyes. Vigor through his thin

blood. In a brief moment the weight of years fell from him like a cloak. Tired, bent, little old man that he was, he smiled, straightened, tapped impressively against his teeth with a toil-stained finger, and bccame that enviable emblem of American life: a business man.

"You be Miz Hicks, huh, honey? 'Course we can't both use the same name. I'll be J. Lucius Jones. J. Lucius. All them real big doin' men use their middle names. Jus' kinda looks big doin', doncha think, hon? Looks like money, huh? J. Lucius." He uttered a sound that was like the proud cluck of a strutting hen. "J. Lucius." It rolled like oil from his tongue.

His daughter twisted impatiently. "Now, Poppa—I mean Mr. Jones, sir—please begin. I am ready for dictation, sir."

He was in that office on Boylston Street, looking with visioning eyes through its plate-glass windows, tapping with impatient fingers on its real mahogany desk.

"Ah—Beaker Brothers, Park Square Building, Boston, Mass. Ah—Gentlemen: In reply to yours of the seventh instant would state—"

Evcry night thereafter in the weeks that followed, with Daisy packed off to bed, and Net "gone up to Pa's" or nodding inobtrusively in her corner, there was the chameleon change of a Court Street janitor to J. Lucius Jones, dealer in stocks and bonds. He would stand, posturing, importantly flicking imaginary dust from his coat lapel, or, his hands locked behind his back, he would stride up and down, earnestly and seriously debating the advisability of buying copper with the market in such a fluctuating state. Once a week, too, he stopped in at Jerry's and, after a preliminary purchase of cheap cigars, bought the latest trade papers, mumbling an embarrassed explanation: "I got a little money. Think I'll invest it in reliable stock."

The letters Millie typed and subsequently discarded, he rummaged for later, and under cover of writing to his brother in the South, laboriously, with a great many fancy flourishes, signed each neatly typed sheet with the exalted J. Lucius Jones.

Later, when he mustered the courage, he suggested ten-

tatively to Millie that it might be fun—just fun, of course!
—to answer his letters. One night—he laughed a good deal
louder and longer than necessary—he'd be J. Lucius Jones,
and the next night—here he swallowed hard and looked a
little frightened—Rockefeller or Vanderbilt or Morgan—
just for fun, y'understand! To which Millie gave consent. It
mattered little to her one way or the other. It was practice,
and that was what she needed. Very soon now she'd be in
the hundred class. Then maybe she could get a job!

He was growing very careful of his English. Occasionally
—and it must be admitted, ashamedly—he made surreptitious ventures into the dictionary. He had to, of course. J.
Lucius Jones would never say "Y'got to" when he meant
"It is expedient." And, old brain though he was, he learned
quickly and easily, juggling words with amazing facility.

Eventually he bought stamps and envelopes—long, im-
portant-looking envelopes—and stammered apologetically
to Millie, "Honey, Poppa thought it'd help you if you
learned to type envelopes, too. Reckon you'll have to do
that, too, when y'get a job. Poor old man"—he swallowed
painfully—"came round selling these envelopes. You know
how 'tis. So I had to buy 'em." Which was satisfactory to
Millie. If she saw through her father, she gave no sign.
After all, it was practice, and Mr. Hennessey had promised
the smartest girl in the class a position in the very near
future. And she, of course, was smart as a steel trap. Even
Mr. Hennessey had said that—though not in just those
words.

He had got in the habit of carrying those self-addressed
envelopes in his inner pocket where they bulged impressively. And occasionally he would take them out—on the
car usually—and smile upon them. This one might be from
J. P. Morgan. This one from Henry Ford. And a million-
dollar deal involved in each. That narrow, little spinster,
who, upon his sitting down, had drawn herself away from
his contact, was shunning J. Lucius Jones!

Once, led by some sudden, strange impulse, as an outgoing car rumbled up out of the subway, he got out a letter,
darted a quick, shamed glance about him, dropped it in an

adjacent box, and swung aboard the car, feeling, dazedly, as if he had committed a crime. And the next night he sat in the sitting-room quite on edge until Net said suddenly, "Look here, a real important letter come today for you, Pa. Here 'tis. What you s'pose it says," and he reached out a hand that trembled. He made brief explanation. "Advertisement, hon. Thassal."

They came quite frequently after that, and despite the fact that he knew them by heart, he read them slowly and carefully, rustling the sheet and making inaudible, intelligent comments. He was, in these moments, pathetically earnest.

Monday, as he went about his janitor's duties, he composed in his mind the final letter from J. P. Morgan that would consummate a big business deal. For days now letters had passed between them. J. P. had been at first quite frankly uninterested. He had written tersely and briefly. Which was meat to J. Lucius. The compositions of his brain were really the work of an artist. He wrote glowingly of the advantages of a pact between them. Daringly he argued in terms of billions. And at last J. P. had written his next letter would be decisive. Which next letter, this Monday, as he trailed about the office building, was writing itself on his brain.

That night Millie opened the door for him. Her plain face was transformed. "Poppa—Poppa, I got a job! Twelve dollars a week to start with! Isn't that *swell*!"

He was genuinely pleased. "Honey, I'm glad. Right glad," and went up the stairs, unsuspecting.

He ate his supper hastily, went down into the cellar to see about his fire, returned, and carefully tidied up, informing his reflection in the bathroom mirror, "Well, J. Lucius, you c'n expect that final letter any day now."

He entered the sitting-room. The phonograph was playing. Daisy was singing lustily. Strange. Net was talking animatedly to—Millie, busy with needle and thread over a neat little frock. His wild glance darted to the table. The pretty little centerpiece, the bowl and wax flowers all neatly arranged: the typewriter gone from its accustomed place. It seemed an hour before he could speak. He felt himself trembling. Went hot and cold.

"Millie—your typewriter's—gone!"

She made a deft little in-and-out movement with her needle. "It's the eighth, you know. When the man came today for the money, I sent it back. I won't need it no more —now!—The money's on the mantelpiece, Poppa."

"Yeh," he muttered. "All right."

He sank down in his chair, fumbled for the paper, found it.

Net said, "Your poppa wants to read. Stop your noise, Daisy."

She obediently stopped both her noise and the phonograph, took up her book, and became absorbed. Millie went on with her sewing in placid anticipation of the morrow. Net immediately began to nod, gave a curious snort, slept.

Silence. That crowded in on him, engulfed him. That blurred his vision, dulled his brain. Vast, white, impenetrable. . . . His ears strained for the old, familiar sound. And silence beat upon them. . . . The words of the evening paper jumbled together. He read: J. P. Morgan goes—

It burst upon him. Blinded him. His hands groped for the bulge beneath his coat. Why this—this was the end! The end of those great moments—the end of everything! Bewildering pain tore through him. He clutched at his heart and felt, almost, the jagged edges drive into his hand. A lethargy swept down upon him. He could not move, nor utter sound. He could not pray, nor curse.

Against the wall of that silence J. Lucius Jones crashed and died.

# Wedding Day

## Gwendolyn Bennett

Many black writers and musicians fled to Paris during and after the 1920s to escape racism in America. Bennett's story of Paul Watson, a black prizefighter living in Paris during and after World War I, explores the complex feelings of a black man fueled by hatred of whites as that hate intersects with his need for love. The story reinforces the strength of taboos around interracial relationships but is more compassionately focused on the double victimization of Watson's character. Bennett's story was first published in 1926 in *Fire!!,* a magazine she helped to form at the height of the Harlem Renaissance. The conversational tone of the story and its use of repetition bears the clear influence of Gertrude Stein, Bennett's contemporary.

HIS NAME WAS PAUL WATSON, and as he shambled down rue Pigalle, he might have been any other Negro of enormous height and size. But as I have said, his name was Paul Watson. Passing him on the street, you might not have known or cared who he was, but any one of the residents about the great Montmartre district of Paris could have told you who he was as well as many interesting bits of his personal history.

He had come to Paris in the days before colored jazz bands were the style. Back home he had been a prizefighter. In the days when Joe Gans was in his glory, Paul was following the ring, too. He didn't have that fine way about him that Gans had, and for that reason luck seemed to go against him. When he was in the ring, he was like a mad bull, especially if his opponent was a white man. In those days there wasn't any sympathy or nicety about the ring, and so pretty soon all the ringmasters got down on Paul, and he found it pretty hard to get a bout with anyone. Then it was that he worked his way across the Atlantic Ocean on a big liner—in the days before colored jazz bands were the style in Paris.

Things flowed along smoothly for the first few years with Paul's working here and there in the unfrequented places of Paris. On the side he used to give boxing lessons to aspiring youths or gymnastic young women. At that time he was working so steadily that he had little chance to find out what was going on around Paris. Pretty soon, however, he grew to be known among the trainers, and managers began to fix up bouts for him. After one or two successful bouts a little fame began to come into being for him. So it was that after one of the prize-fights, a colored fellow came to his dressing room to congratulate him on his success as well as invite him to go to Montmartre to meet "the boys."

Paul had a way about him and seemed to get on with the colored fellows who lived in Montmartre, and when the first Negro jazz band played in a tiny Parisian café, Paul was among them playing the banjo. Those first years were without event so far as Paul was concerned. The members of that first band often say now that they wonder how it was that nothing happened during those first seven years, for it was generally known how great was Paul's hatred for American white people. I suppose the tranquillity in the light of what happened afterward was due to the fact that the café in which they worked was one in which mostly French people drank and danced, and then too, that was before there were so many Americans visiting Paris. However, everyone had heard Paul speak of his intense hatred of American white folks. It only took two Benedictines to make him start talking about what he would do to the first "Yank" that called him "nigger." But the seven years came to an end, and Paul Watson went to work in a larger café with a larger band, patronized almost solely by Americans.

I've heard almost every Negro in Montmartre tell about the night that a drunken Kentuckian came into the café where Paul was playing and said:

"Look heah, Bruther, what you all doin' ovah heah?"

"None ya bizness. And looka here, I ain't your brother, see?"

"Jack, do you heah that nigger talkin' lak that tah me?"

As he said this, he turned to speak to his companion. I have often wished that I had been there to have seen the thing happen myself. Every tale I have heard about it was different, and yet there was something of truth in each of them. Perhaps the nearest one can come to the truth is by saying that Paul beat up about four full-sized white men that night besides doing a great deal of damage to the furniture about the café. I couldn't tell you just what did happen. Some of the fellows say that Paul seized the nearest table and mowed down men right and left, others say he took a bottle, then again the story runs that a chair was the instrument of his fury. At any rate, that started Paul Watson on his siege against the American white person who brings his native prejudices into the life of Paris.

It is a verity that Paul was the "black terror." The last syllable of the word nigger never passed the lips of a white man without the quick reflex action of Paul's arm and fist to the speaker's jaw. He paid for more glassware and café furnishings in the course of the next few years than is easily imaginable. And yet, there was something likable about Paul. Perhaps that's the reason that he stood in so well with the policemen of the neighborhood. Always some divine power seemed to intervene in his behalf, and he was excused after the payment of a small fine with advice about his future conduct. Finally, there came the night when in a frenzy he shot the two American sailors.

They had not died from the wounds he had given them, hence his sentence had not been one of death but rather a long term of imprisonment. It was a pitiable sight to see Paul sitting in the corner of his cell with his great body hunched almost double. He seldom talked, and when he did, his words were interspersed with oaths about the lowness of "crackers." Then the World War came.

It seems strange that anything so horrible as that wholesale slaughter could bring about any good, and yet there was something of a smoothing quality about even its baseness. There has never been such equality before or since such as that which the World War brought. Rich men fought by the side of paupers; poets swapped yarns with dry-goods salesmen, while Jews and Christians ate corned beef out of the same tin. Along with the general leveling influence came France's pardon of her prisoners in order that they might enter the army. Paul Watson became free and a French soldier. Because he was strong and had innate daring in his heart, he was placed in the aerial squad and cited many times for bravery. The close of the war gave him his place in French society as a hero. With only a memory of the war and an ugly scar on his left cheek, he took up his old life.

His firm resolutions about American white people still remained intact, and many chance encounters that followed the war are told from lip to lip proving that the war and his previous imprisonment had changed him little. He was the same Paul Watson to Montmartre as he shambled up rue Pigalle.

Rue Pigalle in the early evening has a somber beauty—gray as are most Paris streets and otherworldish. To those who know the district, it is the Harlem of Paris and rue Pigalle is its dusky Seventh Avenue. Most of the colored musicians that furnish Parisians and their visitors with entertainment live somewhere in the neighborhood of rue Pigalle. Sometime during every day each of these musicians makes a point of passing through rue Pigalle. Little wonder that almost any day will find Paul Watson going his shuffling way up the same street.

He reached the corner of rue de la Bruyere, and with sure instinct his feet stopped. Without half thinking he turned into "the Pit." Its full name is The Flea Pit. If you should ask one of the musicians why it was so called, he would answer you to the effect that it was called "the pit" because all the "fleas" hang out there. If you did not get the full import of this explanation, he would go further and say that there were always "spades" in the pit, and they were as thick as fleas. Unless you could understand this latter attempt at clarity, you could not fully grasp what the Flea Pit means to the Negro musicians in Montmartre. It is a tiny café of the genus that is called *bistro* in France. Here the fiddle players, saxophone blowers, drumbeaters, and ivory ticklers gather at four in the afternoon for a porto or a game of billiards. Here the cabaret entertainers and supper musicians meet at one o'clock at night or thereafter for a whiskey and soda, or more billiards. Occasional sandwiches and a "quiet game" also play their parts in the popularity of the place. After a season or two it becomes a settled fact just what time you may catch so-and-so at the famous "Pit."

The musicians were very fond of Paul and took particular delight in teasing him. He was one of the chosen few that all of the musicians conceded as being "regular." It was the pet joke of the habitues of the café that Paul never bothered with girls. They always said that he could beat up ten men but was scared to death of one woman.

"Say fellow, when ya goin' a get hooked up?"

"Can't say, Bo. Ain't so much on skirts."

"Man alive, ya don't know what you're missin'—somebody little and cute telling ya sweet things in your ear. Paris is full of women folks."

"I ain't much on 'em all the same. Then too, they're all white."

"What's it to ya? This ain't America."

"Can't help that. Get this—I'm collud, see? I ain't got nothing for no white meat to do. If a woman eva called me nigger, I'd have to kill her, that's all!"

"You for it, son. I can't give you a thing on this Mr. Jefferson Lawd way of lookin' at women."

"Oh, tain't that. I guess they're all right for those that wants 'em. Not me!"

"Oh, you ain't so forty. You'll fall like all the other spades I've ever seen. Your kind falls hardest."

And so Paul went his way—alone. He smoked and drank with the fellows and sat for hours in the Montmartre cafés and never knew the companionship of a woman. Then one night after his work he was walking along the street in his queer shuffling way when a woman stepped up to his side.

*"Voulez-vous."*

"Naw, gowan away from here."

"Oh, you speak English, don't you?"

"You an 'merican woman?"

"Used to be 'fore I went on the stage and got stranded over here."

"Well, get away from here. I don't like your kind!"

"Aw, Buddy, don't say that. I ain't prejudiced like some fool women."

"You don't know who I am, do you? I'm Paul Watson, and I hate American white folks, see?"

He pushed her aside and went on walking alone. He hadn't gone far when she caught up to him and said with sobs in her voice:—

"Oh, Lordy, please don't hate me 'cause I was born white and an American. I ain't got a sou to my name, and all the men pass me by 'cause I ain't spruced up. Now you come along and won't look at me 'cause I'm white."

Paul strode along with her clinging to his arm. He tried to shake her off several times, but there was no use. She clung all the more desperately to him. He looked down at her frail body shaken with sobs, and something caught at his heart. Before he knew what he was doing he had said:—

"Naw, I ain't that mean. I'll get you some grub. Quit your cryin'. Don't like seein' women folks cry."

It was the talk of Montmartre. Paul Watson takes a woman to Gavarnni's every night for dinner. He comes to the Flea Pit less frequently, thus giving the other musicians plenty of opportunity to discuss him.

"How times do change. Paul, the woman-hater, has a Jane now."

"You ain't said nothing, fella. That ain't all. She's white and an 'merican, too."

"That's the way with these spades. They beat up all the

white men they can lay their hands on, but as soon as a gang of golden hair with blue eyes rubs up close to them, they forget all they ever said about hatin' white folks."

"Guess he thinks that skirt's gone on him. Dumb fool!"

"Don' be no chineeman. That old gag don' fit for Paul. He cain't understand it no more'n we can. Says he jess can't help himself, every time she looks up into his eyes and asks him does he love her. They sure are happy together. Paul's goin' to marry her, too. At first she kept saying that she didn't want to get married 'cause she wasn't the marrying kind and all that talk. Paul jus' laid down the law to her and told her he never would live with no woman without being married to her. Then she began to tell him all about her past life. He told her he didn't care nothing about what she used to be jus' so long as they loved each other now. Guess they'll make it."

"Yeah, Paul told me the same tale last night. He's sure gone on her all right."

"They're gettin' tied up next Sunday. So glad it's not me. Don't trust these American dames. Me for the Frenchies."

"She ain't so worse for looks, Bud. Now that he's been furnishing the green for the rags."

"Yeah, but I don't see no reason for the wedding bells. She was right—she ain't the marrying kind."

. . . and so Montmartre talked. In every café where the Negro musicians congregated, Paul Watson was the topic for conversation. He had suddenly fallen from his place as bronze God to almost less than the dust.

The morning sun made queer patterns on Paul's sleeping face. He grimaced several times in his slumber, then finally half-opened his eyes. After a succession of dream-laden blinks he gave a great yawn and, rubbing his eyes, looked at the open window through which the sun shone brightly. His first conscious thought was that this was the bride's day and that bright sunshine prophesied happiness for the bride throughout her married life. His first impulse was to settle back into the covers and think drowsily about Mary and the queer twists life brings about, as is the wont of most bride-grooms on their last morning of bachelorhood. He put this impulse aside in favor of dressing quickly and rushing downstairs to telephone to Mary to say "happy wedding day" to her.

One huge foot slipped into a worn bedroom slipper and then the other dragged painfully out of the warm bed were the courageous beginnings of his bridal toilette. With a look of triumph he put on his new gray suit that he had ordered from an English tailor. He carefully pulled a taffeta tie into place beneath his chin, noting as he looked at his face in the mirror that the scar he had received in the army was very ugly—funny, marrying an ugly man like him.

French telephones are such human faults. After trying for about fifteen minutes to get Central 32.01 he decided that he might as well walk around to Mary's hotel to give his greeting as to stand there in the lobby of his own, wasting his time. He debated this in his mind a great deal. They were to be married at four o'clock. It was eleven now, and it did seem a shame not to let her have a minute or two by herself. As he went walking down the street toward her hotel, he laughed to think of how one always cogitates over doing something and finally does the thing he wanted to in the beginning anyway.

Mud on his nice gray suit that the English tailor had made for him. Damn—gray suit—what did he have a gray suit on for, anyway. Folks with black faces shouldn't wear gray suits. Gawd, but it was funny that time when he beat up that cracker at the Periquet. Fool couldn't shut his mouth he was so surprised. Crackers—damn 'em—he was one nigger that wasn't 'fraid of 'em. Wouldn't he have a hell of a time if he went back to America where black was black. Wasn't white nowhere, black wasn't. What was that thought he was trying to get ahold of—bumping around in his head—something he started to think but couldn't remember it somehow.

The shrill whistle that is typical of the French subway pierced its way into his thoughts. Subway—why was he in the subway—he didn't want to go anyplace. He heard doors slamming and saw the blue uniforms of the conductors swinging on to the cars as the trains began to pull out of the station. With one or two strides he reached the last coach as it began to move up the platform. A bit out of breath he stood inside the train, and looking down at what he had in his hand, hc saw that it was a tiny pink ticket. A first class ticket in a second class coach. The idea set him to laughing. Everyone in the car turned and eyed him, but that did not bother him. Wonder what stop he'd get off—funny how these French said descend when they meant get off—funny he couldn't pick up French—been here so long. First class ticket in a second class coach!—that was one on him. Wedding day today, and that damn letter from Mary. How'd she say it now, "just couldn't go through with it," white women just don't marry colored men, and she was a street woman, too. Why couldn't she have told him flat that she was just getting back on her feet at his expense. Funny that first class ticket he bought, wish he could see Mary—him a-going there to wish her "happy wedding day," too. Wonder what that French woman was looking at him so hard for? Guess it was the mud.

# Sanctuary
## NELLA LARSEN

# Mrs. Adis
## SHEILA KAYE-SMITH

Nella Larsen's career was soaring after the critical and commercial success of her only two published novels, *Quicksand* and *Passing,* when the story "Sanctuary" appeared in the January 1930 issue of *Forum.* The simple tale about a man who takes sanctuary in the home of a friend's mother after a shooting was itself unextraordinary. However, in the subsequent issue of *Forum,* a reader's letter noted what it called the story's "striking resemblance" to a story published eight years earlier by a white writer, Sheila Kaye-Smith, in an issue of *The Century Magazine,* which had since become *Forum.* The letter noted similarities in plot, character, and dialogue. After checking the two stories, *Forum* editors agreed that the coincidences were unusual and asked Larsen to respond to the letter. That response was one of Larsen's last published works. Though her letter makes a convincing case that Larsen worked "Sanctuary" up from a story she overheard years earlier, the charges shook the young writer's confidence enough that it curtailed her literary career. Here the two stories are printed together, along with the accusing letter and Larsen's response. Readers should note the marked difference between Kaye-Smith's pure melodrama, and Larsen's attempt to make the relationship between Mis' Poole and the outlaw Jim Hammer a symbol of black kinship in the face of early twentieth-century white justice, which rarely recognized the civil rights of black criminals.

# Sanctuary

## I

ON THE SOUTHERN COAST, between Merton and Shawboro, there is a strip of desolation some half a mile wide and nearly ten miles long between the sea and old fields of ruined plantations. Skirting the edge of this narrow jungle is a partly grown-over road which still shows traces of furrows made by the wheels of wagons that have long since rotted away or been cut into firewood. This road is little used, now that the state has built its new highway a bit to the west and wagons are less numerous than automobiles.

In the forsaken road a man was walking swiftly. But in spite of his hurry, at every step he set down his feet with infinite care, for the night was windless and the heavy silence intensified each sound; even the breaking of a twig could be plainly heard. And the man had need of caution as well as haste.

Before a lonely cottage that shrank timidly back from the road, the man hesitated a moment, then struck out across the patch of green in front of it. Stepping behind a clump of bushes close to the house, he looked in through the lighted window at Annie Poole, standing at her kitchen table mixing the supper biscuits.

He was a big, black man with pale brown eyes in which there was an odd mixture of fear and amazement. The light showed streaks of gray soil on his heavy, sweating face and great hands, and on his torn clothes. In his woolly hair clung bits of dried leaves and dead grass.

He made a gesture as if to tap on the window, but turned away to the door instead. Without knocking he opened it and went in.

## II

The woman's brown gaze was immediately on him, though she did not move. She said, "You ain't in no hurry, is you, Jim Hammer?" It wasn't, however, entirely a question.

"Ah's in trubble, Mis' Poole," the man explained, his voice shaking, his fingers twitching.

"W'at you done done now?"

"Shot a man, Mis' Poole."

"Trufe?" The woman seemed calm. But the word was spat out.

"Yas'm. Shot 'im." In the man's tone was something of wonder, as if he himself could not quite believe that he had really done this thing which he affirmed.

"Daid?"

"Dunno, Mis' Poole. Dunno."

"White man o' niggah?"

"Cain't say, Mis' Poole. White man, Ah reckons."

Annie Poole looked at him with cold contempt. She was a tiny, withered woman—fifty perhaps—with a wrinkled face the color of old copper, framed by a crinkly mass of white hair. But about her small figure was some quality of hardness that belied her appearance of frailty. At last she spoke, boring her sharp little eyes into those of the anxious creature before her.

"An' w'at am you lookin' foh me to do 'bout et?"

"Jes' lemme stop till dey's gone by. Hide me till dey passes. Reckon dey ain't fur off now." His begging voice changed to a frightened whimper. "Foh de Lawd's sake, Mis' Poole, lemme stop."

And why, the woman inquired caustically, should she run the dangerous risk of hiding him?

"Obadiah, he'd lemme stop ef he was to home," the man whined.

Annie Poole sighed. "Yas," she admitted, slowly, reluctantly, "Ah spec' he would. Obadiah, he's too good to youall no 'count trash." Her slight shoulders lifted in a hopeless shrug. "Yas, Ah reckon he'd do et. Emspecial' seein how he allus set such a heap o' store by you. Cain't see w'at foh, mahse'f. Ah shuah don' see nuffin' in you but a heap o' dirt."

But a look of irony, of cunning, of complicity passed over her face. She went on, "Still, 'siderin' all an' all, how Obadiah's right fon' o' you, an' how white folks is white folks, Ah'm a-gwine hide you dis one time."

Crossing the kitchen, she opened a door leading into a small bedroom, saying, "Git yo'se'f in dat dere feather baid, an' Ah'm a-gwine put de clo's on de top. Don' reckon dey'll fin' you ef dey does look foh you in mah house. An Ah don' spec' dey'll go foh to do dat. Not lessen you been keerless an' let 'em smell you out gittin' hyah." She turned on him a withering look. "But you allus been triflin'. Cain't do nuffin' propah. An' Ah'm a-tellin' you ef dey warn't white folks an' you a po' niggah, Ah shuah wouldn't be lettin' you mess up mah feather baid dis ebenin', 'cose Ah jes' plain don' want you hyah. Ah done kep' mahse'f outen trubble all mah life. So's Obadiah."

"Ah's powahful 'bliged to you, Mis' Poole. You shuah am one good 'oman. De Lawd'll mos' suttinly—"

Annie Poole cut him off. "Dis ain't no time foh all dat kin' o' fiddle-de-roll. Ah does mah duty as Ah sees et 'thout no thanks from you. Ef de Lawd had gib you a white face 'stead o'dat dere black one, Ah shuah would turn you out. Now hush yo' mouf an' git yo'se'f in. An' don' git movin' and scrunchin' undah dose covahs and git yo'se'f kotched in mah house."

Without further comment the man did as he was told. After he had laid his soiled body and grimy garments between her snowy sheets, Annie Poole carefully rearranged the covering and placed piles of freshly laundered linen on top. Then she gave a pat here and there, eyed the result, and finding it satisfactory, went back to her cooking.

## III

Jim Hammer settled down to the racking business of waiting until the approaching danger should have passed him by. Soon savory odors seeped in to him, and he realized that he was hungry. He wished that Annie Poole would bring him something to eat. Just one biscuit. But she wouldn't, he knew. Not she. She was a hard one, Obadiah's mother.

By and by he fell into a sleep, from which he was dragged back by the rumbling sound of wheels in the road outside. For a second fear clutched so tightly at him that he almost leaped from the suffocating shelter of the bed in order to make some active attempt to escape the horror that his capture meant. There was a spasm at his heart, a pain so sharp, so slashing that he had to suppress an impulse to cry out. He felt himself falling. Down, down, down. . . . Everything grew dim and very distant in his memory . . . vanished . . . came rushing back.

Outside there was silence. He strained his ears. Nothing. No footsteps. No voices. They had gone on then. Gone without even stopping to ask Annie Poole if she had seen him pass that way. A sigh of relief slipped from him. His thick lips curled in an ugly, cunning smile. It had been smart of him to think of coming to Obadiah's mother's to hide. She was an old demon, but he was safe in her house.

He lay a short while longer listening intently and, hearing nothing, started to get up. But immediately he stopped, his yellow eyes glowing like pale flames. He had heard the unmistakable sound of men coming toward the house. Swiftly he slid back into the heavy, hot stuffiness of the bed and lay listening fearfully.

The terrifying sounds drew nearer. Slowly. Heavily. Just for a moment he thought they were not coming in—they took so long. But there was a light knock and the noise of a door being opened. His whole body went taut. His feet felt frozen, his hands clammy, his tongue like a weighted, dying thing. His pounding heart made it hard for his straining ears to hear what they were saying out there.

"Ebenin', Mistah Lowndes." Annie Poole's voice sounded as it always did, sharp and dry.

There was no answer. Or had he missed it? With slow care he shifted his position, bringing his head nearer the edge of the bed. Still he heard nothing. What were they waiting for? Why didn't they ask about him?

Annie Poole, it seemed, was of the same mind. "Ah don'

reckon youall done traipsed 'way out hyah jes' foh yo' healf," she hinted.

"There's bad news for you, Annie, I'm 'fraid." The sheriff's voice was low and queer.

Jim Hammer visualized him standing out there—a tall, stooped man, his white tobacco-stained mustache drooping limply at the ends, his nose hooked and sharp, his eyes blue and cold. Bill Lowndes was a hard one too. And white.

"W'atall bad news, Mistah Lowndes?" The woman put the question quietly, directly.

"Obadiah—" The sheriff began—hesitated—began again. "Obadiah—ah—er, he's outside, Annie. I'm 'fraid—"

"Shucks! You done missed. Obadiah, he ain't done nuffin', Mistah Lowndes. Obadiah!" she called stridently. "Obadiah! git hyah an' splain yo'se'f."

But Obadiah didn't answer, didn't come in. Other men came in. Came in with steps that dragged and halted. No one spoke. Not even Annie Poole. Something was laid carefully upon the floor.

"Obadiah, chile," his mother said softly, "Obadiah, chile." Then, with sudden alarm, "He ain't daid, is he? Mistah Lowndes! Obadiah, he ain't daid?"

Jim Hammer didn't catch the answer to that pleading question. A new fear was stealing over him.

"There was a to-do, Annie," Bill Lowndes explained gently, "at the garage back o' the factory. Fellow tryin' to steal tires. Obadiah heerd a noise an' run out with two or three others. Scared the rascal all right. Fired off his gun an' run. We allow et to be Jim Hammer. Picked up his cap back there. Never was no 'count. Thievin' an' sly. But we'll git 'im, Annie. We'll git 'im."

The man huddled in the feather bed prayed silently. "Oh, Lawd! Ah didn't go to do et. Not Obadiah, Lawd. You knows dat. You knows et." And into his frenzied brain came the thought that it would be better for him to get up and go out to them before Annie Poole gave him away. For he was lost now. With all his great strength he tried to get himself out of the bed. But he couldn't.

"Oh Lawd!" he moaned. "Oh Lawd!" His thoughts were bitter, and they ran through his mind like panic. He knew that it had come to pass as it said somewhere in the Bible about the wicked. The Lord had stretched out his hand and smitten him. He was paralyzed. He couldn't move hand or foot. He moaned again. It was all there was left for him to do. For in the terror of this new calamity that had come upon him, he had forgotten the waiting danger which was so near out there in the kitchen.

His hunters, however, didn't hear him. Bill Lowndes was saying, "We been a-lookin' for Jim out along the old road. Figured he'd make tracks for Shawboro. You ain't noticed anybody pass this evenin', Annie?"

The reply came promptly, unwaveringly. "No, Ah ain't sees nobody pass. Not yet."

## IV

Jim Hammer caught his breath.

"Well," the sheriff concluded, "we'll be gittin' along. Obadiah was a mighty fine boy. Ef they was all like him—. I'm sorry, Annie. Anything I c'n do let me know."

"Thank you, Mistah Lowndes."

With the sound of the door closing on the departing men, power to move came back to the man in the bedroom. He pushed his dirt-caked feet out from the covers and rose up, but crouched down again. He wasn't cold now, but hot all over and burning. Almost he wished that Bill Lowndes and his men had taken him with them.

Annie Poole had come into the room.

It seemed a long time before Obadiah's mother spoke. When she did, there were no tears, no reproaches; but there was a raging fury in her voice as she lashed out, "Git outen mah feather baid, Jim Hammer, an' outen mah house, an' don' nevah stop thankin' yo' Jesus he done gib you dat black face."

## Nella Larsen's Story

To the Editor:

Having just finished reading Nella Larsen's story, "Sanctuary," published in the January issue of *The Forum,* I cannot help noting its striking resemblance to a story by Sheila Kaye-Smith entitled "Mrs. Adis," which was published in the *Century* for January 1922. Aside from dialect and setting, the stories are almost identical. The structure, situation, characters, and plot are the same. One often finds in Miss Larsen's story the same words and expressions used by Sheila Kaye-Smith in "Mrs. Adis."

Marion Boyd

*Oxford, O.*

## Editor's Note

*Since receiving this letter and several others to the same effect, we have looked up Sheila Kaye-Smith's story and compared it with Nella Larsen's story. We, too, were impressed by the "striking resemblance" between them and felt it our duty to call the matter to our author's attention, asking her, in fairness to* Forum *readers, to explain how she came by her plot and the circumstances under which her story was written. She not only complied with this request, but also sent us four rough drafts of the story showing just how she worked it out from the plot stage to its final form in which we printed it. A careful examination of this material has convinced us that the story, "Sanctuary," was written by Nella Larsen in the manner she describes. The coincidence is, indeed, extraordinary, but there are many well-authenticated cases of similar coincidences in history. For example, the incandescent lamp was invented almost simultaneously by Thomas Edison and an Englishman who had never heard of Edison. The* Encyclopaedia Britannica *also records how the theory of natural selection was worked out independently, and at precisely the same moment, by Charles Darwin and A. R. Wallace. Nella Larsen's letter of explanation follows in full.*

## The Author's Explanation

To the Editor:

I have your letter with its astonishing enclosure this morning. I haven't as yet seen the *Century* story, but it seems to me that anyone who intended to lift a story would have avoided doing it as obviously as this appears to have been done—judging from the excerpts which you have sent me.

In justice to *The Forum* and to myself, I wish to explain exactly how I came by the material out of which I wrote "Sanctuary." The story is one that was told to me by an old Negro woman who, in my nursing days, was an inmate of Lincoln Hospital and Home, East 141st Street and Southern Boulevard, New York City. Her name was Christophe or Christopher. That was sometime during the years from 1912 to 1915.

All the doctors and executives in this institution were white. All the nurses were Negroes. As in any other hospital, all infractions of rules and instances of neglect of duty were reported to and dealt with by the superintendent of nurses, who was white. It used to distress the old folks—Mrs. Christopher in particular—that we Negro nurses often had to tell things about each other to the white people. Her oft-repeated convictions were that if the Negro race would only stick together, we might get somewhere someday, and that what the white folks didn't know about us wouldn't hurt us.

All this used to amuse me until she told some of us about the death of her husband, who, she said, had been killed by a young Negro, and the killer had come to her for hiding without knowing whom he had killed. When the officers of the law arrived and she learned about her man, she still shielded the slayer, because, she told us, she intended to deal with him herself afterward without any interference from "white folks."

For some fifteen years I believed this story absolutely and entertained a kind of admiring pity for the old woman. But lately, in talking it over with Negroes, I find that the tale is so old and so well known that it is almost folklore. It has many variations: sometimes it is the woman's brother, husband, son, lover, preacher, beloved master, or even her father, mother, sister, or daughter who is killed. A Negro sociologist tells me that there are literally hundreds of these stories. Anyone could have written it up at any time.

When I first thought of writing the story, my idea was to use Harlem with its peculiar tempo and atmosphere as a setting, as well as the Harlemese language. But that little old Negro countrywoman was so vivid before me that I wanted to get her down just as I remembered her. Had I had any idea that there was already a story with a similar plot in existence, I don't think I would have made use of the material at all; or, if I had, I should certainly have taken the city for background and would have told the story exactly as it was told to me, or much more differently than I have done.

Nella Larsen

*New York City*

# Mrs. Adis

IN NORTHEASTERN SUSSEX a great tongue of land runs into Kent by Scotney Castle. It is a land of woods, the old hammer-woods of the Sussex iron industry, and among the woods gleam the hammer-ponds, holding in their mirrors the sunsets and sunrises. Owing to the thickness of the woods, great masses of oak and beech in a dense undergrowth of hazel and chestnut and frail sallow, the road that passes Mrs. Adis's cottage is dark before the twilight has crept away from the fields beyond. That night there was no twilight moon, only a few pricks of fire in the black sky above the trees. But what the darkness hid, the silence revealed. In the absolute stillness of the night, windless and clear with the first frost of October, every sound was distinct, intensified. The distant bark of a dog at Delmonden sounded close at hand, and the man who walked on the road could hear the echo of his own footsteps following him like a knell.

Every now and then he made a futile effort to go quietly, but the roadside was a mass of brambles, and their cracking and rustling sounded nearly as loud as the thud of his feet on the marl. Besides, they made him go slowly, and he had no time for that.

When he came to Mrs. Adis's cottage he paused a moment. Only a small patch of grass lay between it and the road. He went stealthily across it and looked in at the lighted, uncurtained window. He could see Mrs. Adis stooping over the fire, taking off some pot or kettle. He hesitated and seemed to ponder. He was a big, hulking man, with reddish hair and freckled face, evidently of the laboring class, though not successful, judging by the vague grime and poverty of his appearance. For a moment he made as if he would open the window; then he changed his mind and went to the door instead.

He did not knock, but walked straight in. The woman at the fire turned quickly.

"What, you, Peter Crouch?" she said. "I didn't hear you knock."

"I didn't knock, ma'am. I didn't want anybody to hear."

"How's that?"

"I'm in trouble." His hands were shaking a little.

"What you done?"

"I shot a man, Mrs. Adis."

"You?"

"Yes, I shot him."

"You killed him?"

"I dunno."

For a moment there was silence in the small stuffy kitchen; then the kettle boiled over, and Mrs. Adis sprang for it, mechanically putting it at the side of the fire.

She was a small, frail-looking woman, with a brown, hard face on which the skin had dried in innumerable small hair-like wrinkles. She was probably not more than forty-two, but life treats some women hard in the agricultural districts of Sussex, and Mrs. Adis's life had been harder than most.

"What do you want me to do for you, Peter Crouch?" she said a little sourly.

"Let me stay here a bit. Is there nowhere you can put me till they've gone?"

"Who's they?"

"The keepers."

"Oh, you've had a shine with the keepers, have you?"

"Yes, I was down by Cinder Wood seeing if I could pick up anything, and the keepers found me. There was four to one, so I used my gun. Then I ran for it. They're after me; reckon they aren't far off now."

Mrs. Adis did not speak for a moment.

Crouch looked at her searchingly, beseechingly.

"You might do it for Tom's sake," he said.

"You haven't been an overgood friend to Tom," snapped Mrs. Adis.

"But Tom's been an unaccountable good friend to me; reckon he would want you to stand by me tonight."

"Well, I won't say he wouldn't, seeing as Tom always thought better of you than you deserved, and maybe you can stay till he comes home tonight; then we can hear what he says about it."

"That'll serve my turn, I reckon. He'll be up at Ironlatch for an hour yet, and the coast will be clear by then, and I can get away out of the county."

"Where'll you go?"

"I dunno. There's time to think of that."

"Well, you can think of it in here," she said dryly, opening a door which led from the kitchen into the small lean-to of the cottage. "They'll never guess you're there, specially if I tell them I ain't seen you tonight."

"You're a good woman, Mrs. Adis."

She did not speak, but shut the door, and he was in darkness save for a small ray of light that filtered through one of the cracks. By this light he could see her moving to and fro, preparing Tom's supper. In another hour Tom would be home from Ironlatch Farm, where he worked every day. Peter Crouch trusted Tom not to revoke his mother's kindness, for they had been friends since they went together to the national school at Lamberhurst, and since then the friendship had not been broken by their very different characters and careers.

Peter Crouch huddled down upon the sacks that filled one corner of the lean-to and gave himself up to the dreary and anxious business of waiting. A delicious smell of cooking began to filter through from the kitchen, and he hoped Mrs. Adis would not deny him a share of the supper when Tom came home, for he was very hungry and he had a long way to go.

He had fallen into a kind of helpless doze, haunted by the memories of the last two hours, recast in the form of dreams, when he was roused by the sound of footsteps on the road. For a moment his poor heart nearly choked him with its beating. They were the keepers. They had guessed for a certainty where he was—with Mrs. Adis, his old pal's mother. He had been a fool to come to the cottage. Nearly losing his self-control, he shrank into the corner, shivering, half sobbing. But the footsteps went by. They did not even hesitate at the door. He heard them ring away into the frosty stillness. The next minute Mrs. Adis stuck her head into the lean-to.

"That was them," she said shortly—"a party from the castle. I saw them go by. They had lanterns, and I saw old Crotch and the two Boormans. Maybe it 'u'd be better if you slipped out now and went toward Cansiron. You'd miss them that way and get over into Kent. There's a London train comes from Tunbridge Wells at ten tonight."

"That 'u'd be a fine thing for me, ma'am, but I haven't the price of a ticket on me."

She went to one of the kitchen drawers.

"Here's seven shillun'. It's all I've got, but it'll be your fare to London and a bit over."

For a moment he did not speak; then he said:

"I don't know how to thank you, ma'am."

"Oh, you needn't thank me. I am doing it for Tom. I know how unaccountable set he is on you and always was."

"I hope you won't get into any trouble because of me."

"There ain't much fear. No one's ever likely to know you've been in this cottage. That's why I'd sooner you went before Tom came back, for maybe he'd bring a pal with him, and that 'u'd make trouble. I won't say I sha'n't have it on my conscience for having helped you to escape the law, but shooting a keeper ain't the same as shooting an ordinary sort of man, as we all know, and maybe he ain't so much the worse; so I won't think no more about it."

She opened the door for him, but on the threshold they stood still, for again footsteps could be heard approaching, this time from the far south.

"Maybe it's Tom," said Mrs. Adis.

"There's more than one man there, and I can hear voices."

"You'd better go back," she said shortly. "Wait till they've passed, anyway."

With an unwilling shrug he went back into the little lean-to, which he had come to hate, and she shut the door upon him.

The footsteps drew nearer. They came more slowly and heavily this time. For a moment he thought they also would pass, but their momentary dulling was only the crossing of the strip of grass outside the door. The next minute there was a knock. It was not Tom, then.

Trembling with anxiety and curiosity, Peter Crouch put his eye to one of the numerous cracks in the door of the lean-to and looked through into the kitchen. He saw Mrs. Adis go to the cottage door, but before she could open it, a man came quickly in and shut it behind him.

Crouch recognized Vidler, one of the keepers of Scotney Castle, and he felt his hands and feet grow leaden cold. They knew where he was, then; they had followed him. They had guessed that he had taken refuge with Mrs. Adis. It was all up. He was not really hidden; there was no place for him to hide. Directly they opened the inner door they would see him. Why couldn't he think of things better? Why wasn't he cleverer at looking after himself, like other men? His legs suddenly refused to support him, and he sat down on the pile of sacks.

The man in the kitchen seemed to have some difficulty in saying what he wanted to Mrs. Adis. He stood before her silently, twisting his cap.

"Well, what is it?" she asked.

"I want to speak to you, ma'am."

Peter Crouch listened, straining his ears, for his thudding heart nearly drowned the voices in the next room. Oh, no, he was sure she would not give him away, if only for Tom's sake. She was a game sort, Mrs. Adis.

"Well," she said sharply, as the man remained tongue-tied.

"I have brought you bad news, Mrs. Adis."

Her expression changed.

"What? It ain't Tom, is it?"

"He's outside," said the keeper.

"What do you mean?" said Mrs. Adis, and she moved toward the door.

"Don't, ma'am, not till I've told you."

"Told me what? Oh, be quick, man, for mercy's sake!" and she tried to push past him to the door.

"There's been a row," he said, "down by Cinder Wood. There was a chap there snaring rabbits, and Tom was walking with the Boormans and me and old Crotch down from the castle. We heard a noise in the spinney, and there—it was too dark to see who it was, and directly he saw us he made off. But we'd scared him, and he let fly with his gun."

He stopped speaking and looked at her, as if beseeching her to fill in the gaps of his story. In his corner of the lean-to Peter Crouch was as a man of wood and sawdust.

"Tom—" said Mrs. Adis.

The keeper had forgotten his guard, and before he could prevent her she had flung open the door.

The men outside had evidently been waiting for the signal, and they came in, carrying something on a hurdle, which they put down in the middle of the kitchen floor.

"Is he dead?" asked Mrs. Adis, without tears.

The men nodded. They could not find a dry voice, like hers.

In the lean-to Peter Crouch had ceased to sweat and tremble. Strength had come with despair, for he knew he must despair now. Besides, he no longer wanted to escape from this thing that he had done.

"O Tom! and I thinking it was one of them demmed keepers! Tom! and it was you that got it—got it from me! Reckon I don't want to live."

And yet life was sweet.

Mrs. Adis was sitting in the old basket armchair by the fire. One of the men had helped her into it. Another, with rough kindness, had poured her out something from a flask he carried in his pocket.

"Here, ma'am, take a drop of this. It'll give you strength. We'll go around to Ironlatch Farm and ask Mrs. Gain to come down to you. Reckon this is a tur'ble thing to have come to you, but it's the will o' Providence, as some folks say, and as for the man who did it, we've a middling good guess who he is, and he shall swing."

"We didn't see his face," said Vidler, "but we've got his gun. He threw it into an alder when he bolted, and I swear that gun belongs to Peter Crouch, who's been up to no good since the day when Mus' Scales got shut of him for stealing his corn."

"Reckon, though, he didn't know it was Tom when he did it," said the other man, "he and Tom always being better friends than Crouch deserved."

Peter Crouch was standing upright now, looking through the crack of the door. He saw Mrs. Adis struggle to her feet and stand by the table, looking down on the dead man's face. A whole eternity seemed to roll by as she stood there. He saw her put her hand into her pocket, where she had thrust the key of the lean-to.

"The Boormans have gone after Crouch," said Vidler, nervously breaking the silence. "They'd a notion as he'd broken through the woods Ironlatch-way. There's no chance of his having been by here? You haven't seen him tonight, have you, ma'am?"

There was a pause.

"No," said Mrs. Adis, "I haven't seen him. Not since Tuesday." She took her hand out of her pocket.

"Well, we'll be getting around and fetch Mrs. Gain. Reckon you'd be glad to have her."

Mrs. Adis nodded.

"Will you carry him in there first?" she said, and pointed to the bedroom door.

The men picked up the hurdle and carried it into the next room; then silently each wrung the mother by the hand and went away.

She waited until they had shut the door; then she came toward the lean-to. Crouch once more fell a-shivering. He couldn't bear it. No, he'd rather swing than face Mrs. Adis. He heard the key turn in the lock and he nearly screamed.

But she did not come in. She merely unlocked the door, then crossed the kitchen with a heavy, dragging footstep, and shut herself into the room where Tom was.

Peter Crouch knew what he must do, the only thing she wanted him to do, the only thing he could possibly do: he opened the door and silently went out.

# A Possible Triad on Black Notes

## MARITA BONNER

The black migration north after World War I completed the transformation of America's already racially and ethnically diverse cities into struggling hybrid worlds. By the 1930s, Chicago had become the city most emblematic of this complexity. In her collection of short stories *Frye Street and Environs*, Marita Bonner created an imaginary Chicago neighborhood, Frye Street, where the full range of social and class conflict unfolds with compassion and a nuanced appreciation for cultural difference. "A Possible Triad on Black Notes," first published in a 1933 issue of *Opportunity*, shows Bonner's mastery of the comedy and sorrow of everyday life in her imaginary corner of the world. Each vignette addresses a serious social question with bittersweet irony and measured stylistic understatement. Like the book from which it comes, "A Possible Triad" is also notable for rendering African American relationships to other ethnic communities as a dynamic but complex microcosm of America's entangled immigrant history.

## Foreword

NOW, WALKING ALONG *Frye Street, you sniff first the rusty tangy odor that comes from a river too near a city; walk aside so that Jewish babies will not trip you up; you pause to flatten your nose against discreet windows of Chinese merchants; marvel at the beauty and tragic old age in the faces of the young Italian women; puzzle whether the muscular blond people are Swedes or Danes or both; pronounce odd consonant names in Greek characters on shops; wonder whether Russians are Jews, or Jews, Russians—and finally you will wonder how the Negroes there manage to look like all men of every other race and then have something left over for their own distinctive black-browns.*

*There is only one Frye Street. It runs from the river to Grand Avenue where the El is.*

*All the World is there.*

*It runs from the safe solidity of honorable marriage to all of the amazing varieties of harlotry—from replicas of Old World living to the obscenities of latter decadence—from Heaven to Hell.*

*All the World is there.*

## There Were Three

There were three of them.

There was Lucille, there was Little Lou, there was Robbie.

Lucille was the mother of Little Lou and Robbie. She was fat, but most certainly shapely and she was a violet-eyed dazzling blonde. But something in the curve of her bosom, in the swell of her hips, in the red fullness of her lips, made you know that underneath this creamy flesh and golden waviness, there lay a black man—a black woman.

Little Lou and Robbie had a touch of their mother's blondness matched with an ivory tinted flesh in the girl and shaded to a bronze brownness in the boy.

Lots of the women of Frye Street, the colored women— the white women—looked at Robbie's lithe slenderness, small features, and black eyes, with a measuring, waiting, stalking look. Robbie was but sixteen.

"Ku Kaing told me I was the prettiest girl on Frye Street!" Little Lou told Lucille once with the bubbling vanity of flattered fourteen. "And Mr. Davy, that funny Scotchman who keeps the grocery store, said I could be his cashier when I grow up! And Sam Taylor—"

"Don't tell me nothing that feather-bed said!" Lucille had screamed. Then she shot out at Robbie, "Why the hell can't you keep care of your sister when I am out working all night?"

Things were like that at number 12 Frye Street where they lived. There were silk sheets on the beds, there was silk underwear in abundance in the bureau drawers, there were toilet waters, perfumes, and flashy clothes. But sometimes there was no dinner or no breakfast. And unless Robbie or Little Lou took up the broom, the house was always unswept. Moreover, you continually ran the possibility of sitting down on anybody's hat.

A father?

Nobody gave a thought to such a person.

"You're all mine, the both of you!" Lucille had told them once, and neither one of them had ever pushed in behind this for more.

Every night at six thirty Lucille made Little Lou run the bathtub full of warm water.

"Put in half a cup of bath-salts, baby!" Lucille would call from her bedroom while she was undressing.

Little Lou would search out a bottle of heliotrope, jasmine, or rose-verbena and drop the crystals daintily in. She would lean way over the steamy tub and sniff with a hungriness at the warm scent as it swept up.

After she had splashed, powdered, and partly dressed. Lucille always called the other two into her room to talk. They knew at the call that their mother had put on her dress and was doing her nails and finishing her face.

"You all keep in the house and off the streets while I'm at work, you hear?" she usually began.

"Yes, Mama," they never failed to reply readily.

But Robbie stayed out on the corner of Grand Avenue up by the Toot Sweet Music Shop with as much of his gang as was not working, until eleven o'clock.

Little Lou went on visits up and down Frye Street, with this girl—with that. But they never left the house until Lucille had finally cocked her hat, settled her complexion to a suitable finality, and silked out to her taxi—to go to work.

"What kind of woman got to go to work dressed better than Sheba when she visited King Solomon and ridin' in a taxi?" Mrs. Lillie Brown, who lived at number 14, often asked her husband.

The question was purely rhetorical. The women like Mrs. Brown who waddled wearily beneath a burden of too much of what was not needed in Life—and did not know how to escape it—had already settled the answer among them. To them, Lucille was that flamboyant symbol of uncleanness that always sets the psalm-singers of all earth into rhapsodies.

But Lucille taxied out of Frye Street every night and remained within doors and in bed of a day, so that neither the full chorus nor the free-tones and embellishments of the rhapsodies ever reached her.

It was one of these evenings in April when even a city river tries to smell of spring. The three were shut up in Lucille's room.

"—And you two stay in the house!" Lucille had finished as usual, but she was looking at her buffer when she spoke.

Little Lou and Robbie stared at each other.

"I wish I could go uptown and hop bells with Sammy Jackson at the Sumner!" Robbie remarked after a while.

"You stay down here and stay out of hotels!" Lucille blazed. She hurled the buffer back on her dressing table. "I don't want you 'round no hotel! White women are the devil! Ruin you!"

"They haven't ruined Sammy!" protested Robbie.

"No! The colored women done that for him, 'fore he left Frye Street," retorted his mother.

"Sammy doesn't chase after girls, Ma! He always hangs with the gang up to the music store."

"Stay in here and let Sammy alone!" his mother fired. "You hear me?"

"Yes!" Robbie lowered his eyes as he answered.

Before either one of them could speak again, Lucille's taxi tooted, and with a kiss for Little Lou, the mother went to her work.

Little Lou leaned on the bureau gazing absently in the mirror, listening to the diminishing chugs of the taxi.

"You going?" She turned to Robbie with the question when the last sound had been lost in the roar of the El.

"You bet!" answered her brother. He swung his leg down

from the trunk where he had been sitting. "I got Sammy to ast the man if I could work in a guy's place tonight, and believe me I'm going. Gct swell tips!"

"Bring me some strawberry ice-cream!" Little Lou begged.

"Sure! I am gonna make two dollars tips!" Robbie expanded.

"We can go to the show!"

"You mean I can!"

"I'll tell if you don't give me some money!"

"Go ahead!"

Robbie swaggered off and out of the house with that, but both of them knew that Little Lou would get a part of the money.

It was a happy Robbie that perched in the midst of the bell-hops at the Sumner two hours later. By that time he had carried two bags, made fifty cents, cursed a little with the boys, and already promised the captain that he would gamble below stairs with the bunch when the night was finally over. Robbie felt as smart as his cerise uniform.

"You kin make the next run upstairs, kid!" the captain had offered in a glow of approval.

This new kid was promising. Gave signs of being a good fellow.

Robbie kept an eager eye on the little black register above their seat. When number 740 showed a sudden white eye, Robbie was on his feet before the little plunger had been pushed up to make the board black again.

"Two Silver Sprays for 740!" ordered the captain from his 'phone.

Robbie nodded and flew out into the kitchen to get the tray and the bottles.

"Where you going, boy!" the elevator man queried as he closed the doors behind Robbie.

"740!"

"Aw, that's a regular souser, that dame! She always gets her sweeties to start the evening by letting her swim in liquor! That's about the sixth bottle of Silver Spray I see go up there tonight!"

"Hot night!" observed Robbie as he stepped off.

"For some folks!" the other called after him, and shot the car down again.

In his little flurry of excitement, Robbie found himself following the numbers of the rooms in the wrong direction at first. He reversed his march and stopped to catch his breath before he knocked at 740.

"Come in!" called a woman's voice.

Steadying the tray against the door, Robbie slid into the room.

"Over here by the bed!" the woman spoke again.

Robbie closed the door with his foot and kept his eyes on his bottles as he headed in the general direction of the voice.

He had almost reached the table when the bed came within his range of vision. It sort of swam up between the bottles he was watching so closely.

A pair of plump bare legs protruded between a pink comforter and the sheet. A broad creamy thigh showed through a black satin negligee. Robbie halted.

The door which led into the bath flung open quickly.

"How much, boy?" demanded the man who stepped forth.

Robbie sat down his tray. "A dollar and a half, sir," he replied turning around.

"Wait'll I get my trousers!" the man ordered, and walked across the room.

Robbie saw that he must have just bathed for he wore only a silk bathrobe. Even his slippers were lacking.

Robbie stole another look toward the bed.

The woman there had been lying on her side with her back toward the boy, but now she began to stir and finally turned over on her back, drawing the comforter up well all around her.

Her movements among the covers drew the boy's eyes once more.

A pair of violet eyes peering sleepily through tangled blond hair, met his.

Perspiration prickled out all over Robbie.

"Mama!" he whispered hoarsely. "Mama."

"Oh! Jesus!" cried the woman in the bed loudly.

"Mama? Mama!" Robbie began shouting. He tore at the bed clothes. "Mama!!!"

There was a rush of feet across the room.

"Here! what the hell do you mean, you little nigger!" shouted the man as he ran.

Now Robbie was by the window.

It was April.

Even a city river opens up to spring.

The window tried to draw spring in, opened as it was, seven stories above the city pavement.

The man rushed up behind Robbie.

The man struck Robbie to knock him down.

The window was open.

. . . A woman on the third floor said that the boy was screaming for his mother as his body hurtled through the air.

But it was an accident.

It was an accident that could not possibly find its way into the daily papers.

There was a note, though, that a bell boy had lost his balance and fallen to his death while opening a window in the Sumner. There was further note that no parents had yet come to claim the body.

That was all to that.

But—there were three.

Now, up at McNeil Institute where those people stay whose wealthy connections can prevent them from being assigned to an ordinary asylum, there is a stout blond woman patient with violet eyes.

Sometimes she screams: "Take your yellow hands off! Off! Off!"

Again she cries: "Don't smother me—don't smother me —black feather bed!"

Or even: "Take your dirty white hands off! Off! Off!"

Nobody knows what she means.
It's a color fixation, some people say.
But—there were three you see.
Sometimes I wonder which door opened for that third.

# Of Jimmy Harris

Jimmy Harris was dying.

"Can't believe it!" said the "boys."

. . . Every night the "boys" gathered in the Valet de Luxe tailor shop. A day was not completed properly unless the colored men of Frye Street—those who were through with the flesh-pots uptown and just as through with wives with whom they had lived some several years—did not gather in Jimmy's shop from eight until ten. They call themselves the "boys," but every single one of them was well beyond thirty-five. Indeed, Pop Gentry, the one who told the nastiest jokes, strutted the most vibrant impromptu dances, drank the most, cursed the loudest, was sixty.

Rain, sleet, wind, family wars, could not keep one of the "boys" away from the De Luxe.

Of a night—except Sundays—every chair and piece of chair, every box, and even the cutting tables were filled with colored men of all sizes and varieties. Some of those temporarily devoid of funds stood around half-dressed and pressed their own trousers while they guffawed and bantered.

Jimmy Harris had a seal-smooth skin coupled with the straight cast features and hair of a natural smooth waviness that constitutes "a good-looking brown." The clothes which he made for himself sat on his medium-sized figure neatly. He was usually amiable, knew how to listen when the gang wanted to do the talking, had a reputation for good living and money, and minded his business.

Everybody liked Jimmy.

He always sat cross-legged on one of the big black tables, stitching—stitching—stitching—while the others talked.

"Nigger! don't you never lay off workin'?" Pop Gentry

asked this more than once. "Them pantsies an coatsies'll all be 'round here waiting for somebody to wear, and yo'll be wid de worms an daisies, boy! How 'm I talkin'!" He would end in a shout of laughter and slap Jimmy on the back or any handy portion of his anatomy before he sat down.

Usually Jimmy would smile and murmur, "That's right," before he lapsed into silence and went on stitching—stitching—stitching.

It was Pop Gentry who had carried Jimmy's head and shoulders when he pitched head first off of his table one night and laid quiet on the floor in their midst.

"My God! the boy got a stroke!" somebody had chattered after the first dazed moment of speechless surprise.

"It's his liquor maybe!" someone else had suggested.

"Jimmy can carry his 'thout laying on the floor and pavements!"

"Git a doctor!" Pop had shouted.

"Cerebral hemorrhage! Put him in bed at once!" the doctor had ordered.

"No hope, I am afraid!" he added.

. . . "Can't believe it," sobbed his mother, adjusting an ice bag over Jimmy's temples. "I can't believe God's goin' take my boy home yet! He's not but thirty-eight!"

She wiped her eyes on a huck towel which she had in her hand. Then she walked to the window. Seemed as if there could be a little less light in the room.

Would it be all right to lower the lace-edged window shades a few fractions of an inch?

That Louise—Jimmy's wife—was such a durn fool about her house.

"Don't break my John Haviland china! Use the jelly glasses to drink out of! You'll chip my hand-etched goblet! Don't take an ice pick to get the ice cubes out of the Frigidaire! If you slam that oven door, you'll upset my thermostat!" She made Jimmy's mother sweat blood for every hour spent visiting at his house.

"Marm Harris" would have preferred to remain in Luray, Virginia, in her own modest five rooms where a body could feel at home and eat with elbows on the table dressed only in a cotton kimono if the urge seized her.

But she never felt easy about Jimmy.

She never felt easy about Jimmy up in the big city on Frye Street with a tailor shop and a blond wife who said she was colored—and Mary Linn, staying single all the fifteen years that had elapsed since Jimmy forgot her for Louise.

And though she hated Frye Street, hated Louise, hated the smoothness of Jimmy's home, Marm would bundle up herself every year and go north to Jimmy's.

One night in the dark solitude of their bed-chamber, Louise had tried a plaintive air of long-suffering affliction.

"Does your mother have to visit you this year again?" she had asked.

"My mother can come anytime she wants and stay as long as she wants! The other bedroom is for her!"

"Oh, oh! I did not know that!" Louise had retorted stiffly. "I thought that was the spare chamber!"

"Spare hell! It's Ma's!"

Louise had been surprised into silence at the violence of Jimmy's retort. She usually swung the reins of their life together skillfully in one hand. Jimmy had never balked before.

It would not do to carry things to open battle. Sniping is more annoying than straight line firing.

The old lady would find her visit "spare hell."

But Marm came and came again and came when Jimmy was sick and Louise had wired that she herself was unable to take care of him.

"I can't believe Jimmy is dying!" Louise cried to Dr. Whetbone. She sat well in the center of the green satin love-seat which made some visitors unwelcome to her parlor.

"Well, dear lady, I am very sorry but I can offer no hope!" Dr. Whetbone repeated.

"Gosh! A lanky bronze colored man with deep-set gray eyes is a heartache, believe me!" thought Louise, watching the doctor.

Whetbone leaned easily against the mantel.

He was one of those tall men who never sat down unless it was absolutely necessary. Some people said that he stood up so you could see how well his suit fitted him across the shoulders, how well his shoes fitted his feet, how well he himself fitted into any surroundings under any circumstances—in short, what a patrician he was.

That was what some people said.

People say a lot of things about a reasonably decent-looking man who can earn a comfortable living and is still single at thirty-four.

Louise widened her eyes until water flowed into them. "What'll I do?" She lifted her voice and her eyes piteously to Dr. Whetbone.

"Now—now," countered the physician. "Just try to realize that you have done your best for him—kept your home beautifully for him!" He made a sweeping gesture of the room.

"Oh, yes," murmured Louise.

"You tried to make him take more rest and better care of himself!" continued Whetbone soothingly.

"Yes, I made him put in oil-heat so he would not have to shovel coal and buy a car so we could go out for nice rides in the evenings together, and buy an electric refrigerator so I could always keep milk and vegetables fresh for him!"

"Yes, yes!" finished the doctor. "Let's run upstairs and take a look at him."

And Jimmy, fastened inside of his body by a tongue that could no longer speak, saw Louise standing close beside the doctor at his bedside.

Saw her lift and lower her eyes as she talked to him.

Why were they smiling at each other?

He watched them.

The doctor left the room presently.

Louise went to the bureau and smiled into the mirror at herself, pinching first her arm, then her cheek, fluffing out her hair, smoothing down her black satin dress.

Then she went out of the room too.

She did not look toward the bed again.

* * *

"Oh, I can't believe it! Jimmy can't be dying!" a tall thin brown woman cried aloud.

She was walking up a country road in Luray.

"God, don't take him! Oh God!!" She stopped and knelt on a bank that was tangled with rose vines and dead leaves.

But she had stopped and cried and prayed on rose banks for fifteen years—and Jimmy had married Louise and stayed up north on Frye Street and waxed and prospered—though he had no children.

Presently she rose from the rose-vines and went walking on crying and praying.

But God must despise a sniveler.

She had cried and prayed for fifteen years.

Jimmy Harris was dying.


Pain thundered down across Jimmy Harris.

Back and forth it avalanched, dragging him down, sucking him deeply under.

Once he fought through, came up out of the thundering to find himself in his own bed—in his own room. The lavender electric clock on the bureau was flanked by the lavender and green figurines that supported Louise's boudoir lamps there. But everything looked new, distant.

"God!! I've been sick!! Sick!!" Jimmy told himself.

He sent his thoughts here, there, into himself to seek out the sick spot, the weak spot.

But before he had found it, pain tumbled back angrily, smotheringly, sucked him under, dragged him down, pulled—pulled—pulled—.

"I can't fight back! I can't get up over this pain mountain over me!" Jimmy cried within.

He began to sink straightway.

That is what they call being reconciled to die. They call it reconciled when pain has strummed a symphony of suffering back and forth across you, up and down, round and round you until each little fiber is worn tissue-thin with aching. And when you are lying beaten and buffeted, battered and broken—pain goes out, joins hands with Death, and comes back to dance, dance, dance, stamp, stamp, stamp down on you until you give up.

"I can't believe it!" Jimmy cried to himself—and all of the time the Two were dancing, dancing, stamping, stamping.

"I can't believe it! I'll get up! Go out! Go to work! Finish! Finish! Stitch! Stitch!"

—What was that uprooting like a tree in a windstorm?

—What was that bright glowing in his eyes?

—What was that loosing—tearing loose—uprooting—shedding—?

"He's gone!" exclaimed Dr. Whetbone, walking to the bed.

"Gone!" sobbed Marm, kneeling beside the bed.

Louise sat on the steps outside of the room. She had not been able to stay in the room while Jimmy Harris had been breathing, breathing, breathing so that it sounded as if the room were filled with many tubs of water draining off with that gurgling of water settling to waste.

Jimmy Harris was dead.

I guess he'd been happy, though.

He had had his hands on what he wanted.

## Corner Store*

"Some more lachs, Anton? A little matzos and wine? A pickled tomato?" A quiver of appeal, entirely too searing for so simple a thing as an invitation to dally with more food, ran through Esther Steinberg's voice.

Anton Steinberg shook his head vigorously in denial. His hands and mouth were full of lebkuchen. He shook his head because he did not wish more food, nor did he wish to recognize the seeking in Esther's tone. He lowered his eyes so that he would not have to see his wife.

* As originally published, this part of "A Possible Triad on Black Notes" carried the following heading above the title "Corner Store": "Three Tales of Living/*From 'The Black Map'/(A book entirely unwritten)."

Her flabby body, slouched in faded gray house dress and muffled in ragged black sweater, was as dismal as the pallor of her flaccid face. Esther's only beauty had been a head of black hair that seemed to spring in aliveness in each curl.

Working from dawn until midnight for seven years behind the counter of Steinberg's Grocery-Market on Frye Street had made an old woman of Esther at thirty-nine.

Anton crammed crumbs of gingerbread hastily into his mouth, wiped his hands on the apron which he never removed for the noon lunch served in this kitchen in back of their store, and rushed out as the bell tinkled in the shop.

As soon as she was alone, Esther drew a sibilant sobbing sigh and covered her face with both hands.

"Teach me what I should do, Gott!" she prayed in a hoarse whisper.

"Say something, Ma?" called a girl's voice suddenly from a room within.

Esther snatched down her hands and crouched lower in her chair. She said nothing.

A sound of yawning came now from within, then all at once, pushing aside the gunny-sacking which served as a drapery between the two rooms, Meta, daughter of Esther and Anton, stood in the door. She rubbed her eyes and stretched with the elastic abandon of seventeen years.

"Who are you talking to, Ma?" she queried again.

Esther shook her head. "Nobody. I—I was—I was wishing I was back in the old country. In the ghetto," she finished timidly with a swift look at her daughter's face.

Meta made a rapid gesture, shrugged her shoulders and, shaking her black hair out around her, began combing it with quick strokes.

"Oh, for God's sake, Ma! What do you want to be back in that old mud hole for with nothing but Jews, Jews, before you, behind you and beside you? You ought to be glad to get to a free country, for heaven's sake!"

Esther looked first at Meta's high-heeled patent-leather pumps, then at her gun-metal chiffon stockings drawn over nicely turned legs. Her red flannel dress caught her snugly across the bosom and at the hips, but its vivid color brought out the blackness of her curly bob, the rich red of her lips, and the soft molding of her delicate oval face. Jewish girls in the Old World did not dress this way.

"You ashamed to be a Jew?" Esther demanded harshly.

"No, Ma! But for pete's sake, I should think you'd be glad Papa is making good money and spending it here like you never could back there!"

"I want to be near a nice *Schule* and have nice Jewish neighbors!" persisted the mother with a sort of stubborn sullenness.

"Then you don't want the new auto and the fur coat and the flats that we own on the West Side?"

Esther made an exclamation like a cat when it spits. "Tcha! We got just as good in the old country—!"

"Like fun! Don't you think I remember those old cold stone houses with no heat and nothing else in them! Why do you want to go back to a place where dirty German kids wait around to throw mud on you when you go out? No! Give me Frye Street!"

Meta dropped down to the table and helped herself to some of the smoked salmon.

Her mother drew back into her corner—drew back into herself.

Anton's heavy step sounded in the little hall outside the kitchen. He scowled as soon as he saw his daughter.

"You up, you Meta! What for do you sleep all the day when I want that you should help me with the Saturday rush?"

Meta wiped her fingers on a piece of wax paper and licked one daintily. "Don't you think I go to sleep, maybe?"

"Why don't you sleep nights instead of racing the streets? That's what I want to know!"

An angry flush swept the girl's face. "Yah!" she mocked. "Why don't I go to the *Schule* at night—Monday—Tuesday—Thursday again like you! You!! At the *Schule*—"

Her pertness trailed off into a frightened silence. The vein in Anton's left temple was standing out like a rope. His face was swollen a dark purple.

*"Du—du—!"* he choked and lifted his hand.

"Anton! Anton!" shrilled Ester. *"Strafe nicht!"*

Meta stared back at her father. But she did not flinch.

The bell on the door of the shop jangled.

No one moved.

"One comes to buy!" Esther urged in Jewish.

"A customer comes, Anton!" she repeated as he did not move.

Her husband hung an instant on the threshold, then with a snort that was almost a snarl, he went back up the passage to the store.

*"Gott! Was für ein' Mann!"* Esther chattered in an agony of fear. "Ever since we got to this place, he becomes more cold to me! Now he wants to hit you, Liebschen!"

"If he hits me, I'll run off to get married, right away," Meta burst forth passionately.

*"Ja!* David Sorbenstein is one nice boy. Me and Papa chose him for you ourselves! Goes to the *Schule* every week and stays *bei* the shop of his *Vater*." Esther garbled Jewish and such English as she knew. *"Ach, solche ein' Knabe!"*

"David Sorbenstein is a fat greasy slob! A dumbbell! He makes me sick! I wouldn't marry that guy!"

"Meta! He'd make such a goot husband! Such an industry—"

But Meta shook her shoulders impatiently and switched David's virtues to scorn as fast as Esther could tell them off.

"I'd run off to marry Abe Brown!" Meta declared.

"A goy—a Gentile?" Esther could not believe herself.

Meta nodded. "He isn't all goy. His grandfather is a Jew, and his mother is colored. *Schwartze!"*

*"Ein' Schwartze! Du mein' lieber Gott!"* Esther laid her face on her arm and wept aloud and loudly.

Anton came running back again. *"Was ist geschied'?* Na! Na, Esther," he cried as he came.

He rubbed his hands soothingly across his wife's hair.

*"Du!"* He glowered at Meta across Esther's bowed head.

*"Ein' Schwartze!* Meta!" screamed Esther.

Anton's eyes hung in Meta's. *"Du?"* The word was a gasp.

His face whitened. Meta shook her head. "Only Abe," she whispered.

Something desperate oozed out of Anton's face. Vast relief grew there.

"Na na! Esther!" he began again. *"Nichts! Nichts! Es gibt nichts! Du musst dass nicht!* Meta don't mean nothing! She wouldn't marry no Gentile. She wouldn't marry no *Schwartze!*"

The bell on the shop rang loudly.

"I'll go!" Anton announced briskly, and he was out and back by the time Esther's wails had subsided to an incessant hiccoughing.

"Now, Mama! Now, Mama! Our little girl will make *bei* Yom Kippur *mit* Sorbenstein's boy a nice marriage!"

"I won't!" Meta shouted.

"Aah—aah!" began Esther in a rising tone of lamentation.

The shop bell rang.

"You go, Mama! Wait on the custom! Papa will talk to Meta!" Anton ordered.

Esther moved on heavy feet forward to the store. Early twilight was falling thickly over everything. Esther turned back to fumble for the switch box.

"Anton! Anton?" called a woman's voice softly from somewhere near the door.

Esther's hand froze uplifted as it reached the switch. Who was this woman who dared to stand in her store calling Anton by his name with that soft, urgent, intimate lift of the voice?

Esther shot on all of the lights and stepped out on to the floor.

Standing by the butcher block was a woman. Her limbs curved heavily beneath a pink cotton house dress, her black hair shone in a series of braids coiled high around a lovely head. On first glance, she was Semitic. It was not until Esther was upon her that she saw that she was a colored woman.

"You want something?" demanded Esther brusquely.

"No—" the other replied hesitatingly.

Heavy steps padded from the rear. "I'll attend the custom, Mama!" Anton nearly shouted as he bounded forward.

"Mama—Mama!" he gabbled. "Meta wants that you should come there. She will tell you something."

*"Noch der Schwartze?* (Is it still to be the black man)," his wife queried.

*"Möglich!* We must be patient, though after a little— *verleicht*—David Sorbenstein! We'll see! *Nun!"*

Esther sped along the hall to the kitchen, but Meta was back in the inner room talking on the telephone.

—"So listen, Abe darling,—I just told him that you were Ella's nephew and that you knew already about his going to the *Schule*—ha! ha!—every night. And he says to me, 'Well, maybe then I'll talk to Mama and tell her to wait a little, but don't you do nothing about marrying, yet awhile!'— What? Sure! He's crazy about her! She's out there now! Ella's out in the store talking to him now—What? Sure! Makes a swell whip to hold over Papa!"

Standing in the kitchen, Esther stared slowly around her, listening. As the words bore into her, she began to stare wildly, shaking her head from side to side—side to side.

This wasn't Meta talking!

That was not Anton outside!

This room was not home. Only stone houses in ghettoes are homes.

The narrow kitchen with its barren huddled air was closing her in.

—"She's out there now! Yah! Ella!!"—

—"Anton?" a woman's voice had called softly with a caress in it that searched like a gentle hand seeking to find something loved in a dark place. . . .

Esther tore back up the hall toward the store.

Anton stood beside his block, a cleaver trailing idly from one hand talking, talking, looking down into the woman's face.

There they stood.

Close together.

Her head tilted back, her eyes veiling, then lifting.

Esther rushed back, and standing in the hall between the shop and the kitchen—she lifted up her voice and screamed and screamed.

She caught hold of the sacking. It tore down from its place between the doors. She fell as it ripped and lay prone on the floor, the sack cloth around her and screamed and screamed.

"Like a wild thing in a forest, you holler!" Anton came running to swear at her.

"Like one who moans for Israel!" replied Esther—and lay and sobbed in her sack cloth.

# The Gilded Six-Bits

## ZORA NEALE HURSTON

"All that is gilded is not gold" could well be the moral of this parable of marriage and fidelity. Hurston's 1933 story, first published in *Story, no. 3,* is typical of her pointed, sympathetic portraits of black love. It characteristically introduces everyday temptation and the lure of a better life as potential bumps in the road toward domestic happiness. Hurston's dialect voice is stronger here than in "Drenched in Light," and her writing style more confident. Four years after publication of this story, her breakthrough novel *Their Eyes Were Watching God* would synthesize all of her developing talents and officially launch her career as a major American fiction writer.

IT WAS A NEGRO YARD around a Negro house in a Negro settlement that looked to the payroll of the G. and G. Fertilizer Works for its support.

But there was something happy about the place. The front yard was parted in the middle by a sidewalk from gate to doorstep, a sidewalk edged on either side by quart bottles driven neck down into the ground on a slant. A mess of homey flowers planted without a plan but blooming cheerily from their helter-skelter places. The fence and the house were whitewashed. The porch and steps scrubbed white.

The front door stood open to the sunshine so that the floor of the front room could finish drying after its weekly scouring. It was Saturday. Everything clean from the front gate to the privy house. Yard raked so that the strokes of the rake would make a pattern. Fresh newspaper cut in fancy edge on the kitchen shelves.

Missie May was bathing herself in the galvanized wash-tub in the bedroom. Her dark-brown skin glistened under the soapsuds that skittered down from her washrag. Her stiff young breasts thrust forward aggressively like broad-based cones with the tips lacquered in black.

She heard men's voices in the distance and glanced at the dollar clock on the dresser.

"Humph! Ah'm way behind time t'day! Joe gointer be heah 'fore Ah git mah clothes on if Ah don't make haste."

She grabbed the clean meal sack at hand and dried herself hurriedly and began to dress. But before she could tie her slippers, there came the ring of singing metal on wood. Nine times.

Missie May grinned with delight. She had not seen the big, tall man come stealing in the gate and creep up the walk, grinning happily at the joyful mischief he was about to commit. But she knew that it was her husband throwing silver dollars in the door for her to pick up and pile beside her plate at dinner. It was this way every Saturday afternoon. The nine dollars hurled into the open door, he scurried to a hiding place behind the cape jasmine bush and waited.

Missie May promptly appeared at the door in mock alarm.

"Who dat chunkin' money in mah do'way?" she demanded. No answer from the yard. She leaped off the porch and began to search the shrubbery. She peeped under the porch and hung over the gate to look up and down the road. While she did this, the man behind the jasmine darted to the chinaberry tree. She spied him and gave chase.

"Nobody ain't gointer be chunkin' money at me and Ah not do 'em nothin'," she shouted in mock anger. He ran around the house with Missie May at his heels. She overtook him at the kitchen door. He ran inside but could not close it after him before she crowded in and locked with him in a rough and tumble. For several minutes the two were a furious mass of male and female energy. Shouting, laughing, twisting, turning, tussling, tickling each other in the ribs; Missie May clutching onto Joe and Joe trying, but not too hard, to get away.

"Missie May, take yo' hand out mah pocket!" Joe shouted out between laughs.

"Ah ain't, Joe, not lessen you gwine gimme whateve' it is good you got in yo' pocket. Turn it go, Joe, do Ah'll tear yo' clothes."

"Go on tear 'em. You de one dat pushes de needles round heah. Move yo' hand, Missie May."

"Lemme git dat paper sack out yo' pocket. Ah bet it's candy kisses."

"Tain't. Move yo' hand. Woman ain't got no business in a man's clothes nohow. Go way."

Missie May gouged way down and gave an upward jerk and triumphed.

"Unhhunh! Ah got it. It 'tis so candy kisses. Ah knowed you had somethin' for me in yo' clothes. Now Ah got to see whut's in every pocket you got."

Joe smiled indulgently and let his wife go through all of his pockets and take out the things that he had hidden there for her to find. She bore off the chewing gum, the cake of sweet soap, the pocket handkerchief as if she had wrested them from him, as if they had not been bought for the sake of this friendly battle.

"Whew! Dat play-fight done got me all warmed up," Joe exclaimed. "Got me some water in de kittle?"

"Yo' water is on de fire and yo' clean things is cross de bed. Hurry up and wash yo'self and git changed so we kin eat. Ah'm hongry." As Missie said this, she bore the steaming kettle into the bedroom.

"You ain't hongry, sugar," Joe contradicted her. "Youse jes' a little empty. Ah'm de one whut's hongry. Ah could eat up camp meetin', back off 'ssociation, and drink Jurdan dry. Have it on de table when Ah git out de tub."

"Don't you mess wid mah business, man. You git in yo' clothes. Ah'm a real wife, not no dress and breath. Ah might not look lak one, but if you burn me, you won't git a thing but wife ashes."

Joe splashed in the bedroom, and Missie May fanned around in the kitchen. A fresh red and white checked cloth on the table. Big pitcher of buttermilk beaded with pale drops of butter from the churn. Hot fried mullet, crackling bread, ham hocks atop a mound of string beans and new potatoes, and perched on the windowsill, a pone of spicy potato pudding.

Very little talk during the meal, but that little consisted of banter that pretended to deny affection but in reality flaunted it. Like when Missie May reached for a second helping of the tater pone. Joe snatched it out of her reach.

After Missie May had made two or three unsuccessful grabs at the pan, she begged, "Aw, Joe, gimme some mo' dat tater pone."

"Nope, sweetenin' is for us men-folks. Y'all pritty lil frail eels don't need nothin' lak dis. You too sweet already."

"Please, Joe."

"Naw, naw. Ah don't want you to git no sweeter than whut you is already. We goin' down de road a lil piece t'night, so you go put on yo' Sunday-go-to-meetin' things."

Missie May looked at her husband to see if he was playing some prank. "Sho nuff, Joe?"

"Yeah. We goin' to de ice-cream parlor."

"Where de ice-cream parlor at, Joe?"

"A new man done come heah from Chicago and he done got a place and took and opened it up for a ice-cream parlor, and bein' as it's real swell, Ah wants you to be one de first ladies to walk in dere and have some set down."

"Do Jesus. Ah ain't knowed nothin' 'bout it. Who de man done it?"

"Mister Otis D. Slemmons, of spots and places—Memphis, Chicago, Jacksonville, Philadelphia, and so on."

"Dat heavy-set man wid his mouth full of gold teethes?"

"Yeah. Where did you see 'im at?"

"Ah went down to de sto' tuh git a box of lye, and Ah seen 'im standin' on de corner talkin' to some of de mens, and Ah come on back and went to scrubbin' de floor, and he passed and tipped his hat whilst Ah was scourin' de steps. Ah thought Ah never seen *him* befo'."

Joe smiled pleasantly. "Yeah, he's up to date. He got de finest clothes Ah ever seen on a colored man's back."

"Aw, he don't look no better in his clothes than you do in yourn. He got a puzzlegut on 'im, and he so chuckle-headed, he got a pone behind his neck."

Joe looked down at his own abdomen and said wistfully: "Wisht Ah had a build on me lak he got. He ain't puzzlegutted, honey. He jes' got a corperation. Dat make 'm look lak a rich white man. All rich mens is got some belly on 'em."

"Ah seen de pitchers of Henry Ford and he's a spare-built man, and Rockefeller look lak he ain't got but one gut. But Ford and Rockefeller and dis Slemmons and all de rest kin be as many-gutted as dey please, Ah's satisfied wid you jes' lak you is, baby. God took pattern after a pine tree and built you noble. Youse a pritty man, and if Ah knowed any way to make you mo' pritty still, Ah'd take and do it."

Joe reached over gently and toyed with Missie May's ear. "You jes' say dat cause you love me, but Ah know Ah can't hold no light to Otis D. Slemmons. Ah ain't never been nowhere, and Ah ain't got nothin' but you."

Missie May got on his lap and kissed him and he kissed back in kind. Then he went on. "All de womens is crazy 'bout 'im everywhere he go."

"How you know dat, Joe?"

"He told us so hisself."

"Dat don't make it so. His mouf is cut crossways, ain't it? Well, he kin lie jes' lak anybody else."

"Good Lawd, Missie! You womens sho is hard to sense into things. He's got a five-dollar gold piece for a stickpin, and he got a ten-dollar gold piece on his watch chain, and his mouf is jes' crammed full of gold teethes. Sho wisht it wuz mine. And whut make it so cool, he got money 'cumulated. And womens give it all to 'im."

"Ah don't see whut de womens see on 'im. Ah wouldn't give 'im a wink if de sheriff wuz after 'im."

"Well, he told us how de white womens in Chicago give

'im all dat gold money. So he don't 'low nobody to touch it at all. Not even put dey finger on it. Dey tole 'im not to. You kin make 'miration at it, but don't tetch it."

"Whyn't he stay up dere where dey so crazy 'bout 'im?"

"Ah reckon dey done made 'im vast-rich, and he wants to travel some. He says dey wouldn't leave 'im hit a lick of work. He got mo' lady people crazy 'bout him than he kin shake a stick at."

"Joe, Ah hates to see you so dumb. Dat stray nigger jes' tell y'all anything and y'all b'lieve it."

"Go 'head on now, honey, and put on yo' clothes. He talkin' 'bout his pritty womens—Ah want 'im to see *mine*."

Missie May went off to dress, and Joe spent the time trying to make his stomach punch out like Slemmons's middle. He tried the rolling swagger of the stranger, but found that his tall bone-and-muscle stride fitted ill with it. He just had time to drop back into his seat before Missie May came in, dressed to go.

On the way home that night Joe was exultant. "Didn't Ah say ole Otis was swell? Cain't he talk Chicago talk? Wuzn't dat funny whut he said when great big fat ole Ida Armstrong come in? He asted me, 'Who is dat broad wid de forte shake?' Dat's a new word. Us always thought forty was a set of figgers but he showed us where it means a whole heap of things. Sometimes he don't say forty, he jes' say thirty-eight and two, and dat mean de same thing. Know whut he tole me when Ah wuz payin' for our ice cream? He say, 'Ah have to hand it to you, Joe. Dat wife of yours is jes' thirty-eight and two. Yessuh, she's forte!' Ain't he killin'?"

"He'll do in case of a rush. But he sho is got uh heap uh gold on 'im. Dat's de first time Ah ever seed gold money. It lookted good on him sho nuff, but it'd look a whole heap better on you."

"Who, me? Missie May, youse crazy! Where would a po'man lak me git gold money from?"

Missie May was silent for a minute, then she said, "Us might find some goin' long de road sometime. Us could."

"Who would be losin' gold money round heah? We ain't

even seen none dese white folks wearin' no gold money on dey watch chain. You must be figgerin' Mister Packard or Mister Cadillac goin' pass through heah."

"You don't know whut been lost 'round heah. Maybe somebody way back in memorial times lost they gold money and went on off and it ain't never been found. And then if we wuz to find it, you could wear some 'thout havin' no gang of womens lak dat Slemmons say he got."

Joe laughed and hugged her. "Don't be so wishful 'bout me. Ah'm satisfied de way Ah is. So long as Ah be yo' husband, Ah don't keer 'bout nothin' else. Ah'd ruther all de other womens in de world to be dead than for you to have de toothache. Less we go to bed and git our night rest."

It was Saturday night once more before Joe could parade his wife in Slemmons's ice-cream parlor again. He worked the night shift, and Saturday was his only night off. Every other evening around six o'clock he left home, and dying dawn saw him hustling home around the lake, where the challenging sun flung a flaming sword from east to west across the trembling water.

That was the best part of life—going home to Missie May. Their whitewashed house, the mock battle on Saturday, the dinner and ice-cream parlor afterward, church on Sunday nights, when Missie outdressed any woman in town —all, everything, was right.

One night around eleven the acid ran out at the G. and G. The foreman knocked off the crew and let the steam die down. As Joe rounded the lake on his way home, a lean moon rode the lake in a silver boat. If anybody had asked Joe about the moon on the lake, he would have said he hadn't paid it any attention. But he saw it with his feelings. It made him yearn painfully for Missie. Creation obsessed him. He thought about children. They had been married more than a year now. They had money put away. They ought to be making little feet for shoes. A little boy-child would be about right.

He saw a dim light in the bedroom and decided to come in through the kitchen door. He could wash the fertilizer dust off himself before presenting himself to Missie May. It would be nice for her not to know that he was there until he slipped into his place in bed and hugged her back. She always liked that.

He eased the kitchen door open slowly and silently, but when he went to set his dinner bucket on the table, he bumped into a pile of dishes, and something crashed to the floor. He heard his wife gasp in fright and hurried to reassure her.

"Iss me, honey. Don't git skeered."

There was a quick, large movement in the bedroom. A rustle, a thud, and a stealthy silence. The light went out.

What? Robbers? Murderers? Some varmint attacking his helpless wife, perhaps. He struck a match, threw himself on guard, and stepped over the doorsill into the bedroom.

The great belt on the wheel of Time slipped and eternity stood still. By the match light he could see the man's legs fighting with his breeches in his frantic desire to get them on. He had both chance and time to kill the intruder in his helpless condition—half in and half out of his pants—but he was too weak to take action. The shapeless enemies of humanity that live in the hours of Time had waylaid Joe. He was assaulted in his weakness. Like Samson awakening after his haircut. So he just opened his mouth and laughed.

The match went out, and he struck another and lit the lamp. A howling wind raced across his heart, but underneath its fury he heard his wife sobbing and Slemmons pleading for his life. Offering to buy it with all that he had. "Please, suh, don't kill me. Sixty-two dollars at de sto'. Gold money."

Joe just stood. Slemmons looked at the window, but it was screened. Joe stood out like a rough-backed mountain between him and the door. Barring him from escape, from sunrise, from life.

He considered a surprise attack upon the big clown that stood there, laughing like a chessy cat. But before his fist could travel an inch, Joe's own rushed out to crush him like a battering ram. Then Joe stood over him.

"Git into yo' damn rags, Slemmons, and dat quick."

Slemmons scrambled to his feet and into his vest and coat. As he grabbed his hat, Joe in his fury overrode his intentions and grabbed at Slemmons with his left hand and struck at him with his right. The right landed. The left grazed the front of his vest. Slemmons was knocked a somersault into the kitchen and fled through the open door. Joe found himself alone with Missie May, with the golden watch charm clutched in his left fist. A short bit of broken chain dangled between his fingers.

Missie May was sobbing. Wails of weeping without words. Joe stood, and after a while he found out that he had something in his hand. And then he stood and felt without thinking and without seeing with his natural eyes. Missie May kept on crying and Joe kept on feeling so much; and not knowing what to do with all his feelings, he put Slemmons's watch charm in his pants pocket and took a good laugh and went to bed.

"Missie May, whut you cryin' for?"

"Cause Ah love you so hard and Ah know you don't love *me* no mo'."

Joe sank his face into the pillow for a spell, then he said huskily. "You don't know de feelings of dat yet, Missie May."

"Oh Joe, honey, he said he wuz gointer give me dat gold money, and he jes' kept on after me—"

Joe was very still and silent for a long time. Then he said, "Well, don't cry no mo', Missie May. Ah got yo' gold piece for you."

The hours went past on their rusty ankles. Joe still and quiet on one bed-rail and Missie May wrung dry of sobs on the other. Finally the sun's tide crept up on the shore of night and drowned all its hours. Missie May, with her face, stiff and streaked, towards the window saw the dawn come into her yard. It was day. Nothing more. Joe wouldn't be coming home as usual. No need to fling open the front door and sweep off the porch, making it nice for Joe. Never no more breakfasts to cook; no more washing and starching of Joe's jumper-jackets and pants. No more nothing. So why get up?

With this strange man in her bed, she felt embarrassed to get up and dress. She decided to wait till he had dressed and gone. Then she would get up, dress quickly, and be gone forever beyond reach of Joe's looks and laughs. But he never moved. Red light turned to yellow, then white.

From beyond the no-man's-land between them came a voice. A strange voice that yesterday had been Joe's.

"Missie May, ain't you gonna fix me no breakfus'?"

She sprang out of bed. "Yeah, Joe. Ah didn't reckon you wuz hongry."

No need to die today. Joe needed her for a few more minutes anyhow.

Soon there was a roaring fire in the cookstove. Water bucket full and two chickens killed. Joe loved fried chicken and rice. She didn't deserve a thing and good Joe was letting her cook him some breakfast. She rushed hot biscuits to the table as Joe took his seat.

He ate with his eyes in his plate. No laughter, no banter.

"Missie May, you ain't eatin' yo breakfus'."

"Ah don't choose none. Ah thank yuh."

His coffee cup was empty. She sprang to refill it. When she turned from the stove and bent to set the cup beside Joe's plate, she saw the yellow coin on the table between them.

She slumped into her seat and wept into her arms.

Presently Joe said calmly, "Missie May, you cry too much. Don't look back lak Lot's wife and turn to salt."

The sun, the hero of every day, the impersonal old man that beams as brightly on death as on birth, came up every morning and raced across the blue dome and dipped into the sea of fire every evening. Water ran down hill and birds nested.

Missie knew why she didn't leave Joe. She couldn't. She loved him too much, but she could not understand why Joe didn't leave her. He was polite, even kind at times, but aloof.

There were no more Saturday romps. No ringing silver dollars to stack beside her plate. No pockets to rifle. In fact, the yellow coin in his trousers was like a monster hiding in the cave of his pockets to destroy her.

She often wondered if he still had it, but nothing could have induced her to ask nor yet to explore his pockets to see for herself. Its shadow was in the house whether or no.

One night Joe came home around midnight and complained of pains in the back. He asked Missie to rub him down with liniment. It had been three months since Missie had touched his body and it all seemed strange. But she rubbed him. Grateful for the chance. Before morning, youth triumphed and Missie exulted. But the next day, as she joyfully made up their bed, beneath her pillow she found the piece of money with the bit of chain attached.

Alone to herself, she looked at the thing with loathing, but look she must. She took it into her hands with trembling and saw first thing that it was no gold piece. It was a gilded half dollar. Then she knew why Slemmons had forbidden anyone to touch his gold. He trusted village eyes at a distance not to recognize his stickpin as a gilded quarter and his watch charm as a four-bit piece.

She was glad at first that Joe had left it there. Perhaps he was through with her punishment. They were man and wife again. Then another thought came clawing at her. He had come home to buy from her as if she were any woman in the long house. Fifty cents for her love. As if to say that he could pay as well as Slemmons. She slid the coin into his Sunday pants pocket and dressed herself and left his house.

Halfway between her house and the quarters she met her husband's mother, and after a short talk she turned and went back home. Never would she admit defeat to that woman, who prayed for it nightly. If she had not the substance of marriage, she had the outside show. Joe must leave *her*. She let him see she didn't want his old gold four-bits too.

She saw no more of the coin for some time, though she knew that Joe could not help finding it in his pocket. But his health kept poor, and he came home at least every ten days to be rubbed.

The sun swept around the horizon, trailing its robes of

weeks and days. One morning as Joe came in from work, he found Missie May chopping wood. Without a word he took the ax and chopped a huge pile before he stopped.

"You ain't got no business choppin' wood, and you know it."

"How come? Ah been choppin' it for de last longest."

"Ah ain't blind. You makin' feet for shoes."

"Won't you be glad to have a li'l baby chile, Joe?"

"You know dat 'thout astin' me."

"Iss gointer be a boy chile and de very spit of you."

"You reckon, Missie May?"

"Who else could it look lak?"

Joe said nothing, but he thrust his hand deep into his pocket and fingered something there.

It was almost six months later Missie May took to bed, and Joe went and got his mother to come wait on the house.

Missie May was delivered of a fine boy. Her travail was over when Joe came in from work one morning. His mother and the old women were drinking great bowls of coffee around the fire in the kitchen.

The minute Joe came into the room, his mother called him aside.

"How did Missie May make out?" he asked quickly.

"Who, dat gal? She strong as a ox. She gointer have plenty mo'. We done fixed her wid de sugar and lard to sweeten her for de nex' one."

Joe stood silent awhile.

"You ain't ast 'bout de baby, Joe. You oughter be mighty proud cause he sho is de spittin' image of yuh, son. Dat's yourn all right, if you never git another one, dat un is yourn. And you know Ah'm mighty proud too, son, cause Ah never thought well of you marryin' Missie May cause her ma used tuh fan her foot round right smart, and Ah been mighty skeered dat Missie May wuz gointer git misput on her road."

Joe said nothing. He fooled around the house till late in the day, then, just before he went to work, he went and stood at the foot of the bed and asked his wife how she felt. He did this every day during the week.

On Saturday he went to Orlando to make his market. It had been a long time since he had done that.

Meat and lard, meal and flour, soap and starch. Cans of corn and tomatoes. All the staples. He fooled around town for a while and bought bananas and apples. Way after a while he went around to the candy store.

"Hello, Joe," the clerk greeted him. "Ain't seen you in a long time."

"Nope, Ah ain't been heah. Been round in spots and places."

"Want some of them molasses kisses you always buy?"

"Yessuh." He threw the gilded half dollar on the counter. "Will dat spend?"

"Whut is it, Joe? Well, I'll be doggone! A gold-plated four-bit piece. Where'd you git it, Joe?"

"Offen a stray nigger dat come through Eatonville. He had it on his watch chain for a charm—goin' round making out iss gold money. Ha ha! He had a quarter on his tie pin, and it wuz all golded up too. Tryin' to fool people. Makin' out he so rich and everything. Ha! Ha! Tryin' to tole off folkses wives from home."

"How did you git it, Joe? Did he fool you, too?"

"Who, me? Naw suh! He ain't fooled me none. Know whut Ah done? He come round me wid his smart talk. Ah hauled off and knocked 'im down and took his old four-bits way from 'im. Gointer buy my wife some good ole lasses kisses wid it. Gimme fifty cents worth of dem candy kisses."

"Fifty cents buys a mighty lot of candy kisses, Joe. Why don't you split it up and take some chocolate bars, too. They eat good, too."

"Yessuh, dey do, but Ah wants all dat in kisses. Ah got a li'l boy chile home now. Tain't a week old yet, but he kin suck a sugar tit and maybe eat one them kisses hisself."

Joe got his candy and left the store. The clerk turned to the next customer. "Wisht I could be like these darkies. Laughin' all the time. Nothin' worries 'em."

Back in Eatonville, Joe reached his own front door.

There was the ring of singing metal on wood. Fifteen times. Missie May couldn't run to the door, but she crept there as quickly as she could.

"Joe Banks, Ah hear you chunkin' money in mah do'way. You wait till Ah got mah strength back, and Ah'm gointer fix you for dat."

# Part of the Pack: Another View of Night Life in Harlem

### Hazel V. Campbell

The Harlem Renaissance quickly gave way to the Depression in black America, which was hit especially hard by the economic downturn. On March 19, 1935, a security guard at a Kress Department Store in Harlem apprehended a black teenager and accused him of shoplifting. Rumors first that the boy was beaten, then false rumors that he had been killed, helped to incite three thousand people to take to the streets of Harlem in protest. More than five hundred policemen were mobilized, four blacks were killed, and property damage was extensive. Published five months later in *Opportunity,* Hazel Campbell's ironically titled story dramatizes the riot from the point of view of a young Harlem couple, to point to the shift from high times to low times in 1930s Harlem and to evoke the tremendous struggle for blacks for jobs, equality, and respect during the Depression. Like the work of her contemporary Richard Wright, Campbell's story shows signs of the popularity of social Darwinist thinking in 1930s America (even the cats in the story are struggling for "supremacy") as blacks and whites battled for dwindling resources. The story is one of the few surviving pieces of African American literature to document so closely the effects on personal lives of the Harlem riots, which helped bring even greater attention to the need for economic relief for black Americans in Roosevelt's New Deal.

STEVE HALL OPENED THE DOOR of his basement home on East 133rd Street. The wooden door cried under its labor. Sucking his teeth, the tall black man bent low and stepped into the dark hallway. The door closed behind him with a bang, and a lone picture hanging on the wall fell to the floor amid a bed of broken glass. The four-room apartment was odorous with the smell of stale cabbage and boiled beef. Steve moistened his lips with one sweep of his tongue and walked back to the cheerless kitchen.

His wife, a tall mulatto woman, was standing over the gas stove stirring a black pot from which steam was issuing.

"You have been stealing again, Lu?" he asked wearily and knitting his brow.

"Sure. Where the hell you think I got this food from?" she answered indifferently, still stirring the pot.

"Aw, we've got to quit this sort of living, Lu. We've got to quit. I'm tired of eating stolen goods," and Steve's voice was strained.

"Ain't satisfied? You don't have to eat it if you don't want to," she snapped, turning toward him. "That will be all the more for tomorrow," she finished.

Steve shifted on his feet. His lean face took on a hurt expression. His pride had been injured, and his heart beat heavily against the ragged shirt covering his bony breast. It hurt him that he could not live up to the word of his promise to her mother, to provide for her in the proper way. Here she was now stooping to the degrading thing of stealing food so that neither he nor she might starve.

"Lu, I wish you wouldn't talk so. Why don't you talk human anymore? You do nothing but snap and snarl like a dog from morn till night." Steve spoke dully.

"Well, what if I do snap and snarl? Maybe I am a dog. I'm part of the pack ain't I, fighting for food and life against the odds," she yelled, throwing a wooden spoon on the table.

"Lu, please," he coaxed, raising his hands as if to quiet her.

"Please, hell! I'm tired of please this and please that. I'm tired of this damn Yankee town anyway. I'm tired of all these damn black Yankees who do nothing but put on airs with their bellies thinking their throat is cut. Yes, look at me! You and these damn gin-soaked, gun-toting, razor-pulling niggers," and Lu's voice rose to a scream.

"Hush, Lu. Please!" he begged raising his hand.

"Hush! Hush! Hush! That's why we are where we are today, cos it is always hush! hush! hush! I tell you I am tired. I am tired of everything from that damn jazz that beats in your ears like the tom-tom of the jungles to the false prophets who walk up and down these streets crying to have faith. Faith in what? I'm going back to the Delta. I'm going back where the music is dull and heavy and kind like the people. At least down there you won't have to fight with dogs and cats over a piece of meat," she finished, her voice growing calmer under memories of pleasant days in the Delta basin.

"It will be only for a while, dear," he tried to say cheerfully, but his voice cracked. "Only for a while. Then there will be plenty of work. In the meantime, dear, why can't you put your pride aside and go to the Home Relief? We just can't go on like this. I hate to see you sneaking like a cat stealing food. You don't have to steal it," and Steve sat on the three-legged stool and hung his head.

"Charity? Did you say charity?" she scoffed.

"Why yes. Yes, of course," he said, looking up.

"Charity! Who the hell wants charity?" she screamed. "A pinch here and a pinch there, and a look of contempt written on everyone's face. Hell, who you think is going to stand for that? I'm going back to the Delta, if I have to crawl on my hands and knees to get there."

"All right! All right!" he said, waving her aside.

"I'd rather steal than take the white man's so-called charity," she snapped.

Steve rubbed his head with both of his hands and shifted in his seat.

Someone was knocking at the door. Neither of them moved.

Again the knock. Lu looked at Steve and Steve looked at Lu.

A look of dismay passed between them. For a while only the tick tock of the clock was heard.

"Well, what you looking at me for?" Lu spoke firmly, pressing her lips together. "You can answer the door, can't you?"

"Yes," Steve spoke slowly, rising from the seat.

"Well, answer it," she said, waving her hand. "You ain't afraid, are you? We've been dodging the landlord and bill collectors for the last few months, so I guess we can face the music now. If it is the landlord, bring him back here so I can give him a piece of my mind. The damn cheat."

Steve walked away from her. His knees felt weak and useless under him. Suppose it was the landlord and he had come to put them out. Where would they go? No rent paid for three months, and no outlook of paying any rent for the next twelve months. He could go to charity, but Lu would rather walk the streets and die from hunger. Queer woman. He opened the door slowly. A short bow-legged man was standing before him. Steve gave a deep sigh as he recognized his best friend, Bradford Hardy.

"Hi, Steve," Brad spoke warmly.

"Come in, Brad. Glad to see you," and the tone of Steve's voice was sincere.

Brad followed Steve to the rear, where Lu was still standing.

She had not moved from her position. Her eyes opened in relief as Brad came toward her.

"Hi, Brad," she greeted.

"Hi, Lu."

"Did you have any luck with that job you went after?" she asked.

"Hell, no," he answered shortly, and taking off his cap, he placed it on the table.

"Gee, that's tough. I'm sorry, old boy," Steve said, patting Brad on the back. "I wonder just what is wrong?"

"What's wrong, man?" sneered Brad, looking at Steve in contempt. "If you must know what is wrong, it is this," and Brad pointed a dirty brown finger to his face. "Just this," and taking the three-legged stool, he sat down.

"You ought to know just what is wrong, Steve, without asking. There is one thing I hate more than poverty and that is a dumb nigger," Lu spoke sharply. "You've been black long enough to know what is wrong. Even a baby could have guessed it was his skin," and Lu looked at him with an air of superiority.

"Not that I couldn't do the work. I've had good training in that field," and a deep frown formed in Brad's forehead. "They always have to give such lame excuses," and his voice shook. Steve caught a hint of rising anger in the tone of his friend's voice. Steve knew that anger. It was a revengeful anger, rising slowly and then suddenly bursting like an eruption. Brad was talking again. "Damn, how long you think this is going to keep up?" and Brad banged his fist on the table. "I'm damn tired of it. Damn it to hell, I wish I were white—hell, no! I wish I were a yaller, bless my soul if I wouldn't cross the line and fool all these old 'ofays.' I'd get the best kind of job, and marry the best kind of them, and fool the hell out of them. Then I'd laugh."

"Would you?" Lu looked at him in amusement. "There would be that something in your blood that would call you back, and, Brad, you wouldn't be able to get away from it."

"Aw, hell!" and Brad put his head on the cupboard.

"Hungry, Brad?" Steve asked.

"Well, I'd be lying if I said no, and I don't want to lie," he laughed, looking up.

"We thought you were the landlord at first, and we had made up our minds to make the best of his verdict," Lu said, going to the dish closet, taking three cracked dishes from the closet and setting them on the table. Brad moved his hat.

"If he came in my place, I'm afraid I'd go in for cannibalism," Brad spoke, watching the dishes on the table.

"You'd go in for what?" laughed Lu.

"Cannibalism."

"Well, as long as you have friends like Steve and I, you won't have to sink that far. Count on us sharing our meager blessings with you," Lu answered. Taking the pot from the stove, she placed it on the table and began filling each plate, giving each a generous portion. When each dish had been filled, she sat down.

"I wish to hell I knew how to pray," Brad spoke mournfully.

"Well, why don't you learn?" Lu asked, looking up from her plate and brushing a long strand of hair from her face.

"Then I'd pray to God from the bottom of my heart, and I'd pray and pray and pray," and Brad jumped from his seat, upsetting the food onto the floor, "and I'd pray to God to give me food, and a job, and to send a Moses to lead us to the land of milk and honey."

Neither Steve nor Lu answered him.

"And I'd pray to God. God, I'd pray to you," went on Brad. "God! oh God! I'd pray for justice, for fairness, and God, I'd pray. Oh hell, I wish I knew how to pray," and Brad tore at his ragged shirt and beat his bony hand against his hairy breast. "God! My God!" he said, sitting down. His foot slipped on the food on the floor. He looked down. His eyes became bewildered.

"Food! God, I'm stepping on food. Good food!" and Brad bent down and picked up the dirty cabbage and beef, scraping the food in his plate. Picking out the splinters and dirt he could see, he began eating again. Lu watched him thoughtfully, as she counted how many times his Adam's apple worked up and down, and his lean face twitched nervously.

When the meal was finished, Brad washed the dishes, Steve dried them, and Lu put the rest of the food on the windowsill.

Above them a woman's voice arose clear and strong.

> It's me, it's me, it's me, oh Lord,
>   Standing in the need of prayer,
> It's me, it's me, it's me oh, Lord,
>   Standing in the need of prayer.

Lu put her hands on her hips and looked at the ceiling.

"Listen to that damn black woman. She's been singing that song all day."

Steve and Brad wiped their hands on a soiled handkerchief. They too listened.

Tain't mah brother
    Tain't mah sister
But me, oh Lord,
    Standing in the need of prayer.

"She's right. She's standing in the need of prayer. We all are," Steve said, putting the dishes on the washtub.

"Well, she doesn't have to shout it from the house tops. What if she is standing in the need of prayer, who the hell she thinks is going to pray for her. Sure, we all are standing in the need of prayer, but are we letting everyone know it? No, we're keeping our hard luck to ourselves, and if we can take it on the chin and not cry to the whole world, that cat up there can too," Lu answered Steve.

"We can't keep it to ourselves much longer," put in Brad.

"Damn right. Damn right," Lu agreed.

Somehow or other they were glad when Brad left them. The afternoon wore on. The woman above them still sang the same song. Out on the river the boats cried and whistled. In the streets the children's laughter and cries shrilled above the noise of the traffic. The clock in the kitchen struck four. Steve paced the rooms in disgust, his wife watching him. Finally he threw himself on the bed and fell asleep. Lu walked to the window and watched with amusement two kittens tumbling over each other. Both of them fighting for supremacy, she thought. For a long time she sat by the window. Steve was snoring, and from her boredom she made a song from his snoring.

Then evening came, and the children in the streets had gone, and the woman above her had ceased her singing. Lu fell across the couch in the living room and slept. It was after nine when she was awakened by someone knocking at the door. She sat up. She heard Steve rise from the bed and his heavy footsteps falling on the wooden, planked floor. By the tone of the voices, she knew Brad had come back. She went to the front door.

"Back again?" she smiled in the dark.

Brad was out of breath.

"What's the matter?" Steve asked, pulling his friend into the living room.

"Race riot," he gasped.

"What?" Lu yelled, opening her eyes wide.

"Fighting down on 125th Street," he went on.

"How'd it start?" Lu asked excitedly.

Brad shrugged his shoulders. "I ran up here as fast as I could, in case you all want to join in the battle. You can hear the noise clean up here."

Lu grabbed Steve's arm.

Brad tugged at the other arm of Steve's. "Come, old man."

Steve knitted his brow and looked at Brad. "Where?"

"To the battlefield. I guess the mob is up near 130th Street by now. They were coming uptown when I came up."

Steve freed his arms, from Lu and Brad. "Who wants to fight?"

"Man alive, they are busting windows like hot cakes. The niggers have gone plumb mad. Nigger heaven has turned into a living hell now. Come on, Steve, we can at least get some of the food from those stores where windows are broken. I'm not in for the fighting either, but if I can get some food and clothes without paying for it, I'm just raring," Brad finished.

"Go on, Steve. You and Brad go out and get food. Keep away from the mob as much as you can, and if you have to fight—damn it, fight. Fighting will make a man of you, Steve. A fighting man, who can snap and snarl along with the pack," Lu said, pushing him from her.

Steve did not answer. He played with the one remaining button on his shirt.

"Go on, Steve. 'Tain't no sin no more nohow to steal. The Lord knows we've got to eat, and if we can't get it honestly, we'll have to take matters into our own hands," Lu was coaxing.

"I'm not going," he said sharply, turning on her. "What's the sense of fighting when you don't have to."

Lu threw back her head. "Well, damn it, if you don't go, I will," she shot at him. "I'll show you, you big coward. I'll be the fighter in this family. I'll get food, and I'll get clothes, and bring it back. You can stay here and nurse your petty feelings. I'll go out and fight and I'll fight like a man, and that is more than you can boast of, you—you, you coward," and switching past him, she took a soiled coat from a nail behind the door, and together she and Brad left him standing in the dark hallway.

Steve did not know what to think. Outside he could hear the murmur of angry voices, mingled with tramping feet. He scratched his head. He wondered why he had let Lu go. She had no business out there. It was his place to fight the battles, if there was any need to fight. Lu could be a regular spit-fire when she wanted to be. She was a woman, and nice women never fought, and Lu was a nice woman. She was his wife. She was good, even though she did drink, and smoke and steal and cuss. He'd go and bring her back. Clenching his fist, he slipped his overcoat on and left the house. The street was crowded. Lu and Brad were nowhere to be seen. He knew they were swallowed up in the crowd. He half walked and half ran toward Lenox Avenue, his eyes fastened on the mob ahead of him, hoping to catch a glimpse of Brad's broad shoulders or the tall figure of Lu. A woman had taken his arm. He looked down and saw that she was a gray-headed woman. She grinned up at him. "We have to go with our men to war," she laughed coarsely. He could smell stale gin coming from her mouth. He did not answer her. She was talking again: "Have you ever fought battles for your rights?"

"Naw," he answered with a shrug of his shoulders.

A crash of glass sounded behind him. A cry went up. "Kill him!"

"Take that 'ofay' and string him up a pole. Kill that cracker," and the cry ran down the street. Steve saw a lone white man speeding and bending low in his car, trying to escape the missiles hurled at him. Steve was glad the man escaped. The street was more crowded now with men and women battling with uniformed men on foot and horse. Knives flashed, guns barked, clubs swung, fists flew, and blood flowed freely in a tumult of misunderstanding and revenge.

All around was broken glass and more glass being broken rang in his ears. He found himself in the midst of the battle, and he began to fight blindly and wondered what he was fighting and why he was fighting. Something heavy struck him on the head. Blood gushed down his face . . . running into his eyes . . . blinding him. He felt darkness engulfing him . . . his head began to swim—he could feel his legs slipping from underneath him. Wiping the blood madly from his face, he groped his way clear of the mob and slumped in a doorway. He could hear tramping feet and angry voices far in the distance.

Lu and Brad came home long after two that morning. Their eyes were blackened and their clothes were torn to shreds, but they were happy. In their arms was food. Lots and lots of food, and more if they wanted to go through the same ordeal they just came through. No one stopped them on their way home. In fact no one would dare, for Lu and Brad would fight.

Lu stumbled in the doorway.

"Steve," she cried.

Silence.

"Steve, wake up."

Only the echo of her voice came back to her from the darkness.

"Hey, you lazy, good-for-nothing character, awaken yourself and see what your mama has brought home to her baby."

Silence.

"Hey, Brad, wake that lazy nigger up," she commanded from the kitchen.

Brad tipped into the bedroom. Turning on the light, he gasped in surprise.

"He ain't here," he yelled.

"Who, Steve?"

"Ain't a sign of him."

"Thank God, he went out to fight. Come in here and get

me some cold water. I want to fix this eye before he comes back."

Morning came. Brad came in late bringing with him the morning paper.

"Steve ain't come home yet," she greeted him.

Brad did not answer.

"What's the matter?" she asked suddenly.

"Steve ain't coming back anymore, Lu," he said, giving her the paper.

"What you mean, he ain't coming back anymore?" she asked, not looking at the paper.

"He just ain't coming back," and Brad shook his head. "I took this paper from the stand," and he shook the paper so that she would take it. "Here," and Brad's voice cracked under the strain he was trying to control.

Lu looked at him, then at the paper. Tears blinded her eyes, but she blinked hard and fast. "Brad—Brad—do you mean—he—is dead? Do you mean the white people killed him? Why, he can't be dead. He was here only a little while ago. Don't you remember? You do remember, Brad. . . . why we left him right out there in the hallway right out there—remember he was standing there all alone—and we left him just like that."

Brad said nothing. He bit his lips, and his face had become grave.

"Brad, do something," Lu screamed all at once. "Oh God! My God!! Bring Steve back to me. White papers say you are dead, but Steve, they lie, they lie, they lie," and Lu was sobbing.

Overheard a voice clear and strong was singing:

> It's me, it's me, it's me, oh Lord
> Standing in the need of prayer.

# Mob Madness

## MARION CUTHBERT

Lynchings became the subject of much black fiction and journalism in the 1930s as African American writers began to mo-
bilize against racism and other forms of oppression. Marion
Cuthbert's short story from a 1936 *Crisis* is loosely based on
the famous 1934 lynching of Claude Neal, a southern black
who was one of literally thousands lynched during and after
the "Jim Crow" reign of terror in the South. Uniquely,
Cuthbert's story is narrated from the perspective of the white
wife of one of the lynchers. Lizzie's disgust at her husband's
brutality opens a window onto white southern racial conscience
rarely seen in African American short fiction. Cuthbert also
considers how racist attitudes imprint from one generation to
the next. The story's stark simplicity and graphic detail make
it a good example of the "social protest" function of much
1930s black writing.

LIZZIE WATCHED JIM stir his coffee. Her eyes were
wide with fever and horror. Around and around he stirred,
and the thin stuff slopped over and filled the saucer. But he
did not notice because he was talking to their son.

"Shore, we got 'im at the very spot I showed you and
Jeff. Lem would o' slit his throat right then, but the fellers
back on the pike was waitin' an' wanted to be in on it, too,
so we drug 'im out o' the brush. The boys wanted ter git at
'im to once, but some o' the more experienced on 'em
cooled us down. You was there last night, so you know as
much o' that end o' it as anybody."

He turned to the neglected coffee now and downed it in great gulps. The thirteen-year-old boy watched, his face set in a foolish grin of admiration and wonder.

"Jeff said he heard a man down to the square say you all got the wrong nigger. Said this one didn't do it."

"Guess he did it all right. An' if he didn't, one of the black ———— stretched out Ole Man Dan'l, an' the smell o' this one roastin' will teach the rest o' 'em they can't lay hands on a white man, b'Gawd!"

"Les see the toe again."

The man took a filthy handkerchief out of his overalls pocket and unwrapped carefully a black object.

Lizzie swayed and, fearing to fall against the hot wood-stove, sank into a chair.

Then Jim and the boy finished breakfast and went out.

For a long time Lizzie sat in the chair. After a while she got up shakily and went in the other room. Little Bessie was still sleeping heavily. She was ailing and her mother had been up with her most of the night.

But she would have been up all of that night, that terrible night, anyway. Neighbors had run in on their way to the square to ask her if she was not going, too.

She was not going.

Jim had come in long past midnight, little Jim with him. His eyes were bloodshot. She would have believed him drunk, but there was no smell of liquor on him. The boy was babbling incoherently.

"Maw, you should a seed it!"

Big Jim shut him up. The two fell into bed and slept at once.

After a time it was day, and Lizzie moved like a sick woman to get breakfast.

She stood looking down now on little Bessie. The child's yellow hair had fallen across her face. This she brushed back and looked for a long time on the thin little oval of a face. The purple-veined eyelids were closed upon deep blue-gray eyes. Lizzie's own mother had said she was the living image of little Bessie when she was a child. Delicate and finicky. But when she was sixteen, she had married six-foot, red-faced Jim. He was always rough, but men seemed all like that. She did not know then that he would . . .

After a little the child awoke. She gave her some breakfast, but would not let her get up. Allie Sneed from next door ran in.

"Everything's as quiet as kin be this mornin'. Not a nigger on the street. Lizzie, you missed it last night!"

Jim drove the truck for the store. He had gone to Terryville and did not come for lunch. Little Jim came in, swallowed his food, and was off. It was cold, so Lizzie kept the woodstove going smartly. She held little Bessie in her arms and rocked back and forth. All day she had not eaten, but she was not hungry. She rocked back and forth . . .

. . . they got It down in the brush on the other side of the branch . . . they took It into the woods . . . at dark they tied It to a car and dragged It back to the town . . . at the square they piled up a huge bonfire . . .

. . . Jim had helped by bringing crates from the store . . .

. . . they had cut parts of It away. . . .

. . . Jim had something black in a handkerchief . . .

. . . then they put what was left of It on the fire . . . Their house was quite a way from the square, but she had heard the shouting. Every house around was emptied . . .

. . . once her brother had had an argument with another man. They fought, and pulled knives on each other. Both were cut pretty badly, and they feared the other man would die. But she never shrank from her brother after that. All hot words and anger. He did not shout, crazy. Afterward he did not brag . . .

. . . they did not fight It . . . they caught It like an animal in the brush . . . if It had been an animal they would have killed It at once . . . but This they took in the woods . . . before they killed It outright they cut off Its fingers and toes . . .

. . . Jim had something black in a handkerchief . . .

She put the child back in bed and went out in the yard to pump some water. She leaned her hot face against the porch post. In the dark by the fence something moved. It came nearer.

"Mis' Lizzie? O my Gawd, Mis' Lizzie! Dey burned me out las' night. Ah bin hidin' in de shacks by de railroad. Waitin' fo' de dahk. You allays good to us po' cullud people. Hope yo' Jim put me in de truck an' take me to Terryville tonight. Tell 'im he'p me, Mis' Lizzie, tell 'im he'p me!"

She could only stare at her. The voice of the black woman seemed far away, lost in the shouting in her head.

Their home was quite a way from the square, but she had heard the shouting.

The voice of the black woman seemed to go away altogether. So Lizzie went inside and began supper.

Soon after, Jim came home and ate his supper. He was weary and dour. As soon as he was through he went to bed, and the boy, too.

Lizzie sat by the fire. Little Bessie was better and sleeping soundly.

. . . if Jim had not been so tired he would have come to her . . .

. . . he did not yet know she was going to have another child. This child, and little Bessie, and little Jim, had a father who helped catch a Thing in the brush . . . and cut off the quivering flesh. It seemed that all the men in the town had thought this a good thing to do. The women, too. They had all gone down to the square . . .

. . . little Jim was like his father. The other day he had spoken sharp to her. As big Jim so often did. He said she was too soft and finicky for her own good. Most boys were like Jim. When little Bessie grew up, she would marry a boy like this . . .

. . . when little Bessie grew up . . .

. . . some boy who could touch her soft, fair flesh at night, and go forth into the day to hunt a Thing in the brush, and hack at Its flesh alive . . .

Lizzie looked and looked at the child. She remembered things which she had thought were true when she was a child. She was a woman now, and she knew that these things were not true. But she had thought they were true when she was a child.

The fire in the stove went down, then out. She made no effort to replenish it. Toward morning she went to the table drawer and took something out. She went in the other room and looked down on the uncouth figures of the sprawling man and boy. It was over the boy that she finally bent, but she straightened at once, remembering that the man and the boy were one. So she turned to the little girl, and the lifted blade of steel did not gleam anymore.

Jim had had a good rest and awakened early. He found the bodies, already cold.

When the shock of the first terror let him find his voice, he declared he would kill with his own hands every black man, woman, and child within a hundred miles of the town. But the sheriff made him see that it was not murder. All this she had done with her own hand.

"She didn't touch me, ner the boy. When they go mad like this, sometimes they wipes out all."

Out in the yard Allie Sneed said to an awestruck group, "I knew it was somethin' wrong with her when she held back from seein' the burnin'. A rare, uncommon sight, that, and she hid in her house missin' it!"

# Conjure Man

OCTAVIA B. WYNBUSH

Conjuring is the art of manipulation and prophecy based on superstitious use of talismans, herbs, and personal totems. It has its roots in the blend of Voodoo and Christian ritual that emerged out of the slave trade. Charles Chesnutt's famous collection of antebellum stories, *The Conjure Woman,* describes the power of conjuring for American slaves, who often sought supernatural remedies for their everyday sufferings. Wynbush's 1938 *Crisis* story uses the conjuring tradition as a backdrop for a more contemporary fable of greed, murder, jealousy, and revenge. The story is meant as an entertaining diversion but also raises questions about the social circumstances that drive people to desperate measures.

HER BEADY OLD EYES glittering through narrow slits of lids as she peered through an opening in the leafy screen, Maum Samba sat behind the matted honeysuckle vines framing her front porch. Across the dusty strip of road in front of her rickety fence, a group of men was assembled in the semicircular clearing in front of Devil's Swamp. The eldest of the group, a tall, muscular fellow, weathered by the Louisiana sun to a blackish hue, appeared to be giving orders.

What worried Samba was the fact that the men were carrying implements suggestive of digging. What could it mean? Was the gossip which had come to her ears of late about to become a truth?

"Mornin', Maum Samba."

Startled, Samba looked up. By her rocker stood the grinning twelve-year-old son of a neighbor.

"Lawd, boy! Don' never come on me like dat agin. What you want, anyhow?"

"Ma done sent me for your risin' sun quilt patte'n. She say len' it to her, please."

Rising stiffly, Samba stepped into the house, from which she returned soon, bearing the pattern tied in a neat package. Before giving it to the boy, she queried: "What's goin' on 'cross the road, Luther?"

"Mistah Wesson's goin' build his new home 'cross from you, Maum Samba," grinned the boy, watching the old woman with a queer gleam in his eye.

The mottled yellow hand plucking the string around the package stopped suddenly, as if stricken with paralysis.

"Yes?" The tone was as unconcerned as Samba could make it.

"Yas'm. He bought dat strip of clearin' from Big Jim Handy, an' is goin' to live there with his fambly an' Miz Amanda."

"I reckon yo' ma's waitin' fo' dis patte'n, boy. Run 'long home."

When the boy had gone, Samba resumed her seat behind the vines. So it had come to this! Mark Wesson was going to bring his wife and Amanda to flaunt themselves and their prosperity in her face the rest of her life. Their new home would be across the road from her own dilapidated cabin with its run-to-weeds garden in which she had lost interest since the death of her husband two years ago.

What a reversal of the picture as she had painted it in her youth! Samba's mind flew back to that happy time, so hazy now that she often wondered whether it had happened to her, or to someone she had once known. She moaned softly to herself. Surely what she had done did not demand life-long punishment.

She was beginning to believe what Nana Marshall had hinted to her once.—"God hain't punishing you, Samba. Hit's yo' bitter enemy what's put a spell on you, an' dey's on'y one human in dis parish what kin tek hit offen you—

dat's ol' Elias, what lives close to de cypress swamp. He kin tek hit off, or put a worser one on yo' enemy. An' you know who dis enemy is."

Samba sighed. How could she help it, if Bob had turned from Amanda Pierre to her, forty-odd years ago, even after his word had been given to Amanda? He hadn't been able to help himself when the sprightly, beautiful girl from St. Martinville had danced into his life on the occasion of her visit to her aunt and uncle at Eglanville.

Maum Samba—Seremba they called her then—had been beautiful in her youth, with her olive complexion, flashing, black eyes, blue-black hair sweeping below her waist, slender ankles, and dainty feet that outdanced the best of the belles of Eglanville. She hadn't meant to take big Bob Moore completely away from his "promised" bride, at first. It had just been fun to see the big fellow fall so desperately for her. But Amanda's furious jealousy and bitter words had spurred the visitor to do her utmost.

Never would she forget the thrill of that evening on the outskirts of the swamp, just where the clearing was now. It was all thicket and trees, then. Bob and she had stopped under the live-oak, since felled by lightning, and there Bob had proposed. Samba recalled her own demurring because of Amanda. Even now she heard again his vehement declaration that Amanda had long since ceased to interest him. Even in her present state of mind, she could not forbear a tender, reminiscent smile.

Then, acres and acres of the rich soil had been Bob's, even the land upon which they had become engaged. And now, Amanda's son-in-law was building his home upon that spot—a home to which he could bring his children, his mother-in-law, Amanda, and his wife, Rose Ellen.

Thought of Rose Ellen stirred the fire in Samba's soul to fiercer heat. With what vengeance had Amanda retaliated!

Of all their six children, Bob and Samba had held their daughter, Lucille, most dear, partly because she was the only girl, and partly because she was such a delicate creature. When Mark Wesson, superior in every way to the young fellows of Eglanville, had come from up the river to settle and open a combined store and "refreshment parlor," he had taken immediately to Lucille.

In a short time they became engaged. Samba had been wild with joy. Every girl in the village, Rose Ellen especially, had made desperate efforts to get this man, whose energy and ability marked him as distinctly different from the indolent, shiftless fellows of their acquaintance.

Even now nausea and weakness swept over Samba as she remembered—Lucille, slim, brown, lovely in her wedding finery, standing before the mirror, taking the last look at herself before starting for the church—Hannah Washington, frowsy, dusty, excited, and perspiring, rushing in and blurting out the brutal fact that Rose Ellen and Mark Wesson had slipped off to the next town that morning and had married. Samba had never been able to forgive Hannah for her tactlessness in blurting out the truth before Lucille. The scorching humiliation which had finally burned up Lucille's vitality and killed her, had shriveled Samba into a mummified version of her former self.

Behind the honeysuckle vines Samba stirred and sighed as she wiped her eyes with one corner of her blue-checked apron. Then she rose resolutely and stood a moment, her fists balled tightly at her temples. Resolve shone in her eyes, as she straightened at last.

"Tonight, at fust dark, I'll do it," she muttered.

The last rays of the sun had been conquered by the night rising from the earth, and the peculiarly velvety darkness that precedes the rising of the moon in Louisiana lay thick on Devil's Swamp. Samba, standing with her hand on the latch of her sagging gate, looked sharply up and down the road, listening for any sound of approaching footsteps. Assured that no one was coming, she swung open the gate and stepped into the road. After carefully closing and latching the rickety barrier between her weedy yard and the open highway, she began walking along in the dust, as fast as her wizened legs could carry her thin body. She must get off the main road before the moon rose. It was a long way to the big oak where she could take the snake-trail.

"I'm goin' to do it! I'm goin' to do it!" she muttered continually, savagely, as she strode along.

"I'm goin' to do it! I'm goin' to do it!" her footsteps seemed to echo back as she moved forward through the powdery dust. The close heat of the night, unfavorable for her pace, soon sent streams of perspiration coursing over her body.

For once fortune favored her. When the moon rose, she was deep in the woods through which wound the crooked little snake-path that began at the base of the big oak by the main road. The big, yellow, eyelike moon made the trees stand in sharp, black outline. Deeper and deeper into their midst went Samba, following the narrow path which led finally to a natural lane of pine trees, ending abruptly before a long, low shanty in a small clearing.

In the light of the moon, the cabin was oddly fantastic. Its roof appeared to be made of bits of tin, tar-paper, and slate. The sides were pieced together from scraps of timber, boxes, and boards from box-cars, the latter still bearing their legends of weight and capacity.

From one window of the shanty came a feeble ray of light. Creeping up to the window, Samba looked in. She could see a crudely made table covered with a dirty, much-marred oil cloth on which stood a flickering smoky lamp. At one end of the table, his face buried in his hands, sat an old man deeply absorbed in thought. Standing tip-toe, Samba craned her neck from side to side. She could discover no one else in the room. Elias was evidently alone. Samba was satisfied.

Mounting the two rickety steps leading to a little stoop before the door, she knocked cautiously and softly. The door was cracked. A rasping old voice inquired,

"Who dat?"

Samba's reply, though soft, was somewhat scornful.

"You oughta know. It's part of yo' trade."

The door was opened still wider. Old Elias peered out, the beams of the moon falling over his fuzzled white head, his black, wrinkled face with its two sharp, ferrety red eyes, and his ragged, open-at-the-neck shirt and tattered, dirty overalls.

"Maum Samba! Well, I *is* surprised! Come in."

The room in which Samba found herself was as grotesque as the outside of the shack. From the rafters, over which the shadows of herself and Elias sprawled in gargantuan proportions, hung all sorts of curious and startling things. Bunches of dried herbs, curiously tied packages dangling from long strings, animal skins, gourds, and three dried snake skins were distinguishable in the dim light.

The walls, bare and unplastered, with nothing to obliterate entirely the fact that they were simply the outside boards seen from the inside, were hung here and there with more of the things which dangled from the ceiling. Over the bunk with its grimy bedclothes hung a horseshoe and a wool-card. On a small table in one corner stood a collection of bottles and jars filled with weird-looking roots. Besides them lay a rabbit's foot, a crystal for gazing, and a luck stone.

Samba looked directly at the man in front of her.

"Elias, you knows I don' hol' much wid yo' trade. I bases my life on de Bible an' prayer, but I needs yo' help now fo' a quick act."

"Set down."

Samba took the stool Elias drew from under the oilcloth-covered table and plunged immediately into her recital.

"Elias, I wants you to help me get shet of a enemy."

"A enemy?"

"Yes. I name no name, an' I bear no blame."

"You bring anything belongs to yo' enemy?"

Samba's face fell.

"I didn't know I had to."

"How kin I wuk 'thout sumpin' to wuk on?"

"But you is done it, ain't you?"

"Not on no one ez pow'ful ez yo' enemy bes. Hit ain't so s'cessful. But I'll give you a luck ball twell you brings me sumpin'."

Elias went to the corner table where reposed his magic potions.

"What mus' I bring?" Samba's voice was guarded and low. Even the rafters might hear.

"Some of yo' enemy's haih, a piece of yo' enemy's clo'es, an' sumpin' yo' enemy's done wrote."

Samba's rigid back did not reveal her dismay. Getting these things from an enemy she had not spoken to in over forty years! Getting them from Amanda Pierre! Well, this was her problem. She would solve it. Impatiently she awaited Elias's return from his table.

When he finally returned to Samba, Elias laid before her a round, evil-smelling black ball and a coarse brown bag containing something hard and pungent.

"Now," he began, "put dis yere black ball somewheah on yo' enemy's grounds, somewheah he'll have to walk over it. Put dis bag away somewheah in yo' own house, an' when you gits back home, sprinkle a cupful o' mustahd seed on youah walk an' do' step, to keep off de evil sperrits yo' enemy might send agains' you at night. Dis will gib you a little pertection, but it ain't gwine be complete twell you brings me de haih, de piece o' clo'es, an' de writin'."

Samba stood up and fumbled in her apron pocket, a question in her eyes.

"One dollah only, bein' as it's you," Elias replied to the unspoken query, "an' to complete the work, it'll cos' you twenty-five dollahs."

"Twenty-five dollars!" Samba's voice rose in a screech. "Wheah you think I kin get twenty-five dollars?"

"Oh, you kin git it, all right. You kin go dis minute an' lay yo' han's on fo' times dat much. Don' look at me lak you's s'prised. I knows dat. Hain't it paht of my trade?"

Elias laughed heartily at the opportunity to fling Samba's words back at her.

"And 'sides," he added after a moment, "de chahms you already has is 'versible. Dey kin wu'k against you ef de one what gave 'em to you wills, as well as fo' you, you knows. W'en will I be favored wid you' comp'ny agin, ma'am? Thanks fo' de dollah."

"Sometime ve'y soon."

Gathering up the ball and the bag and thrusting them

into her pockets, Samba moved toward the door. Gallantly Elias stepped forward to open it. Samba breathed a long sigh of relief as she stepped outside and descended the rickety steps. Pausing for a moment on the ground in front of the shack, she expelled the rancid air of the hut from her lungs and filled them with the sharp fragrance of the pine grove.

Before Samba's problem of obtaining the hair, the piece of clothing, and the writing of her enemy had reached its solution, the finishing touches were being put on the Wesson house. The hot days of summer were giving way to slightly cooler autumn weather when a garden party given by Samba's friend, Teresa Claudin, furnished the occasion.

It was a beautiful night when Samba joined the crowd flocking over the broad expanse of unfenced, grassy ground Teresa pleased to call her "lawn." Elbowing her way through the crowd, Samba, a little black silk bag dangling from her left wrist, a short thin shawl over her shoulders, went straight to a group of which Teresa was one. Greetings over, Samba refused the hostess's offer to escort her to the room where the women had left their wraps.

"Thank you, thank you, Teresa, but you knows I knows ev'y inch of yo' house. I'll go by myself."

Up the path to the house went Samba, greeting friends right and left. It was just a step across the long front porch of the house into the room where lay all the light wraps brought by the women in anticipation of the cool breezes that often sprang up after sundown in the autumn.

Approaching the bed on which the garments lay—an assortment of scarfs, jackets, and coats—Samba stood quietly searching with her eyes for one particular wrap. There it was! Amanda's black silk shawl with the red embroidered roses, and the deep, heavy black fringe. Mark had brought it to her from Baton Rouge.

Opening the bag on her wrist, Samba drew out a pair of tiny scissors. Making sure that she was unobserved, she began clipping a bit of fringe from each of several bunches of the knotted silk. Snip, snip, hurriedly yet carefully, the work was done. The clipped fringe and the tiny scissors reposed in the black bag.

Removing her own shawl, Samba placed it on the bed with the other wraps and moved leisurely to join the group on the lawn. Once there, she moved around slowly, until she found herself next to Amanda, who was receiving congratulation from a number of friends, who were loud in their praises of the new home. All of Samba's hot hatred boiled in her breast, but she was outwardly beaming as she joined the group. Uncomfortable silence fell as she sidled up to Amanda.

"I des wants to add my compliments to de res', Miz Pierre," she began. "It's a mighty fine house, an' I'm glad you's buildin' it in front of me. It gits awful lonesome sometimes fo' me now, 'specially at night. I kin hardly wait fo' you all to move in. Seems to me we mought as well be frien's, sence we's goin' to be neighbors. An' it ain't any better time to staht than right now."

An approving chorus arose from the listeners as Samba finished speaking and laid her hand beseechingly on Amanda's arm. For a moment Amanda stood stiff and frozen. Then, with as good grace as possible, she thanked her erstwhile enemy for her good wishes and expressed her willingness to be friends.

Samba stood awhile, laughing and chatting with the others, and receiving congratulations along with Amanda. Then, excusing herself, she withdrew to a darker part of the yard, shaded by a huge magnolia tree. With the tree trunk between her and the people she had just left, she opened the bag. Something, clutched tightly between her thumb and forefinger, was dropped lightly within. It was a long, coarse gray hair she had found lying on Amanda's shoulder.

The night moved on. The guests grew merrier and merrier. Refreshments were served—all sorts of meats, preserves, chicken, cakes, and cream. Samba ate sparingly, complaining of "not havin' felt well in my stummick since day fo' yestiddy."

Suddenly a commotion arose in the group where she was

sitting. Samba had fainted. One big husky young fellow picked her up and carried her into the house. No one noticed that even in her faint Samba clutched the little black bag tightly in her hands. The crowd, gathered on the outside of the house and pressing up to the screen door, whispered, prayed, or giggled, according to their various natures.

"Lawd, I hope she ain't done got her las' sickness!"

"Mebbe dat's why she mek up wid Miz Pierre. Mebbe she done had a warning."

Presently Teresa came to the door, and called, "Miz Pierre, come dis way, please ma'am."

Ejaculations and comments followed Amanda's progress to the door. In a few minutes every one knew just why she had been called. Samba had expressed a belief that this was truly her last sickness. She wanted Amanda to do her one favor to show that all was well between them. Amanda must write a letter to her son, Andrew, bearing his mother's last words.

When the letter was completed, Samba suddenly took a turn for the better. She was soon able to rise from the bed where she lay and to set out for home in the rattling Ford belonging to one of the guests. The letter to Andrew lay in the black bag along with the fringe and the hair.

For three days Samba was in bed to all visitors, but the fourth day found her up and about. She spent the morning behind her vines watching the men who had come to unload the furniture for the new house. Mark Wesson had gone his limit in building this new house. "Spot cash" had been paid for everything, even for the new furnishings, almost to the complete depletion of his bank account. He had not yet insured the house. That would be taken care of in a few days, after the family had moved in.

On the night of the fourth day, Samba set out on her second journey to the hut of Elias. The sky was covered with scudding clouds that intermittently cut off the light of the moon. They promised rain, but rain that would not come before morning. The darkness necessitated Samba's carrying a lantern to light her way. Arrived at the cabin, she knocked softly. The door opened, and Elias's woolly head appeared.

"Who dat?"

"Me, Samba," in a breathless whisper.

"Come on in."

"Anybody else inside?"

"No."

Quietly Samba stepped over the threshold into the miserable, foul-smelling room. After locking the door behind her, Elias stepped to the table, rubbing his hands and chuckling as if at some joke known only to himself. He peered at Samba, his red eyes glowing with malicious pleasure.

"You got dem t'ings?"

"Heah dey is." Samba placed in his outstretched hands a brown paper parcel. Placing the parcel on the table, Elias bent over it to untie its careful wrappings. The strand of gray hair, the knot of fringe, and the letter lay before him.

"You played pretty slick to git dese, Samba." Elias's ragged, yellow teeth gleamed in a crooked smile.

"Oh, it didn't take no oncommon amount of brains," disclaimed the woman, bridling nevertheless at the compliment. "Now, what's de nex' step?"

Elias's rheumatically knotted, dirt-encrusted hands, that had been playing idly with the contents of the package, came to a sudden stop. He folded them across his chest and stared long and searchingly at Samba, who began to grow uneasy under his gaze.

"Dat is right," he began musingly, stroking his chin with one dirty hand, "dat is de nex' 'sideration. Set down."

The rickety chair creaked as Samba adjusted her meager body to it. Elias took the stool at the end of the table opposite the woman. He gazed and gazed at her with a steady, unfathomable look. To Samba, whose nerves were already a-tingle, the look took on a quality of deepest penetration. Elias was seeing through her, beyond her, into her present and—past. He was seeing everything that she had ever thought, said, or done.

Finally Elias arose, walked over to the table where were spread his roots, charms, and other mysteries. Picking up the crystal, he turned to his seat. Placing it on the table in front of him, he stared intently at it. In the silence Samba could hear the rustling of the trees outside, as tiny breaths of air passed over them. The ticking of the Ingersoll watch in Elias's pocket was like the beating of a drum to her. At last the old conjurer began to speak in his slowest, deepest, most mysterious tones.

"Samba, I sees a heap in dis yeah crystal. Hit's tekin' me 'way back to de pas'. Hit's tekkin' me back twenty yeahs, an' some ovah. I sees a low, shackly buildin'—low an' long. De front is lak a sto'.—Yes, I sees de wo'ds, 'Gin'ral Sto'' on a long, uster-be-white boa'd crost de front.—Don' move, you clouds my vision.

"Hit's fo' noon on a hot day. I sees a man—hit looks lak Bob, yo' husban', comin' in de do'. He got up to de countah; he speakin' to de white man behin' de countah. De man is cloudy. Now he's comin' cleah. Hit's Mistah Thornton. Don' jump like dat, Samba! You 'sturbs me. Mistah Joe Thornton, what owned de gin'ral sto' heah long time ago. De two men talks. Dey is gittin' angry, somehow. Bob seems to be speakin' mighty imperdent to Mistah Joe. Mistah Joe jump ovah de countah—an' lams Bob in de face. Bob, he sprawls in de flo'. Now he's pickin' hisse'f up. He goes out. He done learn hit's dang'ous speakin' back to a white man in Louisiana."

" 'Tain't so, Elias, 'tain't so! I'm goin' out fum heah! Let me out!" Samba had arisen swiftly and was even then on her way to the door.

"Set down!" Elias's bellow filled the little shack and rolled back from every rafter and corner. Samba shrank back to her seat. Elias resumed his steady gazing at the crystal.

"Hit's mighty cloudy, now, 'cause you done broke in. Now, now hit's clearin' once mo'. Hit's black night—no moon, no stahs, I sees two figgahs, a man an' a woman—"

Samba moaned.

"—creepin' up to de side of de gin'ral sto'. Dey looks in

de back winder, what's pahtly open. I sees Mistah Joe sprawled ovah a table—he drunk, as usual. He done fogot hisse'f, too, fo' de big safe whut stan's in dis room be open. De two at de winder waits an' watches. Now de man be climbin' in. What's dat he got in his han'? I b'lieve my soul hit's—a—club. Dat's what hit is!"

"You're makin' that up, Elias!"

Ignoring the woman's wildly shrieked words, the old man went on: "He bring hit down on Mistah Joe's haid. Mistah Joe falls ovah—daid. De man grabs de big sack o' money outen de safe, an' passes hit thoo de winder to de 'ooman. Now he's settin' fiah to de room, now he's climbin' outen de winder. Him an' de 'ooman goes back o' de sto', an' down to de woods, but not fo' I done seen dey faces—in de crystal. Dey is—"

"No! No!" Samba fled shrieking to the door. She rattled it, shook it, but the lock held fast.

Unperturbed, Elias continued. "Dey is Bob an' you, Samba. Lucky fo' you two, de fiah done swep' de shack clean as a whistle, an burn de dead man to ashes, 'fo hit was put out. Ev'ybody thinks to dis day dat Mistah Joe done upsot his lamp an' burn hisse'f to death. Dey thinks de little box o' coin an' bills dey foun' in de safe was all he had, 'cause he was always close-mouthed 'bout hisse'f.

"But two folks knows bettah, doesn't dey? An' dey's 'fraid to make no display wid de money dey's stole, so dey meks 'way wid hit. I can't see whah, jes' now, 'cause yo' noise done clouded dis ball. Come here an' set down agin."

Whimpering, Samba sat down once more. Elias eyed her sternly.

"Samba, yo' whole life's done been cursed by dat evil deed. Now listen to me. Dey is one way fo' you to end yo' days in peace, an' git de bes' o' yo' enemies. Does you want to know dat way?"

Samba's "yes" was smothered in sobs.

Elias nodded his head slowly, sagely.

"Now, dis ve'y night, aftah you leaves heah, walk back de way you come twell you reaches de end of dis lane of trees right befo' my do'. Den take de path dat leads to yo' right.

Follow hit twell you gits to de aidge of de bayou in de cypress swamp by de big cypress what was struck by lightnin' las' summah. Now, when you git there, follow dese directions close.—Is you listenin'?"

Samba nodded mutely.

"Fust, call on de sperrits of de air three times. Name de place whah dat money's hid, an' lif' de curse f'um hit. Jest say, 'Go to—name de place—an' bless what's there. Den, name aloud three times whatever hit is you wants done dis night by de spell I puts on dese token you done brung. Aftah de third time, drop dem in de bayou. Wait right whah you is at on de bayou aidge fo' forty-five minutes. Den go home, an' when you gits da, what-so-never you want did will be did. You got a watch?"

"No."

"Well, heah's my turnip. Dat lantern you got will he'p you see de watch face. You kin return my timepiece in de mornin'."

Samba slipped the watch into her apron pocket. Her hands trembled so that she almost dropped it. At a sign from Elias she arose from the table.

"Remembah, Samba, ef you does one little thing wrong, de curse what you brings on yo' enemy will bounce back on you. Onnerstan'?"

Again Samba nodded. She was past the power of speech. "You's sho'? Well, den, you may go, as soon as—"

Elias paused with a cough intended to be delicately suggestive of what he expected the next step to be.

Turning her back to him, Samba drew from her bosom a bulging, tightly tied handkerchief. Loosening the knots with teeth and fingers, she finally untied it. Holding it carefully by the four corners, she placed the handkerchief on the table and revealed its contents, a pile of quarters, fifty-cent pieces, silver dollars, and an occasional dollar in currency. Together they counted the pile—twenty-five dollars, exactly.

Smiling grimly, Elias said, "T'anks. Now do as I said, an' repo't to me in de mornin', or sometime tomorrow night, ef hit suits yo' modesty bettah."

Mumbling that she would, Samba passed out of the door into the cloudy night. As she moved down the obscured path, the numbing sensation which had enveloped her body seemed now to invade her very brain. She could not think —she dared not. Her mind was a jungle of bewilderment, fear, hate, and wonderment. How had Elias found out all this? Was it really through the crystal, or had he known it all these years—that terrible secret Samba had thought buried with Bob?

Why had Elias directed her to take this path, when the one leading from the west side of his shanty was the shortest and the most direct route? He had made her take the longest and most indirect way, through dense bushes and tall, darkly towering trees. For a moment she was tempted to try the shorter path, but fear of what might be the consequence of such disobedience held her feet in the path Elias had said she must follow.

It was a journey of torture. There was no light save that of her lantern, which served only to make the darkness more dark. The clouds in the sky were now like a heavy black curtain, a canopy drawn close around the earth, shutting out moonlight, starlight, and air. Not daring to look back, hardly daring to go on, fearing almost to put her feet on the ground because of the possibility of stepping on some unseen, fearful night creature that might be in the way, she moved forward. Once, in a pine thicket, some drifting needles sifted against her cheek. She choked back a terrified scream. Again, a dark figure very much like a black cat, scudded across her path into the underbrush.

At last, sheer in her path, like one leg of a black giant whose body reared above the clouds, and whose other leg might be forty leagues away, there rose the trunk of a mighty cypress tree, which had been excoriated by lightning. To Samba, the marks left by the lightning danced and wriggled in the lantern light like so many snakes. On either side of her there spread a dense mass of bushes, tangled grasses, dipping willows whose feathery leaves caressed the black bayou waters, indistinguishable now in the blackness. At the foot of the tree Samba stood still. The deathly silence filled her ears and her heart. The trees and the bushes, save for those that had lately been stirred by her passing, stood like immovable shadows, merging into indissoluble blackness. The yellow flame of the lantern lighted up the ripples in the stygian waters at her feet. A few paces away a bull-frog croaked and plopped suddenly into the inky depth.

Samba tried to stand bravely erect, but the horror and fear of the place bore down her shoulders. A cold, unseen hand was pressing her down, down, upon her knees. She opened her mouth to speak the charm. Once—twice—thrice—before the words finally came:

"Speerits of the air, go to my bedroom, lif' up de hearth-stones, an' lif' de curse, an' bless what's hid beneath it."

Half expecting a ghostly reply, she stopped. A bird roused by the unaccustomed noise chirped sleepily from the trees.

After the third cry, Samba sank down breathless. Would she have the courage to call on the spirits of the air to put the curse upon her enemy? For five minutes she sat at the foot of the cypress tree, panting, gasping, striving to command her voice. At last, she cried:

"Sperrits of the air, set fire to Mark Wesson's new house tonight an' burn it to ashes!"

Utterance of the wish gave strength to her vindictive nature, so that the second and the third times her voice was strong and confident.

When the preying, crouching silence had sprung upon and overpowered the last echo of her voice, Sambra rose to her feet. Bracing herself against the tree trunk, she dropped the three tokens into the water. The hair slid from her grasp like something alive, twining and clutching at her fingers. The pebble-weighted fringe met the water with a soft splash. A thin, swishing sound told of the meeting of the water and the letter.

As the last token fell, Samba was startled by the sudden snapping of a twig behind her. For a second she forgot her perilous position on the edge of the bayou. Then, cautiously, she stepped out of danger and looked around.

Nothing was visible beyond the circle of light cast by the lantern. Picking up the lantern, she turned to go, only to remember that she must remain where she was for forty-five minutes more of fear and terror.

She sank down at the foot of the giant tree, took the watch out of her pocket, and waited—waited—waited. Thrice she screamed aloud; once when an owl in a nearby tree hooted, another time when something long and black with shiny eyes slithered by her in the bayou waters, and a third time when a sudden breeze shook the willow tree close beside her.

But all things come to an end. When forty-five minutes finally crept away, Samba discovered by the watch that it was exactly midnight. Trembling and quivering, she made her way back, muttering, laughing, crying, babbling. When she reached the familiar open road, her legs doubled under her body, and she sank weak and helpless in the dust. Great sobs shook her, and tears rained down to mingle with the powdery yellow dust.

Suddenly, her sobbing ceased. A distant, angry red glow in the skies attracted her attention. The fiery red was in the direction of home. Chuckling, Samba scrambled to her feet. It was a fire, that's what it was. It must be Mark Wesson's place. The charm was undoubtedly working.

A sudden ecstasy made her forgetful of the experience through which she had passed. Wild, mad exultation lent speed to her feet. However, when she arrived at the scene of the fire, the crowd was already scattering. Nothing remained of Wesson's house but a few charred rafters, glowing tin, and red hot nails.

Samba mingled with the crowd so naturally that each group thought she had been with some other group during the entire excitement. She was one of the most sympathetic who spoke to Mark and his family, and she even wrung Amanda's hand in commiseration.

Day was breaking when Samba, the last of the spectators, turned her back on the smoking ashes and smoldering rafters, to enter her own house. As she stepped into her bedroom, her first impulse was to turn up the irregular stones forming the hearth, in order to ascertain whether her treasure still rested in its hiding place. Exhaustion lay so heavily upon her, however, that after a glance to satisfy herself that the stones were in their usual position, she made ready for bed.

It was noon when a sudden loud sound, repeated at irregular intervals, aroused Samba out of a heavy sleep. Drowsily, stupid with fatigue, she raised herself on her elbow to listen. The door was slamming in the kitchen. Climbing out of the high bed, she padded barefoot into the next room. A high wind had risen and was playing havoc with the things in the kitchen, as the rear door swung noisily to and fro. Pulling the door shut, Samba attempted to lock it. A sudden look of surprise swept over her countenance. Then dismay and fear struggled for mastery of her senses.

"Fo' God, dis lock's been broke!"

What did it mean? She knew that she had locked the door before leaving. Never in all the years of her life had she failed to do so. Had someone broken in, under cover of the fire? She had nothing anyone would want. A sudden constriction of her throat made her gasp for breath. Suppose—

Loosing her hold on the door, Samba flew back to her bedroom, knelt by the hearth, and began wildly pawing the stones out of place. Finally they were all thrown back, all over the small room. To Samba's eyes was revealed what had once been a hole, filled with fresh dirt. Screaming, she sprang to her feet and seized a small fire-shovel leaning in one corner of the chimney. As she picked it up, she became aware of bits of fresh, damp dirt clinging to it. Sobbing wildly, talking brokenly, she stuck the shovel into the soil, which, piled loosely, allowed it to sink down, down, down. Desperately she shoveled out pile after pile of loose earth until there was left only a yawning, oblong cavity.

Weak and sick, she sank weeping to the floor. No spirits had done this trick to her. The broken lock, the earth-smeared shovel, and the dirt-filled hole told her better. She had done everything Elias had said. Elias— She checked her sobbing. She sat open-mouthed. Elias—Elias—

With sudden resolution she rose to her feet and began to dress. Now and then she went to the window to look out. Yes, it would rain soon, but she would go. She had to.

A few seconds later, having made the back door fast with a piece of rope, she was on her way to Elias's shack. The first drops of rain were falling as she knocked at his door.

Surprise and great interest shone in Elias's eyes as he opened the door and saw Samba standing on the step. He took her umbrella and assisted her out of the old raincoat she wore.

"Set down! Set down, Samba, I didn't 'spect you 'fo' night. Set down!"

"No, Elias, dis ain't setting down time. I done come to ask you where my treasure be."

"Yo' treasure? Hain't hit whah—"

"No, it ain't, an' somehow I believes you know dat it ain't."

"Now, Samba, I hain't looked in de crystal, an' I hain't t'ought of you sense I put your affair in de hain's of de sperrits. Ef yo' treasure's gone, de sperrits seed fit to tek hit. You bettah thank yo' God dey let you off so easy!"

"Dat's a lie! No sperrits got my money."

"Keerful, keerful! Don't you talk to no conjure man lak dat. Is you lost yo' min'?"

"Los' my min'? Los' my min'?" Samba's voice rose to a shriek. "Los' my min' w'en I ain't got nary a cent in dis worl' an' nary a one to gib me a penny? Los' my min'?"

"Huh! Dat ain't so, an' you knows hit. Whah's dat strappin' boy you still got? Let 'im do somethin' for you."

Samba's voice took on a pleading strain. "Elias, set down an' look in dat crystal an' tell me where my money is."

"Woman, does you want to git found out? How could you 'count for having so much money, even if you knowed who had it now? What kind of a tale would you tell, an' mek any reasonin' person believe it? Ansuh me dat."

Samba sat in silence, head bowed in her hands. Suddenly, a gasp of astonishment tore from between her lips.

With a scream she dropped on her knees and grabbed from the grimy floor an object which had drawn her attention.

"Look! look, Elias!" She waved a long, clumsy, old-fashioned copper key, on whose dull surface glowed three long scratches.

At sight of the key, Elias, who had stepped to Samba's side, recoiled and seized the edge of the table to steady himself. His jaws worked, but he made no sound.

"Dis is de key to dat box, Elias! I knows it by dese scratches what I made de las' time I opened de box. Bob took de key an' de lock from his mother's old armoire."

Samba rose to her feet and faced the conjure man, who was drawing all his wits together for the final cursing of the old woman.

"You got my money yo'self," Samba babbled. "I unnerstan' evahthing now. You wanted me to take de long way to de cypress tree las' night, so's you could go de shortest way and hide behind the bushes an' hear all I was sayin', and then you lit out fo' my house— Gib me back my money!" Her words ended in a wild screech. Elias turned his back on her and walked to the blackened, littered fireplace.

"An' you set fire to Mark Wesson's place, to fool me into thinkin' sperrits did it," Samba wailed, twisting her hands. "You was probably hidin' somewhere about Mistah Joe's house that night they burned it down. You an' he was moughty thick at dat time. You just been waitin' a chance all dese years to git even 'thout hurtin' yo'self. You was too scared of Bob to do anything while he lived. You ain't seed nothin' in de crystal, atall."

Composed once more, Elias turned toward Samba.

"Well, what ef all you say *is* true?" he demanded. "What kin you do about it?"

"Do?" screamed Samba. "Do? I'll have de law on you, an' have yo' 'rested fo' de thievin', house-burnin' scoundrel you is! Dat's what I'll do!"

"An ef you does dat to *me,* jes' what does you 'spec' I'll do to you?" Elias drawled, insolently.

"You—you—wouldn't tell on me, Elias?" quavered the woman.

Clapping his hands to his head, Elias teetered back and forth, roaring with laughter.

"Lissen to dis woman talk. She gwine turn me over to de p'leece, an' yit I mustn't say nothin' 'bout her, under no circumstances. Ain't dat rich!" His voice choked in another outburst of loud laughter.

Samba sank down on the chair. The room with all its grotesque furnishings whirled round and round her. As through a fog, and at an immeasurable distance, she heard Elias's voice.

"Now, I got de upper han', Samba, but I gwine be generous. Oh yes, I gwine be generous. I'll keep de money, an' your secret, too. Youse an ole woman now an' ain't got much longer to live. Dat boy o' yourn kin keep yo' the three, four years yo' got to live. But membah dis," as he shook his dirty finger in her face. "Efn you, or anyone meks one move agin me, I'll tell everything, from A to izzard."

He moved to one side, still keeping his beady eyes on Samba's terrified face.

"Furthermore, I got it all wrote out an' done put it where it kin be got in case anything happens to me, 'fore anything happens to you. Co'se, I won't use it, onless push comes to shove, you onnerstand."

Moaning into her apron, which she had thrown over her face, Samba rocked slowly back and forth.

Crossing the floor, Elias threw open the door, admitting the pelting rain.

"Heah, put on yo' coat, ole woman. Time to be on your way. Come on! Git out! Take your umbrella!"

Samba, her coat hung crookedly about her shoulders, stumbled over the rotted doorsill. The door slammed behind her. Dazedly, mechanically, she raised her umbrella against the slashing rain drops and crept off through the wet grass.

# Justice Wears Dark Glasses

### Grace W. Tompkins

During World War II, African American leaders initiated a "Double Victory" campaign to support the defeat of fascism abroad and the end of discrimination at home. Grace Tompkins's 1944 story, from the short-lived wartime journal *Negro Story*, demonstrates the prevalent mood in the black community that systematic American discrimination could not be forgotten even in wartime. The unflinching story about a black woman's arrest and trial for shoplifting was illustrated by a drawing of a glowering judge in dark glasses brandishing a gavel imprinted with a swastika. Gradually in the 1940s, African American writers broadened their attack on southern social injustice to include the more subtle racial discrimination of the North, where Mamie meets dark justice.

THE GRAY-HAIRED MAN had a kind face, thought Mamie. He would believe her. He removed his glasses and slowly polished them as she nervously shifted from one foot to the other. The big man's hold on her arm tightened as she cleared her throat in an attempt to speak. Carefully replacing his glasses, the man behind the desk spoke,

"Yes, Spraggins?"

"Another one, sir. Stole two dresses."

"I—I—" Mamie's voice died away.

"What are you trying to say?" The man's voice was gentle.

"Mistuh . . . I never stole anything. Just wanted to try on the dresses. . . ."

"Salesgirl saw her duck, sir, caught her with them. Here they are." Spraggins laid the dresses on the desk.

"Yes, sir. I mean, no . . ." Mamie's voice mounted to a wail.

"She wouldn't let me try them on. I asked her, and she . . ."

The gray-haired man held up his hand for silence. He pushed one button in the long row that edged the glass-topped desk. Then he began to write rapidly on a pad of paper. A young woman came in. He detached the sheet and handed it to her, and she left.

An agonizing twitch had set up in Mamie's stomach. She scratched her head nervously and shifted her weight again. The silence only increased her terror. Spraggins cleared his throat, and the sound echoed like a shot in the room.

The man at the desk had not once looked in her direction. She stared hard, trying to catch his eye. You know I didn't steal them, she thought. You're just trying to scare me. She didn't want to wait on me. I didn't steal . . . you know I didn't steal . . . she didn't want to wait to me . . . The sentences chased each other around and around in Mamie's mind, but her throat was dry, and not a word came out.

The office door opened, and the young woman returned with two more. Mamie recognized the salesgirl, but she had never seen the other one.

"Miss Donovan, did you see this theft?"

"Yes, Mr. Feldman."

Mamie was bewildered, for the reply had come from the strange woman.

"And you, too?" He turned to the salesgirl.

"Yes, sir." Her reply was hardly audible, and she reddened.

Mamie found her voice: "No, no. . . . You said I had to ask the floorwalker, and when I tried to talk to him, this man brought me up here!"

"A likely story!" The man behind the desk no longer looked kind and gentle. "You're not only a thief but a liar too. Here are three witnesses who saw you take them.

We're going to teach you . . . you folks to stay out of Manson's, and there's just one way to do it!"

He nodded to Spraggins, who immediately caught Mamie by the arm and started for the door. She struggled. "What are you going to do? What—" Her voice ended in a cry as a vicious upward jerk of her bent arm put an abrupt end to the struggle.

They went down in the freight elevator and out the side door to the rotunda. The blue of the patrol wagon made her wonder who was being arrested. And then she was hustled unceremoniously between two big rough policemen, and the grilled door was slammed shut.

The flies buzzing around a spittoon held Mamie's eyes as she plucked and twisted a corner of her jacket. The mumbled words of the bondsman were lost in the roar of the blood pounding in her ears. A colored policeman stopped to talk to the bondsman. A hopeful gleam lighted Mamie's pain-dulled eyes, but died quickly as the man laughed and sauntered away. After a long wait, she was free to go home until Monday morning. The bondsman had her lone ten-dollar bill in his pocket.

On reaching the street, she found that she did not have carfare. It was a long way to 33rd Street, but she did not have the courage to ask anyone for eight cents. After the first ten blocks she walked in a pain-ridden daze. Passersby thought she was drunk. A man flung a coarse remark at her.

Lena saw her coming and ran down the rickety steps to meet her.

"Mamie! You're sick!"

"I've been arrested."

"Arrested? Jesus!"

Lena helped her into the stuffy bedroom and began taking her street things off. She finally got her to sleep.

Mamie awoke refreshed. Then she remembered, I have to go to court Monday. They arrested me for stealing. I had better get a lawyer, but I haven't any money. She had a strange empty kind of feeling. Lena came in.

"Get dressed," she said. "We're going to see Mr. Clark."

"I ain't got no money to get no lawyer."

"He'll take it in payments. You can't let 'em get away with this."

"They can't do nothin'. I didn't steal them dresses."

"They had you arrested, didn't they? It's a lousy frame! They framed you 'cause they don't want colored people in their damn store. It shoulda been me! You just ain't no fighter!"

"What could I do? The big man grabbed me before you could say 'scat,' and the boss man thought I was lying. Both them women lied. I never even seen the big one with the yellow hair."

"It's a lousy frame. A damn lousy frame!" said Lena.

Mr. Clark was both ponderous and suave. Much of what he said was so veiled in legal terminology that it went over Mamie's head.

"Of course Illinois has a civil rights law under which you may sue when exonerated. Now if you sue for punitive damages the court may award you a dollar. What the hell? It won't pay back what you lose. AND . . . you could go right back in the store again tomorrow and the same thing might happen again. Now if you sue to obtain revocation of license, you won't get to first base. And of course that's all based on your being exonerated."

Mamie looked perplexed.

"Now if they find you guilty—"

"But I ain't," she interrupted him.

"I know, I know." His voice was soothing. "But the law's a funny thing. If those women and the store detective testify under oath that they saw you, then it's your word against three. Of course we can produce character witnesses. Now if you'll . . ."

Court was crowded. Mamie's case was near the end of the docket. Her lawyer sat importantly inside the railing with half a dozen others. She listened carefully to each case, to the testimony of witnesses, to the pleas of the attorneys. Lena patted her hand reassuringly. After six cases in a row had been dismissed for lack of sufficient evidence, she took heart and relaxed a little.

"Manson versus Mamie Jones, shoplifting. Mamie Jones!"

Mamie got to her feet trembling and walked through the enclosure.

As she looked in the face of the judge, her fear left her. To her right stood Spraggins, the two women, and another elderly man, counsel for the store. Her pastor and her doctor had joined her lawyer on the left. Lena stood directly behind her with a protective hand resting on her shoulder. The judge was white haired, and his seamed face was calm. There was an amused twinkle in his eyes as he looked at her, and she almost smiled at him.

Her fear gone, she told her story in a clear steady voice. The judge nodded sympathetically several times as she talked. Then the strange blond woman was talking. She said that she had watched Mamie paw through the dresses on the counter, walk around a bit, and return to the counter. Mamie had taken two dresses and started away.

"Did you say anything to her?" asked the judge.

"No. I thought she was going to approach a salesgirl and try the dresses on."

"Then what happened?"

"She looked around in a furtive sort of way and then started in the direction of the ladies' washroom."

"No . . . I don't even know where the washroom—" began Mamie.

"Please," said the judge.

"A salesgirl accosted her," continued the woman, "and she broke into a run. Mr. Spraggins caught her."

Mamie stared fascinated at the woman as she talked clearly with every evidence of telling the truth. The salesgirl corroborated every word. Spraggins said he had seen the commotion and had arrived in time to see Mamie drop the dresses to the floor.

As Mr. Clark began to talk, Mamie felt a surge of relief.

"Your Honor, this woman had no need to steal. She entered the store in good faith with a ten-dollar bill to buy two of the dresses advertised at $3.99 in the basement sale. She was treated with discourtesy, denied the privilege of trying on her selection, roughly handled by the store detective and the floor walker, and called a liar and a thief by the manager. This woman is respectable. Her reputation is unimpeachable, as these three witnesses will affirm. It is quite obvious that Manson's is trying to intimidate the Negroes who insist upon trading in the store when their publicized policy is not to wait upon colored people."

The last statement brought a quick reprimand and a warning from the judge. He waived the testimony of the character witnesses, and Mamie felt satisfied that she had won.

The lawyer for Manson's was speaking:

"For the past six months, there has been a wave of petty thieving in the store. Women's apparel sections are the hardest hit. We have got to stop it. This woman was caught red-handed. Probably inexperience made her unsuccessful in making away with the merchandise without detection. But the fact remains that three people say the attempt was made. Manson must make an example of her and deter the others with whom she may be associated."

The judge was nodding sympathetically. He turned inquiringly toward Mr. Clark, but the lawyer had nothing to add. The court was very quiet. Mamie was sure every one could hear the pounding of her heart against her ribs. Then the judge began to speak, and his voice was low and friendly:

"I do not believe you are an habitual thief. You work. That is to your credit. Your friends are here in defense of your character as they know it. That is also in your favor. The morale of their working staff must be preserved. I cannot believe that three witnesses have lied under oath. In view of the facts as presented, I have no alternative but to find you guilty and sentence you to thirty days in jail."

In the anteroom, Abe Clark was saying, "My fee is thirty-five dollars. I have a note here for the amount. Will you sign it, please?"

Mamie signed.

# Like a Winding Sheet

## ANN PETRY

The most famous black woman fiction writer of the mid-twentieth century was Ann Petry. Her novels and short stories of the 1940s and 1950s were realistic, socially conscious tales of discrimination and struggle. "Like a Winding Sheet," one of her more famous early stories, is set during wartime, as indicated by the presence of the white female factory manager, probably elevated to that unusual spot because of manpower shortages. Its focus, however, is the effect of racial and class discrimination on the domestic lives of a married couple. Petry subtly demonstrates the disturbing buildup of tensions inside the mind of an otherwise sensitive man provoked into domestic abuse. Petry, like Zora Neale Hurston, was one of the first African American women writers to write explicitly on that theme. Her story shows her commitment to uncompromisingly objective examination of everyday black life. The story first appeared in the November 1945 *Crisis*. It was collected in *Martha Foley's Best American Short Stories of 1946*.

HE HAD PLANNED to get up before Mae did and surprise her by fixing breakfast. Instead he went back to sleep, and she got out of bed so quietly, he didn't know she wasn't there beside him until he woke up and heard the queer soft gurgle of water running out of the sink in the bathroom.

He knew he ought to get up, but instead he put his arms across his forehead to shut the afternoon sunlight out of his eyes, pulled his legs up close to his body, testing them to see if the ache was still in them.

Mae had finished in the bathroom. He could tell because she never closed the door when she was in there and now the sweet smell of talcum powder was drifting down the hall and into the bedroom. Then he heard her coming down the hall.

"Hi, babe," she said affectionately.

"Hum," he grunted, and moved his arms away from his head, opened one eye.

"It's a nice morning."

"Yeah." He rolled over, and the sheet twisted around him, outlining his thighs, his chest. "You mean afternoon, don't ya?"

Mae looked at the twisted sheet and giggled. "Looks like a winding sheet," she said. "A shroud—" Laughter tangled with her words, and she had to pause for a moment before she could continue. "You look like a huckleberry—in a winding sheet—"

"That's no way to talk. Early in the day like this," he protested.

He looked at his arms silhouetted against the white of the sheets. They were inky black by contrast, and he had to smile in spite of himself, and he lay there smiling and savoring the sweet sound of Mae's giggling.

"Early?" She pointed a finger at the alarm clock on the table near the bed and giggled again. "It's almost four o'clock. And if you don't spring up out of there, you're going to be late again."

"What do you mean 'again'?"

"Twice last week. Three times the week before. And once the week before, and—"

"I can't get used to sleeping in the daytime," he said fretfully. He pushed his legs out from under the covers experimentally. Some of the ache had gone out of them, but they weren't really rested yet. "It's too light for good sleeping. And all that standing beats the hell out of my legs."

"After two years you oughta be used to it," Mae said.

He watched her as she fixed her hair, powdered her face,

slipped into a pair of blue denim overalls. She moved quickly, and yet she didn't seem to hurry.

"You look like you'd had plenty of sleep," he said lazily. He had to get up, but he kept putting the moment off, not wanting to move, yet he didn't dare let his legs go completely limp because if he did he'd go back to sleep. It was getting later and later, but the thought of putting his weight on his legs kept him lying there.

When he finally got up, he had to hurry, and he gulped his breakfast so fast that he wondered if his stomach could possibly use food thrown at it at such a rate of speed. He was still wondering about it as he and Mae were putting their coats on in the hall.

Mae paused to look at the calendar. "It's the thirteenth," she said. Then a faint excitement in her voice, "Why, it's Friday the thirteenth." She had one arm in her coat sleeve, and she held it there while she stared at the calendar. "I oughta stay home," she said. "I shouldn't go outa the house."

"Aw, don't be a fool," he said. "Today's payday. And payday is a good luck day everywhere, any way you look at it." And as she stood hesitating, he said, "Aw, come on."

And he was late for work again because they spent fifteen minutes arguing before he could convince her she ought to go to work just the same. He had to talk persuasively, urging her gently, and it took time. But he couldn't bring himself to talk to her roughly or threaten to strike her like a lot of men might have done. He wasn't made that way.

So when he reached the plant he was late, and he had to wait to punch the time clock because the day-shift workers were streaming out in long lines, in groups and bunches that impeded his progress.

Even now, just starting his workday, his legs ached. He had to force himself to struggle past the outgoing workers, punch the time clock, and get the little cart he pushed around all night, because he kept toying with the idea of going home and getting back in bed.

He pushed the cart out on the concrete floor, thinking

that if this was his plant, he'd make a lot of changes in it. There were too many standing-up jobs, for one thing. He'd figure out some way most of 'em could be done sitting down, and he'd put a lot more benches around. And this job he had—this job that forced him to walk ten hours a night, pushing this little cart—well, he'd turn it into a sitting-down job. One of those little trucks they used around railroad stations would be good for a job like this. Guys sat on a seat, and the thing moved easily, taking up little room and turning in hardly any space at all, like on a dime.

He pushed the cart near the foreman. He never could remember to refer to her as the forelady even in his mind. It was funny to have a white woman for a boss in a plant like this one.

She was sore about something. He could tell by the way her face was red and her eyes were half-shut until they were slits. Probably been out late and didn't get enough sleep. He avoided looking at her and hurried a little, head down, as he passed her, though he couldn't resist stealing a glance at her out of the corner of his eyes. He saw the edge of the light-colored slacks she wore and the tip end of a big tan shoe.

"Hey, Johnson!" the woman said.

The machines had started full blast. The whirr and the grinding made the building shake, made it impossible to hear conversations. The men and women at the machines talked to each other, but looking at them from just a little distance away, they appeared to be simply moving their lips because you couldn't hear what they were saying. Yet the woman's voice cut across the machine sounds—harsh, angry.

He turned his head slowly. "Good evenin', Mrs. Scott," he said, and waited.

"You're late again."

"That's right. My legs were bothering me."

The woman's face grew redder, angrier looking. "Half this shift comes in late," she said. "And you're the worst one of all. You're always late. Whatsa matter with ya?"

"It's my legs," he said. "Somehow they don't ever get

rested. I don't seem to get used to sleeping days. And I just can't get started."

"Excuses. You guys always got excuses." Her anger grew and spread. "Every guy comes in here late always has an excuse. His wife's sick or his grandmother died or somebody in the family had to go to the hospital." She paused, drew a deep breath. "And the niggers is the worst. I don't care what's wrong with your legs. You get in here on time. I'm sick of you niggers—"

"You got the right to get mad," he interrupted softly. "You got the right to cuss me four ways to Sunday, but I ain't letting nobody call me a nigger."

He stepped closer to her. His fists were doubled. His lips were drawn back in a thin narrow line. A vein in his forehead stood out swollen, thick.

And the woman backed away from him, not hurriedly but slowly—two, three steps back.

"Aw, forget it," she said. "I didn't mean nothing by it. It slipped out. It was an accident." The red of her face deepened until the small blood vessels in her cheeks were purple. "Go on and get to work," she urged. And she took three more slow backward steps.

He stood motionless for a moment and then turned away from the sight of the red lipstick on her mouth that made him remember that the foreman was a woman. And he couldn't bring himself to hit a woman. He felt a curious tingling in his fingers, and he looked down at his hands. They were clenched tight, hard, ready to smash some of those small purple veins in her face.

He pushed the cart ahead of him, walking slowly. When he turned his head, she was staring in his direction, mopping her forehead with a dark blue handkerchief. Their eyes met and then they both looked away.

He didn't glance in her direction again but moved past the long work benches, carefully collecting the finished parts, going slowly and steadily up and down, back and forth the length of the building, and as he walked he forced himself to swallow his anger, get rid of it.

And he succeeded so that he was able to think about

what had happened without getting upset about it. An hour went by, but the tension stayed in his hands. They were clenched and knotted on the handles of the cart as though ready to aim a blow.

And he thought he should have hit her anyway, smacked her hard in the face, felt the soft flesh of her face give under the hardness of his hands. He tried to make his hands relax by offering them a description of what it would have been like to strike her because he had the queer feeling that his hands were not exactly a part of him anymore— they had developed a separate life of their own over which he had no control. So he dwelt on the pleasure his hands would have felt—both of them cracking at her, first one and then the other. If he had done that, his hands would have felt good now—relaxed, rested.

And he decided that even if he'd lost his job for it, he should have let her have it, and it would have been a long time, maybe the rest of her life, before she called anybody else a nigger.

The only trouble was, he couldn't hit a woman. A woman couldn't hit back the same way a man did. But it would have been a deeply satisfying thing to have cracked her narrow lips wide open with just one blow, beautifully timed and with all his weight in back of it. That way he would have gotten rid of all the energy and tension his anger had created in him. He kept remembering how his heart had started pumping blood so fast he had felt it tingle even in the tips of his fingers.

With the approach of night, fatigue nibbled at him. The corners of his mouth drooped, the frown between his eyes deepened, his shoulders sagged; but his hands stayed tight and tense. As the hours dragged by, he noticed that the women workers had started to snap and snarl at each other. He couldn't hear what they said because of the sound of machines, but he could see the quick lip movements that sent words tumbling from the sides of their mouths. They gestured irritably with their hands and scowled as their mouths moved.

Their violent jerky motions told him that it was getting

close on to quitting time, but somehow he felt that the
night still stretched ahead of him, composed of endless
hours of steady walking on his aching legs. When the whistle finally blew, he went on pushing the cart, unable to
believe that it had sounded. The whirring of the machines
died away to a murmur, and he knew then that he'd really
heard the whistle. He stood still for a moment, filled with a
relief that made him sigh.

Then he moved briskly, putting the cart in the store-
room, hurrying to take his place in the line forming before
the paymaster. That was another thing he'd change, he
thought. He'd have the pay envelopes handed to the people
right at their benches so there wouldn't be ten or fifteen
minutes lost waiting for the pay. He always got home about
fifteen minutes late on payday. They did it better in the
plant where Mae worked, brought the money right to them
at their benches.

He stuck his pay envelope in his pants pocket and followed the line of workers heading for the subway in a slow-
moving stream. He glanced up at the sky. It was a nice
night, the sky looked packed full to running over with stars.
And he thought if he and Mae would go right to bed when
they got home from work, they'd catch a few hours of darkness for sleeping. But they never did. They fooled around—
cooking and eating and listening to the radio, and he always stayed in a big chair in the living room and went almost but not quite to sleep, and when they finally got to
bed, it was five or six in the morning and daylight was already seeping around the edges of the sky.

He walked slowly, putting off the moment when he
would have to plunge into the crowd hurrying toward the
subway. It was a long ride to Harlem, and tonight the
thought of it appalled him. He paused outside an all-night
restaurant to kill time, so that some of the first rush of
workers would be gone when he reached the subway.

The lights in the restaurant were brilliant, enticing.
There was life and motion inside. And as he looked
through the window, he thought that everything within
range of his eyes gleamed—the long imitation marble

counter, the tall stools, the white porcelain-topped tables, and especially the big metal coffee urn right near the window. Steam issued from its top, and a gas flame flickered under it—a lively, dancing, blue flame.

A lot of the workers from his shift—men and women—were lining up near the coffee urn. He watched them walk to the porcelain-topped tables carrying steaming cups of coffee, and he saw that just the smell of the coffee lessened the fatigue lines in their faces. After the first sip their faces softened, they smiled, they began to talk and laugh.

On a sudden impulse he shoved the door open and joined the line in front of the coffee urn. The line moved slowly. And as he stood there, the smell of the coffee, the sound of the laughter and of the voices, helped dull the sharp ache in his legs.

He didn't pay any attention to the white girl who was serving the coffee at the urn. He kept looking at the cups in the hands of the men who had been ahead of him. Each time a man stepped out of the line with one of the thick white cups, the fragrant steam got in his nostrils. He saw that they walked carefully so as not to spill a single drop. There was a froth of bubbles at the top of each cup, and he thought about how he would let the bubbles break against his lips before he actually took a big deep swallow.

Then it was his turn. "A cup of coffee," he said, just as he had heard the others say.

The white girl looked past him, put her hands up to her head, and gently lifted her hair away from the back of her neck, tossing her head back a little. "No more coffee for a while," she said.

He wasn't certain he'd heard her correctly, and he said, "What?" blankly.

"No more coffee for a while," she repeated.

There was silence behind him and then uneasy movement. He thought someone would say something, ask why or protest, but there was only silence and then a faint shuffling sound as though the men standing behind him had simultaneously shifted their weight from one foot to the other.

He looked at the girl without saying anything. He felt his hands begin to tingle, and the tingling went all the way down to his fingertips, so that he glanced down at them. They were clenched tight, hard, into fists. Then he looked at the girl again. What he wanted to do was hit her so hard that the scarlet lipstick on her mouth would smear and spread over her nose, her chin, out toward her cheeks, so hard that she would never toss her head again and refuse a man a cup of coffee because he was black.

He estimated the distance across the counter and reached forward, balancing his weight on the balls of his feet, ready to let the blow go. And then his hands fell back down to his sides because he forced himself to lower them, to unclench them and make them dangle loose. The effort took his breath away because his hands fought against him. But he couldn't hit her. He couldn't even now bring himself to hit a woman, not even this one, who had refused him a cup of coffee with a toss of her head. He kept seeing the gesture with which she had lifted the length of her blond hair from the back of her neck as expressive of her contempt for him.

When he went out the door, he didn't look back. If he had, he would have seen the flickering blue flame under the shiny coffee urn being extinguished. The line of men who had stood behind him lingered a moment to watch the people drinking coffee at the tables, and then they left just as he had without having had the coffee they wanted so badly. The girl behind the counter poured water in the urn and swabbed it out, and as she waited for the water to run out, she lifted her hair gently from the back of her neck and tossed her head before she began making a fresh lot of coffee.

But he had walked away without a backward look, his head down, his hands in his pockets, raging at himself and whatever it was inside of him that had forced him to stand quiet and still when he wanted to strike out.

The subway was crowded, and he had to stand. He tried grasping an overhead strap, and his hands were too tense to grip it. So he moved near the train door and stood there swaying back and forth with the rocking of the train. The roar of the train beat inside his head, making it ache and throb, and the pain in his legs clawed up into his groin so that he seemed to be bursting with pain, and he told himself that it was due to all that anger-born energy that had piled up in him and not been used, and so it had spread through him like a poison—from his feet and legs all the way up to his head.

Mae was in the house before he was. He knew she was home before he put the key in the door of the apartment. The radio was going. She had it tuned up loud, and she was singing along with it.

"Hello, babe," she called out, as soon as he opened the door.

He tried to say hello and it came out half grunt and half sigh.

"You sure sound cheerful," she said.

She was in the bedroom, and he went and leaned against the doorjamb. The denim overalls she wore to work were carefully draped over the back of a chair by the bed. She was standing in front of the dresser, tying the sash of a yellow housecoat around her waist and chewing gum vigorously as she admired her reflection in the mirror over the dresser.

"Whatsa matter?" she said. "You get bawled out by the boss or somep'n?"

"Just tired," he said slowly. "For God's sake, do you have to crack that gum like that?"

"You don't have to lissen to me," she said complacently. She patted a curl in place near the side of her head and then lifted her hair away from the back of her neck, ducking her head forward and then back.

He winced away from the gesture. "What you got to be always fooling with your hair for?" he protested.

"Say, what's the matter with you anyway?" She turned away from the mirror to face him, put her hands on her hips. "You ain't been in the house two minutes and you're picking on me."

He didn't answer her because her eyes were angry and he didn't want to quarrel with her. They'd been married too long and got along too well, and so he walked all the way into the room and sat down in the chair by the bed and stretched his legs out in front of him, putting his weight on the heels of his shoes, leaning way back in the chair, not saying anything.

"Lissen," she said sharply. "I've got to wear those overalls again tomorrow. You're going to get them all wrinkled up leaning against them like that."

He didn't move. He was too tired, and his legs were throbbing now that he had sat down. Besides the overalls were already wrinkled and dirty, he thought. They couldn't help but be, for she'd worn them all week. He leaned farther back in the chair.

"Come on, get up," she ordered.

"Oh, what the hell," he said wearily, and got up from the chair. "I'd just as soon live in a subway. There'd be just as much place to sit down."

He saw that her sense of humor was struggling with her anger. But her sense of humor won because she giggled.

"Aw, come on and eat," she said. There was a coaxing note in her voice. "You're nothing but an old hungry nigger trying to act tough, and"—she paused to giggle and then continued—"you—"

He had always found her giggling pleasant and deliberately said things that might amuse her and then waited, listening for the delicate sound to emerge from her throat. This time he didn't even hear the giggle. He didn't let her finish what she was saying. She was standing close to him, and that funny tingling started in his fingertips, went fast up his arms, and sent his fist shooting straight for her face.

There was the smacking sound of soft flesh being struck by a hard object, and it wasn't until she screamed that he realized he had hit her in the mouth—so hard that the dark red lipstick had blurred and spread over her full lips, reaching up toward the tip of her nose, down toward her chin, out toward her cheeks.

The knowledge that he had struck her seeped through

him slowly, and he was appalled but he couldn't drag his hands away from her face. He kept striking her, and he thought with horror that something inside him was holding him, binding him to this act, wrapping and twisting about him so that he had to continue it. He had lost all control over his hands. And he groped for a phrase, a word, something to describe what this thing was like that was happening to him, and he thought it was like being enmeshed in a winding sheet—that was it—like a winding sheet. And even as the thought formed in his mind, his hands reached for her face again and yet again.

# All That Hair

## MELISSA LINN

Toni Morrison's 1970 novel *The Bluest Eye,* about a young black girl whose esteem suffers because she can't have blue eyes, was the first piece of African American writing to gain popularity while exploring the white standard of beauty and its effects on black women. Melissa Linn's 1946 story "All That Hair" demonstrates that the standard has deep roots. Her sad and profound tale about a young black girl's infatuation with blond hair, and her domestic mother's hurtful response, shows how the glamour, power, and prestige associated with racial characteristics in American culture create fairy-tale identities to which young people especially are always vulnerable. Linn's story took a prize in the 1946 *Negro Story Writer's Digest* contest.

SEVEN-YEAR-OLD MINNIE MAE looked longingly at the sidewalk as she walked from school to her mother's place of work. It was noon. Several little girls passed her without so much as a hello. Minnie Mae knew why they ignored her. She wasn't like them. She didn't have the right kind of hair.

More than anything else in this world, Minnie Mae wanted pretty curly hair crowned by a stiff pink butterfly bow. All the little girls in her room at school had soft, silken, flexible locks, and from her seat in the rear of the room she could look over the room and see all the smooth heads: brown, yellow, black, and red. All of them topped by pink, blue, plaid, or yellow butterfly bows. They were just simply beautiful. Oh, if only she could run a comb through her hair as nonchalantly as Sally Lou and have it leave little rows where the teeth had been! Or to have it fall down into her eyes when she stooped over, or to run in the wind and have it blow before her eyes. But no, she must have these kinky stiff naps that made her cry every time her mother washed them. If only a fairy would come and change her like she did Cinderella! Maybe a fairy would. So Minnie Mae dreamed on as she walked slowly toward the white folks' house where her mother worked and where she ate her lunch every day.

Ever since she could remember she had been going to Mrs. Whitham's to see Mama. Once Mama dressed her up, and she was presented to Mrs. Whitham to speak her Easter piece, then Mrs. Whitham gave her cookies and fifty cents for her new pocketbook. Mrs. Whitham was awfully nice—she was little, almost as little as Minnie Mae. She looked just like a china doll. Her hair was light and curled all over her head in tiny, silken curls. But Mama told Aunt Joe that Mrs. Whitham's hair was false, just like the wigs you wore on Halloween.

Minnie Mae turned up a broad white driveway and followed it around to the back door. She opened a screen door softly and stepped into a clean white kitchen. It was empty. She went on through to the stairs and started softly up. Mama was probably making up the beds, and perhaps she would let her help.

On reaching the top of the stairs, Minnie Mae peered into the first bedroom. It was empty. She tiptoed to the second room and stopped, for there lay Mrs. Whitham, sound asleep. Minnie Mae knew she was asleep, because her eyes were shut and her mouth, hanging loosely open, allowed a thin trickle of saliva to escape and roll down to the pillow. Minnie Mae stared with wide eyes at the white lady because her head was as smooth and shiny as her little baby brother's. It looked just like a new potato that mother had scraped very carefully in order to cream whole.

Close by, on the dresser, where its owner had placed it in order to relieve an aching head, was the wig of beautiful hair, the silken curls shining in the sun. When Minnie Mae saw it, her eyes grew big and she began to breathe harder. If she could just try it on. Oh, if she just dared. She looked again at the sleeping lady, then stepped softly across the room, picked up the wig, and placed it gently on her head.

She looked into the mirror and saw a transformed creature. The inch-long, stubborn, greasy kinks were gone, and silk curls tumbled profusely in their place. Oh, if only she could wear it to school! The kids would like her then. She gave one look at the sleeping lady, then turned and ran quickly out of the room and down the stairs. She stopped. Mama! Where was she? Then she heard a slow boop-a-boop-aboop-aboop—and she knew her mother was washing in the basement. She picked up a piece of cake from the table and ran out of the door. She ran all the way to school, holding the wig on with one hand and thinking all the time. Now maybe Mary Lou, that pretty little fat girl, would play with her at recess. Maybe all the girls, Sally Jane, Lillian, and Ruth, would come and ask her to play jack-stones. Maybe they'd even ask her to come over to their houses after school and play "grown-up." Carried away by her realistic dream, her heart bounded in delightful anticipation, and she reached the school and ran up the steps and into her room.

At first the teacher didn't see her. Then, as a surreptitious tittering arose and gradually grew to open snickering and suppressed laughter, she looked frowningly up. As her eyes focused on Minnie Mae, they widened with incredulity, her large mouth fell open, and red splotches began to spread slowly on her coarse neck. And then the little brown girl, whom class and teacher alike had ignored all year, was suddenly the amused and contemptuous center of attraction.

The child stopped, dismayed. Her eyes, grown enormous, stared in horror and fright from under the white wig. The sound of laughter roared in her ears, and as her heart began to pound with misgivings, the teacher's strident voice cried, "You! Come here!"

At the sound of the angry voice, the laughter ceased, and

it was very quiet in the room. Minnie Mae felt the whole sea of white faces staring, mocking, burning her. Laughing at her. Suddenly everything became blurred, and a greater panic seized upon her, for she felt a wet scalding run down her legs and, to her horror and shame, saw a puddle grow as big as a river at her feet and start rolling down the aisle, under the seats, a long, wide condemning river. They would never like her now!

Shame mingled with the fright, and tears came. Despairing sobs rose in her throat, and she burst into uncontrollable crying. Loud, racking sobs shook her body, and she stood rooted to the spot, her stockings clinging cold and wet to her legs. She bowed her head in the crook of her arm, and the sobs made the absurd white curls of Mrs. Whitham's wig jiggle precariously on the little brown head.

Annoyed and contemptuous, the teacher strode down the aisle, pushed the child into the cloak room, and demanded, "Where did you get that hair?" Minnie Mae was sobbing so much, she couldn't answer, whereupon the teacher half pushed, half shoved her down to the principal's office. That buxom lady gave a glance at the mournful brown girl, her eyes took in the wet soaked stockings, and she told her to go home.

Minnie Mae, crying as though her heart would burst, ran into her mother's place of work, and when that good woman saw her child come in wearing her employer's hair, her heart jumped violently.

"God *a'mighty,* Minnie Mae . . . here—"

Without another word she snatched the wig from the child's head, hastened quick and soft as a cat upstairs where her mistress was still sleeping, and put the wig back in its proper place, then descended rapidly, and shaking the child violently, she whispered fiercely, *"Hush!* Do you want to wake Mrs. Whitham and have her find out you've had her wig, so I'll lose my job? Where would we be then?" She released the child and said, "You go on home, and I'll tend to you tonight after work." She gave the child a shove out the door and turned back to her work, cooking food. She muttered, "Children sure are more bother than they are worth, always doing something to upset folks."

Minnie Mae went slowly out the door, toward her home, and as she walked along in the warm afternoon sun, long shuddering sighs escaped from her heart. By the time she had finished the long walk home, the sighs had stopped, but a new wisdom and sadness was buried deep in a brown child's heart.

# Like One of the Family
# Got to Go Someplace
# Sometimes I Feel So Sorry
# About Those Colored Movies

### Alice Childress

Black female domestics had been literally and figuratively silent in American fiction until Alice Childress found the voice
for the character who inhabits the vignettes in *Like One of the
Family: Conversations from a Domestic's Life*. Published in
1956, the book is a series of imaginary conversations between a
black domestic worker and her friend Marge. The "conversation" ranges, as here, from observations on the subtle pa-
tronization of a white mistress to the more far-reaching topic of
black roles in Hollywood films. Voice is all in these vignettes.
Childress captures the working-class suspicion, the wry satiri-
cal glint, and the potent pride of a relentless rebel for whom
words and talk are the most available means of personal protest and worldly musing.

## Like One of the Family

HI MARGE! I have had me one hectic day. . . . Well, I
had to take out my crystal ball and give Mrs. C . . . a
thorough reading. She's the woman that I took over from
Naomi after Naomi got married. . . . Well, she's a pretty
nice woman as they go, and I have never had too much
trouble with her, but from time to time she really gripes me
with her ways.

When she has company, for example, she'll holler out to
me from the living room to the kitchen: "Mildred dear! Be
sure and eat *both* of those lamb chops for your lunch!"
Now you know she wasn't doing a thing but tryin' to prove

to the company how "good" and "kind" she was to the servant, because she had told me *already* to eat those chops.

Today she had a girlfriend of hers over to lunch, and I was real busy afterward clearing the things away, and she called me over and introduced me to the woman. . . . Oh no, Marge! I didn't object to that at all. I greeted the lady and then went back to my work. . . . And then it started! I could hear her talkin' just as loud . . . and she says to her friend, "We *just* love her! She's *like* one of the family and she *just adores* our little Carol! We don't know *what* we'd do without her! We don't think of her as a servant!" And on and on she went . . . and every time I came in to move a plate off the table, both of them would grin at me like chessy cats.

After I couldn't stand it anymore, I went in and took the platter off the table and gave 'em both a look that would have frizzled a egg. . . . Well, you might have heard a pin drop, and then they started talkin' about something else.

When the guest leaves, I go in the living room and says, "Mrs. C . . . , I want to have a talk with you."

"By all means," she says.

I drew up a chair and read her thusly: "Mrs. C . . . , you are a pretty nice person to work for, but I wish you would please stop talkin' about me like I was a *cocker spaniel* or a *poll parrot* or a *kitten*. . . . Now you just sit there and hear me out.

"In the first place, you do not *love* me; you may be fond of me, but that is all. . . . In the second place, I am *not* just like one of the family at all! The family eats in the dining room, and I eat in the kitchen. Your mama borrows your lace tablecloth for her company, and your son entertains his friends in your parlor, your daughter takes her afternoon nap on the living room couch, and the puppy sleeps on your satin spread . . . and whenever your husband gets tired of something you are talkin' about, he says, 'Oh, for Pete's sake, forget it.' So you can see I am not *just* like one of the family.

"Now for another thing, I do not *just adore* your little

Carol. I think she is a likable child, but she is also fresh and sassy. I know you call it 'uninhibited,' and that is the way you want your child to be, but *luckily* my mother taught me some inhibitions, or else I would smack little Carol once in a while when she's talkin' to you like you're a dog, but as it is, I just laugh it off the way you do because she is *your* child and I am *not* like one of the family.

"Now when you say, 'We don't know *what* we'd do without her,' this is a polite lie . . . because I know that if I dropped dead or had a stroke, you would get somebody to replace me.

"You think it is a compliment when you say, 'We don't think of her as a servant,' but after I have worked myself into a sweat cleaning the bathroom and the kitchen . . . making the beds . . . cooking the lunch . . . washing the dishes and ironing Carol's pinafores . . . I do not feel like no weekend house guest. I feel like a servant, and in the face of that I have been meaning to ask you for a slight raise, which will make me feel much better toward everyone here and make me know my work is appreciated.

"Now I hope you will stop talkin' about me in my presence and that we will get along like a good employer and employee should."

Marge! She was almost speechless, but she *apologized* and said she'd talk to her husband about the raise. . . . I knew things were progressing because this evening Carol came in the kitchen, and she did not say, "I want some bread and jam!" but she did say, *"Please,* Mildred, will you fix me a slice of bread and jam."

I'm going upstairs, Marge. Just look . . . you done messed up that buttonhole!


## Got to Go Someplace

MARGE, I AM VERY SORRY and you will have to excuse me, but I don't feel like devilin' any more eggs, neither do I feel like makin' any more potted ham sandwiches, and furthermore I ain't so hot on goin' on no picnic. . . . Yes,

I know it was my idea, and please don't jump so salty, because I am goin'. No, indeed I would not stand Eddie up. I only said I didn't feel like goin'.

Yes, my mind is disturbed. Now you know I have never been a fearful woman. In fact I have always prided myself on how I'll stand up to anybody, but to tell the God honest truth, I get scared thinkin' of what might happen when you go on a picnic.

It gives me the shivers when I think how they been killin' up our people left and right, and how the law is always lettin' the murderers get away with it! Do you know what happened on the picnic last year? . . . No, not the picnic you went on, but the other one! Well, Stella and Mike, Pearl and Leo and me were drivin' along singin' songs and havin' a nice time, when all these cars came drivin' past us. Guess what? . . . I'll tell you. They were all flyin' Confederate flags and singin' Dixie! They slowed down as they passed us and jeered and hollered a lot of ugly names! There must have been seven or eight cars, and every one of 'em was loaded with screechin' hoodlums! I was some scared. I was afraid that Leo and Mike was gonna get in trouble, especially when I heard Leo say, "Okay, Mike, here's where we take somebody with us, 'cause damn if I'm gonna leave this world by myself!"

Stella started cryin' but Pearl reached down in the lunchbox, got the box of black pepper, and hollered back to me, "The first mother's son that sticks his or her head in this car is gonna get both eyes full of black pepper!" Well, it looked for a while like we was gonna be run off the road, but Leo held that car steady and wouldn't budge a inch. Pearl yelled, "Honey, we gonna hit!" But Leo still held fast to the center of the right lane. Oh yes, they went on after a while, when it looked like it might mean they was gonna crash too!

No, that wasn't all. After we got to the picnic grounds, all we could see was motorcycles roarin' back and forth with Confederate flags on the handlebars. Well, you can imagine how long it took us to get ourselves together, but as hard as it was, we managed to try and enjoy ourselves. When we went to the locker rooms I pointed up to the wall and showed the girls where somebody had written, "niggers not wanted." No, we didn't mention it to the fellas 'cause our day was spoiled enough already. Yes, we had a swim and ate our lunch, even though I couldn't taste it. Afterward when we was drivin' home, we didn't sing, and just before we crossed the tollbridge, a white fella rolled down his car window and asked Leo if he'd give him a match. Leo gave him a dirty look and said, "Hell no!" He looked at us real funny, but we didn't pay him one bit of mind.

Marge, do you remember those two men that was killed in Yonkers just 'cause they went in a bar to buy a drink? . . . No, nothin' at all was done about it except to let the one who did it just go right on about his business! Search your mind and tell me if you remember one time when a white person got the chair or was hanged for killin' one of our folks. Well, if it's ever happened, I've never heard of it!

Don't it give you the goose pimples when you realize that white people can kill us and get away with it? Just think of it! We are walkin' targets everywhere we go—on the subway, in the street, everywhere.

Now I am a good woman, but if I was not, the law is so fixed that I can't go around killin' folks if I want to live myself. But white folks can kill me. And that is why we got to be so cautious even on a picnic.

Of course I'm goin'! I shall take my life in my hands and go to the beach. After all we got to go somewhere . . . sometime.

## Sometimes I Feel So Sorry

YOU OUGHTA HEAR Mrs. B . . . moanin' and groanin' about her troubles. I tell you, if you listen long enough, you just might break down and cry your heart out. That woman don't have nothin' but one problem on top of the other! If it ain't her, it's her husband or her brother or her friends or some everlastin' sorrow tryin' her soul. She's got sixty-'leven jars of face cream and lotions and stuff, but she's gettin' a big frown creased 'cross the front of her forehead just the same.

Girl, you oughta see all the stuff she's got! A handsome mink coat, a big old apartment overlookin' the river, me and a cook and a nurse for the children, a summer cottage in the country, and a little speedboat that she can chug up and down the river in any time she might take the notion. . . . Hello! And what did you say! . . . Yes, indeed, that just should be me!

Today she was almost out of her mind about her brother. Her brother's name is Carl, and he is a caution! Seems like he doesn't know whether to paint pictures or write books, and it just keeps his mind in torment and turmoil. Whenever the problem gets too much for him, he drinks up a case of whiskey and goes into the shakes.

Whenever this happens, they get him into a private home that costs about three hundred dollars a week. He will hang around there while the doctors study his mind for about seven or eight weeks, and then he'll come out again to go through the same merry-go-round all over again.

. . . You ain't heard nothin' yet! She also had a very close friend who was a awful successful actress, but she got to be a dope addict, and Mrs. B—— told me that she got that way 'cause she had so much work and personal appearances 'til it drove her to the drugs. I told her that she could turn down some of that work and do just enough to take it kinda easy-like, but all Mrs. B—— said about that was, "Oh, the poor thing, I feel so sorry for her."

Another time her mother's arm broke out in a little rash, and that thing developed into the biggest long drawn out to-do! The doctors had to analyze that woman's mind for almost a year and even then they couldn't tell whether she had a rash because of her dog's fur or on account of her husband's personality. No, I don't know if the thing is straightened out yet.

This mornin' Mrs. B—— was all tore up because Carl wants to get married. Marge, she is in a pacin'-up-and-down fit! She thinks the girl will aggravate Carl's condition because she can paint pretty pictures, and it will hurt Carl because he can't. Honey, she worries my soul-case out with all them troubles. I have listened to more tales of woe comin' out of that woman. . . . No, she won't want no advice 'cause she never listens to a word you say. I do believe it would break her heart half-in-two if anybody told her somethin' that would end all the misery 'cause she's so used to it by now she wouldn't know what to do without it!

That woman has a pure-artful knack of turnin' the simplest things into a burnin' hellfire *problem*! When she gives a dinner party, she worries herself to death about whether she's invited the *wrong* people and left out the *right* ones! If her daughter ain't laughin' and talkin' every single minute of every single day, she turns herself inside-out worryin' if somethin' is the matter with her. If her husband sneezes, she annoys him to death until he goes to the doctor for a complete check-up. She will eat too much lobster salad and then swear she's got a heart ailment when one of them gas pains hit her in the chest. . . .

Whenever things go kinda smooth-like, she takes time out to worry about the stockmarket and who's gonna be our next president! That poor woman has harried herself into the shadow of a wreck!

Marge, sometimes I think that all she would need to cure her is one good-sized real trouble. You know, like lookin' in your icebox and seein' nothin' but your own reflection! I guess she'd know what trial and trouble really was if she had a child with a toothache, no money, and a dispossess all at the same time! . . . That's what happened to Gloria last spring! . . . Sure, I guess Gloria cried a little, but she took that child to the clinic, and then they moved with her brother for a while, and her brother only had four rooms for his wife and their four children!

. . . Sure, I remember the time you lost your uncle and he didn't have any insurance! And what about the time I had to send all my little savin's down home so that my niece could stay in college? You know everybody's so busy talkin' 'bout us gettin' into these schools 'til it never crosses their mind what a hard time we have stayin' there. It costs money!

I bet Mrs. B—— would think twice about what trouble is if she had one dollar in the house and had to fix dinner for a bunch of kids, like Mrs. Johnson who lives downstairs. She'd also think twice if *her* husband had lost his job 'cause the boss had to cut down and decided to let the colored go first.

. . . Marge, you may be right, perhaps their troubles are as real to them as ours are to us. I don't know about that though. I don't think I'd be goin' through the same miseries if I was in her shoes.

I've seen some trouble in my life, and I know that if I was to call up my aunt and tell her that I'd been too quiet all day or had a hang-over or didn't know whether to paint or write or something like that, she'd say, "Girl, are you out of your mind! Don't be botherin' me with no foolishness!"

## About Those Colored Movies

YOU KNOW ONE THING, Marge, I get really salty sometimes when I listen to some of my people yammerin' away 'bout, "What's wrong with the Negro?", "The trouble with us is we *don't* do this or that," or, "Oh, Lord, when will we learn?" . . . and a whole gang of other remarks like that!

Honestly, Marge, it just bugs me to death! Now it is very true that everyone can stand some correction sometimes, but it gets awful wearisome when it begins to look like we're to blame for everything that happens to us.

For an example, I go to see a lot of movies about colored people, in fact almost all that they put out. I also have seen quite a few of them where they show colored maids and handymen and such. I'm beginnin' to get a little warm under the collar 'bout what they say!

How 'bout them pictures where people are always passin' for white? You know, they are always about some colored person bringin' misery down on themselves by passin' for white. Only the person actin' out the part *is* always white! The one who is tryin' to pass, and I say tryin' 'cause look like they never get away with it in spite of us knowin' that a heap of folks do, well, that person is supposed to make everybody break down and have a good cry 'cause they look white but ain't! I guess the folk who make the movies think that Jim Crow is all right for darker people but is awful unjust if it happens to somebody who is light-complected. It strikes me as awful strange how they wrap everything up so neat and tidy at the end. . . . Well, white people will come to the rescue and point out to the "passer" that it is more honorable to *be what you are* and improve yourself in spite of the fact. Everyone feels real happy in the end 'cause the whites can go away feelin' no fear of bein' married to, bein' the son of, the mother of, or the wife, sister, aunt or cousin of a Negro who lacked the *honor* to inform them of his race. Girl, you know that we know better than that!

Well, the whole situation is sorry enough without them askin' us to believe that them white actors are passin' when we know that they don't *need* to be passin' for white if they *are* white!

I remember seein' another picture that had a colored soldier in it. . . . Oh, no, Marge, he wasn't *passin'* for white, but he was real touchous 'bout bein' *colored*. He got so that he would have spells and things, and finally it bugged him so much that he couldn't walk 'til a nice white doctor called him a nasty name, then he got up and walked! . . . No, Marge, he didn't pop him in the mouth, he just walked. That's psychology.

. . . Yes, I saw that picture 'bout Africa. Wasn't that the one that showed how good white folk can't help no colored folk 'cause they will kill good white people instead of thankin' them? . . . Yes, and didn't it also show how we just won't do right, and it ended up with a nice white man givin' another one some money to help little African boys? . . . Sure, Canada Lee was in that. . . . Yes, he's dead now. He sure was a good actor, but what I liked best was the time I saw him on the stage in a play that was about Haiti. . . . Yes, that was a show where colored folk was doin' right.

No, those kinda movies don't make me as mad as some

'cause at least you do get a chance to see colored playin' all the way through a picture instead of comin' and goin' so quick 'til you could hardly tell they was in it at all. Sometimes when I think on all those little-bitsy parts, it's more than I can understand how they all are so much alike and keep sayin' the same words all the time.

As soon as I see a colored maid that's workin' for somebody, I know that she will have a conniption-fit 'cause the lady she works for won't eat her dinner and before long the maid will say, "You eatin' just like a bird!" Or, "Somethin's worryin' you, chile, and I won't rest 'til I find out what it is!" I know that maids don't be carryin' on like that over the people they work for, at least none of 'em that I've ever met!

I will also bet that we'd never be able to figure out how much brass railin' we have polished up in movin' pictures and how many dishes we've washed and all such as that. Yes, pictures and plays will pretty much show the same kind of thing. It seems that the maid can never be married, or if she is, her husband always has to be no good, but contrary to real life, she likes him 'cause he's that way and will say somethin' like, "I don't know why I *likes* that man. I guess it's 'cause he keeps me laughin' all the time! He won't come home, and I hate to tell it, but I don't think he's none too crazy 'bout workin', but Lord! when that man hears music, he just can' keep still, he ain't much good, but I guess he's all I got, and no matter how he does, I just can' do without him!" Ain't that disgustin'?

What gets me is how the audience seems to go for that stuff and will be blowin' their noses and wipin' their eyes 'cause they're so *touched*. . . . Yes, anybody that believes all that mess is *touched*, all right, touched in the head!

. . . No, Marge, they're not pinnin' as many bandana handkerchiefs on our heads these days, but they get the same result in other ways. Sometimes they will dress up the maid in a frumpy old black dress and a black straw hat sittin' up on top of her head, and she will walk right nice and dignified-like, but when you boil everything down to the nitty-gritty she'll be talkin' the same old line!

Yes, I bet a whole lot of folks is real disappointed 'cause the maids they hire ain't like that at all! If the truth was to be known, they'd be searchin' a devilish long time before they found one, too!

Why, it gets so that every time I see colored comin' on in a picture, I kind of hold my breath 'cause I don't know if I can stand how they gonna have him actin'! Ain't that a shame? Who writes all that mess anyway? . . . I know it can't be the actors 'cause they sure would like to look better than that! It's a sin and shame the way they show colored people!

. . . No, I don't mean just us either! I can't see why a white man always got to play the part of a American Indian. I'm that tired of lookin' at blue-eyed Indian chiefs! Seems awful mean that they can't have a Indian play the Indian *sometimes.* And you never get to see no Chinese unless they're comical or lurkin' 'round in the shadows, waitin' to jump somebody or somethin' like that.

. . . How 'bout that! Sure, they show these pictures and plays all over the world! Marge, can you imagine some of these things bein' shown in countries where they have never had the chance to meet any colored? I bet they think that we act just the way the pictures and the plays show! . . . That's right and if they ever meet *me,* they gonna get on the wrong side of my list almost as soon as they open their mouth!

They're gonna come walkin' up to me expectin' me to laugh and grin, sing 'em a song, do a little jig for 'em, act simple and foolish, be lovable and childish, be bowin' and scrapin', and keep 'em laughin' at every word I say. I can tell you now that if that was to happen, I would most likely forget that they got them notions from some play or book, I would be too mad to be calm and cool and explain to them just what kind of person I am! I would probably cuss 'em out before I could do anything else. "What's the matter with you?" I would say. "Don't come walkin' up to me and actin' like I'm some puppy-dog or pet bird or somethin'! Are you out of your mind?" And then they would back up from me and say to their friends, "They're not like we thought they was at all. Here we was thinkin' that they laugh and play all the time and the truth is, they are *mean*!"

Yes, that would be a shame, Marge. But it's not my fault that they got all the wrong notions 'bout me, and before I could feel sorry for what they don't know, we would have had a big fuss and busted-up friendship before we even got to be friends!

. . . Yes, that's true, too! We have seen some nice plays in the churches and halls here in Harlem. But hardly anybody ever gets to see 'em but us!

. . . Oh, girl, stop talkin' 'bout the Federal Theatre, or people will find out our right age! . . . Sure, I recall some of the plays they did. Remember one called *Turpentine*? . . . That's right they did have one called *Noah* and another named *Sweet Land,* and how 'bout when they did *Macbeth*! . . . You sure are good at rememberin' names. Yes, there was Lionel Monagus, Mercedes Gilbert, Georgette Harvey, Thomas Mosely, Frank Wilson, Bebe Townsend, Hayes Pryor, A. B. DeComathier, Laura Bowman, Alberta Perkins, and Jacqueline Andre. . . . Oh, no, Marge, all of them wasn't on the Federal Theatre. You must have seen some of 'em someplace else! . . . Do you remember Monty Hawley? . . . Yes, a lot of 'em were *great* actors. . . . When I get to thinkin' 'bout how some folks never got to see them at all, it just tears me up. Didn't they miss somethin'!

Marge, a number of those actors are dead now. . . . I only wish that all the old-timers that are livin' and these new actors that are comin' up now will make some pictures and plays sometimes that we could be real proud about. . . . Yes, I know that *they* don't pick out the stories, but, after all, *somebody* does.

# Has Anybody Seen
# Miss Dora Dean?

ANN PETRY

Ann Petry's mastery of the classically well-wrought short story
merges with her gift for biting social criticism in this story, first
published in a 1958 *New Yorker*. The mystery at the heart of
"Has Anybody Seen Miss Dora Dean?" may be read as many
things: a symbol of the relative rarity of black suicide; shame
and denial in a community that has lost one of its own; a
strong woman's need to keep hidden a husband's secret; the
psychological cost for the traditionally black servant class in
America that must, in Paul Laurence Dunbar's famous coin-
age, "wear the mask that grins and lies" in the face of white
power and property. Petry invites readers to consider all of
these questions through a narrator herself distant from the life
of the story's deceased main character. Even the title of the
story, and the object of the song it refers to, are riddles Petry
suggests contain keys to the hidden injuries and desires of
some African American lives. The story is also contained in
*Miss Muriel and Other Stories* (1971).


ONE AFTERNOON LAST WINTER, when the telephone rang in my house in Wheeling, New York, I started
not to answer it; it was snowing, I was reading a book I had
been waiting for weeks to get hold of, and I did not want to
be disturbed. But it seemed to me that the peals of the bell
were longer, more insistent than usual, so I picked up the
phone and said, "Hello."

It was Peter Forbes—and neither that name nor any
other is the actual one—and he was calling from

Bridgeport. He said abruptly, and wheezily, for he is an asthmatic, "Ma is terribly ill. Really awfully sick."

He paused, and I said I was very sorry. His mother, Sarah Forbes, and my mother had grown up together in a black section of Bridgeport.

Peter said, "She's got some dishes she wants you to have. So will you come as soon as you can? Because she is really very sick."

I had heard that Sarah, who was in her seventies, was not well, but I was startled to learn that she was "terribly ill," "really very sick." I said, "I'll come tomorrow. Will that be all right?"

"No, no," he said. "Please come today. Ma keeps worrying about these dishes. So will you please come—well, right away? She is really terribly, terribly ill."

Knowing Sarah as well as I did, I could understand his insistence. Sarah had an unpleasant voice; it was a querulous, peevish voice. When she was angry or irritated, or wanted you to do something that you did not want to do, she talked and talked and talked, until finally her voice seemed to be pursuing you. It was like a physical pursuit from which there was no escape.

I said, "I'll leave right away," and hung up.

It took me three hours to drive from Wheeling to Bridgeport, though the distance is only forty-five miles. But it is forty-five miles of winding road—all hills and sharp curves. The slush in the road was beginning to freeze, and the windshield wiper kept getting stuck; at frequent intervals I had to stop the car and get out and push the snow away so that the wiper could function again.

During that long, tedious drive, I kept thinking about Sarah and remembering things about her. It was at least two years since I had seen her. But before that, over a period of twenty years, I had seen her almost every summer, because Peter drove over to Wheeling to go fishing, and his mother came too. She usually accompanied him whenever he went out for a ride. He would leave her at my house, so that she could visit with me while he and his two boys went fishing.

I thoroughly enjoyed these visits, for Sarah could be utterly charming when she was so minded. She was a tall woman with rather bushy black hair that had a streak of gray near the front. Her skin was a wonderful reddish brown color and quite unwrinkled, in spite of her age. She would have been extremely attractive if she hadn't grown so fat. All this fat was deposited on her abdomen and behind. Her legs had stayed thin, and her feet were long and thin, and her head, neck, and shoulders were small, but she was huge from waist to knee. In silhouette, she looked rather like a pouter pigeon in reverse. Her legs were not sturdy enough to support so much weight, and she was always leaning against doors, or against people, for support. This gave her an air of helplessness, which was completely spurious. She had a caustic sense of humor, and though she was an old woman, if something struck her as being funny, she would be seized by fits of giggling just as if she were a very young and silly girl.

I knew a great deal about Sarah Forbes. This knowledge stemmed from a long-distance telephone call that she made to my mother thirty-three years ago, when I was nine years old. I overheard my mother's side of the conversation. I can still repeat what she said, word for word, even imitating the intonation, the inflection of her voice.

In those days we lived in the building that housed my father's drugstore, in Wheeling. Our kitchen was on the ground floor, behind the store, and the bedrooms were upstairs, above it. Just as other children sat in the family living room, I sat in the drugstore—right near the front window on a bench when the weather was cold, outside on the wooden steps that extended across the front of the building when the weather was warm. Sitting outside on those splintery steps, I could hear everything that went on inside. In summer, the big front door of the store stayed wide open all day, and there was a screen door with fancy scrollwork on all the wooden parts. There were windows on either side of the door. On each window my father had painted his name in white letters with the most wonderful curlicues and flourishes, and under it the word "Druggist." On one window it said "Cold Soda," and on the other window "Ice Cream," and over the door it said "Drug Store."

Whether I sat inside the store or outside it, I had a long, sweeping view of the church, the church green, and the street. The street was as carefully composed as a painting: tall elm trees, white fences, Federal houses.

If I was sitting outside on the steps, listening to what went on in the store, no one paid any attention to me, but if I was sitting inside on the bench near the window, my mother or my father would shoo me out whenever a customer reached the really interesting part of the story he was telling. I was always being shooed out until I discovered that if I sat motionless on the bench, with a book held open in front of me, and did not glance up, everyone forgot about me. Occasionally, someone would stop right in the middle of a hair-raising story, and then my father would say, "Oh, she's got her nose in a book. She's just like she's deaf when she's got her nose in a book. You can say anything you want to, and she won't hear a word." It was like having a permanent season ticket in a theater where there was a continuous performance and the same play was never given twice.

My special interest in Sarah dates from a rainy afternoon when I was sitting inside the store. It was a dull afternoon—no customers, nothing, just the busy sound of rain dripping from the eaves, hitting the wooden steps. The wall telephone rang, and my mother, wiping her hands on her apron, came to answer it from the kitchen, which was just behind the prescription room of the store. Before she picked up the receiver, she said, "That's a long-distance call. I can tell by the way the operator is ringing. That's a long-distance call."

I sat up straight, I picked up my book, and I heard the tinkling sound of money being dropped in at the other end. Then I heard my mother saying, "Why, Sarah, how are you? . . . What? What did you say? . . . Found him? Found him where?" She listened. "Oh, *no!*" She listened again. "Oh, my dear! Why, how dreadful! Surely an accident. You think—!" A longer period of listening. "Oh, no. Why that's impossible. Nobody would deliberately—" She didn't finish what she was going to say, and listened again. "A letter? Forbes left a letter? Tear it up! You mustn't let anyone know that—" There was a long pause. "But you must think of Peter. These things have an effect on—excuse me."

She turned and looked at me. I had put the book down on the bench, and I was staring straight at her, breathing quite fast and listening so intently that my mouth was open.

She said, "Go out and play."

I kept staring at her, not moving, because I was trying to figure out what in the world she and Sarah Forbes had been discussing. What had happened that no one must know about?

She said again, her voice rising slightly, "Go out and play."

So I went the long way, through the back of the store and the prescription room and the kitchen, and I slammed the back door, and then I edged inside the prescription room again, very quietly, and I heard my mother say, "He must have had a heart attack and fallen right across the railroad tracks just as the train was due. That's the only possible explanation. And, Sarah, burn that letter. Burn it up!" She hung up the phone, and then she said to herself, "How dreadful. How perfectly dreadful!"

Whether Sarah took my mother's advice and burned Forbes's letter I do not know, but it became common knowledge that he had committed suicide, and his death was so reported in the Bridgeport newspapers. His body had been found on the railroad tracks near Shacktown, an outlying, poverty-stricken section of Bridgeport, where the white riffraff lived and the lowest brothels were to be found. He was the only person that my father and my mother and my aunts had ever known who had killed himself, and they talked about him endlessly—not his suicide but his life as they had known it. His death seemed to have put them on the defensive. They sounded as though he had said to them, "This life all of us black folk lead is valueless; it is disgusting, it is cheap, it is contemptible, and I am throwing it away, so that everyone will know exactly what I think of it." They did not say this, but they sounded perplexed and uneasy whenever they spoke of Forbes, and they seemed to feel that if they could pool their knowledge of him, they might be able to reach some acceptable explanation of why he had killed himself. I heard Forbes and Sarah discussed, off and on, all during the period of my growing up.

I never saw Forbes. The Wingates, an enormously wealthy white family for whom he worked, had stopped coming to Wheeling before I was born, and he had stopped coming there too. But I heard him described so often that I knew exactly what he looked like, how he sounded when he talked, what kind of clothes he wore. He was a tall, slender black man. He was butler, social secretary, gentleman's gentleman. When Mr. Wingate became ill, he played the role of male nurse. Then, after Mr. Wingate's death, he ran the house for Mrs. Wingate. He could cook, he could sew, he could act as coachman if necessary; he did all the buying and all the hiring.

The Wingates were summer residents of Wheeling. Their winter home was in Bridgeport. In Wheeling, they owned what they called a cottage; it was an exact replica of an old Southern mansion—white columns, long graveled driveways, carefully maintained lawns, brick stables, and all within six hundred feet of Long Island Sound.

During the summer, Forbes rode a bicycle over to my father's drugstore every pleasant afternoon. He said he needed the exercise. Whenever I heard my family describing Forbes, I always thought how dull and uninteresting he must have been. There would never be anything unexpected about him, never anything unexplained. He would always move exactly as he was supposed to when someone pulled the proper strings. He was serious, economical, extremely conservative—a tall, elegant figure in carefully pressed black clothes and polished shoes. His voice was slightly effeminate, his speech very precise. Mrs. Wingate was an Episcopalian, and so was Forbes.

But one day when my father was talking about Forbes, some six months after his death, he suddenly threw his head back and laughed. He said, "I can see him now, bicycling down the street, with those long legs of his pinched up in those straight tight pants he wore, pumping his legs up and down, and whistling 'Has Anybody Seen Miss Dora Dean?' with his coattails flying in the wind. I can see him now." And he laughed again.

At the time, I could not understand why my father should have found this funny. Years later, I learned that the tune Forbes whistled was one that Bert Williams and George Walker, a memorable team of black comedians, had made famous along with their cakewalk. They were singing "Dora Dean" in New York in about 1896. Dora Dean, the girl of the song, played the lead in a hit show called *The Creole Show,* which was notable for a chorus of sixteen beautiful brown girls. I suppose it amused my father to think that Forbes, who seemed to have silver polish in his veins instead of good red blood, should be whistling a tune that suggested cakewalks, beautiful brown girls, and ragtime.

Mrs. Wingate's name entered into the discussions of Forbes because he worked for her. It was usually my mother who spoke of Mrs. Wingate, and she said the same thing so often that I can quote her: "Mrs. Wingate always said she simply couldn't live without Forbes. She said he planned the menus, he checked the guest lists, he supervised the wine cellar—he did everything. Remember how she used to come into the store and say he was her mind, her heart, her hands? That was a funny thing to say, wasn't it?" There would be a pause, and then she would say, "Wasn't it too bad that she let herself get so fat?"

It was from my mother that I learned what Mrs. Wingate looked like. She was short and blond, and her face looked like the face of a fat china doll—pink and white and round. She used rice powder and rouge to achieve this effect. She bought these items in our drugstore. The powder came wrapped in thin white paper with a self stripe, and the rouge came in little round cardboard boxes, and inside there was a round, hard cake of reddish powder and a tiny powder puff to apply it with. She must have used a great deal of rouge, because at least once during the summer she would send Forbes up to the drugstore with a carton filled with these little empty rouge boxes. He would put them on the counter, saying, in his careful, precise, high-pitched voice, "Mrs. Wingate thought you might be able to use these." My father said he dumped them on the pile of rubbish in back of the store, to be burned, wondering what in the world she thought he would or could use them for. They smelled of perfume, and the reddish powder had discolored them, even on the outside.

Mrs. Wingate grew fatter and fatter, until, finally, getting her in and out of carriages, and then, during a later period, in and out of cars—even cars that were specially built—was impossible unless Forbes was on hand.

Forbes was lean, but he was wiry and tremendously strong. He could get Mrs. Wingate in and out of a carriage or a car without effort; at least he gave the illusion of effortlessness. My father said it was Mrs. Wingate who panted, who frowned, whose flesh quivered, whose forehead was dampened with sweat.

My father always ended his description of this performance by saying, "Remember how he used to have that white woman practically on his back? Yes, sir, practically on his back."

After I heard my father say that, I retained a curious mental picture of Forbes—a lean, wiry black man carrying an enormously fat pink and white woman piggyback. He did not lean over or bend over under the woman's weight; he stood straight, back unbent, so that she kept sliding down, down, down, and as he carried this quivering, soft-fleshed Mrs. Wingate, he was whistling "Has Anybody Seen Miss Dora Dean?"

I don't know that Forbes was actually looking for a reasonable facsimile of Dora Dean, but he found one, and he fell in love with her when he was forty years old. That was in 1900. He was so completely the perfect servant, with no emotional ties of his own and no life of his own, that my family seemed to think it was almost shocking that his attention should have been diverted from his job long enough to let him fall in love.

But it must have been inevitable from the first moment he saw Sarah Trumbull. I have a full-length photograph of her taken before she was married. She might well have been one of those beautiful girls in *The Creole Show*. In the photograph, she has a young, innocent face—lovely eyes, and a pointed chin, and a very pretty mouth with a quirk at the corner that suggests a sense of humor. Her hair is slightly frizzy, and it is worn in a high, puffed-out pompadour, which serves as a frame for the small exquisite face. She is wearing a shirtwaist with big stiff sleeves, and a tight choker of lace around her throat. This costume makes her waist look tiny and her neck long and graceful.

My mother had been born in Bridgeport, and though she was older than Sarah, she had known her quite well. Sarah was the only child of a Baptist minister, and, according to my mother's rather severe standards, she was a silly, giggling girl with a reputation for being fast. She was frivolous, flirtatious. She liked to play cards and played pinochle for money. She played the violin very well, and she used to wear a ring with a diamond in it on her little finger, and just before she started to play, she would polish it on her skirt, so that it would catch the light and wink at the audience. She had scandalized the people in her father's church because she played ragtime on the piano at dances, parties, and cakewalks. (I overheard my father say that he had always heard this called "whorehouse music"; he couldn't understand how it got to be "ragtime.")

Anyway, one night in 1900 Forbes had a night off and went to a dance in New Haven, and there was Sarah Trumbull in a white muslin dress with violet ribbons, playing ragtime on the piano. And there was a cakewalk that night, and Forbes and Sarah were the winners. I found a yellowed clipping about it in one of my mother's scrapbooks—that's how I know what Sarah was wearing.

I have never seen a cakewalk but I have heard it described. About fourteen couples took part, and they walked in time to music—not in a circle but in a square, with the men on the inside. The participants were always beautifully dressed, and they walked with grace and style. It was a strutting kind of walk. The test of their skill lay in the way they pivoted when they turned the corners. The judges stopped the music at intervals and eliminated possibly three couples at a time. The most graceful couple was awarded a beautifully decorated cake, so that they had literally walked to win a cake.

In those days, Sarah Trumbull was tall, slender, and graceful, and John Forbes was equally tall, slender, and graceful. He was probably very solemn, and she was probably giggling as they turned the corners in a cakewalk.

A year later, they were married in the Episcopal church (colored) in Bridgeport. Sarah was a Baptist and her father was a Baptist minister, but she was married in an Episcopal church. If this had been a prize fight, I would say that Mrs. Wingate won the first round on points.

When my family discussed Forbes, they skipped the years after his marriage and went straight from his wedding to Sarah Trumbull in an Episcopal church (colored) to his death, twenty-four years later. Because I knew so little of the intervening years, I pictured him as being as ageless as a highly stylized figure in a marionette show—black, erect, elegantly dressed, effeminate, temperamental as a cat. I had never been able to explain why our cats did the things they did, and since there did not seem to be any reasonable explanation for Forbes's suicide, I attributed to him the unreasonableness of a cat.

The conversations in which my parents conjectured why Forbes killed himself were inconclusive and repetitive. My mother would sigh and say that she really believed Forbes killed himself because Sarah was such a slovenly housekeeper—that he just couldn't bear the dirt and the confusion in which he had to live, because, after all, he was accustomed to the elegance of the Wingate mansion.

My father never quite agreed. He said, "Well, yes, except that he'd been married to Sarah for twenty years or so. Why should he suddenly get upset about dirt after all that time?"

Once, my mother pressed him for his point of view, and he said, "Maybe he was the type that never should have married."

"What do you mean by that?"

"Well, he'd worked for that Mrs. Wingate, and he waited too long to get married, and then he married a young girl. How old was Sarah—twenty, wasn't she? And he was forty at the time, and—"

"Yes, yes," my mother said impatiently. "But what did you mean when you said he was a type that never should have married?"

"Well, if he'd been another type of man, I would have said there was more than met the eye between him and Mrs. Wingate. But he was so ladylike there couldn't have been. Mrs. Wingate thought a lot of him, and he thought a lot of Mrs. Wingate. That's all there was to it—it was just like one of those lifetime friendships between two ladies."

" 'Between two ladies'!" my mother said indignantly. "Why, what a wicked thing to say! Forbes was— Well, I've never seen another man, white or black, with manners like his. He was a perfect gentleman."

"Too perfect," my father said dryly. "That type don't make good husbands."

"But something must have *happened* to make him kill himself. He was thrifty and hard-working and intelligent and honest. Why should he kill himself?"

My father tried to end the conversation. "It isn't good to keep talking about the dead like this, figuring and figuring about why they did something—it's like you were pulling at them, trying to pull them back. After all, how do you know but you might succeed in bringing them back? It's best to let them alone. Let Forbes alone. It isn't for nothing that they have that saying about let them rest in peace."

There was silence for a while. Then my mother said softly, "But I do wish I knew why he killed himself."

My father said, "Sarah told you he said in the letter he was tired of living. I don't believe that. But I guess we have to accept it. There's just one thing I'd like to know."

"What's that?"

"I keep wondering what he was doing in Shacktown. That seems a strange place for a respectable married man like Forbes. That's where all those barefooted foreign women live, and practically every one of those orange-crate houses they live in has a red light in the window. It seems like a strange part of the city for a respectable married man like Forbes to have been visiting."

By the time I was ten, Forbes's death had for me a kind of reality of its own—a theatrical reality. I used to sit on the steps in front of the drugstore and half close my eyes so that I could block out the church green and the picket fences and the elm trees and the big old houses, and I would pretend that I was looking at a play instead. I set it up in my mind's eye. The play takes place on the wrong side of the railroad tracks, where the land is all cinders, in a section where voluptuous, big-hipped foreign women go barefooted, wrap their heads and shoulders in brilliant red and green shawls, and carry bundles on their heads—that is, those who work. Those who do not work wear hats with so many feathers on them, they look as if they had whole turkeys on their heads. The houses in this area are built entirely of packing cases and orange crates. There is the sound of a train in the distance, and a thin, carefully dressed black man, in a neat black suit and polished shoes, walks swiftly onstage and up the slight incline toward the railroad tracks—no path there, no road. It is a winter's night and cold. This is Forbes and he is not wearing an overcoat.

As narrator for an imaginary audience, I used to say, "What is he doing in this part of town in his neat black suit and his starched white shirt? He could not possibly know anyone here in Shacktown, a place built of cinders and packing cases. Bleak. Treeless. No road here. What is he doing here? Where is he going?"

The train whistles, and Forbes walks up the embankment and lies down across the tracks. The train comes roaring into sight, and it slices him in two—quickly, neatly. And the curtain comes down as a telephone rings in a drugstore miles away.

This picture of Forbes remained with me, unchanged; I still see him like that. But in the intervening years Sarah changed. My first distinct recollection of her was of a stout middle-aged woman with a querulous voice, which was always lifted in complaint. Her complaint centered on money —the lack of it, the importance of it. But even in middle age there were vestigial remains of the girl who scandalized the religious black folk of Bridgeport by pounding out whorehouse music on the piano, and who looked as though she had just stepped out of the chorus line of *The Creole Show:* the wonderful smooth reddish brown skin, the giggle over which she seemed to have no control, and the flirtatious manner of a Gay Nineties beauty. The coyness and the fits of giggling she had as an old woman were relics of these mannerisms.

I got to Bridgeport just at dusk. As I rang the bell of the two-story frame house where Sarah lived, I remembered something. This was the house that Mrs. Wingate had given to Forbes and Sarah as a wedding present. They had lived in it together exactly three weeks, and then Forbes went back to live at the Wingate mansion. Mrs. Wingate had asked him to come back because she might want to go out at night, and how could she get in and out of a car without him? It would be very inconvenient to have to wait for him to come all the way from the other side of town. (The Wingate mansion was at the south end of the city, and the dark brown, two-story taxpayer was at the north end of the city.) Mrs. Wingate had said that Sarah would, of course, stay where she was. She increased Forbes's wages and promised to remember him most generously in her will.

"It was a funny thing," my mother once said. "You know,

Sarah used to call Forbes by his first name, John, when he was courting her, and when they were first married. After he went back to live at Mrs. Wingate's, she called him Forbes. All the rest of his life, she called him by his last name, just as though she was talking to Mrs. Wingate's butler."

One of Peter Forbes's gangling boys—Sarah's younger grandson—opened the door, and I stopped thinking about the past. He was a nice-mannered, gentle-looking boy, tall and thin, his face shaped rather like Sarah's in the old photograph—a small-boned face. His skin was the same wonderful reddish-brown color. I wondered why he wasn't in school and immediately asked him.

"I've finished," he said. "I finished last June. I'm eighteen, and I'm going in the Army."

I said what most people say when confronted by evidence of the passage of time. "It doesn't seem possible."

He said, "Yeah, that's right," took a deep breath, and said, "Nana's in the bedroom. You'd better come right in."

He seemed to be affected by the same need for haste that had made his father urge me to come see Sarah right away. I did not pause even long enough to take my coat off; I followed him down a dark hall, trying to remember what his real name was. Sarah had brought Peter's children up. Peter had been married to a very nice girl, and they had two boys. The very nice girl left Peter after the second baby was born and never came back. Sarah had given nicknames to the boys; the older was called Boodie, and the younger was Lud. It was Lud who had answered the door. I could not remember anything but the nickname—Lud.

We entered a bedroom at the back of the house. The moment I saw Sarah, I knew that she was dying. She was sitting slumped over in a wheelchair. In the two years since I had seen her, she had become a gaunt old woman with terrible bruised shadows under her eyes, and she was so thin that she looked like a skeleton. Her skin, which had been that rich reddish brown, was now overlaid with gray.

Lud said, "Nana, she's here. She's come, Nana."

Sarah opened her eyes and nodded. The eyes that I had

remembered as black and penetrating were dull, and their color had changed; they were light brown. I bent over and kissed her.

"I'm not so bright today," she said, and the words came out slowly, as though she had to think about using the muscles of her throat, her tongue, her lips—had to think, even, before she breathed. After she finished speaking, she closed her eyes and she looked as though she were already dead.

"She isn't asleep," Lud said. "You just say something to her. She'll answer—won't you, Nana?"

Sarah did not answer. I took off my coat, for the heat in the room was unbearable, and I looked around for a place to put it and laid it on a chair, thinking that the room had not changed. It was exactly as I remembered it, and I had not been in it for twenty years. There was too much furniture, the windows were heavily curtained, there was a figured carpet on the floor, and a brass bed, a very beautiful brass bed; one of the walls was covered with framed photographs.

A white cat darted through the room, and I jumped, startled, remembering another white cat that used to dart through these same rooms—but that was twenty years ago. "That's surely not the same cat, Lud? The one you've always had?"

"We've had this one about three years."

"Oh. But the other cat was white, too, wasn't it? It was deaf, and it had never been outside the house—isn't that right? And it had blue eyes."

"So's this one. He doesn't go outside. He's deaf and he's got blue eyes." Lud grinned and his face was suddenly lively and very young. "And he's white," he said, and then laughed out loud. "Nana calls him our white folks."

"What's the cat's name?"

"Willie."

That was the name of the other cat, the one I had known. And Willie, so Sarah Forbes had said (boasted, perhaps?) —Willie did not like men. I wondered if this cat did.

"Is he friendly?"

"No," Lud said.

"Doesn't like men," Sarah Forbes said. Her voice was strong and clear, and it had its old familiar querulousness. The boy and I looked at her in surprise. She seemed about to say something more, and I wondered what it was going to be, for there was a kind of malevolence in her expression.

But Peter Forbes came into the room, and she did not say anything. We shook hands and talked about the weather, and I thought how little he had changed during the years I had known him. He is a tall, slender man, middle-aged now, with a shaggy head and a petulant mouth that had deeply etched lines at the corners.

At the sight of Peter, Sarah seemed to grow stronger. She sat up straight. "Wheel me out to the dining room," she ordered.

"Yes, Ma," he said obediently. The wheelchair made no sound. "You come, too," he said to me.

"There's some china . . ." Sarah's voice trailed off, and she was slumping again, almost onto one arm of the wheelchair, her arms, head, and neck absolutely limp. She looked like a discarded rag doll.

We stood in the dining room and looked at her, all three of us. I said, "I'd better go. She's not well enough to be doing this. She hasn't the strength."

"You can't go," Peter said, with a firmness that surprised me. "Ma has some dishes she wants you to have. She's been talking about them for days now. She won't give us a minute's peace until you have them. You've got to stay until she gives them to you." Then he added, very politely and quite winningly, "Please don't go."

So I stayed. The dining room was just as hot as the bedroom. It, too, was filled with furniture—a dining room set, three cabinets filled with china and glassware, a studio couch, and in a bay window, a big aquarium with fish in it.

Willie, the white cat, ran into the room from the hall, clawed his way up the draperies at the bay window, and sat crouched on the cornice, staring into the fish tank. His round blue eyes kept following the movements of the fish, back and forth, back and forth.

"Doesn't he try to catch the fish?" I asked.

Lud said, "That's what he wants to do. But he can't get at them. So he just watches them."

"Why, that's terrible," I said. "Can't you—"

Sarah had straightened up again. "Open those doors," she said.

"Yes, Ma." Peter opened one of the china cabinets.

"Get my cane."

"Yes, Ma." He went into the bedroom and came back with a slender Malacca cane. She took it from him in a swift snatching movement and, holding it and pointing with it, was transformed. She was no longer a hideous old woman dying slowly but an arrogant, commanding figure.

"That," she said, "and that," pointing imperiously to a shelf in the china cabinet where a tall chocolate pot stood, with matching cups and saucers, covered thick with dust.

"Get a carton and some newspapers." She pointed at Lud, and she jabbed him viciously in the stomach with the cane. He jumped, and said, "Oh, oo-ooh!" pain and outrage in his voice.

"Go get the carton," Peter said matter-of-factly.

While we waited for Lud to come back, Sarah seemed to doze. Finally, Peter sat down and motioned to me to sit down. He picked up a newspaper and began to read.

Something about the way Sarah had ordered him around set me to wondering what kind of childhood Peter had had. He must have been about twelve years old when Mrs. Wingate died and left thirty-five thousand dollars to Forbes.

With this money, Forbes took what he called a flyer in real estate; he acquired an equity in six tenement houses. My mother had disapproved. She distrusted the whole idea of mortgages and loans, and she felt that Forbes was gambling with his inheritance; if his tenants were unable to pay the rent, he would be unable to meet the interest on his notes and would lose everything.

During this period, Mother went to see Sarah fairly often, and she always came away from these visits quite disturbed. She said that Sarah, who had at one time cared too much about her looks, now did not seem to care at all. The house was dreadful—confused and dusty. She said that Forbes had changed. He was still immaculate, but he was now too thin—bony—and his movements were jerky. He seemed to have a dreadful, almost maniacal urge to keep moving, and he would sit down, stand up, walk about the room, sit down again, get up, walk about again. At first she used to say that he was nervous, and then she amended this and enlarged it by saying he was distraught.

Mrs. Wingate had been dead exactly two years when Forbes committed suicide. Immediately, all of Sarah's friends predicted financial disaster for her. Forbes's money was tied up in heavily mortgaged real estate, and shortly after his death the Depression came along, with its eviction notices and foreclosures.

I glanced at Sarah, dozing in the wheelchair, her chin resting on her chest. At twenty, she had been a silly, giggling girl. And yet somewhere under the surface there must have been the makings of a cold, shrewd property owner, a badgering, browbeating fishwife of a woman who could intimidate drunks, evict widows and orphans—a woman capable of using an umbrella or a hatpin as a weapon. She had made regular weekly collections of rent, because she soon learned that if she went around only once a month, the rent money would have gone for food or for liquor or for playing the numbers. Peter went with her when she made her collections. He was tall, thin, and asthmatic and wore tweed knee pants and long stockings—a ridiculous costume for a boy in his teens.

It was during those years that Sarah perfected her technique of leaning against people and began to develop a whining voice. She began to get fat. Her behind seemed to swell up, but her legs stayed thin, like pipestems, so that she walked carefully. She was what my father called spindle-shanked.

I suppose she had to whine, to threaten, to cajole, perhaps cry, in order to screw the rent money out of her tenants; at any rate, she succeeded. Years later, she told

Mother that she had not lost a single piece of property. She finally sold all of it except the two-story taxpayer where they lived. She said that the bank that held the mortgages and notes had congratulated her; they told her that no real estate operator in Bridgeport had been able to do what she had done—bring all his property through the Depression intact.

Sarah straightened up in the wheelchair and pointed with her cane. "That," she said. Peter hesitated. "That" seemed to be some white cups and saucers with no adornment of any kind. Sarah threatened Peter with the cane, and he took them out of the cabinet and put them on the table.

"Perfect," she said to me. "Six of them. All perfect. Belonged to my grandmother. Handed down. They're yours now. You hand them down."

I shook my head. "Wait a minute," I said, slowly and distinctly, in order to be sure she understood. "What about your grandsons? What about Lud and Boodie? These cups should belong to Lud and Boodie."

"They will run with whores," she said coldly. "Just like Peter does. Just like Forbes kept trying to do, only he couldn't. That's what he was after in Shacktown that time, and when he found he couldn't—just wasn't able to—he laid himself down on the railroad track." She paused for a moment. "I cried for three days afterward. For three whole days." She paused again. "I wasn't crying because of what happened to him. I was crying because of what had happened to me. To my whole life. My whole life."

I could not look at Peter. I heard him take a deep breath.

Sarah said, "Those cups are yours. I'm giving them to you so that I'll know where they are. I'll know who owns them. If they should stay here . . ." She shrugged.

Lud came back with the carton and a pile of newspapers, and Sarah did not even glance in his direction. She said, "The chocolate cups belonged to a French king. Mrs. Wingate gave them to me for a wedding present when I married her Forbes. I want you to have them so that I'll know who owns them."

We wrapped the pieces of china separately and put wads

of crumpled newspaper in between as we packed the carton. Sarah watched us. Sometimes she half closed her eyes, but she kept looking until we had finished. After that, her head slumped and her breathing changed. It was light, shallow, with pauses in between. I could hear the thumping of her heart way across the room.

I said, "Good-bye, Sarah," and kissed the back of her neck, but she did not answer or move.

It was still snowing when Lud carried the carton out to the car for me, held the door open, and closed it after I got in. I thought he did it with a kind of gracefulness that he couldn't possibly have acquired from Peter; perhaps it was something inherited from Forbes, his grandfather.

Lud said, "Did those cups really belong to one of the kings of France?"

"Maybe. I really don't know. I wish you'd put them back in the house. This whole carton of china is more yours than it is mine. These things belonged to your grandmother, and they should stay in your family."

"Oh, no," he said hastily, and he stepped away from the car. "I don't want them. What would I do with them? Besides, Nana's ghost would come back and bug me." He laughed uneasily. "And if Nana's ghost bugged anybody, they'd flip for sure."

When I got home, I washed the chocolate set, and having got rid of the accumulated dust of fifty years, I decided that it could easily have belonged to one of the kings of France. It was of the very old, soft-paste type of porcelain. It had been made in the Sèvres factory, and it was exquisitely decorated in the lovely color known as rose pompadour.

I was admiring the shape of the cups when the telephone rang. It was Peter Forbes. He said, "Ma died in her sleep just a few minutes after you left."

# A Sound of Crying

## ANITA R. CORNWELL

African American literature written during the civil rights era provides dramatic accounts of the personal costs of America's most momentous struggle for personal freedom. Anita Cornwell's story about a black college student's moment of decision to sacrifice all for justice reveals the complex web of emotion and responsibility that such decisions entail. The ripple effect of political commitment on family is captured in his mother's reaction to his decision. This compact, explosive story illuminates in a flash the moment many Americans switched from a position of compliance to resistance in the civil rights struggle. The story first appeared in *Negro Digest* magazine in June 1964, at the height of civil rights activity.

THE AFTERNOON WAS ABOUT GONE, and Amanda Stonecutter wondered if she could finish ironing her last bundle before it was time to start supper. It was Friday, and she liked to finish up before supper-time, so she would have the weekend to do her own chores. Then a sudden noise from the back porch pulled her head up, and she saw her husband rushing through the door waving the evening paper.

"You see here, Manda, them fool kids done gone and got throwed outta school," he shouted. "We told Hal not to hang round them trouble-making demonstrators, yet there he was leading the pack!"

For a moment she stared at him, then slowly cut her iron off and came to gaze at the newspaper spread on the kitchen table. "I heard the news on the radio," she said finally. "They didn't give names, but deep in my heart I guess I knew Hal would be in it somewhere." She sighed, sitting down, her legs suddenly too weary to hold her up.

"He was one of the main ones; it's right here in the paper," Jim declared, pounding the paper vigorously. "Mr. Allen showed it t' me, and he said Hal ought not to come back as Haycroft ain't gonna stand for that mess!"

Amanda's face turned a dull gray as the blood drained from it. "They never did like Hal, them white folks here didn't. They'll be laying for him now, that's for sure," she said in a flat, lifeless tone which seemed to deepen the look of sadness in her eyes. Then anxiety and an overpowering sense of utter helplessness propelled her to her feet. Hugging her folded arms tight against her narrow, palpitating chest, she wandered up into the living room and stood at the window, half-expecting to find a mob already gathered in the front yard.

"Jim, what are we going to do?" she asked, suddenly turning to face her husband, who had followed her into the crowded, boxlike room. "He's nearing twenty; they won't let him get away with the things he did when he was growing up."

"Don't upset yourself, Manda," he began, and she knew by the set of his mouth that he had news of some kind that he hadn't told before. "Mr. Allen lent me money and I telegramed it to Hal. I told him to go on up to New York to be with his sister Helen till this thing blows over."

"You—you think he'll do that?" she asked hopefully.

Jim nodded, his small round head bobbing like a top. "He'll listen. He's older now, Manda; he knows people here don't want things all stirred up."

His wishful thinking and the placid look on his childlike face were almost too much for her to endure. And the feeble ray of hope struggling in her bosom quietly expired as the scattered veins of fear darting through her body converged into the hard lump which settled in her chest. She leaned one bony elbow against the peeling window frame and wondered in silent desperation what would happen to the other children if their eldest son came back and started offending the white people who nowadays seemed more easily provoked than ever.

Finally, shaking her head as if to clear away some dense fog, she turned from the window to see that Jim was already comfortably stretched out on the couch. "I guess I'd better go start supper before the children come," she said, trying without success to suppress another weary sigh.

Out in the kitchen, she lifted the half-ironed shirt from the board with tired, work-knotted fingers. And for a moment she stared at it with blurred eyes: a white shirt, a white man's shirt. In the eyes of her country she was only a black woman who took in washing. She was not supposed to have problems or feelings to care about those problems. She was expected to be a workhorse, not a mother who loved her children, who worried about their well-being. Then, relaxing her fingers, the shirt dropped into the basket, and she took the board down. She would have to finish the bundle after supper now, and Jim could take it by Mrs. Baines's on his way to work tomorrow morning.

Then, yawning and stretching, Jim entered the kitchen, "I reckon I'd better set this out," he said, lifting the wicker clothes basket and taking it out to the back porch. She watched him, moving stiffly like a tired old man, and marveled at the swift, cruel passing of time.

The children had always kept her so busy, she had never had time to wonder whether the years were good or bad. Even when Hal was about ten and started his fighting campaign to reform the world, her hands were plenty full for the twins, Mike and Ike, were only five and Annie Ruth just a baby. Then, at long last, with the help of the good Lord and Rev. Mills, the kindly old minister who had baptized all the children, and Mr. Waterman, the principal who had once taught Jim, Hal finished High with honors and a scholarship. And she had thought the problem solved for good when he went off to Florida to AM&I. But now here he was expelled in his senior year, and only God in His Heaven knew what was coming next.

What came next, the following day in fact, was Hal himself. Just as they were sitting down for the noonday meal, he strolled into the kitchen, plunking his suitcases down onto the freshly scrubbed floor. Saddened but not surprised, Amanda quickly looked at Jim, who, for the moment, was ashy white and quite speechless. But not the children; they whooped for joy and rushed to embrace him, their conquering hero home in person.

"You got th' wire—?" Jim finally asked.

"Sure, Pop, I got it." Hal grinned, tossing his cap onto one of the suitcases. "But I figured what the hell, Harlem can wait. I'll liberate Mississippi first."

The children whooped again, and Amanda felt rather than saw Jim sag in his chair. Then Hal came over and bent down to kiss her. "You're looking great, Mom," he said, but his eyes wondered if she understood why he had acted contrary to his father's command. And to her utter despair, she knew her own eyes assured him that she did understand. But, oh how her heart ached for him!

Food was forgotten as the twins told Hal about the special assembly yesterday when Mr. Lacker, their new principal, warned them not to start that sit-in bit in Haycroft if they wanted to stay at good old Booker T. High.

The handsome, mobile face quivered with emotion as he began pacing the floor. "Yeah, I am very well acquainted with the educated Uncle Tommies," he declared. " 'Wait, go slow, it takes time,' they cry, joining hands with their great white brethren to quote from that venerable script someone wrote coming back from Lincoln's funeral. Well, I'm here to tell you that crap is from Squaresville; they've got to get some new material. Sure a lot of us got thumped on our behinds and kicked out of school too, but we have started something. And they ain't seen nothing yet. Just wait till we hit that second thrust. They're going to realize we're shooting for the moon, not just for the front of the bus!"

Jim stared in speechless fascination, and the twins whistled and banged the table with fists and silverware. Annie Ruth ran to Hal and hugged him again and again, while Amanda, holding her throbbing head tight in her hands, frantically prayed: Dear God, please send him North or shut him up before it's too late.

News of Hal's homecoming spread around town like an epidemic, and a few of the more curious souls came to see with their own eyes. First on the scene was one of Amanda's insurance men, Harry Bicker, who ordinarily collected on Tuesday. Jim had gone back to work, and the rest of them were still in the kitchen listening to Hal tell about the sit-ins in Florida when Harry Bicker came back. And right off Hal wanted to know what was wrong with the doorbell, but Amanda hushed him up and took Harry Bicker up front.

But Hal followed them, staring at the white man while he collected his money and marked up the book. Then, after his hasty, rather nervous departure, Hal turned on his mother. "Why don't you pay those vultures by mail? Every week, here they come, a pack of white-shirted hypocrites. It would kill one of them to sit next to you at the drugstore counter, yet they're living off us just as sure as buzzards picking a dead man's guts."

Then Amanda, as impetuous as he in many respects, got angry too. "Why'd you come back if you hate it so much here? You know what it's like. Why you think you can change 'em?"

Annie Ruth, followed by the twins, came in then, and Hal flopped down into a chair, his mouth clamped shut. And Amanda, tight-lipped and bone-weary, put the insurance book back on top of the mantel and was heading back to the kitchen when the horn started blasting out front. She froze, and for a moment dead silence prevailed as they stared at one another, knowing that none of their colored friends had cars, and if they did, they wouldn't blow quite like that.

But Annie Ruth, the youngest and therefore the least frightened, jumped up and ran to the window. "Mama, it's Mis Baines," she said, turning to face them. "You want me to run out and tell her Daddy took her clothes this morning?"

Ike, the taller twin, looked at his mother. "Why can't she come in here if she wants to see somebody?"

Mike snorted. "She's scared a little color might rub off on her and she'll lose nine-tenths of her privileges, man."

"Shut up," Amanda snapped, but the little tableau was not lost on her. She realized the twins were only trying to impress Hal, but she also knew they were apt to keep trying as long as he remained home. Somehow, she had to get him out of town. And suddenly the thought came to her that perhaps God had sent Lucy Baines to help her.

Standing beside the new blue convertible, Amanda glanced at Mrs. Baines somewhere between her thin, up-turned nose and her long, ducklike neckline and wondered how it felt to be white and therefore right. Envy was not in her heart, but the rank taste of fear fouled her mouth. By now she was most adept at ignoring the fear, for it usually erupted when a white face ventured too close. Vaguely, she knew it sprang from a rockbed of hate, and she resented the hate even more than she did the fear.

God didn't put man here to hate, she thought despairingly, but what were you to do when people pushed you to the ground and kept you there till you were dead and buried? Then her eyes strayed into the pale blue eyes of Lucy Baines, and she saw fear there too. It was only a flash, but Amanda caught a glimpse of it. And she knew she couldn't ask Mrs. Baines to help with Hal. For if Lucy Baines was scared, then she hated too.

Finally, Amanda realized Mrs. Baines was saying something about odd jobs for Hal to keep him out of further trouble, and she nodded her head, grinning the foolish grin that was expected of her. She promised to talk to Hal about the work, but he probably would be going away soon. Helen—did Mrs. Baines remember Helen who useta help her out after school?—well, Helen was looking for Hal to come up to New York to visit with her any day now.

Back in the house, Amanda motioned for Hal to follow her out to the kitchen, where she told him what Mrs. Baines had said and what she had said to Mrs. Baines. But Hal would not be compromised. "Mama," he began patiently, "I know they don't like me here because I don't grin like an ape when they come sneaking around. Well, I'm not an ape, and I'm not going to act like one—"

"Hal," Amanda interrupted sharply, "how can you have so much education and yet be so dumb? You can't fight a whole town, and neither can you change it by agitation. They'll just be waiting for you to start something now. Why your head so hard, boy?"

He backed away from her as though she had struck him, throwing his hands toward the ceiling. "All right, so I'm an agitator. So I want to look up at the sun and go where every man but one with a black face can go in his own country. Is that so wrong? Look at that Barry Roth who came here from Germany years ago. He practically owns the town now. A Jew-hating Nazi can have the country, but I have to stand up to eat a lousy hamburger at the bus terminal! You think that's something to grin about? You think I ought to run up to New York and rot in Harlem and call myself a man? Is that what you want—?"

Amanda clutched at his swinging arms. "You are wrong to stay here and get yourself killed," she cried. "What good would it do? Answer me? What good would it do, Hal?"

But he would not answer her. Perhaps he could not. He was flesh of her flesh, blood of her blood, but not of her generation. And through her tears she watched as he finally left the kitchen and retired to his old room upstairs at the back of the house, where he stayed for the rest of the day, banging away on the portable typewriter Helen had given him when he finished High. Several times she had a notion to go back there to try talking with him again, but since she had no real plan formulated yet, she decided to wait until she had one.

At church next morning Amanda found it virtually impossible to concentrate on the sermon. More than once she caught herself up sharply as Rev. Thornton pounded the lectern, bringing enthusiastic "Amens" from the congregation. The children, sitting in the pew ahead of them, were somewhat more fidgety than usual, but Jim sat quietly be-

side her, moving not an eyelash. Then her restless eyes
fastened on the tall, lanky man pacing the pulpit.

He was young, not much older than Hal, and Amanda
realized now that she had never really felt comfortable in
his presence. He reminded her of Mr. Lacker, the new
principal, in manner more than looks. The town had certainly changed, she thought ruefully, the old faces gone,
replaced by bright eager young men in dark gray suits and
button-down collars. They always had the right word at the
right time, but somehow she felt they were lacking in many
of the old virtues. Rev. Mills or Mr. Waterman would have
taken Hal aside and maybe talked some sense into his
head. But these new people were different; they were probably afraid of a boy who talked too much. They seemed
more interested in hanging on to a job than going out of
their way to risk hanging from a tall strong oak. And who
was she to condemn them?

Leaving the tiny, red brick church, smiling and nodding
at friends, evading their questions concerning Hal as best
she could, Amanda walked along beside her silent husband
more heavy of heart now than when she left the house. But
she attributed this more to the restless wanderings of her
mind than to any defects of the service. Then when they
reached home and she saw the sheriff's car parked out
front, she thought, "Already God is punishing me for not
listening to His Word in church."

Sheriff Osborne and his deputy, young Timmy Updyke,
who had once received two black eyes from Hal for calling
him a nigger, got out of the black, mudstained vehicle as
they came up. Amanda looked at Jim and saw his face turn
whiter than either of the two other men. Then, seeing him
scared like that, her own fear left her, and she reached out
to take his trembling hand in hers.

Timmy said nothing, in fact he barely looked at them,
but Amanda felt the antipathy in him. And the way he
fingered his nightstick in a sort of unconscious caress, while
his dull gray eyes stared out into some eternal void, chilled
her to the bone. She knew that if they didn't soon get Hal

out of Haycroft, Timmy Updyke would see that they carried him feet first to the graveyard.

Reluctantly, Amanda's eyes moved on to the sheriff, who was now saying what he had come to say in plain, good old Mississippi English. And even before he had finished, Jim was vigorously nodding his head and promising up and down that "Hal wasn't thinking o' starting no trouble heah in Haycroft. No sir. Not Hal!"

The sight of Jim grinning and bowing tore Amanda's heart, and she could have wept knowing that somewhere in the house Hal watched, wretched with indignation. But God must have heard her plea, for he did not come out to intervene. They waited until the car disappeared around the corner in a faint cloud of dust, then went into the house to find Hal sitting in the living room staring at his feet propped up on the piano stool. He nodded to them but made no mention of the sheriff's visit, and somehow, his silence was more disturbing to Amanda than any of his long speeches had ever been.

And while she and Jim changed their clothes upstairs, her searching mind finally landed on the same old question: Should they all move North? The subject was first discussed when Helen was born, and they had rejected the idea, agreeing that the North was too crowded with people and covered with cement everywhere and no place for children to grow up in as the tall buildings blotted out every last drop of God's good sunshine.

Later, however, she came to realize that most important of all, a child needed a good emotional climate. But Jim was rooted now and too removed from reality to think clearly about troublesome situations. Nevertheless, she did voice the question once again.

Jim was about ready to go downstairs, but he stopped near the door and surprised her by not flying off the handle. "What would happen to us up there, Manda?" he asked, his eyes squinting in the little face which had screwed up like that of a worried child. Then he answered his own question, "Relief probably. I'm near fifty with not much education. . . ."

He came back and sat on the bed, his small, yet powerful, work-stained mechanic's hands spread upon his thighs. "I reckon relief ain't no worse than this though. All these years hearing Hal shoot off at the mouth, I wouldn't listen 'cause I knowed he was right. I wanted to be a man too when I was his age. I didn't like looking at the ground and grinning like a fool every time Mr. Charley walks by. They do something to your insides here, and when you gets to be as old as me, it's like walking round dead."

It was such a rare thing, him unburdening himself like that, until Amanda, in the midst of rebraiding her hair, hardly knew what to do. Then she let the long braid fall and moved forward, her eyes seeing what they had not noticed in many a long year: a man, a human being with hopes and fears, yet a longing to live in his own way. And for the moment, Hal was forgotten as she reached out her arms to her husband.

By eleven o'clock Monday morning, Amanda's first wash hung on the line, swinging under the hard October sun which climbed toward high noon, and she decided to take a break and look in on Hal. An idea had popped into her head earlier that morning, and the more she thought on it, the better it seemed to her. They had a cousin in Atlanta, and if she could persuade Hal to go there, he might keep out of trouble and also finish his schooling. It was risky, for they were sitting-in there too, but anything was better than having him stay in Haycroft.

She dried her hands on her apron as she trotted up the back steps, her mind suddenly urging her feet to move faster. If Hal were around tomorrow when all those insurance men came, anything might happen. He never had liked them or they him. At the foot of the stairs in the living room, she rested one hand lightly on the newel post and called up to him. Uneasy when he did not immediately respond, she walked partway up the steps and saw his door standing wide open. Fear clogged her breath, and she dashed up the remaining steps so fast, her slippers nearly threw her.

On the foot of his bed she saw a worn, pocket-size New

Testament and in the center was a stack of neatly typed papers. Edging over almost furtively, she bent down to read the top sheet:

AND NOW I SIT ME DOWN
A Novel
by
Harold Lawson Stonecutter

So that's what he's been typing, she thought in some confusion. But about what? she wondered, slowly picking up another page, which she started to read:

"This is the day, Tom thought as he stood at the window idly examining the withered branches of the dying peach tree while another part of his mind remembered how it had been back at Collegetown.

"You were scared to death sitting there with the snarling mob at your back. Every hair stood out on your neck, and you prayed like crazy asking God to give you courage enough not to swing at one of them. Then peace came as renewed strength flowed through your trembling body, and you knew God was with you. In the mirror you saw the contorted faces filled with ignorance, and you knew they were the lost souls. Then you prayed again, asking God to show them the way.

"He turned from the window, a slight smile on his face as he knelt by his bed.

"Then finally he got up, got his cap, and left the room.

"This was the day!"

Suddenly Amanda gasped, holding her throat as if about to strangle. "Hal," she cried softly, "Oh, Hal, how could you—?"

Blindly she fled from the room, down the steps, and out into the bright sunlit day. Yet she knew it was too late, even as she prayed with every breath in her body. Even as she heard the screeching sirens in the distance, she knew it. But she kept on running and calling his name.

# Neighbors

## Diane Oliver

Diane Oliver's promising literary career was cut short when she was killed in an automobile accident at the age of twenty-three. This story about a family's brave and conflicted response to enrolling their son in an all-white school personalizes the social drama that attended the integration of American schools after the 1954 *Brown* v. *Board of Education* ruling that declared segregation unconstitutional. "Neighbors" is a true and heartfelt snapshot of representative—not heroic—black Americans at risk for the courage of their convictions. Originally published in *The Sewanee Review* in 1966, the year of Oliver's death, the story was included in *Prize Stories 1967: The O. Henry Awards*.

THE BUS TURNING THE CORNER of Patterson and Talford Avenue was dull this time of evening. Of the four passengers standing in the rear, she did not recognize any of her friends. Most of the people tucked neatly in the double seats were women, maids and cooks on their way from work or secretaries who had worked late and were riding from the office building at the mill. The cotton mill was out from town, near the house where she worked. She noticed that a few men were riding too. They were obviously just working men, except for one gentleman dressed very neatly in a dark gray suit and carrying what she imagined was a push-button umbrella.

He looked to her as though he usually drove a car to work. She immediately decided that the car probably wouldn't start this morning, so he had to catch the bus to and from work. She was standing in the rear of the bus, peering at the passengers, her arms barely reaching the overhead railing, trying not to wobble with every lurch. But every corner the bus turned pushed her head toward a window. And her hair was coming down too, wisps of black curls swung between her eyes. She looked at the people around her. Some of them were white, but most of them were her color. Looking at the passengers at least kept her from thinking of tomorrow. But really she would be glad when it came, then everything would be over.

She took a firmer grip on the green leather seat and wished she had on her glasses. The man with the umbrella was two people ahead of her on the other side of the bus, so she could see him between other people very clearly. She watched as he unfolded the evening newspaper, craning her neck to see what was on the front page. She stood, impatiently trying to read the headlines, when she realized he was staring up at her rather curiously. Biting her lips, she turned her head and stared out of the window until the downtown section was in sight.

She would have to wait until she was home to see if they were in the newspaper again. Sometimes she felt that if another person snapped a picture of them she would burst out screaming. Last Monday reporters were already inside the preschool clinic when she took Tommy for his last polio shot. She didn't understand how anyone could be so heartless to a child. The flashbulb went off right when the needle went in and all the picture showed was Tommy's open mouth.

The bus pulling up to the curb jerked to a stop, startling her and confusing her thoughts. Clutching in her hand the paper bag that contained her uniform, she pushed her way toward the door. By standing in the back of the bus, she was one of the first people to step to the ground. Outside the bus, the evening air felt humid and uncomfortable and her dress kept sticking to her. She looked up and remembered that the weatherman had forecast rain. Just their luck—why, she wondered, would it have to rain on top of everything else?

As she walked along, the main street seemed unnaturally quiet, but she decided her imagination was merely playing tricks. Besides, most of the stores had been closed since five o'clock.

She stopped to look at a reversible raincoat in Ivey's window, but although she had a full-time job now, she couldn't keep her mind on clothes. She was about to continue walking when she heard a horn blowing. Looking around, half-scared but also curious, she saw a man beckoning to her in a gray car. He was nobody she knew, but since a nicely dressed woman was with him in the front seat, she walked to the car.

"You're Jim Mitchell's girl, aren't you?" he questioned. "You Ellie or the other one?"

She nodded yes, wondering who he was and how much he had been drinking.

"Now honey," he said leaning over the woman, "you don't know me, but your father does, and you tell him that if anything happens to that boy of his tomorrow, we're ready to set things straight." He looked her straight in the eye, and she promised to take home the message.

Just as the man was about to step on the gas, the woman reached out and touched her arm. "You hurry up home, honey, it's about dark out here."

Before she could find out their names, the Chevrolet had disappeared around a corner. Ellie wished someone would magically appear and tell her everything that had happened since August. Then maybe she could figure out what was real and what she had been imagining for the past couple of days.

She walked past the main shopping district up to Tanner's, where Saraline was standing in the window peeling oranges. Everything in the shop was painted orange and green, and Ellie couldn't help thinking that poor Saraline looked out of place. She stopped to wave to her friend, who pointed the knife to her watch and then to her boyfriend standing in the rear of the shop. Ellie nodded that she understood. She knew Sara wanted her to tell her grandfather that she had to work late again. Neither one of them could figure out why he didn't like Charlie. Saraline had finished high school three years ahead of her, and it was time for her to be getting married. Ellie watched as her friend stopped peeling the orange long enough to cross her fingers. She nodded again, but she was afraid all the crossed fingers in the world wouldn't stop the trouble tomorrow.

She stopped at the traffic light and spoke to a shriveled woman hunched against the side of a building. Scuffing the bottom of her sneakers on the curb, she waited for the woman to open her mouth and grin as she usually did. The kids used to bait her to talk, and since she didn't have but one tooth in her whole head, they called her Doughnut Puncher. But the woman was still, the way everything else had been all week.

From where Ellie stood, across the street from the Sears and Roebuck parking lot, she could see their house, all of the houses on the single street white people called Welfare Row. Those newspaper men always made her angry. All of their articles showed how rough the people were on their street. And the reporters never said her family wasn't on welfare, the papers always said the family lived on that street. She paused to look across the street at a group of kids pouncing on one rubber ball. There were always white kids around their neighborhood mixed up in the games, but playing with them was almost an unwritten rule. When everybody started going to school, nobody played together anymore.

She crossed at the corner, ignoring the cars at the stoplight, and the closer she got to her street, the more she realized that the newspaper was right. The houses were ugly, there were not even any trees, just patches of scraggly bushes and grasses. As she cut across the sticky asphalt pavement covered with cars, she was conscious of the parking lot floodlights casting a strange glow on her street. She stared from habit at the house on the end of the block, and except for the way the paint was peeling, they all looked alike to her. Now at twilight the flaking gray paint had a luminous glow, and as she walked down the dirt sidewalk, she noticed Mr. Paul's pipe smoke added to the hazy atmosphere. Mr. Paul would be sitting in that same spot waiting until Saraline came home. Ellie slowed her pace to speak to the elderly man sitting on the porch.

"Evening, Mr. Paul," she said. Her voice sounded clear and out of place on the vacant street.

"Eh, who's that?" Mr. Paul leaned over the rail. "What you say, girl?"

"How are you?" she hollered louder. "Sara said she'd be late tonight, she has to work." She waited for the words to sink in.

His head had dropped, and his eyes were facing his lap. She could see that he was disappointed. "Couldn't help it," he said finally. "Reckon they needed her again." Then as if he suddenly remembered, he turned toward her.

"You people be ready down there? Still gonna let him go tomorrow?"

She looked at Mr. Paul between the missing rails on his porch, seeing how his rolled-up trousers seemed to fit exactly in the vacant banister space.

"Last I heard this morning we're still letting him go," she said.

Mr. Paul had shifted his weight back to the chair. "Don't reckon they'll hurt him," he mumbled, scratching the side of his face. "Hope he don't mind being spit on though. Spitting ain't like cutting. They can spit on him, and nobody'll ever know who did it," he said, ending his words with a quiet chuckle.

Ellie stood on the sidewalk, grinding her heel in the dirt waiting for the old man to finish talking. She was glad somebody found something funny to laugh at. Finally he shut up.

"Good-bye, Mr. Paul." She waved. Her voice sounded loud to her own ears. But she knew the way her head ached intensified noises. She walked home faster, hoping they had some aspirin in the house and that those men would leave earlier tonight.

From the front of her house, she could tell that the men were still there. The living room light shone behind the yellow shades, coming through brighter in the patched places. She thought about moving the geranium pot from the porch to catch the rain but changed her mind. She kicked a beer can under a car parked in the street and stopped to look at her reflection on the car door. The tiny flowers of her printed dress made her look as if she had a strange tropical disease. She spotted another can and kicked it out of the way of the car, thinking that one of these days some kid was going to fall and hurt himself. What she wanted to do, she knew, was kick the car out of the way. Both the station wagon and the Ford had been parked in front of her house all week, waiting. Everybody was just sitting around waiting.

Suddenly she laughed aloud. Reverend Davis's car was big and black and shiny just like, but no, the smile disappeared from her face, her mother didn't like for them to say things about other people's color. She looked around to see who else came and saw Mr. Moore's old beat-up blue car. Somebody had torn away half of his NAACP sign. Sometimes she really felt sorry for the man. No matter how hard he glued on his stickers, somebody always yanked them off again.

Ellie didn't recognize the third car, but it had an Alabama license plate. She turned around and looked up and down the street, hating to go inside. There were no lights on their street, but in the distance she could see the bright lights of the parking lot. Slowly she did an about face and climbed the steps.

She wondered when her mama was going to remember to get a yellow bulb for the porch. Although the lights hadn't been turned on, usually June bugs and mosquitoes swarmed all around the porch. By the time she was inside the house, she always felt like they were crawling in her hair. She pulled on the screen and saw that Mama finally had made Hezekiah patch up the holes. The globs of white adhesive tape scattered over the screen door looked just like misshapen butterflies.

She listened to her father's voice and could tell by the tone that the men were discussing something important again. She rattled the door once more, but nobody came.

"Will somebody please let me in?" Her voice carried through the screen to the knot of men sitting in the corner.

"The door's open," her father yelled. "Come on in."

"The door is not open," she said evenly. "You know we stopped leaving it open." She was feeling tired again, and her voice had fallen an octave lower.

"Yeah, I forgot, I forgot," he mumbled, walking to the door.

She watched her father almost stumble across a chair to let her in. He was shorter than the lightbulb, and the light seemed to beam down on him, emphasizing the wrinkles around his eyes. She could tell from the way he pushed open the screen that he hadn't had much sleep either. She'd overheard him telling Mama that the people down at the shop seemed to be piling on the work harder just because of this thing. And he couldn't do anything or say anything to his boss because they probably wanted to fire him.

"Where's Mama?" she whispered. He nodded toward the back.

"Good evening, everybody," she said looking at the three men who had not looked up since she entered the room. One of the men half stood, but his attention was geared back to something another man was saying. They were sitting on the sofa in their shirt sleeves, and there was a pitcher of ice water on the windowsill.

"Your mother probably needs some help," her father said. She looked past him, trying to figure out who the white man was sitting on the end. His face looked familiar, and she tried to remember where she had seen him before. The men were paying no attention to her. She bent to see what they were studying and saw a large sheet of white drawing paper. She could see blocks and lines, and the man sitting in the middle was marking a trail with the eraser edge of the pencil.

The quiet stillness of the room was making her head

ache more. She pushed her way through the red embroidered curtains that led to the kitchen.

"I'm home, Mama," she said, standing in front of the back door, facing the big yellow sun Hezekiah and Tommy had painted on the wall above the iron stove. Immediately she felt a warmth permeating her skin. "Where is everybody?" she asked, sitting at the table where her mother was peeling potatoes.

"Mrs. McAllister is keeping Helen and Teenie," her mother said. "Your brother is staying over with Harry tonight." With each name she uttered, a slice of potato peeling tumbled to the newspaper on the table. "Tommy's in the bedroom reading that Uncle Wiggily book."

Ellie looked up at her mother, but her eyes were straight ahead. She knew that Tommy only read the Uncle Wiggily book by himself when he was unhappy. She got up and walked to the kitchen cabinet.

"The other knives dirty?" she asked.

"No," her mother said. "Look in the next drawer."

Ellie pulled open the drawer, flicking scraps of white paint with her fingernail. She reached for the knife, and at the same time a pile of envelopes caught her eye.

"Any more come today?" she asked, pulling out the knife and slipping the envelopes under the dish towels.

"Yes, seven more came today." Her mother accentuated each word carefully. "Your father has them with him in the other room."

"Same thing?" she asked, picking up a potato and wishing she could think of some way to change the subject.

The white people had been threatening them for the past three weeks. Some of the letters were aimed at the family, but most of them were directed to Tommy himself. About once a week in the same handwriting, somebody wrote that he'd better not eat lunch at school because they were going to poison him.

They had been getting those letters ever since the school board made Tommy's name public. She sliced the potato and dropped the pieces in the pan of cold water. Out of all those people, he had been the only one the board had accepted for transfer to the elementary school. The other children, the members said, didn't live in the district. As she cut the eyes out of another potato, she thought about the first letter they had received and how her father just set fire to it in the ashtray. But then Mr. Belk said they'd better save the rest, in case anything happened—they might need the evidence for court.

She peeped up again at her mother. "Who's that white man in there with Daddy?"

"One of Lawyer Belk's friends," she answered. "He's pastor of the church that's always on television Sunday morning. Mr. Belk seems to think that having him around will do some good." Ellie saw that her voice was shaking just like her hand as she reached for the last potato. Both of them could hear Tommy in the next room mumbling to himself. She was afraid to look at her mother.

Suddenly Ellie was aware that her mother's hands were trembling violently. "He's so little," she whispered, and suddenly the knife slipped out of her hands, and she was crying and breathing at the same time.

Ellie didn't know what to do, but after a few seconds she cleared away the peelings and put the knives in the sink. "Why don't you lie down?" she suggested. "I'll clean up and get Tommy in bed." Without saying anything, her mother rose and walked to her bedroom.

Ellie wiped off the table and draped the dishcloth over the sink. She stood back and looked at the rusting pipes powdered with a whitish film. One of these days they would have to paint the place. She tiptoed past her mother, who looked as if she had fallen asleep from exhaustion.

"Tommy," she called softly, "come in and get ready for bed."

Tommy sitting in the middle of the floor did not answer. He was sitting the way she imagined he would be, cross-legged, pulling his earlobe as he turned the ragged pages of *Uncle Wiggily at the Zoo.*

"What you doing, Tommy?" she said, squatting on the floor beside him. He smiled and pointed at the picture of the ducks.

"School starts tomorrow," she said, turning a page with him. "Don't you think it's time to go to bed?"

"Oh Ellie, do I have to go now?" She looked down at the serious brown eyes and the closely cropped hair. For a minute she wondered if he questioned having to go to bed now or to school tomorrow.

"Well," she said, "aren't you about through with the book?" He shook his head. "Come on," she pulled him up, "you're a sleepyhead." Still he shook his head.

"When Helen and Teenie coming home?"

"Tomorrow after you come home from school, they'll be here."

She lifted him from the floor, thinking how small he looked to be facing all those people tomorrow.

"Look," he said, breaking away from her hand and pointing to a blue shirt and pair of cotton twill pants, "Mama got them for me to wear tomorrow."

While she ran water in the tub, she heard him crawl on top of the bed. He was quiet, and she knew he was untying his sneakers.

"Put your shoes out," she called through the door, "and maybe Daddy will polish them."

"Is Daddy still in there with those men? Mama made me be quiet so I wouldn't bother them."

He padded into the bathroom with bare feet and crawled into the water. As she scrubbed him, they played Ask Me a Question, their own version of Twenty Questions. She had just dried him and was about to have him step into his pajamas when he asked: "Are they gonna get me tomorrow?"

"Who's going to get you?" She looked into his eyes and began rubbing him furiously with the towel.

"I don't know," he answered. "Somebody I guess."

"Nobody's going to get you," she said. "Who wants a little boy who gets bubblegum in his hair anyway—but us?" He grinned, but as she hugged him, she thought how much he looked like his father. They walked to the bed to say his prayers, and while they were kneeling, she heard the first drops of rain. By the time she covered him up and tucked the spread off the floor, the rain had changed to a steady downpour.

When Tommy had gone to bed, her mother got up again and began ironing clothes in the kitchen. Something, she said, to keep her thoughts busy. While her mother folded and sorted the clothes, Ellie drew up a chair from the kitchen table. They sat in the kitchen for a while listening to the voices of the men in the next room. Her mother's quiet speech broke the stillness in the room.

"I'd rather," she said, making sweeping motions with the iron, "that you stayed home from work tomorrow and went with your father to take Tommy. I don't think I'll be up to those people."

Ellie nodded. "I don't mind," she said, tracing circles on the oilcloth-covered table.

"Your father's going," her mother continued. "Belk and Reverend Davis are too. I think that white man in there will probably go."

"They may not need me," Ellie answered.

"Tommy will," her mother said, folding the last dish towel and storing it in the cabinet.

"Mama, I think he's scared," the girl turned toward the woman. "He was so quiet while I was washing him."

"I know," she answered, sitting down heavily. "He's been that way all day." Her brown wavy hair glowed in the dim lighting of the kitchen. "I told him he wasn't going to school with Jakie and Bob anymore, but I said he was going to meet some other children just as nice."

Ellie saw that her mother was twisting her wedding band around and around on her finger.

"I've already told Mrs. Ingraham that I wouldn't be able to come out tomorrow." Ellie paused. "She didn't say very much. She didn't even say anything about his pictures in the newspaper. Mr. Ingraham said we were getting right crazy, but even he didn't say anything else."

She stopped to look at the clock sitting near the sink. "It's almost time for the cruise cars to begin," she said. Her mother followed Ellie's eyes to the sink. The policemen circling their block every twenty minutes were supposed to make them feel safe, but hearing the cars come so regularly and that light flashing through the shade above her bed only made her nervous.

She stopped talking to push a wrinkle out of the shiny red cloth, dragging her finger along the table edges. "How long before those men going to leave?" she asked her mother. Just as she spoke, she heard one of the men say something about getting some sleep. "I didn't mean to run them away," she said, smiling. Her mother half-smiled too. They listened for the sound of motors and tires and waited for her father to shut the front door.

In a few seconds her father's head pushed through the curtain. "Want me to turn down your bed now, Ellie?" She felt uncomfortable staring up at him, the whole family looked drained of all energy.

"That's all right," she answered. "I'll sleep in Helen and Teenie's bed tonight."

"How's Tommy?" he asked, looking toward the bedroom. He came in and sat down at the table with them.

They were silent before he spoke. "I keep wondering if we should send him." He lit a match and watched the flame disappear into the ashtray, then he looked into his wife's eyes. "There's no telling what these fool white folks will do."

Her mother reached over and patted his hand. "We're doing what we have to do, I guess," she said. "Sometimes, though, I wish the others weren't so much older than him."

"But it seems so unfair," Ellie broke in, "sending him there all by himself like that. Everybody keeps asking me why the MacAdams didn't apply for their children."

"Eloise." Her father's voice sounded curt. "We aren't answering for the MacAdams, we're trying to do what's right for your brother. He's not old enough to have his own say so. You and the others could decide for yourselves, but we're the ones that have to do for him."

She didn't say anything but watched him pull a handful of envelopes out of his pocket and tuck them in the cabinet drawer. She knew that if anyone had told him in August that Tommy would be the only one going to Jefferson Davis, they would not have let him go.

"Those the new ones?" she asked. "What they say?"

"Let's not talk about the letters," her father said. "Let's go to bed."

Outside they heard the rain become heavier. Since early evening she had become accustomed to the sound. Now it blended in with the rest of the noises that had accumulated in the back of her mind since the whole thing began.

As her mother folded the ironing board, they heard the quiet wheels of the police car. Ellie noticed that the clock said twelve-ten and she wondered why they were early. Her mother pulled the iron cord from the switch, and they stood silently waiting for the police car to turn around and pass the house again, as if the car's passing were a final blessing for the night.

Suddenly she was aware of a noise that sounded as if everything had broken loose in her head at once, a loudness that almost shook the foundation of the house. At the same time the lights went out, and instinctively her father knocked them to the floor. They could hear the tinkling of glass near the front of the house, and Tommy began screaming.

"Tommy, get down," her father yelled.

She hoped he would remember to roll under the bed the way they had practiced. She was aware of objects falling and breaking as she lay perfectly still. Her breath was coming in jerks, and then there was a second noise, a smaller explosion but still drowning out Tommy's cries.

"Stay still," her father commanded. "I'm going to check on Tommy. They may throw another one."

She watched him crawl across the floor, pushing a broken flower vase and an iron skillet out of his way. All of the sounds, Tommy's crying, the breaking glass, everything was echoing in her ears. She felt as if they had been crouching on the floor for hours, but when she heard the police car door slam, the luminous hands of the clock said only twelve-fifteen.

She heard other cars drive up and pairs of heavy feet trample on the porch. "You folks all right in there?"

She could visualize the hands pulling open the door, because she knew the voice. Sergeant Kearns had been responsible for patrolling the house during the past three weeks. She heard him click the light switch in the living room, but the darkness remained intense.

Her father deposited Tommy in his wife's lap and went to what was left of the door. In the next fifteen minutes policemen were everywhere. While she rummaged around underneath the cabinet for a candle, her mother tried to hush up Tommy. His cheek was cut where he had scratched himself on the springs of the bed. Her mother motioned for her to dampen a cloth and put some petroleum jelly on it to keep him quiet. She tried to put him to bed again, but he would not go, even when she promised to stay with him for the rest of the night. And so she sat in the kitchen, rocking the little boy back and forth on her lap.

Ellie wandered around the kitchen, but the light from the single candle put an eerie glow on the walls, making her nervous. She began picking up pans, stepping over pieces of broken crockery and glassware. She did not want to go into the living room yet, but if she listened closely, snatches of the policemen's conversation came through the curtain.

She heard one man say that the bomb landed near the edge of the yard, that was why it had only gotten the front porch. She knew from their talk that the living room window was shattered completely. Suddenly Ellie sat down. The picture of the living room window kept flashing in her mind, and a wave of feeling invaded her body, making her shake as if she had lost all muscular control. She slept on the couch, right under that window.

She looked at her mother to see if she too had realized, but her mother was looking down at Tommy and trying to get him to close his eyes. Ellie stood up and crept toward the living room trying to prepare herself for what she would see. Even that minute of determination could not make her control the horror that she felt. There were jagged holes all along the front of the house, and the sofa was covered with glass and paint. She started to pick up the picture that had toppled from the book shelf, then she just stepped over the broken frame.

Outside her father was talking, and curious to see who else was with him, she walked across the splinters to the yard. She could see pieces of the geranium pot and the red blossoms turned face down. There were no lights in the other houses on the street. Across from their house she could see forms standing in the door and shadows being pushed back and forth. "I guess the MacAdams are glad they just didn't get involved." No one heard her speak, and no one came over to see if they could help; she knew why and did not really blame them. They were afraid their house could be next.

Most of the policemen had gone now, and only one car was left to flash the revolving red light in the rain. She heard the tall skinny man tell her father they would be parked outside for the rest of the night. As she watched the reflection of the police cars returning to the station, feeling sick on her stomach, she wondered now why they bothered.

Ellie went back inside the house and closed the curtain behind her. There was nothing anyone could do now, not even to the house. Everything was scattered all over the floor, and poor Tommy still would not go to sleep. She wondered what would happen when the news spread through their section of town and at once remembered the man in the gray Chevrolet. It would serve them right if her father's friends got one of them.

Ellie pulled up an overturned chair and sat down across from her mother, who was crooning to Tommy. What Mr. Paul said was right, white people just couldn't be trusted. Her family had expected anything, but even though they had practiced ducking, they didn't really expect anybody to try tearing down the house. But the funny thing was the house belonged to one of them. Maybe it was a good thing her family were just renters.

Exhausted, Ellie put her head down on the table. She didn't know what they were going to do about tomorrow—in the daytime they didn't need electricity. She was too tired to think anymore about Tommy, yet she could not go to sleep. So she sat at the table trying to sit still, but every few minutes she would involuntarily twitch. She tried to steady her hands, all the time listening to her mother's sing-songy voice and waiting for her father to come back inside the house.

She didn't know how long she lay hunched against the kitchen table, but when she looked up, her wrists bore the imprints of her hair. She unfolded her arms gingerly, feeling the blood rush to her fingertips. Her father sat in the chair opposite her, staring at the vacant space between them. She heard her mother creep away from the table, taking Tommy to his room.

Ellie looked out the window. The darkness was turning to gray, and the hurt feeling was disappearing. As she sat there she could begin to look at the kitchen matter-of-factly. Although the hands of the clock were just a little past five-thirty, she knew somebody was going to have to start clearing up and cook breakfast.

She stood and tipped across the kitchen to her parents' bedroom. "Mama," she whispered, standing near the door of Tommy's room. At the sound of her voice, Tommy made a funny throaty noise in his sleep. Her mother motioned for her to go out and be quiet. Ellie knew then that Tommy had just fallen asleep. She crept back to the kitchen and began picking up the dishes that could be salvaged, being careful not to go into the living room.

She walked around her father, leaving the broken glass underneath the kitchen table. "You want some coffee?" she asked.

He nodded silently, in strange contrast she thought to the water faucet that turned with a loud gurgling noise. While she let the water run to get hot, she measured out the instant coffee in one of the plastic cups. Next door she could hear people moving around in the Williamses' kitchen, but they too seemed much quieter than usual.

"You reckon everybody knows by now?" she asked, stirring the coffee and putting the saucer in front of him.

"Everybody will know by the time the city paper comes

out," he said. "Somebody was here last night from the *Observer.* Guess it'll make front page."

She leaned against the cabinet for support, watching him trace endless circles in the brown liquid with the spoon. "Sergeant Kearns says they'll have almost the whole force out there tomorrow," he said.

"Today," she whispered.

Her father looked at the clock and then turned his head.

"When's your mother coming back in here?" he asked, finally picking up the cup and drinking the coffee.

"Tommy's just off to sleep," she answered. "I guess she'll be in here when he's asleep for good."

She looked out the window of the back door at the row of tall hedges that had separated their neighborhood from the white people for as long as she remembered. While she stood there, she heard her mother walk into the room. To her ears the steps seemed much slower than usual. She heard her mother stop in front of her father's chair.

"Jim," she said, sounding very timid, "what we going to do?" Yet as Ellie turned toward her, she noticed her mother's face was strangely calm as she looked down on her husband.

Ellie continued standing by the door listening to them talk. Nobody asked the question to which they all wanted an answer.

"I keep thinking," her father said finally, "that the policemen will be with him all day. They couldn't hurt him inside the school building without getting some of their own kind."

"But he'll be in there all by himself," her mother said softly. "A hundred policemen can't be a little boy's only friends."

She watched her father wrap his calloused hands, still splotched with machine oil, around the salt shaker on the table.

"I keep trying," he said to her, "to tell myself that somebody's got to be the first one, and then I just think how quiet he's been all week."

Ellie listened to the quiet voices that seemed to be a

room apart from her. In the back of her mind she could hear phrases of a hymn her grandmother used to sing, something about trouble, her being born for trouble.

"Jim, I cannot let my baby go." Her mother's words, although quiet, were carefully pronounced.

"Maybe," her father answered, "it's not in our hands. Reverend Davis and I were talking day before yesterday how God tested the Israelites. Maybe he's just trying us."

"God expects you to take care of your own," his wife interrupted. Ellie sensed a trace of bitterness in her mother's voice.

"Tommy's not going to understand why he can't go to school," her father replied. "He's going to wonder why, and how are we going to tell him we're afraid of them?" Her father's hand clutched the coffee cup. "He's going to be fighting them the rest of his life. He's got to start sometime."

"But he's not on their level. Tommy's too little to go around hating people. One of the others, they're bigger, they understand about things."

Ellie still leaning against the door saw that the sun covered part of the sky behind the hedges, and the light slipping through the kitchen window seemed to reflect the shiny red of the tablecloth.

"He's our child," she heard her mother say. "Whatever we do, we're going to be the cause." Her father had pushed the cup away from him and sat with his hands covering part of his face. Outside Ellie could hear a horn blowing.

"God knows we tried but I guess there's just no use." Her father's voice forced her attention back to the two people sitting in front of her. "Maybe when things come back to normal, we'll try again."

He covered his wife's chunky fingers with the palm of his hand, and her mother seemed to be enveloped in silence. The three of them remained quiet, each involved in his own thoughts, but related, Ellie knew, to the same thing. She was the first to break the silence.

"Mama," she called after a long pause, "do you want me to start setting the table for breakfast?"

Her mother nodded.

Ellie turned the clock so she could see it from the sink while she washed the dishes that had been scattered over the floor.

"You going to wake up Tommy, or you want me to?"

"No," her mother said, still holding her father's hand, "let him sleep. When you wash your face, you go up the street and call Hezekiah. Tell him to keep up with the children after school. I want to do something to this house before they come home."

She stopped talking and looked around the kitchen, finally turning to her husband. "He's probably kicked the spread off by now," she said. Ellie watched her father, who without saying anything walked toward the bedroom.

She watched her mother lift herself from the chair and automatically push in the stuffing underneath the cracked plastic cover. Her face looked set, as it always did when she was trying hard to keep her composure.

"He'll need something hot when he wakes up. Hand me the oatmeal," she commanded, reaching on top of the icebox for matches to light the kitchen stove.

# Not Your Singing, Dancing Spade

JULIA FIELDS

Fields's story of a black entertainer married to a white woman was published at the height of the black nationalist movement in 1967. That context helps illuminate the theme of Fields's small gem of a story. The social-climbing main character of the story is caught between his sense of his own status in the white world he overvalues and the judgment of blacks who see deeper than he is able. The story brings to light the intense, underlying reactions to interracial relationships that is still a feature of American society, while striking a somewhat ironic stance toward black men who value themselves through the color of their female companions. The story first appeared in *Negro Digest* in 1967 and was reprinted in the 1968 anthology *Black Fire*.

IT WAS RIDICULOUS to have an issue of such an insipidly written magazine in the apartment, he knew. Nevertheless, he picked it up again and began to read the article written about himself. The audacity of it, and the incredible and insane arrogance it suggested, made him feel helpless against the terrible tide of consciousness so established and so knowledgeable to him and to his people. His brains were sealed, signed for, and delivered, just as his body would have been in the previous century.

He focused his eyes and finished the article, his black hands and black eyes drooping wearily over the side of the plush gold sofa. Then he lay down upon it, keeping his shoes on. It was not very comforting at all.

The article stated clearly that his childhood dream had been to pursue and to possess a "blond goddess," that he could never be happy without her. It made fun of a black entertainer he had dated. It said he paid her to give him his "freedom." There was no picture of her. But there was a listing and pictures of national and international ladies with fair hair to whom he had been linked romantically at one time or another.

There was a picture of him with his wife—his wife bright and grinning, and his teeth matching her fairness kilometer for kilometer. His hair was falling into his eyes. It always seemed to be fallen into his eyes, whenever he was playing golf, or driving, or dancing, or singing. And he always had to toss his head, give his neck a quick snappy jerk in order to keep his tumbling hair neat. It always got into his eyes. He bent over to light a cigarette. The hair fell into his eyes. He used his free hand to brush it back, knowing that it would tumble into his eyes again.

His wife entered the room. She was very, very white. He had asked her to stay out of the sun. And the black maid entered with a tray of beverages. The children liked the maid and his wife liked the maid. He hated her. She was almost as black as himself, and her hair was short. He always felt like singing an old down-home blues whenever he saw her . . . "I don't want no woman if her hair ain't no longer'n mine; she ain't nothing but trouble and keep you worried all the time." But no matter how much hatred he showed toward her, the woman was always kind and serene; yet there was the very faintest hint of laughter and incredible mockery in her eyes when she looked at him. He knew the look. He himself had given it to others many times. He remembered the party in Greenwich Village, the interracial party with all the loud music and the loud dancing, which belonged to a younger time than now.

There was a colored girl there, he was told, but all the girls looked of the same race, because there was not the brightest lighting. Still he thought that he would know a "Sapphire" if he saw one. The girl's white date had laughed at him for saying this, and slapped him on the back. He had felt so clever, so able to take "it," so "free," so optimistic, so "in," and that was when he knew that he could make it if he chose to make it in the big world of the American dream. And this world, as he knew it, was not white. It was a gray world with room in it for all the people. He felt so "in" that he almost blessed Emma Lazarus.

A group of them were laughingly trying to sing a foolish ditty with dirty words. They were all so happy and drunk. And there was a girl whose hands kept going to her temple and down behind her ears with long locks of hair, which she pushed over her shoulder. Then she would toss her hair, or attempt to, but the long hair barely moved. The long strands did not move freely. They seemed waxen, stuck around her face like fetters. His hands went to his own head in sudden derision, and stuck in the Dixie Peach. The girl swung her head again and caught his eyes. He looked into her eyes as deeply as he could, and his bitterness spilled like a white sizzle across to her in mockery and despair and a tender, compassionate hatred.

The boy who had slapped him on the back moved toward the girl, caught her by the hand, and began to dance with her, his hips swaying, brutally ungraceful in mock-Negro.

He went to the window. Dawn was moving up to the river and over the roofs. It was time for him to go. He knew that he would never go to another party with a Negro. No matter what color the Negro was—they were all embarrassing. He might go if he were the only one. Only if he were.

He knew that his wife somehow resulted from this promise which he had made to himself a long time ago at the Village party. He had come a long way. His name, his picture, his life, were on the lips and the life-sized posters of the world. Subway bums, whores, and dogs could lean against his photograph in most of the world's swinging cities. And he was very wealthy. He had his own entourage of jesters and the best hairdresser in the world—one who kept him well stocked with the best pomade.

The article in the magazine shouldn't have bothered him so much, he told himself. It wasn't the first time, nor would it be the last. He had to pay the price. They were requiring it of him, and he had to make it. He had to keep making it.

It was too late to stop. Where would he go? There was no place elsewhere but down. Down to scorn. Back, slowly but certainly, to a world which had become alien, black, strange, and nameless. The wolves would chew him black.

Back to black indeed. Never. What did it matter? The whites had begun their assaults late; the blacks had berated him all his life. "Black bastard. Black bastard. Bad hair." "Boy, get a brush." And comparisons: "Almost Bunky's color." "No, not quite as black as Bunky." "Child, I couldn't see nuthin' but eyes and teeth." "I like him, sure, but my daddy would kill me if I married a man that black." "Child, I wouldn't want to mess up my children with that color." He was recalling the words of parents, relatives, and lovers. His yellow mother. His jet-black father who was his mother's footstool. His mother's freckles. Her rituals with Black and White ointment. Her "straight" nose. He hated his flat nose. All of his pictures were in profile. Except the one in the magazine. In that one, all of his black faults were on view. In that picture, the heat had turned the expensive pomade on his hair to plain and simple shining grease. Ah, chicken-eaters of the world, unite. You have nothing to lose except your shame.

He began to dress, immaculately as always, for there was, his agent had said, a chance to make another million. Melanin and millions. Millions and melanin.

Numbly, he moved about the dressing room, larger than his parents' living room had been.

Mutely, he dressed. Dejectedly, he faced himself in the mirror. Silently, the green gall of self-revulsion passed through his psyche and soul. Swiftly, he recalled the chance to make a million and the wife who would spend it on furs, jewels, fun, cosmetics, and servants. And the whole world would see what black bastards with millions and melanin could do. Yes, they would.

The agent's smooth voice, on the phone, reassured him about the million. There was nothing to reassure him about himself. Nothing. Nothing.

Down the stairs, voices were shrill suddenly. His little girl was sobbing. He heard the maid say, "Be quiet. You'll wake up your mama."

"But Cathy said my daddy's a nigger monkey."

"What do you care what Cathy says?"

"And Daddy puts gasoline in his hair to make it nice like her daddy's hair. Isn't Daddy's hair nice?"

"Of course it's nice. That little sickly Cathy with those strings hanging 'round her face. Don't pay her no attention. She's just jealous because your daddy's got the original beauty."

"The what?"

"The first, best beauty in the world. Black. Your daddy's a pretty man. That's why everybody likes him. Where've you seen Cathy's daddy's pictures? Not nearly's many places as your daddy. Your daddy is a beautiful man."

"Is he?"

"Yes. Of course he don't know how pretty he is. Anyhow, it's easy to be pale. Like milk. It ain't got nothing in it. Like vanilla ice cream. See? Now take any other flavor. Take chocolate. Milk with cocoa. You love chocolate malt, don't you?"

"Yes."

"Take strawberry. Any ice cream. It's nothing as just plain milk. What goes in makes it beautiful. It can be decorated, but by itself, it lacks a lot. Your daddy was born decorated. Born a pretty king. Born beautiful. Don't believe Cathy. She's dumb."

"Born beautiful. Daddy was born beautiful. That silly Cathy. She's a dumb one. My daddy is pretty. I always thought so."

"Yes, I always thought so, too."

Numbly, he stood there. He had to listen. The annihilated searching, seeking to be. Terror. Who had first given assumption and such supreme arrogance to the captives? He knew she had read the article that had denied her existence. A black female. The race and sex that, according to them, could never move him to love, to cherish, to desire. *Caldonia, Caldonia, what makes your big head so hard?*

He remembered his boyhood. And all the lyrics that

laughed at and lamented black womanhood. Blackness. Black manhood. Black childhood. Black.

They had made the world for him, had set all the traps. He had been born to it. The horror of blackness. They had outdone themselves. They had outdone him. And it was not meant that he should ever be saved. He must believe. And they could assume postures and lies. And they could believe in his self-hatred. And they could rest comfortably, believing that he believed, and continue their believing.

They were so arrogant, so stupefied by history and circumstances that they could accept any incredible thing they said about him. Terror. Who was the bondsman? Who was the freed man? He knew.

Life began to flow again. His blood sang vital and red. Freedom. Power, even. Yes, I *am* beautiful. Born black. Born with no lack. Decorated. Born decorated.

At the foot of the stairs, he could hear the maid again, angrily muttering. With dancer's feet, he moved nearer. Nearer to hear, nearer to self, to recovery.

"Lies, lies, lies. Sometimes we have to lie to make it. Even to live. We got to lie to ourselves, to our friends and to our enemies. To those we loves and to those we hates. If they so smart, they ain't got to b'lieve us."

He saw her throw the movie magazine clear down his long, sumptuous living room. And he heard his little daughter laughing as she went to get the magazine.

"Here. Put it in the trash can."

"But it's got Daddy's picture. Daddy's picture's in it."

"Your daddy's picture's everywhere. Besides, that's not a good picture of him. Some fool took it. Here." The child obeyed.

"Arrogant, uppity folks'll believe anything. Let 'em pay. And pay. White bastards."

"What? What?" the child questioned.

"Nothing. Go on to the playroom until I call you for lunch. I got to vacuum up this room."

Then he was there, standing in the beautiful, luxurious room facing the black woman with the short hair.

"Humph," he heard her say as she turned to push a low,

red, incredulously plush, and ridiculously expensive chair aside for her vacuuming.

"Here, let me be of service," he said.

"Never mind."

"Let me!" he said again, and gently pushed her aside.

"Humph," she said again. But he got a glimpse of her face, which had years of anger and defiance and hope written in chicken-scratch wrinkles and crow's-feet. And there was the mockery he always saw there. And yet a kindness, a laughter which was very sweet and strong. And the barest hint of tears in the eyes, tears like monuments to despair.

When he replaced the chairs and kissed his wife and child, he said his good-bye to the black woman and sang a snatch of his latest recording as he walked to the elevator. He felt light—weightless and yet strong and pretty. "I feel pretty," he thought. Well, not that kind of pretty, he mocked himself. But it was surprising that he sang, for he had promised himself that he was only an entertainer, that he wasn't your singing, dancing spade, that he, a professional only, wouldn't be caught dead, drunk, or straitlaced, singing off the stage or away from the TV cameras, or dancing like some ham-hocking jigaboo.

Nevertheless, his chauffeur smiled happily when he cut a step from his latest musical sensation as he entered the limousine with the sacrilegious words, "I feel pretty," floating, cakewalking from his lips.

# A Revolutionary Tale

## Nikki Giovanni

The black nationalist movement of the late 1960s charged black men and women to revolutionary action against years of social and racial oppression. The protagonist of Nikki Giovanni's story, a magna cum laude college graduate, is representative of a generation of young blacks of her time at a crossroads between full-time commitment to revolutionary aims and the more comfortable road to career and conformity. The unforgettable voice of Kim is the voice of a black generation at the height of self-affirmation and energetic intellectual growth. Her problems are as varied as were the black nation's in the 1960s, as are her explosive responses. Typically, Giovanni mixes social criticism with wry satire and dry irony characteristic of her career as poet, essayist and, less often, short story writer. The story was first published in *Negro Digest* and reprinted in Giovanni's *Gemini: An Extended Autobiographical Statement on My First 25 Years as a Black Poet.*

THE WHOLE DAMN THING is Bertha's fault. Bertha is my roommate and a very Black person, to put it mildly. She's a Revolutionary! I don't want to spend needless time discussing Bertha, but it's sort of important. Before I met her, I was Ayn Rand–Barry Goldwater all the way. Bertha kept asking how could Black people *be* conservative? What have they got to conserve? And after a while (realizing that I had absolutely nothing, period) I came around. But not as fast as she was moving. It wasn't enough that I learned to like the regular mass of colored people—as a whole, as it were—but she wanted me to like the individual colored people that we knew. I resisted that like hell but eventually came around. Bertha is the sort of Black person where eventually you come around. Now just be patient, you want to know why I'm late; don't you? So I got an Afro and began the conference beat and did all those Black things that we were supposed to do. I even gave up white men for The Movement . . . and that was no easy sacrifice. Not that they were that good—nobody comes down with a sister like a brother, but they were a major source of support for me. I agreed that they shouldn't be allowed to support The Movement, but I believe in income being passed around, and if anyone has income to spare, whiteys do. So I cut myself off from a very important love of mine—money— and that presented a problem. No I'm not going round-robinhood'sbarn, this is a part of it. So when my income was terminated for ideological reasons, you'd think she'd say something like, "I'll take over the rent and your gas bill since you've sacrificed so much for The Movement." You'd really think that, wouldn't you? But no, she asked me about a job! A job, for Christ's sake! I didn't even know anybody who worked but her! And here she was talking 'bout a job! I calmly suggested that I would apply for relief. You see, I believe society owes all of its members certain things like food, clothing, shelter, and gas, so I was going to apply to society since individual contributions were no longer acceptable. She laughed that cynical laugh of hers and offered to go down with me. No, says I, I can do it myself. So I went down at the end of the week.

Now I'm a firm believer in impressions. I think the first impression people make is very important, and since I would have to consider welfare my job from now on, for Bertha's sake at least, I got dressed up and went down. I'm sure you've applied for relief at least once, so you know the procedure. I went to Intake and met an old civil servant; the kind who's been on the job since Hayes set the system up. She asked me so many questions about my personal life I thought she was interviewing me for a possible spot in heaven. Then we got to my family. I told her Mommy was a supervisor in the Welfare Department and that Daddy was a social worker. She shook her head and looked disgusted —just plain disgusted with me—huffed up her flat chest, and said, "Young lady, you are not eligible for relief!" And stormed away! I started after her. "What the hell do you mean 'eligible'?" I asked. "I'll take somebody's job who really needs it. Somebody with skills or the ability to be trained, with a wife and kids, or maybe just an unwed mother will be put out of work! What kind of jive agency are you! You sure don't give a damn about people!" As she turned the corner, I had to run to keep up with her. "And who are you to decide what I need? You nothing but a jive petty bourgeoisie bullshit civil servant." Yes I did. I told her exactly that. I mean, that's what she is! "Going 'round deciding people's needs! You got needs yourself. Who decides how your needs gonna be filled? You ain't God or Mary or even the Holy Ghost—telling me what I'm eligible for," and I was laying her out. The nerve! I'd come all the way down there and didn't have on Levi's or my miniskirt but looked nice! I mean really clean, and she says I'm not eligible. Really did piss me off. At the end of the corridor where she was hurrying to, I saw this figure. It looked real small and pitiful like. It was Mommy. I guess someone had recognized me and called her to come down. I went over to put my arms around her. "Don't cry, Mommy. It'll be all right." But she just cried and cried and kept saying, "Oh Kim. Why can't you be like other daughters?" I got so involved with soothing her that the servant got away. "Mom," I said as I walked her to her office, "there's going to be a Black Revolution all over the world, and we must prepare for it. We've got to determine our own standards of eligibility. That's all." She quit crying a little and just looked at me pitifully. Then she put her arms around me and said, "Oh Kim. I love you. But why can't you just get married and divorced and have babies and things like other daughters? Why do you have to disgrace us like this? I didn't mind when you got kicked out of school for drinking, and I even got used to all those men I didn't like. And remember the time you made the front page for doing that go-go dance at the Democratic Convention? I've been a Democrat all my life! You know that. But I was proud that in the middle of Johnson's speech you jumped on the table, shoes and all, to dance your protest to the war in Vietnam. But this is my job! Your father and I have worked very hard to give you everything we could." "Mom," I cut her off, "I'm not against your job. I tried to explain it wasn't personal even when I had to throw that rock through your window that time. We didn't fire bomb, did we? 'No,' I told the group, 'don't fire bomb the welfare department.' And when we had to turn the director's car over, you noticed that he didn't get hurt? I told the group, 'Be sure not to hurt the director.' That's what I told them. But Mom, I'm broke now. All my savings are gone, and if I don't get on relief, I'll have to take a job. Oh Mommy, what will I do if I take a job? Locked up in a building with all those strangers for eight hours every day. And people saying, 'Good morning, Kim. How's it going?' or 'Hey Kim, what you doing after work?' I mean getting familiar with me and I don't even know them! How could I stand that?" Then for the first time in the twenty-three years I've known her she looked me dead in the eye—I mean exactly straight—and said, "You'll either have to work or go to grad school." It floored me. I mean she's never made a decision like that all the time I've known her. "Mom," I said, "you don't mean it. You've been talking to Bertha. You're angry with me for what I told that civil servant. I'll apologize. I'll make it up somehow. I swear! I'll get my hair done!" But she would not budge. "Kim, it's school or a job." "Mom, 'member when I went back and graduated from college? Magna cum laude and all. 'Member how proud you and Daddy were that I had the guts to go back after all they did to me in college? 'Member what you said? 'Member how you said I had done ALL you wanted me to do? 'Member how you kept saying you wouldn't ask me for nothing else? 'Member, Mom? Mom? 'Member?" But she wouldn't budge. I tell you it's something when your own mother turns against you. She knew I was working for The Revolution. "What would happen to The Revolution if I quit to take a job?

What would my people do?" I asked her. And she looked at me and said, rather coldly if I recall, "Your people need you to lead the way. Not just toward irresponsible acts but toward a true Revolution." "There's nothing irresponsible about chaos and anarchy. We must brush our teeth before eating a meal." "Kim, I've read everything you've written. I've heard on tape all your speeches. And what are you talking about now? Program. I've read Frantz Fanon and Stokely Carmichael. I especially enjoyed *Burn the Honky* by Rap Brown—he's got an amazing sense of humor. I've read Killens and Jones and Neal and McKissick. I've read most of the books on those lists you gave us. Haven't I always tried to understand you and sympathize with you? When I was going to get Mother a cookbook, did I buy *La Gastro-nomique*? No! I bought the *Ebony Cook Book,* even though Mother has forgotten more than Frieda McKnight could ever have known. When your father and I went to the So-cial Work Convention in Detroit last year, did we stay with the other delegates at the Hilton? No! We stayed at the Rio Grande. I've done all I could for The Revolution, and I'll probably do more. But I'm not going to allow you this be-havior. You will get a job, or you will go to school." "Aw Mom," I protested, "you just don't understand. . . ." "Kim, that's all there is to it. I'll give you a surprise when you tell me something definite." I was crushed. Absolutely crushed. My own mother turned against me. I must have looked terribly hurt because she kissed me again and said, "Oh Kim. It's best—really it is. If I can read your people and try to understand your way, you can try mine." I called my father.

I asked him to take me to lunch. I think he knew. He didn't know when I called him, but by the time we met for lunch—he knew. 'Course being a social worker and relating to people and all for a living, he didn't just burst in and say, "I agree with your mother." No. He sat down and ordered me a drink. He doesn't drink anymore since he and his liver made an intellectual decision that Negroes shouldn't get high. That is his sacrifice for The Movement. Of course he quit five years ago when he was in the hospital; he considered it a religious-conversion thing. His own special sacrifice to Jesus. We used to ask about it, but he always just said Jesus had spoken to him through his liver. And nothing would shake him. He quit church after a couple of months, but he continued to tithe every month faithfully and never drank again. His tennis game improved, and he got to be a good swimmer again. He took up golf and to tell the truth had gotten so damned clean-cut-american Mommy began sneaking gin into his eggs every morning just to keep him from becoming a real bastard. He doesn't know that, however. So we sat down and I had a drink and we ordered lunch. "What's on your mind, chicken?" (He always calls me some sort of animal or inanimate object. I'm not sure what his message is.) I didn't want to throw it on him right away. "DADDY MOMMYSAYSI'VEGOT-TAGOTOSCHOOLORTAKEAJOBANDIDON'TTHINK THAT'SFAIR," I said. "Uhmm. Would you say that again in English . . . I mean American?" "Mommy says I have to go to school or get a job." "Good, lambie-pie. Which one is it?" "Daddy, you don't understand. I don't think it's fair." "Of course not, sugar lump. She shouldn't have said it like that. You just get yourself a nice job. You don't even have to consider school. I'll call up Harry White and see what he can do for you. 'Course you can get one on your own . . . you just let me know what you would like." "Oh Daddy," I said, "you're on her side, and she's been talking to Bertha, and nobody ever understands me." "I try to understand you, angel cake. I've read almost all those books on your lists and everything you've written, and I've heard all your speeches. I think you're doing fine work, but you must set an example, too. You just show your people that new systems can be created. If you want to destroy something, you must first learn how it works and what need it's filling. After the—how you say 'Black Flame'?—encases the world, you'll want your people to work for The Black Nation. How can you encourage that if you have no idea of what you're asking of them? That's one thing I noticed about everyone from Nkrumah to Ben Bella to Brown. They don't really know what they're asking everyday people to do. Not that they don't work—and hard—but do they punch a time clock? Do they have a thirty-minute lunch hour? Do they dig ditches? Work in a mine? Not that they have to do every one of those; but have they labored? Have they punched a time clock? It's important that they do. And all the reading and writing in the world doesn't give a true understanding of time clocks. Maybe they'll do away with time clocks, but they must first understand what purpose they serve before they do."

"Oh, Daddy, not that many Black folks ever punch a clock!" "I'm not talking just about a clock, and you know it. I'm talking about going to work on time, eating lunch on time, getting off on time, going home on time. All those meetings, conferences, and rallies—even if they are on time —are scheduled to your and their convenience—not the people's. Get up at 6:30 or 7:00, go downtown, eat lunch with a couple of thousand people, relate to your supervisor, relate to your clients, relate to the people in your office or sewer, get off at 4:30 or 5:00, rush home, read your paper while your wife cooks dinner, talk to your children, listen to their troubles, put them to bed; talk to your wife, listen to her troubles, take her to bed; and in your spare time watch TV, say hello to your neighbor, run to the store, go to a rally, try to read a book. Try that and you might understand why The Revolution, as you call it, moves so slowly." "Oh Daddy, I didn't want a lecture. I just wanted you to be on my side." "Is that my name now? Ohdaddy? I am on your side, brown sugar. That's why I'm telling you this. Get yourself a job, then do all the things you're doing. You may readjust your methods." "I won't change! I won't let the bourgeoisie system get me!" "I didn't say your thinking, Kim. I didn't say you would readjust your thinking. I said you *may* change your methods." Lunch was ruined for me. I went home to type a résumé, and that wasn't easy. It had been that kind of a day.

I have this really neato pink IBM—it was a gift; though when I got it it was a down payment. It's always worked right. I've had it for two and a half years and never had a bit of trouble. Once a year I call the people and they clean and service it—that's it. It's a dream. But that day, of all days, it just wouldn't work right. The "s" was skipping, and the "a" was hitting twice, plus the magic margin wouldn't click in, and it was just a fucky day. I quit and stretched out on the floor. I fell sort of half asleep. I couldn't decide between school or an agency job, and it must have been on my mind 'cause I had this really terrible dream. There was this university chasing me down the streets. I turned the corner to get away from it and ran right into the mouth of an agency. It gobbled me up, but it couldn't digest me. When it tried to swallow me, I put up such a fight that it belched me back into life. As I hit the street, there was this university again, waiting for me like a big dyke that has run her prey into a corner, with a greasy smile on her lips. I woke up screaming. Both of them would destroy me! And furthermore, what did I need with a master's degree? As I brooded on my future, the image of educational institutions kept coming back. Going to school is like throwing the rabbit into a briar patch. There would be scores of students that I could convert. And because of "academic freedom" the school would have to accept and support me; or at least leave me alone unless I flunked out, drank a lot, or smoked in public. And if I applied in social work, both Mommy and Daddy would be pleased 'cause I'd get a degree and agency training and an inadequate paycheck to boot. So I sat down at my pink IBM to type a letter for an application blank. Surprisingly enough the typewriter was fixed. I mailed it immediately and sat back while others stronger and wiser than I would determine my fate.

Geeze you've got a one-track mind! I'm trying to get around to explaining about the delay. I was, you know, accepted in school. I thought everyone would be happy and leave me alone. That was February, and I had nine months of Freedom before enrollment day. And I fully intended to use them. I got my acceptance letter on a Tuesday. That was so upsetting that all I could do for a long time was just gnash and growl. It didn't bother Bertha a bit 'cause she just started running 'round the house singing "Kim's going to school . . ." You know, like she was happy. My mood wasn't too positive, so I told her, dead calmly, that if she didn't get the fuck out of my half of the apartment, I'd kill her. She laughed one of those grand "ha ha ha" type things, then spread her arms and pirouetted out the door. It was hard to take. After these years of freedom of choice and movement I was going back to school. I just cried and cried. Then I thought: What the hell! Hadn't I survived the time we were playing The Prince of Wales? Hadn't I survived the Wisconsin Sleeper? Hadn't I been to Harlem? Hadn't I refused to screw a white boy when we were in Mississippi on the big march? Why wouldn't I survive now? I was really talking it up to myself. Much worse things had happened to me, and here I was acting like a cry baby. Why wouldn't I survive, I asked myself bravely; boldly, perhaps —brazenly! Why would I not survive? BECAUSE!! came the answer, and I just cried and cried.

I've got to tell you this. No—don't be that way—listen, if ever something happens to you that makes you real unhappy, and you've just got to cry about it, don't cry in the same spot. Move around. That's what I learned. After I cried and cried, there was this shiny puddle around my feet, and there were these blood-red eyes looking up at me. I learned then, never cry in one spot. But I was cool with it. I never really became emotionally involved in it. I cleaned up the mess, took a shower, got dressed to a "T," then went out walking the streets. I stopped by this bar I know and had a drink. One of my brothers, soul brothers, bought me a drink, and we started discussing what would have to come down. He and I got into a real deep thing, and we talked until the bar closed. He kept wanting to kill toms, and I still think that's not who we have to kill. Toms, I told him, only have power if we let them have power. I mean, if a tom says get off the streets and you get off the streets, then that's your fault, not his. If, on the other hand, a tom tells you to get off the streets and you don't—well then the power structure has no use for him—plus if you can encourage him in a physical way to come on over to your side, then you've made a friend. I mean you can beat anyone or boycott them or something besides killing a brother to get him to either help you or get out the way. There are too few brothers on this shore already to be killing each other off. We need to get rid of whitey. I mean, if we can't kill a whitey, how can we ever justify killing a brother? That's a hell of a cop-out to me. Talking 'bout killing brothers—and sisters, too—and not being able to kill a whitey. The only way we can ever justify offing a brother is if we have already offed twenty whiteys—that's the ratio, I told him, for offing a brother. So we went to his place to talk further.

The next morning all my problems were solved, I thought. I had figured it all out. Now this much I knew about social work school—they will put up with anything at all except heterosexual relations—I mean anything at all. And the school where I was accepted was founded by two ladies who had adopted children. I just knew if I wrote them and explained that I had not only been screwing but had enjoyed it—well, I thought, they'd write a nice letter explaining the mistake in accepting me and that would be the end of that. So I jumped up and dashed home to compose a letter. Then I thought that won't get to them soon enough—I'd better send a wire—so I did.

TO THE SCHOOL OF SOCIAL WORK
DIRECTOR OF PLACEMENT
PLEASE BE ADVISED STOP I HAVE
SCREWED STOP IT WAS GOOD STOP SO
THERE EXPLANATION POINT
                    YOURS IN FREEDOM
                    KIM

I thought the minute they receive that they would really be sick of me. I got a long involved letter explaining how proud they were that I was so open to new things and that they were very pleased at my level of honesty. I tell you, I was pissed. That's the only way to describe it. And what the fuck did she mean "new things"? I'd been screwing since I was twelve, ten if you want to count the times before it was serious. And he wasn't new, anyway. I was truly indignant, but Bertha discouraged me from expressing my feeling to the school by just demoralizing my whole intellectual thing.

Well, yes, it was a calculated intellectual involvement. You see, I never act on my unabridged emotions. Emotions are to be controlled by the intellect. Even when I act in what could be considered an emotional manner, I have thought it out before and have *decided* this will be the way I act. So to have my whole intellectual bag blown sky high right before my eyes, well that was frightening. I started to give Bertha a quick punch in the gut, but my whole action-reaction syndrome began to reek of emotion, so I just cooled it a bit and dropped a half teaspoon Drano in her coffee later during the day.

Strange about that. I was only playing a little joke, and there was plenty of milk on hand, you see, to help offset the effects. So Bertha drank her coffee and went to the john and never once indicated that anything was wrong. Later, when I asked, she did say it had been awfully runny, but that was all. I'm a failure, I told myself—a failure. Oh goody! I'm a failure . . . I don't have to deal with it anymore. I dashed a telegram off to the director of placement:

PLEASE BE ADVISED STOP HAVE PUT DRANO IN ROOMMATE'S COFFEE STOP SHE LIVES STOP I AM A FAILURE YOU MUST REJECT ME STOP

Those ridiculous people up there just considered it a bid for attention. I got a nice long letter explaining how they realized I hadn't received my placement yet, and they were sorry but that they had a lot of work and sometimes even the best of us get tied down, etc. Plus, if you can dig it, they think I have ingenious ways of letting them know my needs. I mean, really! Ingenious! Goddamnit, I am a failure. If I don't find a decent quick way out of this, why I'll end up in an institution—a part of an agency—being decent, responsible—all those ugly, sick things that I hate. I'd really have to think of a scheme.

It was way in the middle of April before it even dawned

on me. I mean, it was so simple that I was overlooking the obvious. What is the one thing we know for damned sure about white people? I mean, you know, beside the fact that they hate Negroes, children, and sex. What is the one thing we know absolutely and positively about any honkie anywhere in the world? That he worships money. He's got such a case on money he's transferred it to anything green. That's why you see those goddamn KEEP OFF THE GRASS signs. Not that he cares about grass but that it's green. What's the quickest way to turn a honkie off? Ask him for money. He's as nice as he can be as long as he thinks he'll get your money—but the minute you ask him for some, well that's like asking a hippie for his pot or a Negro for his knife; I mean they get hostile. You don't believe it? Go into any bank and deposit five bucks. Then go back in a week and withdraw it. When you go to deposit it, they're all smiles. The V.P. will come out and shake your hand. The teller smiles and welcomes you to the family. And that's only five bucks I'm talking about. When you go to withdraw it, the first thing is the teller will say, "You realize this will close your account." Just like you didn't know that if you deposit five bucks and you withdraw five bucks that you were closing your account, and you just smile at him and say, "Yeah, groovy." He'll frown and say, "This will cost you one dollar." And you say, "Cool. Gimme my four bucks." Then he says, "This will take a minute." That's when you look at him very menacingly and say, "I should surely hope the hell not." Then he'll slam your money down and scream, "NEXT," or he'll slap the NEXT WINDOW PLEASE sign up and turn his back on you. And this is a Black teller I'm talking about. So knowing this I wrote the director of placement and told her I had no money; that I needed a stipend and a tuition grant. I just knew for whatever my charm or whatnot that they weren't going to pay me to go to their school. I mean as tight as they are they are not about to give me any money. I was as happy as a ten-year-old turkey the day before Thanksgiving—I knew I now had them by the ass—I was just naturally too tough to handle. I walked a little taller, breathed a little deeper, felt a little prouder. I was so happy that I went back to my Revolutionary Work. Not that I hadn't been working for Revolution all along—but I had really been hung up on this thing about a job.

We set up a Black Arts Festival, and I was working my you know what off. You may have heard about me being on the radio telling all the honkies not to come. I'm sure you heard about Lonnie going into the honkie neighborhood with his sign saying, YOU'RE NOT READY. It was great advertisement for us, and we were all really sorry about that kid. However, though the papers played it down after the first day it is not true that Lonnie tore his leg from the joint—he only fractured it. And contrary to first reports the kid will walk again. I personally tell all the brother Black Belts I know that they shouldn't provoke white kids, then beat on them. But, well, you're not always able to control Folk, even if they do take a lot of your advice. But that was the only incident that could be, in some quarters, considered unfortunate. It was a groovy set. The blue beasts foamed at the mouth, but it was our day! I say again, it was Revolutionary! Slavetown, U.S.A., was back in the movement 'cause the Kim was back into her thing.

I really forgot all that shit about school and jobs and do. I just put it out of my mind. Our underground press, yes it does have something to do with why I'm late. You see, we were putting out a magazine called *Love Black*. It was a group thing, you know, but it really belonged to all the people. We had learned the secret of why the folks don't read. C'mon, see do you know? You jive, they can too read. But nobody ever writes for them or writes anything they can relate to. So having figured that out through the very difficult process of stopping every brother we could on the corner one day asking them what they would enjoy reading, we went about getting *Love Black* out. See, most folks don't read, honkies especially, but people, too. You think they really read *GH* or *Time*? They look at the pictures and will scan any article they can see the end of. Most people like to read what they can see the end of. So we started a Black mag on $8\frac{1}{2} \times 11$ with articles that ran a page or less. Also it doesn't run over twenty pages all toto. Therefore a brother can read the whole damned thing, which is a legit mag, and really do two things: learn something positive about himself and complete something he started. Now don't start breaking into my explanation. It may well be propaganda, but all pieces of paper with writing are propaganda, and if I have to deal in mind control, it's much better to be Black-Washed. I mean the honkie press and stuff just naturally fucks with any Black man's mind 'cause first it doesn't recognize that there is a Black mind. It does what it can to a Black mind—it whitewashes it—it flushes it out of his head —that's what it does. But we were giving the people something, and we were getting a lot. One issue we were late, and all kinds of soul stepped up and told me if I didn't get my thing together and get the mag out, well, they would look upon that with disfavor. And they also sent articles in. Like we'd get slightly used toilet tissue with an article on it or brown paper bags with short sayings or just a note to say they dig us. Some of it looked like our ancestral writing, Egyptian, and we really had to work at deciphering it, but when you saw how the man changed after he had "published," well it would really hit you. You see, the brother will read if he's writing it or if he knows people who are, and *Love Black* was strictly ours. It wasn't the prettiest thing in the world, and sometimes it wasn't too clear. I've always maintained that if we lose the Revolution it'll be because we don't know nothing about machinery—but it was ours. It talked about Slavetown and what the brother thought and felt, and the brother was digging it. You got to understand the whole concept of writing.

Like in the East everything is dishonest. They do a lot of things, but mostly it's three thousand per cent B. S. The people are so used to talking Black, buying Black, and thinking Black, they don't get shook no more. Every hustler (why is it a Black capitalist is called a hustler?) and every panhandler is Black, so Black don't mean nothing. It's taken for granted. And one Black thing is like another. They've been saturated with a program that has never come off. Between Garvey and Malcolm, Harlem should be owned lock, stock, and barrel by us—but we still trying to get rat control and jobs, and paying rent to circumcised honkies. In the Dupont plantation state they even passed a law that said if building codes aren't lived up to, you can deposit your money in one of the company banks and leave it there till the cat comes round. Ain't that the jivest shit you ever heard of? I mean, paternalism with a capital WHITE. No, wait a minute. If you live in a house or apt. and something is wrong with it and you living there every day the good lord makes you Black, well you should fix that place up and what's left over from rent should go in your pocket. So the old witch from the Welfare Dept. comes down and tries to explain that she'll have to hold your check if you don't pay your rent to the rightful owner. And that's when you come out of your thing so righteously and whip it on her so beautifully. You just light up a joint and calmly explain, "Honkies have made women, bombs, and Kellogg's corn flakes, but they have never made a piece of land. The land is one bitch that is everybody's woman, and I, being man and all, have got a right to a piece of her." You see, the honkies' whole sex thing is tied up to land. No lie. Land is their love. All land, except Germany, is female. The motherland, her, she—all land is woman. And they do anything to prove that they are worthy to be land's man. Only land don't give a shit about white people. See, land has this memory thing. Land remembers god stepped out on space and looked around and said, I'LL MAKE ME A MAN. God reached down into land, a woman, and formed this thing—you know, a man. Now land has always been Black. And you know god well enough to know that he goes first class. So god got the best land he could find, which had to be the Blackest land he could find. You just don't know about no white land. Snow, maybe, some white sand, maybe; but you just don't know about no white land. And land is hip to that. Land is very put out that we are making her prostitute herself for the beast. You didn't hear about no land being raped until the beast came along. We live in harmony with land because we are a part of land and we are out of land. The honkie came from sand and snow.

Now what is that? That's nothing. It has a place on earth, but it's nothing. Snow freezes land, and sand dries her up; both destroy land and land wants to live and recreate. You run it on down to where you are going to free land so that she can go about woman's work of taking care of her children—the Black people of the earth. Now she'll send the law out, but that don't mean nothing, either. The law only means something if you think it does. So she'll send out the law to make you pay, and you smile sincerely and promise to get it in next week. After you're alone with your piece of land, you remove very carefully anything that cannot be replaced; like pictures of your first lay, your joints, etc., and you throw kerosene on everything else. You see, it's yours and if you can't enjoy it in freedom and peace, then land wants you to destroy it. You can't destroy land because it'll always be there, but you can destroy the rapist's claim stake. The only thing about that land that makes the beast think he owns it is the claim he's staked, a house, a building, a fence, so you destroy that. That's when you burn. You don't burn to get the thief to fix it up, you burn when you've staked your claim and they try to steal it from you. And I really believe that after you've fixed it up and made it yours, you'll kill for it.

That's the one thing we've got to understand. This Revolution isn't to show what we're willing to die for, Black people have been willing to die for damn near everything on earth, it's to show what we're willing to kill for. Yes it is! Do we love life enough to deal righteously with key honkies? We don't have to deal with King and Young and those other three or four if we don't want to. We have got to deal with the folk who send them up. Which means we have to control ourselves. I have got to control me, and you have got to control you. Like if I see something that needs to be done and you see something else, we don't got to argue about what to do. You do yours, and I'll do mine. It's like we're on a road that forks off, then comes back together. We just had different priorities, and that don't make one right or wrong, just different. But if I use the fact that you want to do something I don't want to do to keep from doing what I have to do, then I'm not together. I'm B.S.'ing, and I know it. See, you and I are never in a conflict situation 'cause we're after the same thing—we're after the same honkie, and however we get him is our business. All that jive about coordination and keeping people in line and Elites and shit don't really mean nothing. That's not Revolution—that's not anarchy! And anarchy is what we want. This country doesn't have anything that we can't build again if we need it. But to even try to think of taking over and preserving GM or something, what for? Nobody's trying to make the system Black, we're trying to make a system human so that Black folks can live in it. That means we're trying to destroy the system. It's not even a question of can Black folks run it better than white folks. We don't have to prove to whites that we can—and if we take over their system, that'll be the reason. We haven't got to prove nothing to honkies 'cause they are nobody's authority on nothing.

Look here, we take over their system, give Black folks jobs and property, and what'll we have? We'll still have troops in Asia, we'll still be raping Africa, we'll still be controlling and killing folks in South America 'cause that's what makes the system run. You can't rape Europe 'cause her legs are spread and her mouth is wet just waiting to suck in Black people. No, that's one whore we'd better avoid. She's not even good from what I heard. She wants to blow you, but that's nothing new 'cause America has been blowing your mind for half a century or more. And the latest reports from Hanoi do indicate to me that some folks' minds are hanging between their legs. We have got to rid ourselves of those needs.

But the whole damn thing I do blame on Bertha. 'Cause I was just as happy sitting at home twittering my toes and masturbating every now and then. I didn't even know that I was colored let alone anything about Blackness. But she kept bringing those beautiful Black people home, and they kept talking that talk to me, and as I moved, I moved toward Black Power, and I recognized the extent of white power, which is so pervasive that the American solution cannot be Black Power at all, though as a world solution it is a possibility, but must be Revolution—anarchy, total chaos—and this should not be so hard for us since we have worked so diligently in every other cause we can now work for our own. We have sacrificed our lives and interests for white power, and now we can save ourselves through Revolution—our baptism by fire. But as I worked this out, people kept calling me a hater, and really I'm a lover. No one knows how much I do love all that is lovable. Then Bertha chimed in to ask do I love Black folks enough to trust them to TCB, and do I trust Black people to do those things necessary by any means necessary, recognizing that the means is in fact the ends. She kept saying if they and I are one, then I should get out of the way and see where they would go without me. And since Revolution ages you so quickly, and having watched the summer I had to admit that I was old and tired and recognized that already we were moving beyond my vision, so maybe I should step aside and regroup.

So I packed and made arrangements to come to school, and everybody cheered and was really pleased with my decision, and I kept telling myself that it would be good and that I was dealing with the best the system had to offer and that if I couldn't relate meaningful enough to them for me to accept them, then I could easily go back to destroying it in a very real manner. So having made my decision, I decided to walk. I mean, it would have been much too easy to hop a flight or thumb a ride. And though physical punishment of myself doesn't negate the total import of my act, it did serve as a human extension of myself to help offset my total feeling of wasting my time. And I had no idea you were so far away from Uncle Tom's Cabin in Slavetown. I had thought I could make it in a day or two, but it's taking much longer. I'm really sorry about holding you up and all, but it's done now, and here I am. See can you handle it.

# Gorilla, My Love

## Toni Cade Bambara

Black female adolescent experience was barely a subject in
American literature until Zora Neale Hurston captured Isie
Watts in "Drenched in Light." Since Hurston's time,
Gwendolyn Brooks, Alice Walker, and especially Toni Cade
Bambara have used the short story form to explore the lives of
young black girls testing out ideas of womanhood for themselves. Such is the case with Bambara's masterpiece story here
about a precocious girl's challenge to adult claims on truth and
reality. Hazel is as memorable for her wonderfully sassy voice
as she is for her knowing wisdom about how adults routinely
create expectations that only children are innocent enough to
take seriously. This is the title story of Bambara's important
1972 collection of short stories, which helped spur a renaissance in short story writing by black women throughout the
1970s and 1980s.

THAT WAS THE YEAR Hunca Bubba changed his name.
Not a change up, but a change back, since Jefferson Winston Vale was the name in the first place. Which was news
to me cause he'd been my Hunca Bubba my whole lifetime,
since I couldn't manage Uncle to save my life. So far as I
was concerned it was a change completely to somethin
soundin very geographical weatherlike to me, like somethin
you'd find in a almanac. Or somethin you'd run across
when you sittin in the navigator seat with a wet thumb on
the map crinkly in your lap, watchin the roads and signs so
when Granddaddy Vale say "Which way, Scout," you got

sense enough to say take the next exit or take a left or whatever it is. Not that Scout's my name. Just the name Granddaddy call whoever sittin in the navigator seat. Which is usually me cause I don't feature sittin in the back with the pecans. Now, you figure pecans all right to be sittin with. If you thinks so, that's your business. But they dusty sometime and make you cough. And they got a way of slidin around and dippin down sudden, like maybe a rat in the buckets. So if you scary like me, you sleep with the lights on and blame it on Baby Jason, and so as not to waste good electric, you study the maps. And that's how come I'm in the navigator seat most times and get to be called Scout.

So Hunca Bubba in the back with the pecans and Baby Jason, and he in love. And we got to hear all this stuff about this woman he in love with and all. Which really ain't enough to keep the mind alive, though Baby Jason got no better sense than to give his undivided attention and keep grabbin at the photograph which is just a picture of some skinny woman in a countrified dress with her hand shot up to her face like she shame fore cameras. But there's a movie house in the background which I ax about. Cause I am a movie freak from way back, even though it do get me in trouble sometime.

Like when me and Big Brood and Baby Jason was on our own last Easter and couldn't go to the Dorset cause we'd seen all the Three Stooges they was. And the RKO Hamilton was closed readying up for the Easter Pageant that night. And the West End, the Regun, and the Sunset was too far, less we had grownups with us which we didn't. So we walk up Amsterdam Avenue to the Washington and *Gorilla, My Love* playin, they say, which suit me just fine, though the "my love" part kinda drag Big Brood some. As for Baby Jason, shoot, like Granddaddy say, he'd follow me into the fiery furnace if I say come on. So we go in and get three bags of Havmore potato chips which not only are the best potato chips but the best bags for blowin up and bustin real loud so the matron come trottin down the aisle with her chunky self, flashin that flashlight dead in your eye so you can give her some lip, and if she answer back and you already finish seein the show anyway, why then you just turn the place out. Which I love to do, no lie. With Baby Jason kickin at the seat in front, egging me on, and Big Brood mumblin bout what fiercesome things we goin do. Which means me. Like when the big boys come up on us talkin bout Lemme a nickel. It's me that hide the money. Or when the bad boys in the park take Big Brood's Spaudeen way from him. It's me that jump on they back and fight awhile. And it's me that turns out the show if the matron get too salty.

So the movie come on and right away it's this churchy music and clearly not about no gorilla. Bout Jesus. And I am ready to kill, not cause I got anything gainst Jesus. Just that when you fixed to watch a gorilla picture you don't wanna get messed around with Sunday school stuff. So I am mad. Besides, we see this raggedy old brown film *King of Kings* every year and enough's enough. Grownups figure they can treat you just anyhow. Which burns me up. There I am, my feet up and my Havmore potato chips really salty and crispy and two jawbreakers in my lap and the money safe in my shoe from the big boys, and here comes this Jesus stuff. So we all go wild. Yellin, booin, stompin, and carryin on. Really to wake the man in the booth up there who musta went to sleep and put on the wrong reels. But no, cause he holler down to shut up and then he turn the sound up so we really gotta holler like crazy to even hear ourselves good. And the matron ropes off the children section and flashes her light all over the place and we yell some more and some kids slip under the rope and run up and down the aisle just to show it take more than some dusty ole velvet rope to tie us down. And I'm flingin the kid in front of me's popcorn. And Baby Jason kickin seats. And it's really somethin. Then here come the big and bad matron, the one they let out in case of emergency. And she totin that flashlight like she gonna use it on somebody. This here the colored matron Brandy and her friends call Thunderbuns. She do not play. She do not smile. So we shut up and watch the simple ass picture.

Which is not so simple as it is stupid. Cause I realize that just about anybody in my family is better than this god they always talkin about. My daddy wouldn't stand for nobody treatin any of us that way. My mama specially. And I can just see it now, Big Brood up there on the cross talkin bout Forgive them Daddy cause they don't know what they doin. And my Mama say Get on down from there you big fool, whatcha think this is, playtime? And my Daddy yellin to Granddaddy to get him a ladder cause Big Brood actin the fool, his mother side of the family showin up. And my mama and her sister Daisy jumpin on them Romans beatin them with they pocketbooks. And Hunca Bubba tellin them folks on they knees they better get out the way and go get some help or they goin to get trampled on. And Granddaddy Vale sayin Leave the boy alone, if that's what he wants to do with his life we ain't got nothin to say about it. Then Aunt Daisy givin him a taste of that pocketbook, fussin bout what a damn fool old man Granddaddy is. Then everybody jumpin in his chest like the time Uncle Clayton went in the army and come back with only one leg and Granddaddy say somethin stupid about that's life. And by this time Big Brood off the cross and in the park playin handball or skully or somethin. And the family in the kitchen throwin dishes at each other, screamin bout if you hadn't done this I wouldn't had to do that. And me in the parlor trying to do my arithmetic yellin Shut it off.

Which is what I was yellin all by myself which make me a sittin target for Thunderbuns. But when I yell We want our money back, that gets everybody in chorus. And the movie windin up with this heavenly cloud music and the smart-ass up there in his hole in the wall turns up the sound again to drown us out. Then there comes Bugs Bunny which we already seen so we know we been had. No gorilla my nuthin. And Big Brood say Awwww sheeet, we goin to see the manager and get our money back. And I know from this we business. So I brush the potato chips out of my hair which is where Baby Jason like to put em, and I march myself up the aisle to deal with the manager who is a crook in the first place for lyin out there sayin *Gorilla, My Love* playin. And I never did like the man cause he oily and pasty at the same time like the bad guy in the serial, the one that got a hideout behind a push-button bookcase and play "Moonlight Sonata" with gloves on. I knock on the door and I am furious. And I am alone, too. Cause Big Brood suddenly got to go so bad even though my mama told us bout goin in them nasty bathrooms. And I hear him sigh like he disgusted when he get to the door and see only a little kid there. And now I'm really furious cause I get so tired grownups messin over kids just cause they little and can't take em to court. What is it, he say to me like I lost my mittens or wet on myself or am somebody's retarded child. When in reality I am the smartest kid P.S. 186 ever had in its whole lifetime and you can ax anybody. Even them teachers that don't like me cause I won't sing them Southern songs or back off when they tell me my questions are out of order. And cause my Mama come up there in a minute when them teachers start playin the dozens behind colored folks. She stalk in with her hat pulled down bad and that Persian lamb coat draped back over one hip on account of she got her fist planted there so she can talk that talk which gets us all hypnotized, and teacher be comin undone cause she know this could be her job and her behind cause Mama got pull with the Board and bad by her own self anyhow.

So I kick the door open wider and just walk right by him and sit down and tell the man about himself and that I want my money back and that goes for Baby Jason and Big Brood too. And he still trying to shuffle me out the door even though I'm sittin which shows him for the fool he is. Just like them teachers do fore they realize Mama like a stone on that spot and ain't backin up. So he ain't gettin up off the money. So I was forced to leave, takin the matches from under his ashtray, and set a fire under the candy stand, which closed the raggedy ole Washington down for a week. My Daddy had the suspect it was me cause Big Brood got a big mouth. But I explained right quick what the whole thing was about and I figured it was even-steven. Cause if you say Gorilla, My Love, you suppose to mean it.

Just like when you say you goin to give me a party on my
birthday, you gotta mean it. And if you say me and Baby
Jason can go South pecan haulin with Granddaddy Vale,
you better not be comin up with no stuff about the weather
look uncertain or did you mop the bathroom or any other
trickified business. I mean even gangsters in the movies say
My word is my bond. So don't nobody get away with nothin
far as I'm concerned. So Daddy put his belt back on. Cause
that's the way I was raised. Like my Mama say in one of
them situations when I won't back down, Okay Badbird,
you right. Your point is well-taken. Not that Badbird my
name, just what she say when she tired arguin and know
I'm right. And Aunt Jo, who is the hardest head in the
family and worse even than Aunt Daisy, she say, You absolutely right Miss Muffin, which also ain't my real name but
the name she gave me one time when I got some medicine
shot in my behind and wouldn't get up off her pillows for
nothin. And even Granddaddy Vale—who got no memory
to speak of, so sometime you can just plain lie to him, if
you want to be like that—he say, Well if that's what I said,
then that's it. But this name business was different they
said. It wasn't like Hunca Bubba had gone back on his word
or anything. Just that he was thinkin bout gettin married
and was usin his real name now. Which ain't the way I saw
it at all.

So there I am in the navigator seat. And I turn to him
and just plain ole ax him. I mean I come right on out with
it. No sense goin all around that barn the old folks talk
about. And like my mama say, Hazel—which is my real
name and what she remembers to call me when she bein
serious—when you got somethin on your mind, speak up
and let the chips fall where they may. And if anybody don't
like it, tell em to come see your mama. And Daddy look up
from the paper and say, You hear your mama good, Hazel.
And tell em to come see me first. Like that. That's how I
was raised.

So I turn clear round in the navigator seat and say,
"Look here, Hunca Bubba or Jefferson Windsong Vale or
whatever your name is, you gonna marry this girl?"

"Sure am," he say, all grins.

And I say, "Member that time you was baby-sittin me when we lived at four-o-nine and there was this big snow and Mama and Daddy got held up in the country so you had to stay for two days?"

And he say, "Sure do."

"Well. You remember how you told me I was the cutest thing that ever walked the earth?"

"Oh, you were real cute when you were little," he say, which is suppose to be funny. I am not laughin.

"Well. You remember what you said?"

And Grandaddy Vale squintin over the wheel and axin Which way, Scout. But Scout is busy and don't care if we all get lost for days.

"Watcha mean, Peaches?"

"My name is Hazel. And what I mean is you said you were going to marry *me* when I grew up. You were going to wait. That's what I mean, my dear Uncle Jefferson." And he don't say nuthin. Just look at me real strange like he never saw me before in life. Like he lost in some weird town in the middle of night and lookin for directions and there's no one to ask. Like it was me that messed up the maps and turned the road posts round. "Well, you said it, didn't you?" And Baby Jason lookin back and forth like we playin ping-pong. Only I ain't playin. I'm hurtin and I can hear that I am screamin. And Grandaddy Vale mumblin how we never gonna get to where we goin if I don't turn around and take my navigator job serious.

"Well, for cryin out loud, Hazel, you just a little girl. And I was just teasin."

" 'And I was just teasin,' " I say back just how he said it so he can hear what a terrible thing it is. Then I don't say nuthin. And he don't say nuthin. And Baby Jason don't say nuthin nohow. Then Granddaddy Vale speak up. "Look here, Precious, it was Hunca Bubba what told you them things. This here, Jefferson Winston Vale." And Hunca Bubba say, "That's right. That was somebody else. I'm a new somebody."

"You a lyin dawg," I say, when I meant to say treacherous dog, but just couldn't get hold of the word. It slipped away from me. And I'm crying and crumplin down in the seat and just don't care. And Granddaddy say to hush and steps on the gas. And I'm losin my bearins and don't even know where to look on the map cause I can't see for cryin. And Baby Jason cryin too. Cause he is my blood brother and understands that we must stick together or be forever lost, what with grownups playin change-up and turnin you round every which way so bad. And don't even say they sorry.

# Everyday Use

## ALICE WALKER

Perhaps the most famous and widely read short story by a black woman, "Everyday Use" rewards every reading. Walker's casually understated style makes it difficult to appreciate at first glance her complex interweaving of generational, cultural, and family bonds and divides. Read thoroughly, the story documents an important moment in the late 1960s and early 1970s when black experience became a contested terrain of memory, appropriation, power, and knowledge. The different ways that Dee, Maggie, and their mother think of "everyday use" in the story speak to sudden differences between life paths and personal histories. The objects of the home are markers of everything that holds family together and now suddenly separates its individual members. Ultimately, the story affirms what can't be erased: the power of experience and memory to outlive fashion. Widely anthologized today, "Everyday Use" appeared in Walker's 1973 collection of short stories *In Love & Trouble,* one of the most widely read collection of short fiction by a black woman and one of the most influential.

### For Your Grandmama

I WILL WAIT FOR HER in the yard that Maggie and I made so clean and wavy yesterday afternoon. A yard like this is more comfortable than most people know. It is not just a yard. It is like an extended living room. When the hard clay is swept clean as a floor and the fine sand around the edges lined with tiny, irregular grooves, anyone can come and sit and look up into the elm tree and wait for the breezes that never come inside the house.

Maggie will be nervous until after her sister goes: she will stand hopelessly in corners, homely and ashamed of the burn scars down her arms and legs, eying her sister with a mixture of envy and awe. She thinks her sister has held life always in the palm of one hand, that "no" is a word the world never learned to say to her.

You've no doubt seen those TV shows where the child who has "made it" is confronted, as a surprise, by her own mother and father, tottering in weakly from backstage. (A pleasant surprise, of course: What would they do if parent and child came on the show only to curse out and insult each other?) On TV mother and child embrace and smile into each other's faces. Sometimes the mother and father weep, the child wraps them in her arms and leans across the table to tell how she would not have made it without their help. I have seen these programs.

Sometimes I dream a dream in which Dee and I are suddenly brought together on a TV program of this sort. Out of a dark and soft-seated limousine I am ushered into a bright room filled with many people. There I meet a smiling, gray, sporty man like Johnny Carson who shakes my hand and tells me what a fine girl I have. Then we are on the stage and Dee is embracing me with tears in her eyes. She pins on my dress a large orchid, even though she has told me once that she thinks orchids are tacky flowers.

In real life I am a large, big-boned woman with rough, man-working hands. In the winter I wear flannel night-gowns to bed and overalls during the day. I can kill and clean a hog as mercilessly as a man. My fat keeps me hot in zero weather. I can work outside all day, breaking ice to get water for washing; I can eat pork liver cooked over the open fire minutes after it comes steaming from the hog. One winter I knocked a bull calf straight in the brain between the eyes with a sledge hammer and had the meat hung up to chill before nightfall. But of course all this does not show on television. I am the way my daughter would want me to be: a hundred pounds lighter, my skin like an uncooked barley pancake. My hair glistens in the hot bright lights. Johnny Carson has much to do to keep up with my quick and witty tongue.

But that is a mistake. I know even before I wake up. Who ever knew a Johnson with a quick tongue? Who can even imagine me looking a strange white man in the eye? It seems to me I have talked to them always with one foot raised in flight, with my head turned in whichever way is farthest from them. Dee, though. She would always look anyone in the eye. Hesitation was no part of her nature.

"How do I look, Mama?" Maggie says, showing just enough of her thin body enveloped in pink skirt and red blouse for me to know she's there, almost hidden by the door.

"Come out into the yard," I say.

Have you ever seen a lame animal, perhaps a dog run over by some careless person rich enough to own a car, sidle up to someone who is ignorant enough to be kind to him? That is the way my Maggie walks. She has been like this, chin on chest, eyes on ground, feet in shuffle, ever since the fire that burned the other house to the ground.

Dee is lighter than Maggie, with nicer hair and a fuller figure. She's a woman now, though sometimes I forget. How long ago was it that the other house burned? Ten, twelve years? Sometimes I can still hear the flames and feel Maggie's arms sticking to me, her hair smoking and her dress falling off her in little black papery flakes. Her eyes seemed stretched open, blazed open by the flames reflected in them. And Dee. I see her standing off under the sweet gum tree she used to dig gum out of; a look of concentration on her face as she watched the last dingy gray board of the house fall in toward the red-hot brick chimney. Why don't you do a dance around the ashes? I'd wanted to ask her. She had hated the house that much.

I used to think she hated Maggie, too. But that was before we raised the money, the church and me, to send her to Augusta to school. She used to read to us without pity;

forcing words, lies, other folks' habits, whole lives upon us two, sitting trapped and ignorant underneath her voice. She washed us in a river of make-believe, burned us with a lot of knowledge we didn't necessarily need to know. Pressed us to her with the serious way she read, to shove us away at just the moment, like dimwits, we seemed about to understand.

Dee wanted nice things. A yellow organdy dress to wear to her graduation from high school; black pumps to match a green suit she'd made from an old suit somebody gave me. She was determined to stare down any disaster in her efforts. Her eyelids would not flicker for minutes at a time. Often I fought off the temptation to shake her. At sixteen she had a style of her own: and knew what style was.

I never had an education myself. After second grade the school was closed down. Don't ask my why: in 1927 colored asked fewer questions than they do now. Sometimes Maggie reads to me. She stumbles along good-naturedly but can't see well. She knows she is not bright. Like good looks and money, quickness passed her by. She will marry John Thomas (who has mossy teeth in an earnest face) and then I'll be free to sit here and I guess just sing church songs to myself. Although I never was a good singer. Never could carry a tune. I was always better at a man's job. I used to love to milk till I was hooked in the side in '49. Cows are soothing and slow and don't bother you, unless you try to milk them the wrong way.

I have deliberately turned my back on the house. It is three rooms, just like the one that burned, except the roof is tin; they don't make shingle roofs any more. There are no real windows, just some holes cut in the sides, like the portholes in a ship, but not round and not square, with rawhide holding the shutters up on the outside. This house is in a pasture, too, like the other one. No doubt when Dee sees it she will want to tear it down. She wrote me once that no matter where we "choose" to live, she will manage to come see us. But she will never bring her friends. Maggie and I thought about this and Maggie asked me, "Mama, when did Dee ever *have* any friends?"

She had a few. Furtive boys in pink shirts hanging about on washday after school. Nervous girls who never laughed. Impressed with her, they worshiped the well-turned phrase, the cute shape, the scalding humor that erupted like bubbles in lye. She read to them.

When she was courting Jimmy T she didn't have much time to pay to us, but turned all her faultfinding power on him. He *flew* to marry a cheap city girl from a family of ignorant flashy people. She hardly had time to recompose herself.

When she comes I will meet—but there they are!

Maggie attempts to make a dash for the house, in her shuffling way, but I stay her with my hand. "Come back here," I say. And she stops and tries to dig a well in the sand with her toe.

It is hard to see them clearly through the strong sun. But even the first glimpse of leg out of the car tells me it is Dee. Her feet were always neat-looking, as if God himself had shaped them with a certain style. From the other side of the car comes a short, stocky man. Hair is all over his head a foot long and hanging from his chin like a kinky mule tail. I hear Maggie suck in her breath. "Uhnnnh," is what it sounds like. Like when you see the wriggling end of a snake just in front of your foot on the road. "Uhnnnh."

Dee next. A dress down to the ground, in this hot weather. A dress so loud it hurts my eyes. There are yellows and oranges enough to throw back the light of the sun. I feel my whole face warming from the heat waves it throws out. Earrings gold, too, and hanging down to her shoulders. Bracelets dangling and making noises when she moves her arm up to shake the folds of the dress out of her armpits. The dress is loose and flows, and as she walks closer, I like it. I hear Maggie go "Uhnnnh" again. It is her sister's hair. It stands straight up like the wool on a sheep. It is black as night, and around the edges are two long pigtails that rope about like small lizards disappearing behind her ears.

"Wa-su-zo-Tean-o!" she says, coming on in that gliding way the dress makes her move. The short stocky fellow with the hair to his navel is all grinning, and he follows up with "Asalamalakim, my mother and sister!" He moves to hug Maggie, but she falls back, right up against the back of my chair. I feel her trembling there, and when I look up I see the perspiration falling off her chin.

"Don't get up," says Dee. Since I am stout, it takes something of a push. You can see me trying to move a second or two before I make it. She turns, showing white heels through her sandals, and goes back to the car. Out she peeks next with a Polaroid. She stoops down quickly and lines up picture after picture of me sitting there in front of the house with Maggie cowering behind me. She never takes a shot without making sure the house is included. When a cow comes nibbling around the edge of the yard, she snaps it and me and Maggie *and* the house. Then she puts the Polaroid in the back seat of the car and comes up and kisses me on the forehead.

Meanwhile Asalamalakim is going through motions with Maggie's hand. Maggie's hand is as limp as a fish, and probably as cold, despite the sweat, and she keeps trying to pull it back. It looks like Asalamalakim wants to shake hands but wants to do it fancy. Or maybe he don't know how people shake hands. Anyhow, he soon gives up on Maggie.

"Well," I say. "Dee."

"No, Mama," she says. "Not 'Dee,' Wangero Leewanika Kemanjo!"

"What happened to 'Dee'?" I wanted to know.

"She's dead," Wangero said. "I couldn't bear it any longer, being named after the people who oppress me."

"You know as well as me you was named after your aunt Dicie," I said. Dicie is my sister. She named Dee. We called her "Big Dee" after Dee was born.

"But who was *she* named after?" asked Wangero.

"I guess after Grandma Dee," I said.

"And who was she named after?" asked Wangero.

"Her mother," I said, and saw Wangero was getting

tired. "That's about as far back as I can trace it," I said. Though, in fact, I probably could have carried it back beyond the Civil War through the branches.

"Well," said Asalamalakim, "there you are."

"Uhnnnh," I heard Maggie say.

"There I was not," I said, "before 'Dicie' cropped up in our family, so why should I try to trace it that far back?"

He just stood there grinning, looking down on me like somebody inspecting a Model A car. Every once in a while he and Wangero sent eye signals over my head.

"How do you pronounce this name?" I asked.

"You don't have to call me by it if you don't want to," said Wangero.

"Why shouldn't I?" I asked. "If that's what you want us to call you, we'll call you."

"I know it might sound awkward at first," said Wangero.

"I'll get used to it," I said. "Ream it out again."

Well, soon we got the name out of the way. Asalamalakim had a name twice as long and three times as hard. After I tripped over it two or three times, he told me to just call him Hakim-a-barber. I wanted to ask him was he a barber, but I didn't really think he was, so I didn't ask.

"You must belong to those beef-cattle peoples down the road," I said. They said "Asalamalakim" when they met you, too, but they didn't shake hands. Always too busy: feeding the cattle, fixing the fences, putting up salt-lick shelters, throwing down hay. When the white folks poisoned some of the herd, the men stayed up all night with rifles in their hands. I walked a mile and a half just to see the sight.

Hakim-a-barber said, "I accept some of their doctrines, but farming and raising cattle is not my style." [They didn't tell me, and I didn't ask, whether Wangero (Dee) had really gone and married him.]

We sat down to eat, and right away he said he didn't eat collards and pork was unclean. Wangero, though, went on through the chitlins and corn bread, the greens and everything else. She talked a blue streak over the sweet potatoes. Everything delighted her. Even the fact that we still used the benches her daddy made for the table when we couldn't afford to buy chairs.

"Oh, Mama!" she cried. Then turned to Hakim-a-barber. "I never knew how lovely these benches are. You can feel the rump prints," she said, running her hands underneath her and along the bench. Then she gave a sigh, and her hand closed over Grandma Dee's butter dish. "That's it!" she said. "I knew there was something I wanted to ask you if I could have." She jumped up from the table and went over in the corner where the churn stood, the milk in it clabber by now. She looked at the churn and looked at it.

"This churn top is what I need," she said. "Didn't Uncle Buddy whittle it out of a tree you all used to have?"

"Yes," I said.

"Uh huh," she said happily. "And I want the dasher, too."

"Uncle Buddy whittle that, too?" asked the barber.

Dee (Wangero) looked up at me.

"Aunt Dee's first husband whittled the dash," said Maggie so low you almost couldn't hear her. "His name was Henry, but they called him Stash."

"Maggie's brain is like an elephant's," Wangero said, laughing. "I can use the churn top as a centerpiece for the alcove table," she said, sliding a plate over the churn, "and I'll think of something artistic to do with the dasher."

When she finished wrapping the dasher, the handle stuck out. I took it for a moment in my hands. You didn't even have to look close to see where hands pushing the dasher up and down to make butter had left a kind of sink in the wood. In fact, there were a lot of small sinks; you could see where thumbs and fingers had sunk into the wood. It was beautiful light yellow wood, from a tree that grew in the yard where Big Dee and Stash had lived.

After dinner Dee (Wangero) went to the trunk at the foot of my bed and started rifling through it. Maggie hung back in the kitchen over the dishpan. Out came Wangero with two quilts. They had been pieced by Grandma Dee, and then Big Dee and me had hung them on the quilt frames on the front porch and quilted them. One was in the

Lone Star pattern. The other was Walk Around the Mountain. In both of them were scraps of dresses Grandma Dee had worn fifty and more years ago. Bits and pieces of Grandpa Jarrell's Paisley shirts. And one teeny faded blue piece, about the size of a penny matchbox, that was from Great Grandpa Ezra's uniform that he wore in the Civil War.

"Mama," Wangero said sweet as a bird. "Can I have these old quilts?"

I heard something fall in the kitchen, and a minute later the kitchen door slammed.

"Why don't you take one or two of the others?" I asked. "These old things was just done by me and Big Dee from some tops your grandma pieced before she died."

"No," said Wangero. "I don't want those. They are stitched around the borders by machine."

"That'll make them last better," I said.

"That's not the point," said Wangero. "These are all pieces of dresses Grandma used to wear. She did all this stitching by hand. Imagine!" She held the quilts securely in her arms, stroking them.

"Some of the pieces, like those lavender ones, come from old clothes her mother handed down to her," I said, moving up to touch the quilts. Dee (Wangero) moved back just enough so that I couldn't reach the quilts. They already belonged to her.

"Imagine!" she breathed again, clutching them closely to her bosom.

"The truth is," I said, "I promised to give them quilts to Maggie, for when she marries John Thomas."

She gasped like a bee had stung her.

"Maggie can't appreciate these quilts!" she said. "She'd probably be backward enough to put them to everyday use."

"I reckon she would," I said. "God knows I been saving 'em for long enough with nobody using 'em. I hope she will!" I didn't want to bring up how I had offered Dee (Wangero) a quilt when she went away to college. Then she had told me they were old-fashioned, out of style.

"But they're *priceless*!" she was saying now, furiously; for she has a temper. "Maggie would put them on the bed and in five years they'd be in rags. Less than that!"

"She can always make some more," I said. "Maggie knows how to quilt."

Dee (Wangero) looked at me with hatred. "You just will not understand. The point is these quilts, *these* quilts!"

"Well," I said, stumped. "What would *you* do with them?"

"Hang them," she said. As if that was the only thing you *could* do with quilts.

Maggie by now was standing in the door. I could almost hear the sound her feet made as they scraped over each other.

"She can have them, Mama," she said, like somebody used to never winning anything, or having anything reserved for her. "I can 'member Grandma Dee without the quilts."

I looked at her hard. She had filled her bottom lip with checkerberry snuff, and it gave her face a kind of dopey, hangdog look. It was Grandma Dee and Big Dee who taught her how to quilt herself. She stood there with her scarred hands hidden in the folds of her skirt. She looked at her sister with something like fear, but she wasn't mad at her. This was Maggie's portion. This was the way she knew God to work.

When I looked at her like that, something hit me in the top of my head and ran down to the soles of my feet. Just like when I'm in church and the spirit of God touches me and I get happy and shout. I did something I never had done before: hugged Maggie to me, then dragged her on into the room, snatched the quilts out of Miss Wangero's hands, and dumped them into Maggie's lap. Maggie just sat there on my bed with her mouth open.

"Take one or two of the others," I said to Dee.

But she turned without a word and went out to Hakim-a-barber.

"You just don't understand," she said, as Maggie and I came out to the car.

"What don't I understand?" I wanted to know.

"Your heritage," she said. And then she turned to Maggie, kissed her, and said, "You ought to try to make something of yourself, too, Maggie. It's really a new day for us. But from the way you and Mama still live, you'd never know it."

She put on some sunglasses that hid everything above the tip of her nose and her chin.

Maggie smiled; maybe at the sunglasses. But a real smile, not scared. After we watched the car dust settle, I asked Maggie to bring me a dip of snuff. And then the two of us sat there just enjoying, until it was time to go in the house and go to bed.

# A Ceremony of Innocence

## Arthenia Bates (Millican)

The appeal of Muslim religion to younger black Americans in the 1960s underscored their disillusionment with traditional features of American culture, including Christianity. Arthenia Bates quietly articulates the differences between traditional religion and newfound conversion in this simple vignette about an encounter between old friends. Like "Everyday Use," the story examines emotional nuances and small tensions between generations suddenly at a crossroads. The work comes from Bates's 1975 collection *Seeds Beneath the Snow: Vignettes from the South*.

THE THICK EVERGREENS screened Georgia Ann Mc-Cullum's front porch so well that Tisha did not see her sitting in the porch swing until she reached the top step—the eighth, because she had once measured her age by these steps. She had practiced the salutation "Mother" Georgia to pay honor to this distant cousin who had reached the highest point of distinction for a woman in Chute Bay. She had been made the "mother" of Chute Bay Memorial Baptist Church, which had been built by the people in the Bay on a pay-as-you-go basis during the Depression years.

Tisha stood quietly hugging herself in a full-length Natural Emba Autumn Haze mink coat as she waited for the old woman to recognize her. Even though it was a bright day, the temperature held at 23 degrees above zero and a stiff breeze blew in from the north.

The noise of a truck coming down Bay Road jostled the swinger from an apparent reverie. She slipped from the swing and started forward, then recognized Tisha. Their eyes met and held long enough for the old woman to make a good guess. She fumbled in her mind and grunted, then, caught by pain, she backed back to the swing to steady herself. The swing moved backward, almost causing her to miss her seat.

Tisha rushed to clasp her in a bear hug.

"Don't fall, Mother Georgia—please don't fall," she pleaded.

"Don't tell me," Mother Georgia said, "you Flora Dee's baby. Ain't you, now?"

"Yes, Mother Georgia," she answered, and relaxed her grip, helping the old woman to seat herself in the swing.

"This here Tisha. Sweet little Tisha. Just as pretty, too. You look good enough to eat. Your grandpa still call you his 'little spicy gal'?"

"Grandpa hasn't come close to me since I've been home, Mother Georgia."

"That's your own doings. But thang God. Thang God. Thang God. I talk to Him the other night 'bout you, and here He done sent you already. I ain't scared of you just 'cause you gone astray." She cradled Tisha in her arms and nuzzled her thin cheeks with a bottom lip packed hard with Railroad Mill snuff. Coins hit the porch and began to roll as they reeled in this odd pantomime of genuine affection. She finally held Tisha away at arm's length and, gloating over her, told of the wonders that had come with the title "Mother" Georgia.

Old white men whose shirts she had ironed until arthritis twisted both of her wrists—who had brought shirts to her, even though a one-day service laundry had opened in Crystal Hill—who brought handouts to supplement the $54.00 a month from the "government"—even they used the title of honor "Mother" Georgia, when they had for decades called her "Aunty."

After this rehearsal, Tisha began to pick up the coins

from the floor. She found several nickels and a dime, but Mother Georgia said that that was not all.

"Don't bother yourself," she told Tisha. "Go on in and make yourself at home. You needn' act like company, when this your second home. I'm slow but I'm coming."

Tisha walked into the front room, a room she knew by heart before she left Chute Bay. She glanced about, noticing that it was the same. She waited a minute for Mother Georgia, then brushed the bottom of a chair with her fingers to test it for dust. Her fingertips were black with coal dust. She walked to the door to check on the old woman's delay. She did not want to be caught cleaning the chair. She walked to the door and looked out in time to see Mother Georgia crawling about slowly on her knees and fumbling up and down the porch planks with her drawn hands.

"Mother Georgia, can I help—?"

"No, Sugar, I got all but two pennies. Hope the Lord them two didn't roll off the porch. If it was Mr. Pogue's truck, I'd get my coal if I was a few cents short. But this truck want every cent. I don't know who it b'longt to."

"Come on in, Mother Georgia," Tisha said. "I'll give you what you need for the coal man." She then went out and helped her up from the floor.

"Sugar, they got them ole engines what pull theirself. If they was still using coal like they used to, I'd be out there up and down them tracks with my bucket, picking me up all the coal I want."

"Yes ma'm," Tisha replied. "Now tell me how much the coal cost, and I'll sit out there and wait for the truck."

"No, Sugar. You so dressed up, he might not stop if he don't see me. You just sit tight, and soons he come I'm going to make up a great big fire in the heater. It ain't cold, is it? I got on plenty clothes, and you got on that big fine coat. Don't get hetted up 'cause I got to ask you for myself 'bout that Allie what Flora worried to death 'bout. She worried plumb stiff 'bout that God've yours, just like she can't put you back in your place. Humph. I said send her to me when she come home. I'll get her straight before she go back out yonder."

Tisha pat her feet as Mother Georgia talked, because her toes were getting stiff from cold. A minute later a truck pulled up, and she let Tisha give the driver $1.25 for a crocker sack of coal and a bunch of lightwood splinters. She built a fire in the heater with two splinters and a few lumps of coal. She washed her hands in a basin on the washstand, then sat down to watch Tisha.

"Lord, Sugar, you look good enough to bite on the jaw. The only thing got me bothered is what your ma told me 'bout that Allie. You know you got her nearly distracted? What's that, anyhow, child—talking 'bout goin'ta serve Allie? That ain't no God. You know Mother Georgia ain't goin'ta tell you nothing wrong 'long's I had my hand on the gospel plough. That was 'fore they spanked your ma, so you know I'm a soldier. You got no business turning your back on God."

"Allah, Mother Georgia, is the true God. You see, I know He's the right God because of what He's done for me. Okay?" Tisha started to stand, but the old woman waved her back to her chair. "He helps us to have heaven right here on earth, and that's what I want because I can enjoy life every day of my life."

"What I'm telling you—that is, what Mother Georgia, ambassador to Christ, is telling you—is that ain't no God you found up the road. Your ma learned you 'bout the right God from your cradle, and it ought to be good enough to take you to your grave. You see what He's done for me, don't you, child? That Allie you heard tell of way out yonder is just a make-shift God the crowd hark'ning after. And I'm trying to tell you better 'cause, you, Flora, and every child she got rest close to my heart. We kin as cousins, but I been a mother to her and to y'all before I come a mother to the church. You better turn to the true and living God 'fore it's a day and hour and eternity too late."

Tisha started to let the argument rest, but she felt that she would be a shameful volunteer for Allah if she let this occasion pass without sharing her idea of his worth.

"I'm serving Allah," she persisted, "and I hope to serve Him better. I'm twenty-two now, and I hope to be that many times stronger in His grace before I'm twice that old."

"I'm going on these here knees, little Miss, to the Master I know who'll open your eyes. Look at me." Mother Georgia hoisted her huge frame from the rocker and fastened her sharp bird eyes on Tisha. "I'm seventy-six-odd years old. How you reckon I make it without the Lord? You see that sack of coal? The Lord sent it here. Let me tell you, the Pastor—I reckon you don't know Reverend Sarks—anyway, he come here faithful as the days is long and brings me ration just like he take it home. And Mr. Dwyer—I guess you forgot him—he sends me all the bones from his store to feed these six dogs I got on the yard for company. Some of them oxtails 'n stuff the dogs don't see 'cause I make me a pot've soup."

"Well, let's not get excited," Tisha said. "I brought a present for you. Let's look after that." Tisha handed her a small Christmas-wrapped package which the old woman shook.

"What these? Drawers?" she asked.

Tisha shook her head. "You see," she told Mother Georgia, "we don't have Christmas, but you do."

"You mean Allie don't let y'all have no Christmas? How do you do when you don't ever have no Christmas? How can you live with no Christmas?"

"Every day ought to be important in this life." Tisha had lost her ardor.

"Oh, these them pretty head rags? Well, I'm going to wear this cotton one to Prayer Meeting and the silk one on Communion Sunday." She rewrapped the gift in the same paper.

"That will be nice." Tisha was pleased with her happiness over the small gift. It was one of the things she always cherished about Mother Georgia.

It was warm enough now for Tisha to remove her coat. The old woman got up to leave for the kitchen, but Tisha tried to persuade her to relax or, if she insisted on making coffee, to make it on the heater, but she would not listen.

"You're company now," she maintained, "and a fine lady

at that, so I'll treat you like one, no matter if you did used to help me out. You make yourself at home now while I get straight in the kitchen. And you get up and turn that coat insadouter so's no smoke'll hit it."

"Yes ma'm," she answered.

Tisha sat there remembering the room as she had known it years before. This room was full of furniture. There was an upright grand piano, a three-piece bedroom suite, a washstand, two rocking chairs, and a davenport with sugar-starched crocheted pieces on the arm rests. The center table held a large metal oil lamp on the top and a big family Bible on the bottom tier. The old green wool rug was practically eaten away from the floor, and the wallpaper of unidentified color was smoky and filled with rainwater circles.

There was an array of several pretty vases on the mantelpiece, of odd shapes and sizes, and pictures hung indiscriminately wherever a nail could be placed to hold them. High above the mantel was a picture of Cupid asleep, with the bow and arrow besides him. Glancing around the wall, she found the pictures of undertakers, ministers, church groups, family members, movie stars, and flowers. There was a lone insurance policy hanging above the doorsill going to the middle room. She tried to evaluate the holdings of this room in terms of financial worth—the most valuable possessions in the house secured from a lifetime of satisfactory labor. They hardly added up to dollars and cents.

After a while Mother Georgia came in with a cup of coffee and a plate of cake on a tray.

"I made your coffee on the hot plate. I got 'lectric, you know," and she pointed to the bulb hanging on a suspended wire in the center of the room. "I have my lamp lighted half the time before I remember I can pull that little chain to get some light." She watched Tisha a minute, then encouraged her to eat the five slices of cake because she had baked the cakes herself. They were her specials: raisin, chocolate, pineapple, coconut, and strawberry jelly.

"Mother Georgia," she said, "you remember the time I ate a whole plateful of cake when I was a child? Well, it was the best cake I'd ever had in my life at that time. And since then, I've found out how to enjoy life the way I enjoyed that first plate of cake you gave me. As long as you enjoy this life, there's nothing to worry about."

"I don't want to spoil your appetite, but you're gone from your raising. You're caught in the web of sin. And you know what that mean. You sitting there all pretty, but you dying, Sugar." The old woman shook her head.

Dying! Tisha turned and looked at Georgia Ann McCullum. *She* was dying. The old woman was dying—dying as she had done every day of her life, though she was too good a minstrel man to know it. Her ugly life was death. She no doubt would have a beautiful funeral according to their pattern, with a nice long obituary, good remarks from the deacons, a wailing eulogy from the preacher, and honest tears from unknown visitors at the grave; but her life was, and always had been, an ugly death.

"Thang God you come through, Sugar. Look—put your cake you left in a bag and take it home with you. And when you go back up the road, you'll remember what God has done for me and you'll forget about that Allie and the Mooselims. They'll run the world off the map if you not careful. You were raised to know that no colored folks can't rule the world by theirself. My folks told me white folks is a mess, but a nigger ain't nothing."

"Yes ma'm," Tisha said as she put on her coat to leave. She was not going to argue with the old lady because, more than anyone else, Mother Georgia had given her the final proof that she had chosen the right path—the path away from the religion of the Cross. God, the God of Mother Georgia, the God of her parents, the God who had let His only Son be crucified by wicked men, was uncaring. Then, as now, she told herself, if He was up there, He was oblivious of all the Georgia Ann McCullums in the universe.

She pulled the mink closer to her ears as she faced the cold, crisp air on the walk to her parents' home down Bay Road, happy in the thought that she had learned to praise Allah, who cared for His black children enough to help them find heaven on earth.

# White Rat

## GAYL JONES

Gayl Jones is one of the best writers of short stories that make difficult everyday subject matter truthful and dramatic. This title story of her 1977 collection is a case in point. The narrator is troubled at every turn not only by his skin color but by his entanglement with love and responsibility. The story in some ways transforms the traditional "tragic mulatto" story from one of symbolic social prejudice to hard personal reality. Jones, like her characters and stories, is rarely sentimental.

I LEARNED WHERE SHE WAS when Cousin Willie come down home and said Maggie sent for her but told her not to tell nobody where she was, especially me, but Cousin Willie come and told me anyway cause she said I was the lessen two evils and she didn't like to see Maggie stuck up in the room up there like she was. I asked her what she mean like she was. Willie said that she was pregnant by J.T. J.T. the man she run off with because she said I treat her like dirt. And now Willie say J.T. run off and left her after he got her knocked up. I asked Willie where she was. Willie said she was up in that room over Babe Lawson's. She told me not to be surprised when I saw her looking real bad. I said I wouldn't be least surprised. I asked Willie she think Maggie come back. Willie say she better.

The room was dirty and Maggie looked worser than Willie say she going to look. I knocked on the door but there weren't no answer so I just opened the door and went in and saw Maggie laying on the bed turned up against the wall. She turnt around when I come in but she didn't say nothing. I said Maggie we getting out a here. So I got the bag she brung when she run away and put all her loose things in it and just took her by the arm and brung her on home. You couldn't tell nothing was in her belly though.

I been taking care of little Henry since she been gone but he three and a half years old and ain't no trouble since he can play hisself and know what it mean when you hit him on the ass when he do something wrong.

Maggie don't say nothing when we get in the house. She just go over to little Henry. He sleeping in the front room on the couch. She go over to little Henry and bend down and kiss him on the cheek and then she ask me have I had supper and when I say Naw she go back in the kitchen and start fixing it. We sitting at the table and nobody saying nothing but I feel I got to say something.

"You can go head and have the baby," I say. "I give him my name."

I say it meaner than I want to. She just look up at me and don't say nothing. Then she say, "He ain't yours."

I say, "I know he ain't mine. But don't nobody else have to know. Even the baby. He don't even never have to know."

She just keep looking at me with her big eyes that don't say nothing, and then she say, "You know. I know."

She look down at her plate and go on eating. We don't say nothing no more and then when she get through she clear up the dishes and I just go round front and sit out on the front porch. She don't come out like she used to before she start saying I treat her like dirt, and then when I go on in the house to go to bed, she hunched up on her side, with her back to me, so I just take my clothes off and get on in the bed on my side.

Maggie a light yeller woman with chicken scratch hair. That what my mama used to call it chicken scratch hair cause she say there weren't enough hair for a chicken to scratch around in. If it weren't for her hair she look like she was a white woman, a light yeller white woman though.

Anyway, when we was coming up somebody say, "Woman cover you hair if you ain't go'n' straightin' it. Look like chicken scratch." Sometime they say look like chicken shit, but they don't tell them to cover it no more, so they wear it like it is. Maggie wear hers like it is.

Me, I come from a family of white-looking niggers, some of 'em, my mama, my daddy musta been, my half daddy he weren't. Come down from the hills round Hazard, Kentucky, most of them and claimed nigger cause somebody grandmammy way back there was. First people I know ever claim nigger, 'cept my mama say my daddy hate hoogies (up North I hear they call em honkies) worser than anybody. She say cause he look like he one hisself and then she laugh. I laugh too but I didn't know why she laugh. She say when I come, I look just like a little white rat, so tha's why some a the people I hang aroun with call me White Rat. When little Henry come he look just like a little white rabbit, but don't nobody call him White Rabbit they just call him little Henry. I guess the other jus' ain't took. I tried to get them to call him little White Rabbit, but Maggie say naw, cause she say when he grow up he develop a complex, what with the problem he got already. I say what you come at me for with this a complex and then she say, Nothin, jus' something I heard on the radio on one of them edgecation morning shows. And then I say Aw. And then she say Anyway by the time he get seven or eight he probably get the pigment and be dark, cause some of her family was. So I say where I heard somewhere where the chil'ren couldn't be no darker'n the darkest of the two parent and bout the best he could do would be high yeller like she was. And then she say how her sister Lucky got the pigment when she was bout seven and come out real dark. I tell her Well y'all's daddy was dark. And she say, "Yeah." Anyway, I guess well she still think little Henry gonna get the pigment when he get to be seven or eight, and told me about all these people come out lighter'n I was and got the pigment fore they growed up.

Like I told you my relatives come down out of the hills and claimed nigger, but only people that believe 'em is

people that got to know 'em and people that know 'em, so I
usually just stay around with people I know and go in some
joint over to Versailles or up to Lexington or down over in
Midway where they know me cause I don't like to walk
in noplace where they say, "What's that white man doing in
here." They probably say "yap"—that the Kentucky word
for honky. Or "What that yap doing in here with that nigger woman." So I jus' keep to the places where they know
me. I member when I was young me and the other niggers
used to ride around in these cars and when we go to some
town where they don't know "White Rat" everybody look
at me like I'm some hoogie, but I don't pay them no mind.
'Cept sometime it hard not to pay em no mind cause I hate
the hoogie much as they do, much as my daddy did. I drove
up to this filling station one time and these other niggers
drove up at the same time, they mighta even drove up a
little ahead a me, but this filling station man come up to me
first and bent down and said, "I wait on you first, 'fore I
wait on them niggers," and then he laugh. And then I laugh
and say, "You can wait on them first. I'm a nigger too." He
don't say nothing. He just look at me like he thought I was
crazy. I don't remember who he wait on first. But I guess he
be careful next time who he say nigger to, even somebody
got blond hair like me, most which done passed over anyhow. That, or the way things been go'n, go'n be trying to
pass back. I member once all us was riding around one
Saturday night, I must a been bout twenty-five then, close
to forty now, but we was driving around, all us drunk cause
it was Saturday, and Shotgun, he was driving and probably
drunker'n a skunk and drunken the rest of us hit up on this
police car and the police got out and by that time Shotgun
done stop, and the police come over and told all us to get
out the car, and he looked us over, he didn't have to do
much looking because he probably smell it before he got
there but he looked us all over and say he gonna haul us all
in for being drunk and disord'ly. He say, "I'm gone haul all
y'all in." And I say, "Haul y'all all." Everybody laugh, but
he don't hear me cause he over to his car ringing up the
police station to have them send the wagon out. He turn his

back to us cause he know we wasn goin nowhere. Didn't have to call but one man cause the only people in the whole Midway police station is Fat Dick and Skinny Dick, Buster Crab and Mr. Willie. Sometime we call Buster, Crab Face too, and Mr. Willie is John Willie, but everybody call him Mr. Willie cause the name just took. So Skinny Dick come out with the wagon and hauled us all in. So they didn't know me well as I knew them. Thought I was some hoogie jus' run around with the niggers instead of be one of them. So they put my cousin Covington, cause he dark, in the cell with Shotgun and the other niggers and they put me in the cell with the white men. So I'm drunkern a skunk and I'm yellin' let me out a here I'm a nigger too. And Crab Face say, "If you a nigger I'm a Chinee." And I keep rattling the bars and saying "Cov', they got me in here with the white men. Tell 'em I'm a nigger too," and Cov' yell back, "He a nigger too," and then they all laugh, all the niggers laugh, the hoogies they laugh too, but for a different reason and Cov' say, "Tha's what you get for being drunk and orderly." And I say, "Put me in there with the niggers too, I'm a nigger too." And then one of the white men, he's sitting over in his corner say, "I ain't never heard of a white man want to be a nigger. 'Cept maybe for the nigger women." So I look around at him and haul off cause I'm goin hit him and then some man grab me and say, "He keep a blade," but that don't make me no difrent and I say, "A spade don't need a blade." But then he get his friend to help hole me and then he call Crab Face to come get me out a the cage. So Crab Face come and get me out a the cage and put me in a cage by myself and say, "When you get out a here you can run around with the niggers all you want, but while you in here you ain't getting no niggers." By now I'm more sober so I jus' say, "My cousin's a nigger." And he say, "My cousin a monkey's uncle."

By that time Grandy come. Cause Cov' took his free call but didn't nobody else. Grandy's Cov's grandmama. She my grandmama too on my stepdaddy's side. Anyway, Grandy come and she say, "I want my *two* sons." And he take her over to the nigger cage and say, "Which two?" and she say,

"There one of them," and points to Cov'ton. "But I don't see t'other one." And Crab Face say, "Well, if you don't see him I don't see him." Cov'ton just standing there grinning, and don't say nothing. I don't say nothing. I'm just waiting. Grandy ask, "Cov', where Rat?" Sometime she just call me Rat and leave the "White" off. Cov' say, "They put him in the cage with the white men." Crab Face standing there looking funny now. His back to me, but I figure he looking funny now. Grandy says, "Take me to my other boy, I want to see my other boy." I don't think Crab Face want her to know he thought I was white so he don't say nothing. She just standing there looking up at him cause he tall and fat and she short and fat. Crab Face finally say, "I put him in a cell by hisself cause he started a rucus." He point over to me, and she turn and see me and frown. I'm just sitting there. She look back at Crab Face and say, "I want them both out." "That be about five dollars a piece for the both of them for disturbing the peace." That what Crab Face say. I'm sitting there thinking he a poet and don't know it. He a bad poet and don't know it. Grandy say she pay it if it take all her money, which it probably did. So the police let Cov' and me out. And Shotgun waving. Some of the others already settled. Didn't care if they got out the next day. I wouldn't a cared neither, but Grandy say she didn like to see nobody in a cage, specially her own. I say I pay her back. Cov' say he pay her back too. She say we can both pay her back if we just stay out a trouble. So we got together and pay her next week's grocery bill.

Well, that was one 'sperience. I had others, but like I said, now I jus' about keep to the people I know and that know me. The only other big 'sperience was when me and Maggie tried to get married. We went down to the courthouse and fore I even said a word, the man behind the glass cage look up at us and say, "Round here nigger don't marry white." I don't say nothing just standing up there looking at him and he looking like a white toad, and I'm wondering if they call him "white toad" more likely "white turd." But I just keep looking at him. Then he the one get tired a looking first and he say, "Next." I'm thinking I want to reach in that little winder and pull him right out of that little glass cage. But I don't. He say again, "Around here nigger don't marry white." I say, "I'm a nigger. Nigger marry nigger, don't they?" He just look at me like he think I'm crazy. I say, "I got rel'tives blacker'n your shit. Ain't you never heard a niggers what look like they white?" He just look at me like I'm a nigger too, and tell me where to sign.

Then we get married and I bring her over here to live in this house in Huntertown ain't got but three rooms and a outhouse that's where we always lived, seems like to me, all us Hawks, cept the ones come down from the mountains way back yonder, cept they don't count no more anyway. I keep telling Maggie it get harder and harder to be a white nigger now specially since it don't count no more how much white blood you got in you, in fact, it make you worser for it. I said nowadays sted a walking around like you something special people look at you, after they find out what you are if you like me, like you some kind a bad news that you had something to do with. I tell em I aint had nothing to do with the way I come out. They ack like they like you better if you go on ahead and try to pass, cause, least then they know how to feel about you. Cept nowadays everybody want to be a nigger, or it getting that way. I tell Maggie she got it made, cause at least she got that chicken shit hair, but all she answer is, "That why you treat me like chicken shit." But tha's only since we been having our troubles.

Little Henry the cause a our troubles. I tell Maggie I ain't changed since he was borned, but she say I have. I always say I been a hard man, kind of quick-tempered. A hard man to crack like one of them walnuts. She say all it take to crack a walnut is your teeth. She say she put a walnut between her teeth and it crack not even need a hammer. So I say I'm a nigger toe nut then. I ask her if she ever seen one of them nigger toe nuts they the toughest nuts to crack. She say, "A nigger toe nut is black. A white nigger toe nut be easy to crack." Then I don't say nothing and she keep saying I changed cause I took to drink. I tell her I drink before I married her. She say then I start up again. She say she don't like it when I drink cause I'm quicker tempered than when I ain't drunk. She say I come home drunk and say things and then go sleep and then the next morning forget what I say. She won't tell me what I say. I say, "You a woman scart of words. Won't do nothing." She say she ain't scart of words. She say one of these times I might not jus' say something. I might *do* something. Short time after she say that was when she run off with J.T.

Reason I took to drink again was because little Henry was borned club-footed. I tell the truth in the beginning I blamed Maggie, cause I herited all those hill man's superstitions and nigger superstitions too, and I said she didn't do something right when she was carrying him or she did something she shouldn't oughta did or looked at something she shouldn't oughta looked at like some cows fucking or something. I'm serious. I blamed her. Little Henry come out looking like a little club-footed rabbit. Or some rabbits being birthed or something. I said there weren't never nothing like that in my family ever since we been living on this earth. And they must have come from her side. And then I said cause she had more of whatever it was in her than I had in me. And then she said that brought it all out. All that stuff I been hiding up inside me cause she said I didn't hated them hoogies like my daddy did and I just been feeling I had to live up to something he set and the onliest reason I married her was because she was the lightest and brightest nigger woman I could get and still be nigger. Once that nigger start to lay it on me she jus' kept it up till I didn't feel nothing but start to feeling what she say, and then I even told her I was leaving and she say, "What about little Henry?" And I say, "He's your nigger." And then it was like I didn't know no other word but nigger when I was going out that door.

I found some joint and went in it and just start pouring the stuff down. It weren't no nigger joint neither, it was a hoogie joint. First time in my life I ever been in a hoogie joint too, and I kept thinking a nigger woman did it. I wasn't drunk enough *not* to know what I was saying neither.

I was sitting up to the bar talking to the tender. He just standing up there, wasn nothing special to him, he probably weren't even lisen cept but with one ear. I say, "I know this nigger. You know I know the niggers (He just nod but don't say nothing.) Know them close. You know what I mean. Know them like they was my own. Know them where you s'pose to know them." I grinned at him like he was s'pose to know them too. "You know my family came down out of the hills, like they was some kind of rain gods, you know, miss'ology. What they teached you bout the Juicifer. Anyway, I knew this nigger what made hisself a priest, you know turned his white color I mean turned his white collar backwards and dressed up in a monkey suit—you get it?" He didn't get it. "Well, he made hisself a priest, but after a while he didn't want to be no priest, so he pronounced hisself." The bartender said, "Renounced." "So he 'nounced hisself and took off his turned back collar and went back to just being a plain old every day chi'lins and downhome and hamhocks and corn pone nigger. And you know what else he did? He got married. Yeah the nigger what once was a priest got married. Once took all them vows of cel'bacy come and got married. Got married so he could come." I laugh. He don't. I got evil. "Well, he come awright. He come and she come too. She come and had a baby. And you know what else? The baby come too. Ha. No ha? The baby come out club-footed. So you know what he did? He didn't blame his wife He blamed hisself. The nigger blamed hisself cause he said the God put a curse on him for goin' agin his vows. He said the God put a curse on him cause he took his vows of cel'bacy, which mean no fuckin', cept everybody know what *they* do, and went agin his vows of cel'bacy and married a nigger woman so he could do what every ord'narry onery person was doing and the Lord didn't just put a curse on him. He said he could a stood that. But the Lord carried the curse clear over to the next gen'ration and put a curse on his little baby boy who didn do nothing in his whole life . . . cept come." I laugh and laugh. Then when I quit laughing I drink some more, and then when I quit drinking I talk some more. "And you know something else?" I say. This time he say, "No." I say, "I knew another priest what took the vows, only this priest was white. You wanta know what happen to him. He broke his vows same as the nigger and got married same as the nigger. And they had a baby too. Want to know what happen to him?" "What?" "He come out a nigger."

Then I get so drunk I can't go no place but home. I'm thinking it's the Hawks' house, not hers. If anybody get throwed out it's her. She the nigger. I'm goin' fool her. Throw her right *out* the bed if she in it. But then when I get home I'm the one that's fool. Cause she gone *and* little Henry gone. So I guess I just badmouthed the walls like the devil till I jus' layed down and went to sleep. The next morning little Henry come back with a neighbor woman but Maggie don't come. The woman hand over little Henry, and I ask her, "Where Maggie?" She looked at me like she think I'm the devil and say, "I don't know, but she lef' me this note to give to you." So she jus' give me the note and went. I open the note and read. She write like a chicken too, I'm thinking, chicken scratch. I read: "I run off with J.T. cause he been wanting me to run off with him and I ain't been wanting to tell now. I'm send litle Henry back cause I just took him away last night cause I didn't want you to be doing nothing you regrit in the morning." So I figured she figured I got to stay sober if I got to take care of myself and little Henry. Little Henry didn't say nothing and I didn't say nothing. I just put him on in the house and let him play with hisself.

That was two months ago. I ain't take a drop since. But last night Cousin Willie come and say whcrc Maggie was and now she moving around in the kitchen and feeding little Henry and I guess when I get up she feed me. I get up and get dressed and go in the kitchen. She say when the new baby come we see whose fault it was. J.T. blacker'n a lump of coal. Maggie keep saying "When the baby come we see who fault it was." It's two more months now that I been look at her, but I still don't see no belly change.

# Babies

## BECKY BIRTHA

In the past thirty years black lesbian fiction has become a strong, flourishing part of African American women's writing. Becky Birtha's "Babies," as its title suggests, addresses the issue of childbearing for lesbian couples. The understated story of Lurie and Sabra represents a complex struggle for women in love to preserve that love against social convention and inevitable personal choice. Birtha's story shows intimate familiarity and quiet compassion for the private life of her characters. First published in *Azaleas: A Magazine by Third World Lesbians* in 1979, the story also appears in Birtha's 1983 book *For Nights Like This One: Stories of Loving Women*.

LURIE AWOKE with a sense of satisfaction, contentment, completion. A second to register Sabra's face—awake, watching, loving her—and she closed her eyes again, snuggling into the crook of Sabra's arm, trying to recapture the source of that contentment. Then she remembered:

"I dreamed there was some emergency or disaster going on," she began. "And there were all these refugee children and babies. Someone was asking people to take one, to take care of them. And I picked out a baby and tied it on my back, and came home to you. And you didn't mind at all; you liked it. You even started to play with it."

Lurie smiled, remembering the fat little creature with the wisps of shining black hair and wide, wondering eyes—bringing it home to Sabra like the best surprise of all. Then she let go, opened her eyes to Sabra's reaction—the furrowed brow, mouth drawn tight. Sabra, Lurie remembered, fully awake now, did not like babies. Didn't share that weakness that would draw Lurie's gaze after a toddler on the street, or cause her to stare hungrily for minutes at an infant on a subway.

She knew Sabra was already interpreting her dream. "Never mind, Sabra," she said. "It was only a dream. I can't help what I dream." She tried to joke. "I haven't got a baby in my backpack."

"I know." Sabra's face, her voice, were gentle again. But the uneasiness which Lurie's dream had caused lingered.

Lurie remembered the first time they had talked about children, long ago in their first months together. It had been winter then, too, and they were walking in town at night, idly window-shopping. The streets were deserted, and they walked arm in arm. Lurie had been caught by the display in a children's clothing shop and had stared wistfully into the window, pointing things out while Sabra stood silently behind her. "That's the kind of stuff I'd like to get for my little girl. Those hooded sweaters, and corduroy jumpers like those."

"Your little girl?" Sabra had asked incredulously.

And Lurie had laughed. "No, Sabra, I don't have a little girl I've been hiding from you. I mean someday—when I do."

They'd walked on, but Lurie had realized after a block or two that Sabra was still silent and had not taken her arm again. "What are you thinking, Sabra?" she'd asked.

"I'm thinking about what you said. About a little girl. I don't know what you mean. I thought you were serious about us staying together."

Lurie had been startled. It had not occurred to her that those two plans for her future might be mutually exclusive. "I *am* serious about staying together, but . . . well, I guess I've always wanted to have children. And I hadn't thought about how this might make a difference. Haven't you ever wanted to have children?"

"No," Sabra said, "I never have. In fact, I've always

wanted to *not* have children. I know it's not the same for you, but I've been gay all my life, and I want to be for the rest of my life, and it does make a difference about things like that. I've always felt like kids were a kind of heterosexual problem, one more way women are oppressed by men. And I've always felt good that I'd be free from that."

Lurie had been thoroughly shaken. Now that she had finally found the one person she felt she could love, that person was completely opposed to her most important dream. As they had talked on for hours, it became clear that Sabra felt just as threatened, just as shaken by this new question between them, as she. In the end, they had left it open—Lurie reluctantly accepting the possibility that she might never have a child, and Sabra, equally reluctantly, accepting that someday they might consider it.

In the beginning, Lurie would sometimes bring it up—point out something she noticed about a child on the street, or comment on a book or film in which an issue of child-rearing was raised. She had hoped that perhaps, in time, Sabra's views might change, that she might be able to interest Sabra in children. But Sabra seemed to value very highly a life-style in which children had no place, and Lurie realized that the subject always created tension and bad feelings between them. After a few months, she had stopped mentioning the matter and tried to be careful not to let it show that she still wanted a child.

Now years had passed, in which Lurie's and Sabra's love for each other had deepened and expanded, and in which nothing seemed to be missing. Years when there was plenty of time to be together—to go to films and concerts, to take weekend trips to the seashore, to read aloud together. Time to be apart—for Sabra to practice her music, for Lurie to take evening courses at the local college. Time to make daydreams and plans about writing a book together, moving to the country someday, buying land. They were years in which the fun they had together nearly put out of Lurie's head the images she had held since childhood of her future adult life—full of babies and children and family. Nearly, but not completely. There were still times when she thought about children, about whether she herself would ever have a child.

The morning she related her dream was the first time in three years that Lurie had openly brought up the subject of babies. But once she had, the topic seemed to be open between them again. Lurie would find herself now, often, indulging in thoughts about children, or whimsical fantasies. Like parthenogenesis. She, Lurie, would be the one to carry the child in her body, but the baby would be a biological re-creation of Sabra. Lurie imagined a child who would look exactly as Sabra had in those old snapshots that folded out in accordion pleats from the yellow paper folders. A thin little girl in shorts, with pale brown hair in two braids, bangs across her eyes. Lurie would tie plaid ribbons on the ends of the braids. She would make all the child's clothing herself—long white nightgowns with lace at the neck and sleeves, starchy ruffled pinafores. She pictured the little girl walking into the room where Lurie sat stitching the last hem of a lacey pink dress. And the child taking one look and saying, "I'm not gonna wear that!" Sabra all over again. And Lurie laughed out loud at the prospect. Then Sabra had to know what she was laughing at, and Lurie didn't want to tell her, which made it seem bad, as if she'd been laughing at Sabra. So she did tell her. And, amazingly, Sabra laughed, too.

Sometimes Lurie dreamed of a child who would be both of theirs. Wondered what a cross between the two of them would look like. Brown or white? Large-boned or small? Black, frothy hair or pale, straight hair? She pictured a golden child. Golden skin and soft, fluffy golden hair. She had seen such children and wanted every one. But then, didn't she want every child she saw?

Sometimes, now, they talked about it. Parthenogenesis was not a real possibility, so Lurie talked of artificial insemination. Sabra would counter every argument, half-serious, half-teasing. "The baby would still be some man's. And it might be a boy. And anyway," Sabra said, wrinkling up her nose in a way that always made Lurie laugh, "who'd want to be pregnant?" When Lurie said she wouldn't mind being pregnant, Sabra said she knew some people who thought it was obscene and disgusting. "How do you know," she continued, laughing, "I wouldn't be embarrassed to be seen in public with you?"

At times, Sabra would stop teasing and arguing both and talk about it seriously. "I wish you could understand," she said one afternoon, "why I want *not* to have a child. I think you think the only reasons are selfish ones, for me. It's true the things I do with my time are important to me, like my music and my job and friends—things there might not be time for with a kid. But it's more than that. It's that I believe women in general should be able to care about themselves and their own interests, not always somebody else first. And as a woman, I really value freedom and independence."

Lurie began to smile, and Sabra immediately caught the meaning behind the smile. "I know," she said. "I'm not so independent and free anymore since you came along. But that's another reason: us. The way we live together and are happy together. I want it to always be like that. I want to be able to buy a piece of land, or write our book, or whatever else we want to do. I don't want everything to change. And I know it would."

"You're right," Lurie conceded. "Of course it would. But things always change anyway, and how do we know they wouldn't change for the better?"

Sabra shook her head. "I just don't believe it. I've been around the gay community for a long time, and I've seen what it's like for women who have children—bringing little kids to meetings, or not showing up because they can't get child care. I've heard about women having fights or breaking up with their lovers over the way they're raising the kids. I've seen how women with kids get alienated from the rest of the community. Not just gay women—all women. Like my mother, or your mother. They gave up everything they could have been, their whole identity, just to be mothers, housewives. I wouldn't want that to happen to you— even if you . . . weren't with me. I want you to be able to finish school and be a social worker or anything you want. You know, besides all the other stuff, I think one of the main reasons I don't want us to have a kid is you."

Lurie was quiet for a long time after that. "Sabra," she finally said, "sometimes I think you care about me even more than I care about myself."

Other times, when they talked, Sabra would grow sad and blame herself. "Maybe I'm all wrong," she would say, "acting as if I know more about what's good for you than you do yourself. If you weren't with me, you would probably have a child by now, and it would probably work out fine."

"I'd rather be with you."

"But if you weren't, wouldn't you have figured out some way to get pregnant, and done it?"

"In fact," Lurie told her, "I wouldn't have. I decided, even before I met you, that I didn't want to get pregnant with a child I would have to raise by myself. It didn't seem right, bringing a new child into the world to a less than perfect situation. If I wasn't with you, being alone would have kept me from getting pregnant like it did all those years."

"But," Sabra said, "you still did think about having a child. You must have been counting a whole lot on meeting a man you could do that with."

"Well, no," Lurie answered. "I'd pretty much given up on them, too, even before I met you. I was thinking about being a single parent, by adoption."

She had thought about adoption far more seriously than Sabra knew. In the years before she had met Sabra, she had taken books about it from the library and talked with pediatric social workers. She had even been on the mailing lists of several agencies who sent appealing pictures of wistful little faces starved for love. She knew there were some children whom agencies felt it almost impossible to place. Children who were black or mixed in race, or retarded, emotionally disturbed, or physically handicapped. Those who were over three, or over six. Or children who were all of these things. Even in the years before she was with Sabra, she had wondered whether the desire to have a child, or the love she felt she could offer one, was great enough to overcome obstacles like those. She had tried to imagine a child she might adopt—not an innocent baby, but a child already full of the hurt and rejection, the mistrust and resentment that six or seven years in foster homes and institutions could cause. Lurie wondered, even then, if it would be worth it, to try to take that on by herself.

Now, being with Sabra, she couldn't overlook another fact she knew about adoption agencies. That there were some adults with whom they would not consider placing even such "impossible" children. And that among these adults were lesbians. Even if Sabra agreed to adopt a child, Lurie realized it would be difficult. Probably it would mean lying and deception. Perhaps living apart, denying their lesbianism. Could their relationship survive that? And what if Sabra would never agree to try to have a child? That brought her to the real question. Did she, Lurie, want one, any child, enough to do it by herself, enough to leave Sabra in order to do it? To leave the one person she had found who she knew loved her, for a child she could not be certain of getting, or whose love she could not be certain of, either? She felt the question closing in on her, felt pushed to make some decision, to reach some resolution. She was thirty-two.

On the Saturday morning before Christmas, when she and Sabra were in town doing the last of their shopping, Lurie noticed a woman who looked familiar standing near them at a stationery counter. She stared at the woman a second or two, then recognized her—an old friend from school that she hadn't seen in six years. Lurie introduced her to Sabra, who waited patiently while the other two tried to catch each other up on the events of the past few years. Lurie was brief—she was unable to disclose the changes in her life that really mattered. In turn, the friend told of her marriage, ending by calling a little girl from a few feet away and introducing her as her daughter.

"Your daughter?" Lurie stared at the child of four or five

in the fur-trimmed cape and hood, and then again at her friend who was, she remembered, the same age as she.

As if she could read Lurie's thoughts, the woman asked, "You have any children yet?"

Lurie shook her head. "No, not . . . no."

After another minute or two they parted, to continue with their shopping. Lurie was lost in her own thoughts as they wandered through the rest of the store and out into the street, completely forgetting their intended purchase. Sabra was silent, too, and it was some time before Lurie was startled by Sabra's asking, "Are you ready to go home, or what?"

Lurie nodded, and as they turned the corner, Sabra shoved her free hand into her pocket. Once they were home, Sabra managed to be always in a different room from Lurie, the whole afternoon. Lurie could read Sabra's mood in the way she sat as they lingered at the table after dinner—hunched up with her arms folded in on herself, not sitting back relaxed and open as she usually did. When Sabra asked what she wanted to do that evening, Lurie said she had thought they might visit friends. Seconds later, Sabra abruptly walked out of the kitchen while Lurie was still doing the dishes. Lurie found her later curled up under the afghan on the bed, crying.

She sat on the bed and put her arms around Sabra, afghan and all, and asked what was wrong.

"Nothing."

"Yes, there is. Tell me what it is."

"No, there isn't. If you want to go visit people tonight, why don't you go ahead?" Yet Lurie knew Sabra was not crying about visiting friends.

"Tell me, Sabra." She began to plant kisses, little quiet ones, against the back of Sabra's neck and in her hair. "Please tell me." More kisses, until Sabra finally turned and let it spill.

"I just feel like you don't love me as much as you used to. It feels like I'm not enough for you, that you keep wanting somebody else, somebody more."

"That's not true. You know I only want you. There isn't anybody else. . . ."

"I don't mean another woman," Sabra said. "I mean a baby. I used to think," she went on, "that it was just left over from when you were alone, and that you wanted a kid because you just needed somebody to love. And after we'd been together awhile, you did stop talking about it, and I thought maybe your ideas were changing, and you were appreciating how nice our life is with just us. But now, ever since we brought it up again, you want to talk about it all the time, as if it's all you think about. I've tried to listen to what you say, but I just can't see it that way. And I've tried to tell you how I feel, but it seems like you don't care. Lurie, you mean so much to me, I don't understand why it's not the same for you. You have me, and I thought we were happy. . . ."

"Oh, Sabra. I am happy. You *do* mean a whole lot to me. It's just that . . ." and she felt Sabra stiffen as she said those last three words. How could she explain to Sabra what she had been struggling with in her mind? How could she even suggest the decision she felt compelled to make, one way or the other? Yet she had to be honest. "It's just that I've been thinking about kids a lot these days because I feel like I have to work it out. Wanting a baby doesn't mean I don't love you or don't want to be with you. But I can't help wanting a baby. It's just there, and I can't make it go away. Maybe I'll always want one."

She waited, still holding Sabra, afraid of what Sabra's response might be. But Sabra only said, "Can't I be your baby?"

And Lurie said, "You are. You are my baby." And she held her and rocked her very gently as she would have rocked the child she had always wanted to love.

During the Christmas holidays, Lurie went to spend a day at her mother's house. She had been meaning, for a long time, to go through a closet full of odds and ends left over from her childhood and adolescence. She meant to take what she still wanted to her own home with Sabra, and to throw the rest out.

She pored through old copybooks and social studies papers, boxes of costume jewelry, and picture post cards from nearly forgotten friends. Her mother came in to join her under the pretext of cleaning out a cedar chest full of old clothing that was in the same room. They talked casually about people on the block, about the latest news from relatives.

When Lurie pulled out a small trunk and opened it to find it full of her childhood dolls, her mother came over to join her. Together they went slowly through its contents. There were a dozen dolls, one from every Christmas until Lurie was twelve—babies, toddlers, little girls with impish or pouting or smiling faces. Lurie remembered those Christmas mornings, so different from the quietly happy one that had just passed, when she and Sabra had stayed in bed cuddling and talking long into the morning, when there had been no dolls or toys under their Christmas tree. She still remembered the name of every doll. They had been her children, all those years when she was still certain she would have real babies someday.

Each of the dolls had a complete wardrobe. There were little dresses of plaid and checked and printed fabrics, aprons, nightgowns, coats. Lurie turned them over in her hands, touching the tiny gathers and the fine-stitched seams and hems. She had made them all herself.

At the bottom of the trunk was a soft rag doll, made of brown cotton cloth with black yarn hair in two braids. "Goodness," Lurie's mother said. "There's Sister! I didn't know you'd kept her all these years. I remember when I bought her, the year you were two—couldn't resist her because she reminded me so much of you. You wouldn't part with her then."

"I remember," Lurie said. "I remember Sister." She set the doll gently to one side and began to replace the others in the trunk. "I guess," she said, "we could give these to the Salvation Army."

Her mother looked shocked. "You want to give them away?"

Lurie managed a little laugh. "Well, what am *I* going to do with them? I'm not a little girl anymore."

"I thought," her mother sounded hurt, disappointed, "you were going to save them for your children. That's what you always used to say."

"Did I?" Lurie lingered a second longer over the up-turned faces looking at her forlornly from the tray of the trunk, while her mother seemed to wait for some further answer from her. Then she closed the trunk. She picked up the rag doll she had put aside. "I'm just going to keep this one," she said, and smiled a little self-consciously. "I want to give her to a little girl I know."

On the train she held Sister in her arm as she had held her so many years ago, indifferent now to the quizzical looks of the other passengers. She would give the doll to Sabra, a belated Christmas present.

On New Year's Eve, Lurie and Sabra sat together on the couch, reading aloud by the light of the kerosene lamp. Together, they read lesbian novels, taking turns or reading the dialogue in parts, and they were now finishing the last chapter of this one.

Both sighed in relief that the two women in the story were still together at the end. "It's strange," Lurie finally said. "This is the third book we've read that touches on the issue of lesbian motherhood and child custody." She knew it was dangerous ground, bringing that up, and yet she was not afraid, she wanted to, tonight. She went on, "Having to choose between her child and her lover—what a choice for a woman to have to make."

"I know who I'd choose," Sabra said.

"The other woman, right?"

"Of course." Sabra smiled, seeming to have caught the safety from Lurie's mood. "You know me. It wouldn't be such a hard choice either, if the other woman was you." Then worry crossed out the smile on her face. "Who would you choose?"

"Oh . . . it's hard to say." Lurie tried to make it sound inconsequential, only a story they were analyzing the ending of. But she knew they were serious. She closed the book and wandered across the room, to end up staring at the little rag doll Sabra had instantly loved, who sat now looking so little in the big rocking chair.

"Who, Lurie?" Sabra's voice was insistent, cutting across the small room, then hurt. "You don't have to tell me. I know. You'd choose the little girl, wouldn't you?"

Lurie picked up the doll, turned, and recrossed the room. She put the little doll in Sabra's lap, then sat on the couch again next to Sabra and looked her full in the face. "If I had to choose . . ." she said slowly. "Between a child and the woman I loved. It isn't 'If,' Sabra, it's real. I've had to make that choice, and I've chosen."

# Play It, But Don't Say It

## Ann Allen Shockley

A strong voice in fiction about black lesbians as well as an accomplished literary bibliographer and editor, Ann Allen Shockley is an important contemporary black woman writer. This story is a unique, witty, and distressing tale of political power and sexual identity that, though it hasn't made the papers yet, probably will. Mattie B. Brown is an imposing, complex character whose refusal to be "outed" or to "out" herself preserves her career but potentially destroys her private life. Like the racial passing stories of Dunbar-Nelson and Fauset, Shockley shows how keeping identity—here sexual identity—hidden can exact a major toll. The story appears in her 1980 book *The Black and White of It*.

## I

WITH ALICE SEATED next to her on the front seat, Mattie Beatrice Brown slowly drove her sleek, black polished Lincoln Continental through the grubby niche of rough-tongued street licking out from the fang-toothed mouth of the ghetto. This section was a stunted pygmy of the city, but all hers to handle and manipulate. Possessiveness and pride claimed her as she gazed out the tinted windows at the people walking the streets—constituents to her—those black brothers and sisters.

The dwindling steel gray of a November twilight made the pedestrians blend like phantoms into the asphalt from which they seemed to emerge. To Mattie, they were her voting populace—poor, but significant nonetheless. She was grateful to all of them—the tall, thin, young, old men and women who had made *her.*

When she stopped for a red light, the policeman at the corner saluted in recognition. Directly behind him was a huge billboard with her picture looming big and brassy back at her. Her arm was raised high in a clenched fist, and the lettering on the sign read: *Vote for Mattie B. Brown— U.S. Congresswoman, Third District—Voice of the Black People.* Two flags surrounded her, one the red, green, and black liberation banner, and the other of red, white, and blue.

"I like that billboard," Alice remarked, startling Mattie, whose thoughts were turned upon herself.

"Hon?" She had forgotten Alice was beside her. One good thing about Alice, she knew how to keep quiet when Mattie wasn't in the mood to talk.

"The billboard—" Alice repeated. "I like it best of all."

The picture of Mattie on the panel stared back at her like a twin etched on paper. The drawing depicted her short black hair in tightly curled ringlets peaking above a broad brown face. Her almost flat nose tended to widen at the nostrils, flaring over a tidal wave of a mouth. With her piercing sharp dark eyes, she presented a formidable impression.

Back home in Dolsa, Georgia, they said that she was the spitting image of her father, big Thomas Jeffers Brown. He must have been the meanest black man on George Washington Carver Avenue, where he ran a cluttered corner grocery store stocked with the poor blacks' staples of sodas, bread, crackers, bologna, rice, and beans. Sundays, he was "called to preach" and served as the lay minister for the First Avenue Baptist Church. When Mattie got older, she began to think that his Sunday avocation was an atonement for cheating his own people during the week with marked-up prices and playing backroom politics with the local white rednecks for his own selfish gains.

Mattie hated her father's guts, but later was glad she had inherited them. They were what she needed to survive in the manner she wanted, causing her to emerge victoriously from nothing to something. She had gone to Prairie View

A&M and on to Howard University's Law School with the assistance of her family, work, and scholarships.

When she received her law degree, she returned to Georgia but not to the small town of Dolsa, settling instead in a medium-sized city. In Sanchersville, she opened a storefront law office perforating the heart of the ghetto. Here she made friends, learned to know and talk the tough, subtle everchanging secret language of the inhabitants, and became as hardened and slick as they. She worked to promote a high profile by keeping the pimps, bootleggers, whores, and gamblers out of jail or getting them off with a light sentence. She gave cheap advice and charged minimum fees, hardly ever collecting on past due accounts. All of her machinations finally paid off. She was now U.S. Congresswoman Mattie Beatrice Brown who was on her way to Washington, D.C. She felt like shouting.

"Those people over there are waving to you—" Alice said, pointing.

Mattie's eyes followed the direction of Alice's finger. Upon seeing them, she flashed her big-toothed politician's smile and sounded her horn in appreciation. Jesus, it was *good* to be somebody!

"We really worked hard to win, didn't we?" Alice's small, thin voice came to her again from far away.

"Alice—" Mattie breathed in mock patience, "to win *anything,* you have to work hard." They *had* worked like poor folks' mules. She in particular, morning, noon, and night, holding meetings, giving speeches, shaking hands, garnering money in exchange for favors, making both ethical and unethical deals. A politician had to be a salesperson, wheeler-dealer, and slickster. She had loved all of the grueling campaign, keyed up like a man with a perpetual hard-on. The excitement was there of shrewd maneuvering. Luckily, she had an innate ability to quickly judge people— if they were honest, loyal, tricksters, or leeches. This was difficult to do with black people who were born actors to make it in a white world.

"Well—I'm glad it's over. I'm tired." Alice sighed wearily.

Mattie frowned, glancing at her. Alice did look a little pale and had lost weight, but she shouldn't be all *that* tired. Alice was just thirty-four, six years younger than she, and holding her age well. On the other hand, she surmised, Alice was by nature frail and dainty like her mother back in Dolsa. Maybe that was what had attracted her to Alice when she moved here seven years ago. Alice had an uncanny resemblance to Josie, a gentle, kind tiny woman who taught all grades in a one-room school, only to come home in the evenings to be voiceless in the background of Thomas Jeffers Brown. Alice was lighter in complexion than her mother, but had a similar round pretty face with delicate features. Alice reminded her of those supposed-to-be black dolls that she used to get for Christmas as a child —the ones with keen features, straight hair, and painted brown.

Now on smoother streets leading away from the inner ghetto, Mattie drove faster, basking in the luxurious power of the car. Soon she pulled into the driveway of her house, a modest brick ranch type fringing the edges of her voting district. At this point, the black middle-class domiciles began, sprawling outward away from the stink of the ghetto's mouth with greener pastures harboring fashionable homes.

"Here we are—" Mattie pressed the automatic device on her dashboard, and the garage door eased upward for the Lincoln to slide smoothly in.

When they entered the kitchen from the garage, the loud shrill of the telephone met them, pealing through the house. "Answer the private line for me, Alice," Mattie said, throwing off her coat. The house had already been lighted by the timer she had set. She had a phobia about entering dark houses. Being distrustful had become an intimate part of her nature.

Inside, the thought of food immediately nagged her. She was hungry. Unfortunately, eating was her weakness. Whether this was congenital, stemmed from growing up around a grocery store, or nerve induced, she sometimes wondered. The reasons seldom fretted her too much, for eating gave a soothing pleasure to her, like a cat whose back was being stroked. She had gained ten pounds in three weeks before the election, sending out for hamburgers, french fries, Kentucky Fried Chicken, and thick milk shakes. To add to this conglomerate were the campaign fundraising dinners, extravagant lunches with key people in restaurants noted for their cuisine, and soul food suppers in greasy-smelling joints where the street people frequented. A politician needed a good stomach.

"That was Con on the phone—" Alice disclosed, following her to the kitchen. "He wanted to remind you about your ten o'clock press conference in the morning at the Hyatt."

"Oh yeah—" Mattie grunted abstractedly, totally engrossed in peering at the various plastic containers and bowls in the refrigerator. She finally decided on the ham, potato salad, and deviled eggs. Bringing out the food that she was aware she should shun, a sting of resentment passed through her aimed at Alice. If Alice wouldn't keep her refrigerator stocked with already prepared food, she wouldn't be tempted. She liked to eat, but hated to cook.

"I'm going to get a drink. Want one?" Alice asked, going familiarly to the den off the kitchen.

Alice had helped design the house that Mattie had moved into after making enough money to leave the dark five-room apartment above her law office on Jungle Avenue. Reflecting upon this, Mattie began to speculate that Alice had deliberately positioned the bar near the kitchen for her own convenience.

"Mattie—do you want a drink?" Alice's voice octaved higher.

"Damnit, no!" Mattie yelled back, annoyed. Why in hell did Alice persist in asking? She knew that she didn't give a hoot about liquor, except sometimes for a light, dry wine with a particularly fine meal. Anyway, she had to keep her wits about her. Slicing the meat, the thought occurred to her that she ought to start locking up her booze, for Alice seemed to be hitting the sauce a lot lately.

Mattie piled her plate with food, got a sixteen-ounce bottle of Coca-Cola, and sat down at the kitchen table. "Hey, Alice! You in there trying to drink up all my liquor?"

Alice came in with her usual Chivas Regal and water. She had put on some records, and Roberta Flack's *Killing Me Softly* drifted languidly through the speakers like a creeping mist.

"Hum-m-m, I like that"—Alice murmured, leaning over Mattie, one arm around her shoulders, chin resting feather-light on top of her head—"and *you.*"

"Umph!" Mattie grunted, reaching for more potato salad. It was heavily flavored with onions, the way she liked it.

Alice sipped the drink and began humming with the plaintive sound of the singer who was weaving a euphoric melody of love. "Dance with me—"

"Can't you see I'm eating?" Mattie snapped through a mouthful of food. Christ, stupid! Who wanted to get senti-mental while eating?

Alice's lips brushed warm sunrays at the base of Mattie's neck, while her breath stirred a gentle rose-flung breeze. A spontaneous shiver of delight knifed through Mattie. Her free arm reached out and curved around the smallness of Alice's waist, bringing her to her side. "Babes—why don't you go and get comfortable for me?" Mattie's voice was huskily low.

Alice kept a gown, robe, toothbrush, and other accesso-ries in the private guest room for such times. She had the key to the house and knew more about the management and needs than the three-times-a-week housekeeper.

Suddenly Alice giggled over her glass.

"What's so funny, Babes?" Mattie asked, still using the confidential pet name for her woman.

Alice pulled out a chair and sat down. "I was just think-ing: you were eating the first time I met you. Remember? At the NAACP benefit dinner at Mason Hall. Everybody had finished eating and gone into the auditorium waiting for you."

"Hell—the food was too good to leave. Anyway, it was a

free speech," she snorted, wiping her mouth on a paper napkin.

Alice took another long drink from the tall frosted glass with a curved B on it. "I reminded you that people were waiting—"

A half smile crossed Mattie's lips. "That was my first formal introduction to the black *co-mune-ni-tee-e,* as my fired-up young black activists call it." She laughed. "I gave *some* speech, didn't I? It was on a Black Woman's Search for Justice. Shame I hadn't thought about taping it at the time." Since then, she taped all her speeches, playing the tape over and over for herself and trapped guests. "Later, I got a spread in *Ebony*—Black Female Lawyer in the Ghetto."

Alice pulled out a pack of cigarettes from her jacket. "I was the one who got you that speaking engagement." She would never divulge to Mattie that she had been second choice when Judge T. Templeton could not do it.

Mattie sneered. "Oh, you and your little old committees." Alice was forever serving on community and social committees that investigated, planned, organized, and gave functions. During that time, she was on the NAACP's program committee. Mattie supposed being a social worker required belonging to those frivolous committees that she personally termed as inconsequential in comparison to political committees, which got right down to the nitty gritty—power and control.

Alice inhaled and heaved out a dragon's breath of smoke. The nicotine odor floated over Mattie's food and into her nostrils. "Goddamnit, Alice, you know I can't stand people smoking around me when I'm eating!"

"Sorry—" Alice hurriedly put out the cigarette and got up to empty the ashtray.

The loud rollicking sounds of a female rock group assailed the room: "You got to lo—ve—ve—lo—ve—ve—yeah—yeah—yeah!"

"Yeah—yeah—yeah!" Alice chimed in, snapping her fingers and moving her hips in time with the rocking beat.

"Let's dance—" she invited Mattie, twisting toward her in gyrating movements.

Mattie gulped down the remainder of the Coca-Cola and belched. Alice tugged at her hand. "Com'on—"

The thumping, pulsating music shook the kitchen walls. Laughing, Mattie stood up, moving her heavy body with the rhythm. She was amazingly light on her feet and matched Alice's steps in unison, swinging her hips and bumping her. They got down, shaking, rocking, laughing unrestrainedly.

When the music ended, Alice breathlessly kissed Mattie, who backed away in playful admonishment. "Watch out there. You're now kissing a U.S. Congresswoman!"

"Hum-m-m, and it's sure good!"

"Let's go to bed, Babes, so I can show you how *good* it *can* be!"

## II

Mattie had a king-sized bed with a padded blue velvet headboard. When she made the selection, Alice had facetiously labeled it Mattie's bedtime monument. Now as she snuggled closely to Mattie's full, warm body, she was thankful for the huge bed, which provided plenty of room for loving.

Clad in black silk pajamas, Mattie lay on her side, offhandedly stroking Alice's breast, as she talked in what amounted to a monologue: "I'm going to set that capital on fire when I get there. Those white male congressmen are goin' to know who *this* black woman is inside six months. And the black me—en-n ain't never gonna see-e-e a more black bitch of a woman than this ole Sapphire!"

Alice tried to concentrate on Mattie's words above the wonderful feeling her hand was conferring on her breast. When Mattie got excited, her deep voice became lower, almost like a man's, and when Mattie finally relaxed, she would purposefully lapse into her black English—what she termed her first language. From past night interludes through the years, Alice knew Mattie was wound up and going to talk until she was tired. Shifting slightly, she reached over on the nightstand for her glass, reflected in the small glow of the nightlight like a frosted mirror. Slowly she sipped the liquor, savoring the taste of her relaxer.

"Yes—sir—ree! Those black me—en-n in Congress are going to see one *evil* black woman. Me! They're goin' to meet their match. Just like that Ike Smith who I beat. He ain't ne-ver goin' to forgit that a woman burned his ass in that election!" she guffawed, kicking up her heels beneath the covers. "I sure beat the hell out of that little fag."

Alice continued to drink, wishing Mattie would forget for a while her victories, hates, future, and self, and remember her. "How do you know Ike Smith is a fag?" she pronounced the word distastefully.

"Hell—*everybody* knows it, including his wife!" Mattie retorted, irritated by a question that she deemed a waste of time even to answer. "Goin' 'round all prim and prissy like he's got a stick stuck up in his behind all the time. So neat and clean you're 'fraid to even *breathe* on him. Polite as an undertaker."

"You shouldn't call him that, Mattie—" Alice chastised softly.

"I'll call him what I damn please—" The nerve of *her*. Alice and her not-wanting-to-hurt shit. Another facsimile characteristic of her mother. Nice to people, hiding behind genteelism, masking truth. A middle-class southern black woman's white female social acculturation.

"Suppose"—Alice bit her lip, clutching tightly to the glass balanced on her stomach—"somebody called you—"

*"Called me what?"* Mattie stopped her angrily, sitting upright in the bed like a mountain rumbling with the pent-up fires of an impending volcano. "I dare you to *say* it!" she challenged, forgetting the ambiguity of it all embedded in her previous ruminations on genteelness versus speaking your piece.

Alice froze, closing her eyes against Mattie's wrath. Mattie's daring her to call it began six months after the NAACP dinner, one year after Mattie came to Sanchersville. There had been a snowstorm that evening, and in the South, if it snows, everything stops, for snow paralyzes a southern city. She was over to Mattie's and spent the night. The two of them sharing the one bed in the Jungle Street apartment. Mattie's hands had fumbled out for her in the square bedroom with the faded green paint. Within the circle of Mattie's arms, she had confessed in her ear: "I guessed it all along. That's why I wanted to meet you, to find somebody in this God awful secret black lesbian world with whom I could at least be myself—"

At those words, Mattie had pushed her away, hissing: "What are you *talking* about?"

"About you—me—*us*," Alice replied, a trifle frightened, for that was the first time she had seen the full vent of Mattie's temper.

"There is nothing to say about us," Mattie said coldly, the words as precise and incisive as a surgeon's knife. "As long as we are together—like this—I don't want to discuss it. In other words, don't *say* it."

Now as Mattie towered menacingly above her, a mixture of concern and anger invaded her, gnawing into the fibre of her being. This was representative of the times when she did not understand Mattie, or perhaps understood her too well, perceiving the weakness of her in this vulnerable spot, which precipitated fear and defensiveness. Fear of what might become known and defensiveness against the possible hostility of those who discovered.

Suddenly Alice got up. "I'm going to get a drink—" A task which would involve a passage of time away from Mattie for her to calm down. And too, she wanted another refill. "Let me fix you one—" she suggested, thinking it might help—one way or another.

"You know I don't like the taste of liquor!"

"It's just that you seem to be all tight inside, restless—" Alice tried to explain, turning on the bedlamp to find her way to the den with her empty glass. At the bar, she drank a hasty straight shot before mixing a double scotch and water. When she returned to the bedroom, Mattie was lying on her back, eyes glued to the ceiling, arms flung behind her neck.

"Phew-w-w, that stuff stinks!"

"No more than those damn onions on your breath." The rebuttal came out of Alice's mouth like slippery greased lightning sooner than she had time to think. She placed her glass carefully on the table again and got back into bed. Why did Mattie have to make a profession out of abrasiveness—hardness? Was she afraid of tenderness—softness? Even with her lovemaking, it was strictly physical, insensitive in a way, detached, skillful mechanical movements to wind up a toy for carnal gratification. Had Mattie ever really loved anyone but herself? She doubted it, for love of self was too rooted in the seeds of her growth. She wanted to ask about the others in Mattie's life—those nebulous ghosts of whom she never spoke, but who Alice knew had been there. One has to get started somehow.

Coinciding with her thoughts, a warm feeling of compassion for Mattie flowed through her. "Let me soothe you—" she whispered in Mattie's ear, running her hands over the wide flabby spill of her overly abundant breast. "Help you to relax. Please."

Ignoring her, Mattie sprang up and began to pace back and forth in her lengthy, flatfooted movements on the deep pile of the rug. "The first thing I plan to do in Washington is to get on the committee for—"

With resigned disgust, Alice lay back, submerging herself in the only softness available at that time—the pillow. She was committed to wait for Mattie's urge. Mattie never thought of her—*her* needs. She was always the one who served, not the one to be serviced. She sought her glass and drank. The liquor helped to spin a vapor over what Mattie was saying.

"Shit—who knows? If I work at it hard enough, I might even become the first black and female vice president—"

Ambitious Mattie, Alice ruminated, the alcohol beginning to take a numbing effect, causing a languor that is sometimes miraculously accompanied by penetrating insight. Mattie might even make it as vice president. She had enough guts, coupled with an ego that nurtures the will to succeed.

She, as different from Mattie, did not want to be any more than what she was, nor do any more than she was doing. What she wanted out of life was a lover who offered what a lover was supposed to: love itself. Some time ago, Mattie had told her that she was a dreamer—not pragmatic. Visions of dreamers were too frequently interred with their spirits.

As abruptly as she had gotten out of the bed, Mattie climbed back in. "Turn off the light—" she ordered gruffly.

Alice stole one long drink before rolling over in the boundless bed, fantasizing it as an endless beach of white cloud. Laughing, she snapped off the light.

"What's so funny—" Mattie grunted, arms pulling her close.

"Nothing—" Alice replied truthfully, for nothing was funny. She had simply laughed out of happiness, pleased that the time had come for Mattie to hold and love her. She made funny quick short lip marks on Mattie's face, impressioning herself on Mattie's forehead, eyes, and mouth.

"Hum-m-m," Mattie murmured, smoothing her large hands up and down the length of Alice, "take off that gown—"

Alice struggled out of the flimsy pink nightgown and tossed it at the foot of the bed. Mattie wiggled out of the bottom of her pajamas and dropped them on the floor. Then she began to knead the brown nipples of Alice's breasts.

Alice closed her eyes, wishing Mattie would kiss her. Kisses were important. Soft kisses spoke of tenderness; medium ones of warmth; and the passionate of hunger and fire. Kisses too spoke of love.

"Hum-m-m, Babes—" Mattie moaned against Alice's right breast, lips closed around the nipple. Taking the top of the pear-shaped cone into the wet cavern of her mouth, she sucked, licked, and groaned with pleasure.

Alice's hands entangled into Mattie's hair, stroked and slid down her spine to the amazing flatness of her buttocks. She encircled each bottom cheek, squeezed, and let one lone finger make a singular gliding bird movement from the base of her spine to the part in the twin-mound cleavage.

"Go-o-d, Babes, go-o-d—" Mattie's only term of endearment. She shuddered as Mattie's hand began to roughly work between her legs. Then Mattie sprawled on her back against the pillows and pulled Alice's small body on top of the huge mount of her own.

"OK—Babes—do your thing."

# III

At ten A.M. the next morning, Mattie strode into the lobby of the Hyatt Hotel, impeccably dressed in Alice's wardrobe selection of a stylish beige woolen dress set off by a green jacket and scarf. She had handed Con her cashmere coat to hold, not trusting the coat hanger in the back of the room where the press was waiting.

Poised on the little platform stage in front, she quickly scanned the faces confronting her. The local reporters were recognized by flashing her intimate Tom Jeffers Brown smile. Most of them were white except for the one from *Jet* and another representing the NNPA. One white woman nearby caught her attention. She was husky, medium height, had short straight blond hair that she kept pushing back from her face, and wore large owl-framed glasses. Her tight-fitting jeans and denim jacket caused Mattie to frown disapprovingly, for the attire seemed an affront to her, not in deference to the occasion.

Confidently she turned to face the Third Estate. There was nothing, absolutely nothing, she liked better than being in the limelight before her public—the press and TV cameras. All over the country, people were seeing and listening to *her*—Mattie Beatrice Brown. During these highlighted moments, she could imagine how a dictator felt, armed with the exuberant sensation of power engulfing him—an emotional vise more heady than the pangs of orgasm.

Con stood at the door, her coat draped over his arm, giving orders. He was performing those functions for which she paid him. She had heard that he sometimes called her "frustrating" and "temperamental," but what did she care, as long as he performed capably what he was assigned to do. At this stage, she still needed him. He was part of the black co—mune—ni—tee-e. Although middle-aged, he was youthful in appearance with his suave handsomeness. She wished he would shave off some of that beard encircling his mouth, making his lips look like a pussy. He looked extremely good this morning in his blue silk suit and splashy colorful hand-painted tie. By this, he made her look good too, communicating the fact that she could pick a staff.

The cameras came alive and the questions began, stock ones to which she smoothly gave answers, smiling as she did. She assumed the posture of coolness, confidence, and self-assuredness. The queries were leveled at her:

"How does it feel to be a black woman elected to Congress?"

"Are you going to work with the Black Caucus?"

"What do you expect to accomplish?"

"Are you interested in any particular committees?"

She answered effortlessly, fluently, without hesitancy, aided by her innate gift for words. To the questions parried for which she wasn't ready to commit herself, she gave double meanings that sounded like a plausible reply at the time, but later when the polish wore off, would shatter into puzzled pieces. Answers rolled off her tongue with well-oiled ease. She was a skillful politician, utilizing the most effective tool of her trade—words.

The woman in denim held up her hand. "Congresswoman Brown—"

"Yes?" she smiled warmly, to show her woman-to-woman recognition. She, too, represented the minority of women.

"I'm Cathy Storm of the *Gay Free Press*—"

Mattie's smile froze into ice, body growing rigid from an inward caution warning. *How did she get in here?* she wondered to herself. She glanced reprimandingly at Con, who was standing expressionless by the door.

"Ms. Storm—"

"Do you plan to support legislation in favor of homosexuals that would be especially beneficial to the triple jeopardy associated with black lesbians—"

Perspiration began to dampen Mattie's forehead and under her arms. She blamed the uncomfortable sweat on Alice. She shouldn't have worn the wool dress, but something lighter to cope with the lights and the room, which she had instantly found to be too warm.

The reporter's eyes seemed to have grown as large and round as the brown frames of her glasses. With what Mattie interpreted to be a cynical smile, the woman repeated in a most deliberately explicit manner her question. The room seemed to become submerged in a stagnant pool of waiting.

Drawing herself up to her full five foot six inches, Mattie responded in a voice completely alien to her ears, "This is not my concern. You see, there are no such black women." After the statement, her lips pulled back over her teeth like a gorilla trying to smile.

The woman reporter's mouth flew open as the room was polarized in a split-second of shocked silence. When Mattie saw the woman's mouth open again, she quickly turned to the man whose pencil was half raised and said: "Next question—please."

# IV

The evening's papers mocked her: *Black Congresswoman Claims No Black Lesbians.* Within the sanctity of her home, Mattie had the answering service monitor all her calls and cut off the ring of her private line.

Frantically she paced up and down the kitchen, slapping her forehead and muttering repetitively to Alice: "God, out of all the *important* things that I said, why in hell did they have to pounce on *that*?"

Alice had cooked dinner, beginning early in the day to prepare Mattie's favorite prime beef roast. After she had looked at the press conference on TV, she feared the worst.

She thought the dinner would serve as a partial balm to help soothe what she anticipated would be Mattie's strung-out nerves.

"Well—I think you could have given a better answer—" Alice said, opening the oven door to check on the roast surrounded with potatoes, onions, and carrots. Her at-the-ready glass of scotch was on the counter. She was a little tight, having started drinking after the TV conference, which had been in her opinion a disaster. In her haste to deny, Mattie had made an ass of herself.

"What do *you* mean—*stupid*? I *don't* know any black *les-bi-ans*!" The word came out in a clenched shriek, flung by force. "Do *you*—?"

*She said it!* Alice thought. *She has finally gotten the word out of her mouth.* Alice looked at her contemptuously. Was she real? Or living in a fantasy of wishful make-believe? What were *they*? *Play it—don't say it.*

"Sure, I know some black lesbians and so do you. Only the nice middle-class black women who *are* won't *admit* it. Careers, hiding behind husbands, and social status are more important in black life than admitting a same-sex preference." Alice picked up her glass and shrugged. "Besides, in the long run, what good would it do? Coming out of the closet is more significant to white lesbians. That's why that woman asked you the question. We black women in our struggle against racism planted the seeds for the white women's movement. Now, I guess, it's time for *them* to do *us* a favor. Liberate the so-called sex-crazy black woman from her own hang-ups. Making it so that if she's a lesbian, she won't be afraid to say or feel deep within her that it is as good as shouting black is beautiful."

Mattie stared at Alice as if amazed that Alice could say so much, or even carry a thought. Finally, drawing herself up, she said icily: "I have no concern for black *or* white lesbians."

Alice finished her drink and moved to take the roast out of the oven. "Dinner's ready—"

Seated at the table, Mattie generously began helping herself to the food. "Alice—you realize this shit is ruining my political career before I even get to Washington," she continued, unable to forget what had transpired. "Lesbians —umph!"

"Mattie!" Alice shrilled, slamming her fist down hard on the table. "For God's sake, *what do you think we are?*"

A winter's blizzard crossed Mattie's face to film a sheath of ice. "You fool—" she uttered in disgust. "How do you figure *I* am one of *those?*"

"How do I—?" Alice echoed incredulously. Then in exasperation: *"Face* it—Mattie. You play it; you might as well *say* it."

Without warning, Mattie's hand shot out and struck her. Alice's face snapped around in a half arc from the blow. Surprise traumatized her, offsetting the sting of the slap. She gaped at Mattie, who had calmly returned to eating. "You are unbelievable!" she blurted out incredulously, shaking her head in dismay. "Everybody knows, Mattie. They *know."*

"Know *what?*" Mattie snapped, eyes narrowing. She fought to control her anger and the urge to drag Alice from the chair and shake her until her teeth fell out.

"What you *are.* Why do you think the woman was there —to ask?"

A sneer crawled over Mattie's face. "Alice," she commenced with restrained patience, "they might *think* it, but they don't *know.* And if anybody accuses me publicly, I'll sue like hell!"

"You are denying yourself—"

"And *you*— Not to others?" Mattie struck back triumphantly.

"Actually"—Alice gave a small laugh—"no one has ever *asked."*

"And if they did?"

Alice looked down at her plate, a pinched frown between her eyes. "I don't know. I just don't know—"

"Finish your dinner," Mattie commanded. "It's getting cold!"

"I'm not hungry anymore—I think I'm going home," Alice said, rising from the table.

"Be sure and lock the door behind you—" Mattie flung out to the departing figure. Turning back to her meal, she brought the food closer to her, spooning up second helpings of each dish. As she relished the succulent meal, her thoughts began seeking a plan of action, for Alice had given her a lot to think about.

## V

Mattie phoned Alice early the next morning, inviting her to dinner after she finished work. All night she had explored step by step what she considered a major problem: her relationship with Alice. The problem had to be eradicated, for it threatened her survival as a politician and person.

By early morning, she had arrived at what she considered a workable and safe solution. The disposition settled upon negated her previous plans for Alice to go with her to Washington as a private secretary—of sorts. But if it were true what Alice had said about the knowing, then she had to leave her behind. She could not afford suspicion in an area extremely touchy to blacks. Lesbians were almost lepers. She had to be looked upon with unblemished pride by the black co-mune-ni-tee-e.

Taking Alice with her, whom people considered as her best friend, would lead to too much speculation. She knew a couple of friends elsewhere who lived together under the pretense of sharing an apartment or duplex. Thank goodness she had not succumbed to the idea of having Alice *live* with her.

In a strange way, she felt sad. She liked Alice in an unexciting way and was going to miss her for a while. Alice had been her friend, companion, listening wall, and lover. But after all, people destroyed faithful dogs when they had outlived their lives, didn't they? The cure for that was said to be go get another. What had to be done, had to be done. First things first, and Mattie Beatrice Brown would always be first with her.

When Alice arrived that evening, Mattie could tell that

she had stopped by her after-work haunt, Big Lil's Lounge. The place was a favorite Happy Hour waterhole for the black bourgeois at five o'clock. Big Lil was a tub of a woman with a friendly yellow face who ran her place like a reigning black Pearl Mesta. She was the drinker's friend, confidante, and mother, extending an open ear to problems made more sodden with liquor. Sometimes Mattie wondered about Big Lil—whether she was or wasn't. It was rumored she was.

The lingering odor of scotch and cigarette smoke from Big Lil's clung strongly to Alice, striking Mattie's nose in full force. It was all she could do to keep from blaring out: "You smell like a barroom fly." Resisting the indicting delivery, she graciously conjured up a smile and said: "I'm so-o-o glad you could make it."

Alice returned a little half smile familiar to Mattie, conveying that she was feeling good and guilty about it too. Mattie ignored it, determined that this was going to be a *good* evening. "Let me take your coat, Babes."

At this overture, Alice looked perplexed. She was accustomed to hanging up her own coat. Wasn't this home to her too? She watched Mattie walk over to the closet, her ample form hidden beneath the folds of African lounging attire. Alice had been around Mattie long enough to realize something was in the air. Beware of Mattie when she veered from her true self.

"Fix yourself a drink. I prepared a simply marvelous dinner."

"A drink would be fine—" Alice said, thinking she needed it to help cope with whatever was to come. When Mattie went out of her way to be charming, it was either to ask for something or deliver a swift kick while smiling. She preferred Mattie being her old, mean, self-centered self. That was the most honest part of her.

In the kitchen, Mattie proudly pointed to the food. "Look what I cooked for us—"

Alice held a double strength Chivas Regal for a sustainer. "Looks good—"

"Steak, baked potatoes, broccoli, and a tossed salad—"

"Hum-m-m, nice—" Alice said, unimpressed. The menu was Mattie's only forte in the culinary department, except for bacon and eggs. She was impatient with anything else.

"I even set the table in the dining room—"

"So I see—" Alice remarked, looking into the room. "Best silver, dishes, candles—"

"For *us*, Babes—"

Alice swallowed her drink. Funny, even with all the drinks at Big Lil's, she couldn't get a buzz on yet. Too many warning signs.

"How's Big Lil?" Mattie asked randomly, placing thick steaks under the broiler.

*Jesus-us, how did she guess I had been there? Simple, she knows your habit as you are standing here knowing hers, Alice Ryan,* she apprised herself. "Big Lil's fine."

"I *must* stop by there sometime and thank her for helping me with the campaign." Then slyly: "She's quite a gal, isn't she?"

To this, Alice simply nodded affirmation. Seeing Mattie's quandary about leaving the steaks to finish the salad, Alice said: "Let me help you—"

"Oh, no-o-o! *I'm* doing this. You go on in and sit down."

Alice turned with relief from the mess of the kitchen, with the coffee boiling over and broccoli half burning, to take her seat at the long mahogany table covered with Mattie's best white linen tablecloth. Slowly she sipped her drink, eyes on the flickering candle flames conducive to intimacy, finding a mesmerizing warmth in them.

"Big Lil is a strange person—" Mattie said, bringing in the food.

*Why was she harping on Big Lil?* "Is she?"

"You stop by there quite a lot. Do you like her?"

"How do you mean?" Alice questioned testily.

"Personally—"

"*Everybody* likes Big Lil. She's warm, friendly and honest." *More than some can say about you,* her inner silent voice retorted.

Mattie made needless pilgrimages back and forth to the

kitchen, showing her ineptitude at the task. "It's wonderful Big Lil can run that place all alone without a man's help."

"She has a good business sense—" Alice spread her napkin over her lap. "And I don't know if she's a lesbian," she added perceptively.

Mattie flung her a grim look. "Alice, I didn't ask for that."

"You didn't have to. I just guessed—" Alice said too sweetly. "Shall we eat?

"A very nice dinner," Alice complimented her, watching Mattie put more logs in the living room fireplace. The fire was lit only for Mattie's few special occasions, like the expensive after-dinner brandy she had brought out. It would all have been very nice if she didn't know Mattie as she did.

Leaning back in her favorite chair, Mattie sighed. "Ah-h-h, if this could last forever, Alice. Evenings like this with you."

Alice said nothing. The fire cracked as the flames leaped into a dance of warmth. Mattie moved out of her chair to come over and sit beside her on the couch.

"Babes—it's going to be a long, hard road for me ahead in Washington."

"I know."

"I'm going to have *double* problems now. There and *here*. So, I've been thinking. What I need is someone I can *trust* to take care of *this* end for me—where my voters are."

Alice clutched the brandy glass, then set it down on the coffee table. The taste of it had suddenly turned sour. She needed a cigarette. The inhaling and exhaling would help her breathing, keep her calm.

"I've decided, as much as I hate it, not to take you to Washington with me. I need you *here*—"

The flick of the gold lighter kept on the coffee table was sharp as an electric shock in a room of steel. Alice deliberately took her time, dragging hard on the cigarette before she blew out a reeking stream of smoke directly into Mattie's face.

Mattie did not flinch, nor did the manufactured look of pleading for understanding vanish from her face. "I can *trust* you, Babes, more than anybody. You can keep an eye on Con for me. I believe my soul that he deliberately let that—that woman in the press conference to embarrass me. And, I need you, Babes, to see that the housekeeper does her job and to keep an eye on the office. I'll put you on the payroll." Mattie felt pleased. Paying Alice would make it appear more real and alleviate any twinge of compunction she might develop. This way was the best. Eventually she would get rid of her completely. There would be no one around to cause speculation. If she had to give up sex, she would submerge herself in work.

"In other words," Alice began slowly, frowning, "you're trying to get rid of me. I may become an embarrassment—"

"Of course not, Babes!" Mattie exclaimed, throwing up her hands in feigned bewilderment. "How could you even *think* a thing like that? All we've been together in the past—"

"Because I know *you,* Mattie. How important your work is to you. Your drive—ambition—"

Mattie looked in confusion at Alice, watching her coolly smoking a cigarette. This was an Alice she could not fathom. She had considered Alice to be a trifle light upstairs, but she was presently demonstrating that she had more sense than she had been given credit for having. Alice, as her mother underneath it all knew Thomas Jeffers Brown, understood her.

"There—you see! Since you *do* know how much my work means to me, this proves that I can't do without people I can trust—" Mattie seized upon her words, turning them to her own advantage.

Alice gave her a long disdainful look before putting out her cigarette and getting up. "Don't worry, Mattie. I won't ruin you, and I know how to keep my mouth shut."

"Babes—" Mattie looked at her in abashment, feeling a hollowness in her stomach. She would have rather there been a fight, anger—or even tears and pleadings. These she could deal with, not this deadly coldness exhibited by Alice. It wasn't even a contest.

"I wish you luck—" Alice said, getting her coat.

Mattie went swiftly across the room to her. "You *are* going to take care of this end for me, aren't you?" The question turned itself into an entreaty.

"I don't know. I'll have to think about it." She would not have to ponder long. If there was to be a break, it was best to have it over—clean, no hanging-ons. Mattie would finish it anyway when her usefulness was over. It would have been nice to stay with her, glory in her triumphs, be there to cushion her defeats. Only it takes more than one to make an equation of love.

"Think it over, Babes—" Mattie's arms went about her.

Alice stood rigid in the embrace. The kiss on her mouth was like the surface of a stone. She opened the door, smiling sadly. "Just remember, Mattie, play it—don't say it. And you'll be safe."

Mattie stood for an indeterminable time frowning at the closed door. Then the pangs of hunger as powerful as the cramps unexpectedly seized her. Automatically she went to the kitchen. Without preliminary thought she began to pull out dishes of food and place them on the table. Then she sat down and started to eat. She ate on and on into the night, until the deep hollow well within her had seemingly been filled—for a while. It was only then the lingering thoughts of Alice went away.

# Color Me Real

## J. CALIFORNIA COOPER

J. California Cooper combines a folksy narrative voice with
honest insight into black women's lives in her short fiction. A
kind of cross at times between Zora Neale Hurston and Terry
McMillan, her unique talent for telling stories from inside the
lives and minds of characters is evident in "Color Me Real."
Era, the second-generation victim of racism and sexism, is a
fighter and searcher after a life of fulfillment and love. What is
"real" in "Color Me Real" is everything that inhibits that fulfillment. The story comes from Cooper's 1984 collection *A
Piece of Mine.*

IT DOES NOT MATTER what year it was or where, it
would have been just as terrible and tragic at any time.
Minna, a thirteen-year-old child, was seduced by a grown
white man her mother worked for. She had a man child
that he never recognized. A year later she had a girl child
by the same seducer. It would seem strange and suspect,
this second child, except that money, that old cross, was
almost nonexistent in the child-mother's family, and she
was trying to get money for food from the babies' father,
and he gave it to her "on condition." Minna was in need.
Her whole family was hungry. Her last intention was to sell
her body, but the whole world knows what can happen to
the best intentions in a mother's mind when it comes to her
hungry child, a hungry, sickly grandmother, brothers and
sisters lining the cold hearth and empty cupboard. An
empty coal bin results in a cold stove. Few things are worse

than four or five hungry people alternately staring at and looking away from the others that hold no answers, only needs.

By rights, money was owed them by this particular white man for work done for him, but he had decided to hold off paying. His intent was to have Minna again. After the first time he had seduced her, he thought she would cease holding off in her childlike fear and come sleep in his cold lonely bed, but she did not. So he added hatred to his lust for her. He made his plan and did not pay Minna's mother, nor Minna for helping her, the cooking and cleaning pay for two months. He locked his cupboard and coal bin and everything else they could use or sell, then sat back, picking his teeth and belching after his dinner. He ate at the little greasy Addies Eats diner and gave them just enough for one person to eat and sat and watched them fix it so they would have none in his absence. He watched them grow nervous, hungry, and afraid, but he did not see the anger. I don't know why. His power blinded him, I guess.

He kept them there, working, by saying his money was held up and he would be getting it any day now and would pay. They knew he lied, at least they thought so, but what could they do? The judge and the sheriff were white. So Minna was forced to take her baby boy over to him to ask for help. Money she had already earned. He tied the little boy gently to a wicker chair. The white-skinned child with his own face was his child, he thought, as he finished tying him and patted him on the head. He then lay Minna down on the bed and rode her all morning into the afternoon. The baby, tired from crying, had fallen asleep, head hanging over the ropes tied around him by his father, his gasping breaths jerking his little body as he slept, crying out now and again without even waking up. The second baby, a girl named Era, was born nine months later. During that nine months the sickly grandmother moved out into the woods she knew so well and picked her herbs and roots and puttered over them silently, and somehow they found their way into the white man's house, and somehow he became blind, which was soon followed, somehow, by impotency.

But they, Minna's family, were kind to him. They continued to care for him, and they never had to wait for their money again because they had to do everything for him that involved money. They never cheated him, but he never cheated them again either. He tried to get a wife once, so he could get rid of them. He suspected something but could not be sure of what. No white woman wanted a blind, impotent husband though, so he remained single, and they remained to take care of him in his time of need.

Time passed and the children were growing. Minna worked in the schoolhouse in exchange for letting her children sit in the back of the room to get a general education, and insisted they go even with all the taunts, teasings, and insults they received there from the other children. An older brown-skinned playmate, George, was companion and protector to Era. He lived up the road and was never far from her, going to and from school.

When Era was about seventeen years old, George said he would marry her, but she really didn't see George. Her brother had been running off and coming back home for the past two or three years bringing tales of a bigger and better life. One day while cleaning her father's room, Era went into a box of his cash kept under his mattress and took $400. Packing her few things in a cardboard box, she got George, now working, to drive her to town and left on the bus that came through town headed for New York, checked into the YWCA, and signed up for secretarial school. She had a plan in mind. When she had graduated, near the top of her class, she moved on to Idlewild, where, her brother had told her, the rich men were idle and the women were wild!

Era was a good-looking woman, and she chose to pass for white because it would make her way easier, and she planned to get ahead in life and get a wealthy husband to take care of her. She loved her family at home and planned to send them things and be good to them, but her greatest fear was of being as hungry as she had been at some times in her life. She remembered doing without the smallest things that sometimes make a big difference in daily life.

Well, Era got a job at a brokerage firm and in two years or so had married one of the clients there. He was not rich, but he was on his way. She couldn't invite her mother and family to the wedding. She wrote them about it!

They had a good life for several years. Then, while on a two-day shopping trip in New York, Era got sick and left her friends to come home. When she arrived, she found her husband in her bed with a black woman! Her husband admired her tolerance and understanding attitude toward the black woman and offered her to share, but both black women refused the offer. The black woman was sent away in a cab.

Era was silent and thoughtful because she was hurt. She had loved her husband.

To make a long story short, when they were getting into the freshly cleaned bed, he held Era and kissed her through her tears and made many declarations of love, true love, deepest love . . . and said he didn't know what it was about black women that he liked so much. Just always had! But that they would never compare to her and so on and on. Era let her logic carry her away, and she told him, "If what you really want is a black woman, then you have one. I am a black woman." He stared at her a few moments, then laughed and told her she didn't have to go that far! Era got up and got pictures her mother had sent her over the years, saying, "This is my mother." She smiled at him and the photos. He snatched the photographs and stared at them until he dropped them to the floor. When he turned to her, his fist came with him, and he beat the wife a moment ago he had loved truly, deeply. He refused to have a black woman for a wife, so he settled some money on her in the divorce, and she left the years she had made a life there behind her, and flew home to her mother.

Her mother, Minna, still lived in the broken-down little house. Grandmama was dead and gone. Brother was home at the time but living with a woman at the woman's home. The first thing Era did was buy her mother a better house closer in to the little town, and they made a home of it. She stayed there about a year. George had already moved to town and had his own business as a gardener. He had remained single and was taking care of his mother.

Now, Era was a simple uncomplicated woman, born and raised around growing things and animals, trees and space. These things still pleased her, so George would take her to work with him sometimes to break the monotony for her, but still she didn't really see him. He worked with her in her own yard, and it became one of the best. George loved his work, and his flowers blossomed in all the wealthier white folks' yards. He was reliable and smiled a lot. They liked that, so he prospered. Era took pleasure also in reading to her mother and dressing her in good clothes. She did her hair and gave her facials for fun.

As Minna improved in looks and confidence, several older gentlemen, who at first came to look upon Era, began to turn their faces to this quiet, shy woman who hadn't had much of anything. Not friends, laughter, or male companionship. Minna blossomed and soon became attached to one pleasant man, Arthur. Era stayed until her mother's first and only wedding. The only bad part of the day was when brother beat his black woman after the wedding reception. Later, when he took Era to the station to leave, she stood on the train steps and asked him if he thought he was white, and if that was why he beat his darker-hued wife whom he said he loved? And why didn't he marry her? Because of his daddy? "Well," she continued (before he could answer, because the train was pulling out), "that white man who raped our mama was not just a white man, he was a child molesting, raping, ignorant, slimy, cruel bastard . . . who died alone! Is that who you think you are?"

"At least I ain't try'n to pass for white!" he hollered back at her as the train was gathering a little speed.

"No!" she shouted back at him. "You tryin to pass for a man!" Then the train was too far away to answer her, so they watched each other until the track curved and they could not.

Era chose Chicago this time and, after becoming settled, finding work, looked around for something "meaningful" to do. She volunteered to help in a political campaign for a black man. The headquarters was always full of many people, including lawyers and other politicians. Some bringing something to give, some coming to get something. Now Era was black, and that was that in her mind. However, quite a few men took her to be white. Consequently she had quite a few lunch dates, which she thought was normal. One in particular, Reggie, began to show up when he didn't have to be there. He often told her, "You are my kind of woman!" Which goes to show you everybody can take the same set of words and all go off in their own direction as to what those words mean! Dinner dates were soon added to lunch dates; then cocktails and dancing.

Reggie liked all the attention Era got, the admiring glances from the other lawyers and professional men. Since it is rather obvious to you he was rather shallow, it will stand to reason if I tell you he soon proposed. One night he had the ring, the license, the car, and the gas, and he drove a few counties away, convincing Era all the way of his love for her and how far they would go together. She married him because she thought he was not exactly a fly-by-nighter. He was part of a good law firm, had a nice home (where the bar was filled but the pantry empty), and a boat. The marriage went pretty well the first year or two. But Era discovered her black husband thought she was white, and it seemed so important to him, she didn't tell him the truth right then, and later it became harder to tell. But here was another man, a black man, she could not take home to her mother . . . yet.

The decision was made one night when he had the fellows, those who had white wives, over to his house for cocktails, and the conversation came naturally around to the kind of women black women were. Era was a little tired of going into the kitchen or getting busy somewhere else when these conversations came up, so she just listened and thought. She knew from conversations with the white wives that most of them felt superior to their black men, and one of their fantasies was to picture them, during lovemaking, as slaves; the black skin glistening on the white skin helped multiple orgasms along. So when the black men ridiculed their own black women, saying, among other things, "Black women are not ready, never had been ready, and it would take ten thousand more years before the sister would begin to get ready," the white women smiled, because they knew it was against the rules to laugh out loud at black women in these meetings in front of the other black brothers. But they moved to the kitchen or bedroom, and passing each other, the thrill in their hearts showed in their eyes as they looked at each other.

Era was setting a dish of hors d'oeuvres on the table when her husband said, "Black women will never stop castrating their men, and when I have a son, I'm going to tell him, 'Son, don't be a fool and marry a black woman, get one just like your mama!' "

Era, full of it all, interrupted, "Reggie, do I castrate you?" He patted her on the hip and laughed. "Baby, we not talking about you all, we are talking about black women." Then he looked around for accord from his black brothers. Era didn't laugh.

"Which one of you black brothers got a white mama?" she spoke quietly. "If you don't have a white mama, then it's your own mother you are dragging in mud, all the women in your families who carry the same blood you do!"

Reggie stopped smiling and looked seriously at Era. "Listen," he started to say something.

Era looked around the room at the men, "When you was growin up, who tried to starve you and who tried to feed you? And when you find a foot in your behinds, now that you are grown, what color is it?" Era threw the plate of food against the wall over the record player, and it fell on the turntable and knocked the needle off the Miles Davis record and began to spin and knock against the boards. Reggie jumped up to quiet his wife, acutely conscious of what the others were seeing and hearing. "Baby, baby!"

Then she said, "I am a black woman! I never told you I was white. I knew you didn't want to hear that!"

Reggie stiffened, "I don't want to hear it now!"

But Era didn't care anymore. "What's so big about you, so grand, that you think you aren't stooping down when you try to tear black women down, women your own color? What makes you think you can tear half a thing down and leave the other half up? You weren't freed from slavery any earlier than she was!"

Reggie reached for her, but she moved away, still talking.

"I'm gonna tell you something. Black women don't care if you like white women. What we really resent, and what makes us so disgusted with you, is that you have to stand on our shoulders, tear us down, make us look like nothing, to make yourself big enough to do what you want to do! Just go on and like em if you want to, only stop tearing us down to do it! Some white women are really all right! So, it's O.K.!"

Reggie was beyond anger. His male friends saw that and rounded up their coats and wives, who were trying to remember all the things they had told Era when they thought she was white. They left.

Reggie beat Era, lawyer or not, pushed her down the stairs so she could see the front door, and said, "See that door, black bitch? You be gone out of it when I get back here in a few days." Then he tore her clothes off her and made evil love to her as hard as he could. When he was finished, bitten and scratched, he grabbed his boat keys and left, saying, "I don't want you no more!"

Era lay there and cried and cried until it was far into the night. She wasn't crying for the loss of Reggie or the nice house or the boat. It was the loneliness. She wanted someone to love her, and she wanted to love someone . . . real. She called an ambulance, stayed two days in the hospital, where, fortunately, she learned nothing was broken. Came out, packed her things, went to a lawyer, stopped downtown, and charged a new wardrobe for the country. Mailed back the charge cards to her husband with a note saying, "The cards come back from the black side, the bills will come from the white side of me." Then she drove home to her mother's to recuperate and think about her life and what she was going to do next.

Everything was still the same at home, quiet and peaceful, seeming far removed from big city racing. George was still there and they worked in the garden again, and when Era needed something more to fill the days, she would go with George to work on his jobs. She liked being out in the sun, working in the earth. Sometimes they talked.

"George, you are still doing exactly the same things every time I come home."

"What I'm going to change for? It suits me! Don't give me no black eyes and big bruise!"

Silence would follow. But another time, she would say, "You know, you could make more money. Get a bigger house!"

"I'm doin all right! Do what I want to do! You can't always buy the things you want, you know." He would smile.

Silence. Then George might say, as he put the flower bulbs gently into the ground, "You had a big house . . . twice, far as I know. What they do for you?"

Era would pat the earth down gently around the bulb. "You know what I mean, George."

Another time, "George, why haven't you married? Had children?"

"Era, I'm gonna marry the woman I love. I don't love them women I fool with!"

"Who do you fool with, George?"

He stood up. "This is a small kinda town . . . so when I need a woman, I gets dressed and go up the highway to a nice place I know and spend my money, and when I get back, that's all there is to it! Not nobody gonna be knockin on my door worryin me!"

"Ain't nothing wrong with marriage, George. You need to be married!" She looked up at him.

He bent back to his work, "Ain't done you no good, Era!"

Silence again. Off and on they talked about all the things they felt and thought about life. George was a little deeper than Era had thought, and she found she was not as deep as she thought she was!

Another time. "George, my marriages were different. I tried to make them both work."

"What went wrong then?" He was digging around a tree.

"I was too black, George."

"What that mean, Era?"

"Well," she said thoughtfully, "one husband needed what he did not want . . . the other husband wanted what he did not need."

George stopped digging and looked at Era. "Was you wanting a rich man? How come they picked you?" He picked up the shears and began pruning the tree, spreading the lowered branches apart so he could look at her. She began to drag the branches into a pile, the sunlight blazing down on her now shining, healthy, sun-baked face and body.

She finally answered, "Well, I guess I did, I do. And them? Well they looked at me, and each one saw what he needed to see!"

George lowered his head through the branches. "And you helped them see what they wanted to see?"

"Ain't nothing to say but I guess I did!"

"Era, you ain't always sposed to see what you doing, you sposed to feel it! Seem like all you all did was for the look of things."

"George, how come you know so much about it? You have never been married!"

"But I been in love a long, long time, Era."

"Well," her voice seemed strangled somehow, "why don't you marry her? What's wrong with her?"

As he spoke, everything seemed to become still, suspended in space. "I love you, Era. Always have. Look like I always will. But you not sposed to know that, cause I ain't gonna do a damn thing about it! Ain't got no room for no big heartaches in my life . . . done had one all my life already."

Era's throat tightened, and she could feel her own blood rushing through her body while at the same time the sun seemed to blaze brighter and she had to close her eyes from the glare.

Silence again. The rest of the afternoon they said things like, "You want this?" "No, hand me that."

When George called Era the next morning, she said she didn't believe she would go with him. She expected him to come running by that evening; he didn't. Nor the next, nor the next. She drove by his jobs, and when she saw him and waved, he smiled. She could see his house from her porch, and when he saw her, he waved, smiled, and kept right on going about his business. On the weekend she saw him wash and shine his car all afternoon. Later he came out clean and dressed up. He waved, got in his car, and drove off, to the highway.

Era sat on the porch, thinking and staring at George's house far into the night till he came home, then she went in to bed and stared at the ceiling, feeling. Another week went by. He came by and ran in with some flowers for Minna and grabbed Era by the back of the neck, "Seem like I done lost my helper, Ms. Minna!"

Minna answered, "I don't know why! She ain't doin nothin round here cept reading and lookin out the window and sittin on that porch!"

George let go Era's neck, "Well, people got to read and look out windows too. I got to go!"

Minna asked, "What's your hurry? Stay and have some supper. Era cooked it."

"No, ma'm." George smiled. "Got to get home and clean up. Going to hit the highway this evenin!" He started out the door.

Era spoke sarcastically, "Again? You sure hitting the highway a lot!"

He smiled at her, "How you FEELING, Ms. Era?" He put a lot into that word "feeling."

"You ain't been calling me 'Ms. Era,' call me Era!"

He smiled at her as he got into his truck, "Era, you sound like you don't feel too good." He drove away.

She didn't have to wait on the porch as long this time. He was back after a couple of hours. She started across the street to talk to him. For some reason she was angry. But she changed her mind when she realized she didn't have anything really to say. She went back home to bed. She lay there listening to Minna and Arthur talking and laughing in their bedroom. They made things seem so simple, close, and good. Where was her man, the man she could live with in peace and love—and reality? She thought hard about herself.

The next day she was up early and dressed in her cutest shorts outfit. She went and worked in the garden. When George passed, she smiled and waved him by. For a week she did her yard and helped the neighbors on each side of her, in a new cute shorts outfit every day. She seemed to perk up each time George's truck came by, and he seemed to find more reasons to come home for a minute. On the weekend, when he had cleaned his car and himself and was driving away, he slowed in front of Era's house, where she was painting the fence.

"Good Lord! You are busy Era! You gon paint the house next?"

"If I FEEL like it!"

"That's right!" He smiled. "Always try to do what you feel! Wait for the feeling!"

Era placed her hands on her hips. "You sure feel like hitting that highway a lot!" she screamed at him as he drove away.

He was back early, hardly over an hour. As he parked in his driveway, Era burst through the porch door, slammed it, and with her face set, strode across the street toward his house. He saw her coming and held up his hand and strode to meet her, calling, "I'll meet you halfway!"

They met in the middle of the road.

They were both silent for a time, then George spoke; his voice was soft in the dusky evening on the empty road.

"What's the matter, girl?"

"I don't know, man!" Her voice, angry, trembled.

"Want to talk about it, woman?"

"Yes . . ." She looked up at him. He took her hand, pulling her toward his house. "Wanta sit down?" he asked.

"I want to know if you meant it when you said you loved me?"

"Yes, I meant it. I also meant I don't want no problems."

"Am I a problem to you, George?"

"Do you love me, Era?"

"I want you . . . is that love? I feel you! Is that love?"

"Sometimes."

"Well, what do you want from me, George?"

"Love . . . and a peace of mind."

"How will we know we'll always feel this way? What will I get from you, George?"

"Love . . . and a peace of mind."

"But how do you know?"

"Because I FEEL it, Era. Always have, always will."

They drew close, standing there for a time, then they kissed for the first of many loving and peaceful times.

She was neither white nor black now. She was a woman, his woman. It lasted till death did them part, leaving beautiful brown children on the beautiful brown earth. They worked their garden, which grew abundantly and had mostly . . . love and a peace of mind.

# The Spray Paint King

## RITA DOVE

Though best known for the poems that made her U.S. Poet
Laureate, Rita Dove is also an accomplished short story writer.
This is a complex and original tale about a mixed-race teenager
living in Germany, whose lust for life is expressed in the brilliant and angry graffiti he leaves on a city's ancient face. The
boy's anger and passion are alternately directed at the analyst
who calls his work "asocial," white people, the girl he loves,
and the toll history takes on individuals in the creation and
destruction of civilizations. Dove's story is both sensitive to the
potential genius in youthful alienation and rebellion and wary
of the hostility—against women in particular—that sometimes
accompanies it. The story appeared in *Fifth Sunday: Stories*
(1985).

*WHEN DID YOU FIRST TAKE TO THE STREETS?* Bitch
with pad and pencil, doodling cocks in the margin while
digging at me with that cool soft voice. *What criteria determined your choice of buildings?* Blue eyes trained on some
far-off point as if she were driving her BMW on the Autobahn. *Why do you use black paint?* Blond hair crimped like
a statue's. A down home German girl.

I walk over to the window, casually, and stare down at
the Rhine. I know she wonders just how black I am. She
wonders how many sessions before she can ask me about
my ancestry. *Ach, Mädchen*—when I see you sitting on that
straight-back chair, ankles crossed and pad balanced on

those waffly thighs, I imagine you as my private stenographer. Taking down all my pearls.

If she would look a little further than my crinkly hair, if she would glance over my shoulder, I would point out the Cologne Cathedral, rising from the glass and steel *Hauptbahnhof* like a medieval missile launch; I would show her the three blackened arches of the Hohenzollern Bridge and, farther to the right, upriver from Old St. Alban's, the bare metal stripe that's the Köln-Deutz Autobridge, then the little tower at the tip of the harbor whose name I've forgotten and . . . there it is. Severin Bridge. Saint Severin of the eleventh century, whose bones lie boxed in gold in a church on the south side of the city.

I'll call her Severin, that bitch who calls herself my psychiatrist. Though her ID might show otherwise: Dr. Severin.

How I feel about Diana, she asks. Why don't you guess for a while. Gives you something to do when you're lying alone between the frottee bedsheets, exhausted from your own pleasure but unable to sleep. (I've watched you squirm in that hard chair. I've seen you secretly sniffing your fingers as you put away pad and pencil in the desk drawer.) And if you still can't sleep, you can type up your notes. I see it now: Case History of the Spray Paint King.


Dr. Severin has decided I should keep my journal private until I think I am finished. My first entry shocked her (did you cream in your panties, my bride, my Edeltraut? Did I catch you right?) *Seventeen and already asocial.* She thinks she can take the wind out of my sails. He will tire of these juvenile insults, she thinks, when no one is there to read them. She has provided me with a list of questions. Why did you drop out of high school? When did you join a motorcycle gang? How did you meet Diana? What satisfaction does defacing public buildings give you?

I am forced to do your bidding, but it is not easy. So many questions! I'll need an outline to answer them all:

> ### I. Background
> ### A. Family
> ### B. Sexual experiences
>
> ### II. Onset of Criminal/Artistic Activities
> ### A. My friends above the river
> ### B. Concrete vs. stressed steel
> ### C. Flick of the wrist

This, then, Lady Bockwurst, is for you. Take it in memory of me and the deeds I have wrought upon this blighted city, scab on the banks of the Rhine.

When I was ten my mother sent me to the cellar to haul coal. I was frightened, and the scuttle banged my knee several times in my haste to escape; but by the third trip, I gathered courage to linger. Under the flickering light of the naked bulb swinging, the coal gleamed dimly, like wax, in huge craggy mounds. All that coal dust I had inhaled every winter, all the tenements dulled with soot and the chilling rain and the sky like an iron glove, all that dusty and gingery despair settling on the skin like grit—blackness undiluted, one hundred percent.

But years went by before I unzipped my pants for the first time. I didn't know what would come next—just that it felt good. I couldn't stop, even when my spine threatened to sink between my knees. Then something broke inside me and splattered against the wall of coal. Now I'm going to die, I thought, watching it grow translucent, darken to a gray jelly.

As such, Diana's nothing special. But the way she walks! —as if her head doesn't know what her body is doing . . . and what it does is sensational. Not that she's a knockout. Her breasts are average, but she's so slim that they're . . . well, *there.* And legs like a young boy, legs that don't stop. And a round trim ass. She wears corduroy pants, tight, in orange and pink and lilac; she looks like a tree and the fruit on it.

Diana hung out at the Hi-Fly, our penny-arcade on the east bank. Everyone in the gang was afraid to touch her unless they were high—then sometimes they'd take her for a ride across the Autobahn bridge. Every time she came back, she looked as if she were drowning.

But the oddest thing about Diana, what made me start paying attention to her, was that she read books. Philosophy, anthropology—things like that. She'd sit at a table, a Flair pen between her lacquered fingernails, underlining. I watched her several nights before I went over. The guys liked to kid her, asking her if Sigmund Freud was her great-granddaddy, stuff like that. But when I sat with Diana, I didn't ask her anything. I didn't even talk. I just watched her read. I believe she understood what she read, because when she was reading was the only time her head and body seemed to come together.

It got so I'd sit there until the Hi-Fly closed, watching the Flair pen move under her fingers. I drank one mango juice after another; watching pink ink move through the words. (You wouldn't understand, Dr. Severin, how peaceful I felt.) Then one night—the sky was a deep, tricky blue—Diana finished a book. I had never seen her finish one before. I waited for her to fish the next one out of her handbag; but she clicked the pen shut and threw the paperback on the table. I stared at the cover, something about the phenomenology of space. The author had a French name.

"Let's go for a ride," she said, standing up. I nodded and went for my bike.

We rode every bridge over the river that night, all eight of them. We roared around the square at Neumarkt four times. We teased the prostitutes on Weidengasse and the bums at the *Hauptbahnhof.* Somewhere in Ehrenfeld we got lost and wandered around through the deserted underpasses until we stumbled onto a familiar street and started back into town. Swinging past the radio station, we saw a man in a three-piece suit practicing turns on roller skates. His briefcase lay propped neatly against a balustrade.

"All the white buildings," Diana whispered, and when I turned around, she had that drowned look.

And finally the dingy spires of the cathedral, spotlit to remind us all where we were, the great *Köln am Rhein,* home of toilet water and pale bitter beer.

Anonymous benefactors send me sketch pads and charcoals. Yesterday a packet from Zurich—precision drafting pens and an arsenal of pastels. I distributed them among the guys on my corridor. As if, after painting the town, I would doodle on a slip of paper.

The only decent gift came from a Martin Tauber, Dr. phil., Free University of Berlin. "You keep good company," he wrote inside the front cover. Lithographs by Picasso. I'm not sure what he meant, Dr. phil. Tauber—I'm not academic. But the book's not bad. A series of sketches of a bull caught my eye. First Picasso draws a bull in every detail—cock, balls, muscles, and all. In the next picture, the bull has lost his muscles, but he's still a damned fine beast. Next he loses his hooves and eyes, and the tail's just a swooping line. Then he sports a branch with two leaves sticking to it instead of a cock. By the time Picasso's finished there's only two or three ink strokes on the page. But it's still a bull. Inside the front cover Dr. Tauber had also pasted this newspaper clipping about my sprayings:

> The young artist's style is reminiscent of Picasso in austerity of line, of Matisse in fantasy and social comment. The bitterness, however, the relentless scrutiny of what we so vainly call civilization, the hopelessness which pervades his work, without coquetry nor call for pathos—these qualities are all his own. He is, so to speak, his generation's appointed messenger.

Bingo. The Big Time. Razzmatazz.

Certainly Dr. Severin considers the possibility that I might, one day, pull her onto the shrink-couch: she considers the possibility with a mixture of thrilling curiosity and propitious dread.

There's a term for me—*quadroon*. Every time I say the word, I think of pale chewy cookies and laugh. I'm what girls call a treat—*ein Leckerbissen*. Gray eyes with a slight tilt. Flaring nostrils on a sharp nose. A large, clear brow. Women either shy from me on the street or linger, smiling. Men's eyes narrow.

The Negro blood is more prominent in me, in fact, than in my mother. From a very light baby with a cheesy complexion, I darkened during kindergarten. It began at the ears and descended with frightening rapidity to the neck (pale coffee). Lines appeared in my palms like lemon juice scribblings held over a flame. The hair, so fine and wispy, crinkled. The pink cheeks of my classmates huffed and puffed: *Negerlein, Negerlein*.

My mother, conversely, lightened as she aged. When I was younger she reminded me of some magnificent bird of prey, tall and golden-skinned with an aquiline nose set into the flat strong bones of her face. Her plucked brows perch like talons above her eyes, which are hazel and wide apart. She wears her thick hair tied back with a ribbon, like a girl.

But way back in Aachen, during the last snow-whipped days of 1945, my grandmother—when she studied the caramel-colored face of her new daughter—had been in despair. She had never set eyes on a black person before the soldier from the land of chewing gum and grapefruit spoke to her in his elastic voice. He gave her chocolate bars and promised to return. Then the British arrived, and she packed her things, walking eastward toward her hometown, Dresden, pleading aid from military convoys—the swarthy baby helped. By the time my mother learned to walk, they had gotten as far as the border of the Soviet Occupied Zone and were turned back, placed on a U.S. Army truck headed west. A Negro M.P. was loading the refugees; my mother began to cry when his hands reached for her; she did not stop until, smiling, he drew on white gloves.

\* \* \*

My father works construction; his idea of recreation is to take a streetcar to an unfamiliar quarter of town and to walk his family through it, pointing out buildings that are in need of repair or soon to be torn down. Once, when I was eleven, we took the streetcar as far as Chlodwigplatz; we got out near St. Severin's Gate with its little terracotta tower and strolled through the cobblestone streets. My parents held hands and laughed at my Lancelot-like attempts to spar with the neighborhood dogs. It was one of those September evenings when the sky is rinsed clean and hot, a light that makes you feel exhilarated and melancholic in the same breath. To the right, between crenelated facades, the Rhine glittered like an alchemist's greed; all the sparrows of late summer swooped to the lowest branches and blinked at the earthbound pityingly. We turned down Dreikönigsstrasse, toward the river, and when we could go no further, my father stopped and pointed a blunt finger at the pale green Severin Bridge.

"Like a bird's long dream," he said, "a tribute to modern engineering." And with a proud sigh: "I helped build it— for three years of my life."

The next day I looked it up in my *Kinderlexikon*. Span, 300 meters. Steel box girders braced by three sets of cables passed over the top of the A-shaped tower located near the east bank. I went to the public library to find out more details. *Köln—History of a Modern City*. Five men were buried in one of the cement pilings. . . .

I ran to my mother and found her bent over the bathtub, rinsing sheets. "How could they?" I asked.

"How could they what?" she countered.

"Leave those men to die!"

"Don't tell me," she began, slapping sheets against the side of the tub, "you've been reading those Westerns again." Then she saw the book clutched to my chest, and her hands ceased their convulsive wringing.

"Who are you talking about?" she asked.

"Josef Breit, Mathias Metzger, Winfried—"

"Not their names!" She caught herself shouting, spoke

softer. "I know." The afternoon sun splashing through the blinds and across her face turned her eyes pale gold.

"They fell into a hole while pouring concrete. The others kept pouring. . . ."

For a moment my mother hesitated, her hands quiet in the water. Then her face hardened. "That's your father's territory," she replied. "Ask him." Bending over, she attacked the laundry with renewed energy, wringing the sheets.

"What did you want us to do," Dad said, leaning back in his armchair, "stop production and dig them out?"

Yesterday the street cleaners, under orders from the city, prepared to erase one of my sprayings with XR-3, the chemical abrasive concocted to eliminate political graffiti left over from the student movement. The spraying in question, nicknamed "Space Flower" by the press, blooms on the facade of a prominent bank; this plant with its dagger stamens and cone-shaped appendages arcs in perfect imitation of a statue poised beside it, a bronze replica of the bank's first president.

The street cleaners moved in early—around 6 A.M.—hoping to avoid a confrontation. But news had leaked; already grouped around the statue, in a neat but impenetrable mass, were the apprentices from the art academy, many nonpartisan radicals and some Young Socialists.

Supposedly no one said a word. A fine cold rain began. After a few minutes, the cleaners turned on their heels and drove away.

Diana comes to visit; she wears a blue dress and looks exhausted. I wonder what Dr. Severin has been telling her.

"I knew it was you," she blurts out. "I knew as soon as I saw which buildings you picked. The newspapers. The radio station. The sides of tenements, concrete retaining walls. All white."

Getting the spray cans, easy. The clerk at Hertie's department store couldn't take his eyes off Diana's butt. The youth center ran out of black paint while decorating their float for the *Karneval* parade. But how to explain the drives at night, my bike lubed and polished for the trip? How explain the building calling with its face blank as snow awaiting defilement? Natural canvases.

"It started that night, didn't it?"

We had stopped in the middle of the Severin Bridge; I cut the motor. The bridge was too high for us to hear the movement of the Rhine, but the wind hummed through the cables; it was almost like listening to the water. Five men are buried in this stanchion, I told her, staring into the glittering lights. I recited their names, I repeated what my mother and father had said. She listened, and when I turned around, her eyes were gliding from one side of my face to the other as if I were one of her books. She took my head in her hands; her palms burned but her fingertips were like ice. She kissed me. I was twisted half-backward on my motorcycle—an awkward position—but we did not get off.

Today Diana looks straight into my eyes. The room is brightly lit, and the greenish wallpaper makes me shiver, despite the overheated iron radiators underneath the barred windows. Rush hour traffic roars outside of this "detention home for youthful offenders."

"Why did you paint the Madonna?"

Can I explain what itch built up inside me, how I tried to ignore it at first and *act responsibly,* then learned to welcome its presence and nurture it, prime it, hone the vague desires to a single, jubilant swoop, one vibrant gesture?

"I didn't paint her," I replied. "She painted herself."

The Madonna. When I had finished, I just stood there, looking at her—I would have stood there all night, the stars shone so soft and cool. I didn't give a shit about anything, except for that picture. I didn't budge, even when a pair of young lovers strolled around the corner. For a moment we stood quietly and gazed at her. Then the woman pointed: "The police!"—and I bolted.

"I always thought . . ." Why does Diana look down at her lap, Diana, whose eyes were reputed to batter the most lascivious suitor to a bale of twigs? "I always figured"—a coy swoop of eyelashes—"you drew her after me. You know—tits and ass." She laughs disparagingly.

That's why the dress. Blue, too. Ah, Diana—again you are right, but it means so little. The Madonna is my masterpiece. The councilman in charge of education (a member of the Christian Democratic Party) has called her "the product of a sick and filthy mind." What do you think, Diana? Am I sick, or are you just beautiful?

My mother comes every day and cries. She says it's all her fault. She says she knows how it feels to be always stared at and never loved, how one is never comfortable except in the smallest of spaces, at the stove or bent over a tub of suds. She raves. When it gets too much, I play out the fantasy I had as a child; I am sent down to the cellar for coal. While I am filling the scuttle, the Americans drop the Big Bomb. When I come upstairs again, I am the only German left in the whole country—all because I have to haul coal when other little boys are outside playing.

Dr. Severin will read this and say: "The coal saves you—your black blood." And when I paint, I'm spraying blood on the walls, or semen, a fascinating example of reverse projection. She wants to ease me back into society; she will tell me I have a talent I mustn't squander.

First there is the blue of the air as they fall, open-mouthed, open-eyed, toward a deeper blue. Then the red of impact, the stunned blow as their mouths fill and capillaries pop. And then, for the longest kind of time, the black before death and then the black of dying, the black of metal before it is painted sea green and the black of sea green metal against the sun, an unfinished web. But when most people have forgotten, when those men become no more than a macabre joke at a party, or the niggling conscience of an engineer as he drives to work, they will float up out of the stanchion and through the rain-slick streets of Cologne, looking for a place to tell their story. The newspapers will scoff; the radio station will shrug. Their walls are clean.

The city stands in concrete snow, and even the cathedral's turned white overnight. O citizens who have forgotten, I was there to remind you, I put the stain back on the wall—no outraged slogan, no incoherent declaration of love, but a gesture both graceful and treacherous, a free fall ending in disaster—among the urgent scrawls of history, a mere flick of the wrist.

# A House Full of Maude

## COLLEEN MCELROY

Where do young girls go to find a room of their own? Colleen McElroy's poignant coming-of-age story "A House Full of Maude" recalls the awkward, unforgettable moments of adolescence when children pass through fantasies of adulthood into the real thing. Maude Morgan's house becomes home to rites of passage for two girls learning from and about each other during a time of "forbidden" knowledge and experience in America. Maude's house is full not just of her own magnificent presence but of opportunity to steal away from the influence of parents, convention, and conformity. It is a place to explore. McElroy's story is collected in her 1987 book *Jesus and Fat Tuesday*.

## I

WHAT TO REMEMBER about the house on Ashland and Taylor? Maude's house with its darkness, the wet brown bricks that seemed to shimmer, to suck in light so that the house was more of a gape at the end of the block than a building. The ever present wetness—winter and summer—a mossy velvet covering that seemed to grow, to move in an effort to absorb every inch of brick. And the bricks themselves, shiny with the stuff—a residue that permeated everything, ate its way through the outer surface and into the mortar, the plaster, the wallboards of the house. The yard carried the smell of mold. Moisture seemed to muffle sounds coming from the house or off the street, and Maude's brand-new DeSoto, as round and black as Maude herself, clotted one end of the driveway.

The house couldn't be seen from the south end of Taylor. That end was divided into exacting little postwar plots of bungalows and cottages. And every one of them held a woman who was determined to put her stamp on the property. Upright solid black women like my mama, who would have you believe dirt was a personal enemy and so, the house was a major threat. Their yards held back the power of the house. Each one displaying some peculiar array of potted plants, or cheap weather vanes and brassy street numbers. Each yard with its own degree of tastelessness, the next more awful than the one before, until by the time you reached the house, those overly decorated cottages blurred into one gaudy string of cheap baubles. Each one a little bit of country and a little bit of what the women saw on the Ozzie and Harriet show they watched every evening on their postage-stamp television sets when they weren't watching Ed Sullivan, or listening to the gospel sounds of Rev. Staples and dreaming of pulling that old man out of Memphis and into their parlors. The house intruded its dark presence onto the end of this flashy line-up of neighbors. The house was somber, secretive, and so much bigger than anything else on the street, it blunted Taylor Avenue into a cul-de-sac passageway someone had named Ashland Place but was, in actuality, an alleyway, a shaft of paved road rammed between the house and the patch of city park that completed the north end of the block. And the house, nested in a semicircle of cottonwood and willow trees, pushed forward by a jumble of narrow rooms and add-on storage porches, seemed to be straining to reach the street. Leaning forward as if to step past the thatch of trees and into the sunlight, where it would fling open its windows and all its raunchy secrets would swirl down the street and scare the hell out of its churchified neighbors.

The first time I passed the house, it sent a trail of Maude's laughter through a window, and the sound wound itself around me and held me rooted to the spot. I was wearing a despicable little seersucker dress, all fuzzy dots and pastels, and the laughter tugged at the material, seeping under the sleeves until my armpits were wet, then flicked the hem so that the warm summer air billowed under my skirt and embraced my legs. The laughter buzzed in my ears, its sound so clear it seemed to hold words I could almost understand. Laughter that made me step back, then laugh a little myself. A woman's laughter. Laughter that owned the world. Laughter that knew something I wanted to know.

## II

Violet Nashberry was fourteen years old—technically. At least Violet had been alive a mere fourteen years, but Violet had lived more than her years and looked it. She believed in living. A month in one week, three weeks in one night. Whatever she needed, she took without question. The house accepted her, drew her past its inner ring as if she'd always been there. When she settled into the left wing of the house, when her mother had finally stopped leaping out of the shadows of the trees and snatching the poor girl into the street in an attempt to drag her home, the house had settled in, night cries of its creaking floorboards smoothed into low moans. Violet took the first corner room on the Ashland Place side of the house. It jutted away from the main structure, rounded in the arc of its former sunporch shape. That suited her fancy, gave her a sense of not really being there. Bay windows tempted her to escape and enter without using the front door. But the house welcomed her fugitive habits. When she entered from the street, she turned into the center path between the trees and always stopped for one last look at the rest of the street and its uniform bric-a-brac. Whether she could see them or not, a few hand-laced curtains fluttered as God-fearing eyes marked her passage, and church folks chalked up another sin against Maude's house. Violet's bare brown legs, the light glinting off large hoop earrings, her head shaved past a boyish cut so that her short kinky hair covered the

roundness of her scalp like velvet and invited a hand to
stroke its downy curve. Her already full figure pushed
against whatever cheap blouse and skirt she'd hastily
thrown on, the closure of her blouse more than likely
pinned where she'd popped a button or snapped a stitch.
And more than one teeth-sucking *uh-uh-uh* passed judgment on her slovenly ways. At that point, Violet looked
tired and fed up with the world. Then she'd lunge toward
the house, and as the tree-lined shadows dappled her back
with speckles of light that danced like butterflies or silvery
fish, she seemed to toss the world's damnation into the
debris gathered with the leaves at the base of the trees. I
always felt torn between commenting on Violet's daily
stand against her neighbors' gossip and the mingled smell
of dime-cheap toilet water and mold that swept through the
door with us. For it was Violet who offered me entrance to
Maude's house.

I was eighteen looking twelve, the age I'd been when the
house had first reached for me. In part or entirety, the
house had begun to dominate my life. I knew what I feared
and wanted most rested in that house, seeped into my
dreams until I wasn't sure what I had imagined and what I
had actually seen—a high-ceiling room, an arched threshold, gargoyle downspouts, a yard path slit between over-
hanging trees, windows slick with moisture and winking in
the dim light. At twelve, I had inspected those windows
from the safe distance of the playground in the adjacent
park, swinging so high, I easily cleared the wall and placed
myself in direct view of the upstairs hallway. Sometimes,
with luck, I caught a glimpse of Maude's naked back entering the bathroom, or a hand caressing her bare shoulder.
My dreams filled in the rest. Those fleeting images kept me
pumping that swing to dangerous heights, knees bent until
I flew to the very edge of the trees and then pushed down,
blood rushing to my head, grunting until my weight forced
the swing back instead of flipping me over the rail. At eighteen and out of the playground stage, I grew bolder. I discovered a wrought-iron bench half-buried in the sod beneath one of the willow trees, where, if I sat very still while

the willow branches brushed my face like fingers or the hair of some lover, I could watch Maude's kitchen at the far side of the house. Everyone eventually gathered in the kitchen, and for most of the years of my watching, three brothers dominated the house until one by one they left—the younger first, then the others in reverse order until the oldest was gone. Violet lived in the room the oldest had occupied. I dreamed her in his bed, her figure filling the mirror he'd spent so much time staring into.

And it was Violet who caught me staring at her one afternoon as she leaned from the bay window, teasing the liquor store delivery boy, my next door neighbor's cousin who had spent his first summer after high school running his hands up the dress of any girl careless enough to get close to him. My mama said Peck's head was big because he was the first boy on the block to graduate from the desegregated high school, but Peck had always been a nuisance. At school, he'd had as much trouble fitting in as I'd had, law or no law. But on the block, he didn't have to worry about white folks and teachers. He pestered everybody. I watched Violet giggle and lean farther over the windowsill. Peck's eyes followed the swell of her breasts inside her half-closed robe. A movement startled me. The willow trees bending, swirling near the edge of the sidewalk. A bird or a squirrel scratching a tree trunk or someone tossing water from one of the back windows. I moved. Violet turned, laughed, and called to me in a voice that said she'd known I'd been there all along. "Hey girl."

## III

The downstairs hallway was a singular path. Curved inward from both ends of the house, it converged on a stairwell, a shaft that plunged light into the entryway like a commanding finger. From this central shaft, the hallway spread toward both ends of the house like two arms or, if you looked down, two legs straddling the center entryway and softened by oak paneling buffed smooth as skin. At the top of the stairs and on either side of the entryway, the light, dimmed by turn-of-the-century glass, grew dull and furry, but the steps led to one great window—a mosaic of beveled glass changing light into a carnival of shapes. And the corridor itself was wide enough for ball gowns to pass and only brush each other in the journey. On one side of the hallway there were windows and green shadows whispering against the panes. On the other side, voices were audible behind heavy doors to rooms that faced the back of the house. But neither the doors nor the oblique path of the hall kept out the smells. Thin sad smells and smells that knifed the air. Smells that clashed with those tight family smells I'd brought from my mother's house. The odors in Maude's house left me open to scenes I could barely imagine. The house was ripe with its age. Every corner invaded by one or another of its tenants, and its own decay. It seemed to try on and discard smells as easily as a woman passing rows of perfume bottles on a department store counter. The faint smell of plaster drifted from rips in the wallpaper, one layer stripped to expose another, which in turn had cracked and peeled to the next layer, and below that still another. The jimson smell of old rugs and overstuffed furniture floated at floor level but remained undisturbed unless someone scraped a chair across the carpet or decided to clean a room. Each room had its own smell. Bedroom smells that, at home, were covered by my pious mother with cologne and ammonia. In the house, I found bathrooms of dusting powder, douche, and vinegar, their sources under the sink, hidden by curtains covering the shelves. A kitchen where bacon was fried, even at night, its smokehouse odors barely masking cigarettes and whiskey, chitterlings and jars of pickling. And none of it as pungent as the pomade on the back burner where Maude hot-cooked her hair before choir practice. The flickering light, the smells and noises. The house moving on its foundation, groaning with the life that passed beneath its roof. Wet branches skittering across window glass. Doors that no longer hung level on their frames. The sound of someone coughing or cursing over a game of cards, a moan that could have been male or female, a recording of gospel music—the record stuck in one groove. And no one to tell me I couldn't or I shouldn't.

# IV

Every Wednesday and Sunday night, Maude left the house. On those nights, the Temple Tabernacle God in Christ Church rocked. Maude Morgan led the choir. Everyone sang exactly the way Sister Morgan told them to sing. She bullied them with her hands, bruised them with her voice, drove them from one chorus to another with fierce looks that offered them no salvation until Sister Morgan wore herself out on repetitions of a song. Sister Morgan loved her songs. She believed every song held endless rounds of a soul stomping chorus and wasn't about to fall quiet until she sang every one of them. She was as faithful to the choir as she was to food. When she really had them pitched to her frenzy, when everyone clapped and popped their fingers, shouting, "Yes Jesus. Amen," Sister Morgan would gather her two hundred-fifty pounds and jump straight up and down like a Zulu during fertility rites. The heft of her weight added timbre to the congregation's joy as she thumped them from one "Amen" to the next. Folks on the street feared the whole storefront would collapse when Maude Morgan started prancing. The rather straight-laced Methodists shook their heads at her jungle antics, and the organized Baptists prayed to Jesus to guide her to a quieter worship. After all, the ghosts of those images lived in their houses, and they worked hard to put those ghosts to rest. But just as they mistook her weight for a deterrent to the physical joys of life, they mistook her enthusiasm for singing as pure faith in the ways of religion. "Don't matter what words you say long as you give your spirit to the music," Maude would tell anyone who warned her about overexertion. And she never wiped the sweat from her face. And she never cared whether her hair went bad at the nape of her neck. "That's where it ought to look rough. That's the kitchen and the kitchen is where I do my business," she'd say. And I surely didn't need to find the oldest of those three brothers to help me testify to that.

# V

Maude Morgan was the kind of woman who could be nosy without ever paying attention to what was going on. She always seemed to know what everyone was doing without really being there. A plum-colored woman smelling of spice and talc that seemed to cling to the folds of her dress, the back of her neck and elbows. Her skin was burnished to a high gloss as if someone had worked down the sides and hollows of her flesh in long strokes, ending each stroke in tight circles to add a sheen to her already smooth skin. And Maude loved to touch and be touched, so it was easy to notice when she wasn't around. Before Maude entered, any room seemed like a space just inviting to be filled. "Com'on in," she'd say once she arrived. "Com'on in over here and give me some of your time," she'd laugh, as if you had just been waiting in that lonely room for Maude Morgan to open her arms to your company. Some folks, especially some of the hinkty, upright church women, resented the way Maude could make a stranger snuggle up to her and feel at home, but other folks felt the Lord had blessed them by putting such a loving woman on earth to give them comfort. True enough, it was puzzling to see Maude make a young man turn away from some young woman with aching eyes just because Maude had brushed up against him, but Maude soon sent him back to the source of his admiration. "Some folks can't tell the difference between needing and having," Maude would laugh. "Ain't no reason to be the same fool in 1954 that I been in 1953. Too much in this world for me to be wanting what I need." Then she'd smooth her dress over her hips, wiping the wrinkles out of the material until you could see the flesh push against her hands. And the palms of her hands, plump and pungent, leaving a dewy streak that, invariably, shimmered just enough to force your eyes to follow its trail along her thighs. That movement always made you aware, once again, of Maude's girth, and how much of her was encased in dress, petticoat, and underpants. For no matter how raucous her laughter became, or how many "sweet-loving men folks" she boasted about knowing, Sister Morgan seemed to be full of prissy secrets. She thrived on secrets. When the choir began its chorus of "My Soul Is a Witness for My Lord," or "Didn't My Lord Tell Daniel," her breasts quivered with the excitement of what was not said, what was kept unconfessed, hidden, and in the dark. And when Violet and I sat around the kitchen watching her add a little bite of pepper to a pot of stew, or a little sugar to a deep-dish pie, she'd let us in on a bevy of secrets. "Men is funny," she'd say. "Nothing makes them come to you quicker than to think you're happy. Then they get all into your business trying to find out just what makes you so happy. And you just remember, you don't have to tell them nothing." Then she'd give us a pinch of something to lip-test, and Violet would nod her head just like she understood everything Maude had said. Whenever she told us a story about a bad time she'd had with a man, she'd stop cooking. She never turned the story around to make the man seem worse—not the way my mother and her friends did—she told it straight, her voice low and the words humming in her throat like a gospel. And while she was telling, she'd massage Violet's head, slow and careful, until Violet looked like she was asleep. The first time she rubbed my head that way, it felt so good, I almost cried, but I just closed my eyes and let Maude's fingers pull me against the rise of her belly.

## VI

Violet said, "Girl, this job is driving me crazy." The iron sizzled against the apron of her uniform.

"You only been working there three weeks," I told her.

She burned a brown smear across the waistband. "Don't

matter. Them folks is crazy. Wanting me to work in some greasy spoon for nickels and dimes."

"Better than what I got," I said.

"Who you?" Violet asked.

I watched her burn the cap. "Maybe you ought to go back to school."

"I don't need no school for what I do," she laughed.

"You got to be eighteen, Vi. How you gonna strip tease and you can't even get a drink in a bar?"

"Peck says I look—"

"Peck!"

"Yeah. Peck." The iron slammed against the Shepherd's Burger emblem. "And Peck ain't the only one."

"If your mama finds out, she's gonna be on you like white on rice."

"Damn her!" Violet shouted, then threw the uniform on the bed and yanked the ironing cord out of the socket. I mouthed a Dance Fever tune playing on the radio. Violet and I were heads and tails of a coin. I was an only child, and she the middle one in a nest of brothers and sisters. I spent too much time hiding behind my glasses, and Violet cared less about who saw her do what. But we both agreed on the aggravation of mothers. "Let me show you what I did last night," Vi said. "Bought me some green feathers yesterday, and girl—I'm gonna be the best thing this town has ever seen." She began to undress.

I tried not to watch her—not that it made any difference. Everyone else in the neighborhood could see her through the open windows. Besides, this wasn't the first time I'd seen her undress. Our summer work schedule made it easy for me to visit Violet. My job with the Recreation Department ended at noon. I came directly to the house after I left the park. Vi's job at Shepherd's didn't begin until six, so I had plenty of time to visit before dinner. She was always asleep when I arrived, and sometime during my visit, she'd get ready for work, never bothering to turn her back or dress in the bathroom. When she practiced stripping, she took her time, almost unconsciously falling into her routine. "Come on, Thin. Give me some rhythm," she said. As if on cue, the radio switched to a Little Richard heavy-on-the-drums cut. "And now, Miss Vi Berry," she announced as I turned up the radio and began clapping. She pulled her wig off the lampshade and plunked it on her head. She'd bought it with her first paycheck. A gross brown thing full of oily curls that almost matched the beige tones of her skin. The hair transformed her, hardened her features, made her body seem more suited to the squinty-eyed look she affected. Even the room was right for what she did. The half oval of bay windows a common stage—window panes of old glass, drawn to an uneven thickness, made light turn syrupy and cast rainbows on her skin. Willow limbs cut the light like beacons while Violet's hand snaked out, dropping a garment here, caressing skin there. A caramel doll. A painted trick of eye and imagination. A dream of what I thought I could never become. Even with practice and without the hard thin warnings of my mother echoing in my ears. What kind of a world could grant misery to an eighteen-year-old when it had allowed so many gifts to Violet at fourteen?

## VII

Violet and Maude spent far too much time together. I was the outsider. I was in the house but not of the house. Maude spoke in riddles and Violet answered. My tongue was stuck in my mouth. Roles were reversed. I was the one who should know more, who should have the right answers. But there we were—a girl who wanted to be a woman and an almost woman who had never been a girl. Each day I felt more incomplete. At six o'clock, I entered my mother's house and turned to stone. She wanted to know if I would ever speak again. I waited for morning, for the dreariness of entertaining irresponsible children. They played the same games I'd played—Blind Man's Bluff, Little Sally Walker, 24 Robbers. What would it teach them? What had it taught me? I began to live once I entered the house. No matter that the air was stale, or that I would be trapped for twenty minutes by Mrs. Cole, caught as I walked through the door and made to lead her down the stairs and to the kitchen, one arthritic step at a time. If I was lucky, Violet would be awake when I reached her room. If I was lucky, I would help with her bath, pour in generous amounts of Maude's bath salts, and fill the tub with sudsy water. If I was lucky, she wouldn't mind me sitting beside her, waiting to wash her back. If I was lucky. Or I'd run into Beulah, who had a room near the kitchen and belonged to the Ladies Auxiliary. She knew my mother but didn't like her, so she sent me to the store and gave me beer for running her errands. Her husband pinched my arms whenever she wasn't looking. If I couldn't shake Violet awake, I'd drop in on Maude, who was always in the kitchen fixing her next meal while she finished her last one.

One day, midsummer, I opened the door and found the oldest brother sitting at a table. A face from a distance suddenly close up. I felt chilled as if a breeze had blown through the kitchen, but the air was swamped in smoke and heat. He'd taken off his shirt, and Maude caressed his shoulders. "Ain't the size of the ship that makes the sailor seasick," Maude said. "It's the motion of the ocean." Then she saw me standing in the doorway. "Come in," she beckoned. "Look who's back." "Back in the women's quarters. Ain't nothing like it," he laughed and pressed his head against the soft mound of her belly, his voice so deep his words seemed to rumble into the roar of water Maude had going full blast in the sink. Maude called him Bud, and while she told me where he had been and why he'd come back, he stared at me. Brown eyes ringed in black. A long, square-cut face with a strong jawline and even white teeth. His hair was cut short, almost as short as Violet's, but shaped so it accentuated his strength and neither invited nor discouraged a desire to touch him.

## VIII

"I told your mama. I say, Dorothy Nashberry, you had far too many babies to act the way you do about Violet. By the time I was Violet's age, I'd run off from my first husband. Plenty of girls prettier than me still at home working on pin money for the movies. And look at me now, I say. Got me a big house, plenty of friends. . . . Ain't that right, Bud? Yeah, and the Lord's good music. But you still worrying about Vi, I told her. . . . Now, ya'll wake up. Dealer's choice." We played cards once or twice a week. Bid whist and Violet always bidding as if she could handpick her cards on every deal. Bud watched every move I made, turning now and again to smile at Vi or rub Maude's arm. Violet made far too many mistakes. She barely looked at her cards, and each time she needed to make a bid or play a card, she prolonged the game: calling attention to herself, smoking, laughing, brushing her hands across her wig—which she insisted on wearing all the time these days. "Don't you have to get ready for work?" I'd ask. She'd glare at me and ask Bud another question, acting like I hadn't said a word. And Bud would tell us what destroyer he'd been stationed on, about Florida and Mediterranean ports, and how many young sailors would love to be in the room with him playing cards with such lovely ladies, as he called us. "How about some sailors, Thin?" Violet would ask, but when I wouldn't answer, she'd grunt and turn back to Bud. He'd have just enough time to change his expression before she saw him. But Maude would roar, a deep-throated laugh that threatened the already cracked chandelier. "Bud, you ain't changed a bit," she'd say, and pour some more sweet wine into the water glasses at our elbows. Bud would say, "Yeah," in a detached way and wink. I'd manage to blurt out my bid without looking directly at him. I'd already memorized his smile, the curve of his neck, the toast brown color of his skin. Most of the time, I knew what he would say and how hc would say it, but that didn't seem to matter so much as hearing him speak the words. On other afternoons, we danced. Violet, as usual, starting us with her stripper fantasy and how she'd make everyone re-member her when she was a big star. Then Bud would urge me and Maude to get up. Comic relief, I called it. Maude's bulk shifting like oil and water, like a hippo rising from a bath, while I worked to keep my elbows tucked in and my legs from goose-stepping. But Bud always singled me out, always gathered me into his arms. "Just a handful," he'd whisper as he led me through an achingly slow dance. Vio-let would look sullen, but Maude would laugh and laugh and tell Bud what a stud he was.

Violet missed work more often than not, but one day after I'd persuaded her that she had to go, we tripped down the hall toward her room, both of us more than a little loaded on sweet wine and less than ready for the rest of the bottle Violet had with her. She'd begun to let her hair grow, so after I finally managed to get her wig off, I brushed the soft mass of curls, chiding her about being late for work while I concentrated on aiming the brush for her hair, and not her neck or forehead. We both took swigs from the bottle. She told me Maude wouldn't give Bud a moment of peace. I said yes, and that I'd seen her groping him whenever she had the chance. She told me Bud only stayed because Maude gave him free room and board, and Maude only kept him because it made the other women jealous. I told her she'd better not let Maude catch her leaving Bud's room the way I had the day before.

"Who you telling?" she asked.

"Nobody."

"SO?"

"Nothing."

"You just remember who you came here to see," she said. I was silent. "Hey girl," she said. "That's where it's at, don't you know?" And we rolled on the bed, laughing and drinking wine as if we'd talked about jobs or Peck or Maude's church friends or how many empty rooms there were in the house.

## IX

I couldn't go home smelling of wine, and Violet was in no shape to dress herself. We didn't just give in—we really did try standing up straight, but no amount of effort could keep our knees from buckling. We thought the August heat had made us silly. Lord knows, we'd been sipping Maude's sweet wine all summer without letting it slow us any. Violet tugged at the window and, with my help, managed to open it a crack. The air was sticky warm, worse than the room had been without it, but we didn't have the energy to shove the window down. Finally, we let the wine take us. As I fell into a soggy dream, one arm flung across Vi, who was already asleep, the voices of children drifted from the playground on the other side of Ashland Place. I slept, thinking I was gathering my snaggle-toothed third graders into their favorite ring game, knowing they would collapse in the end, exhausted little rag dolls.

Little Sally Walker, sitting in a saucer.
Rise Sally Rise. Wipe your weeping eyes.
Put your hands on your hips and let your backbone slip—
Oh shake it to the East. Oh shake it to the West.
Oh shake it to the one you love the best.

## X

Violet answered the door. She didn't bother to put on a robe, and Bud took no surprise in seeing her nakedness. "Maude's gone to choir practice," he said.

"Tell ME," Violet laughed. She watched his hand touch her shoulder, then slide to the curve of her waist.

"Yeah," he said.

I only had managed to open one eye, but I grabbed Violet's robe and sat up. "Vi!" I shouted, or tried to shout. What came out sounded like the moan of a dying frog.

Bud placed his palm against the door as if he expected Violet to close it. "Well, look at this."

"Ain't she cute?"

I was all bones. Knees and elbows. Arms that seemed to

extend the length of the bed. I had thrown Violet her robe but left my own body uncovered. Bud smiled. A mister-cool-breeze smile. A piano-player-in-a-blues-club smile. A now-I-see-what-I-want smile. I gulped air. "Oh Jesus," Violet yelled. "She's gonna be sick." I felt her push my head forward. "Com'on, Thin," she said as she rubbed my back. "Don't get sick on me, girl." Bud had conjured up a wet cloth and a waste can at the same time. They sat me on the side of the bed, Violet holding me and Bud wiping my forehead and neck with the cloth. "It's all right," he whispered. "Don't worry." This is jive, I thought. This is not real. I wondered if I should be sick, then let myself go limp as they cooed and cuddled me. Violet let Bud hold me while she lit a cigarette. After a few puffs, she passed the cigarette to him, and he passed it to me. Violet held my hand. Without meaning to, I felt the need to cry. We were shipwrecked. We were lost in a haunted house with no way out. A dog barked outside the window, and two kids yelled at it. A woman's voice, shrill, called someone home. Who could know where we were? The house held us inside its circle. Afternoon breezes skirted evening.

# XI

Bud leaned forward and kissed Violet. "You ain't right," she told him. Her hand gripped mine tighter, and the world rushed past me all at once. "I have to go," I said, and tried pushing my way through the tangle of their arms. Bud pressed his hand against the small of my back and pulled me toward him. Violet giggled, and I shut away my mama's face. I could hear Bud talking, murmuring the way he had when we'd danced. I felt the length of his body, muscles too close to the surface and unwilling to fit my palms the way my own body slipped so easily against my hands. I leaned against him and willed myself to fit the curve of his neck, the width of his shoulder. Inhaled the surly sweetness of his skin. The smell of skin in summer has the same tangy odor of warm, yeasty bread, or the smell of a pillow pulling you awake from a dream. Skin can invite you to touch it, dare you. It can pull you in until the only way to stop yourself from aching is to let it take you. Bud's skin was new leather, the way a fine pair of woman's gloves feel when you take them from their tissue wrapping. So sweet and brand new, you almost don't want to wear them. And Violet, Violet was the present I'd been good for all my life, the package wrapped in secret and hidden somewhere in the house. What I'd get on my birthday or some special day when all my chores were finished and I'd said "yes ma'am" in just the right voice. We helped Bud undress, touching each other for every movement he made. And Bud whispered to us both as we slid over and under him. My hand, clutched in Violet's, was a smudge of ink, a tell-tale shape that could have been an elephant holding an umbrella or cannibals over a stew pot. She led my hand across Bud's chest, his waist and below, and she laughed when I wanted to draw back, to curl my fingers into a fist. When I touched Violet and trembled, Bud helped me, and when I turned away, Violet was always there. The three of us knelt together, our bodies like trees twisting toward the sky in a tangle of limbs. One tree splitting into parts or three feeding off each other. The three of us, somehow, balanced on Violet's rickety bed, Bud's clothes falling away like leaves until, in one motion, we began to fall. One body floating against another like clothes falling in a woman's closet. And then, elbows and knees like weapons. Violet yelled, "SHIT!" Blood on her lower lip and my eye already swelling. At first, only the taste of salt—my own tears. Then Bud kissing me and Violet. Then Violet. My hand moving between Violet's legs. I thought of all the words: muff, poodle, beaver. All too ugly to fit the softness I felt. Our mouths turned to sugar. Bud's hand against the cup of my thighs. Violet's nails stroking his back. My tongue tracing the rise of Violet's breast. The sound of the willow tree rustling like silk, leaves swaying like the rocking motion of Bud's embrace. Wherever we were, no one could find us. No children's games, no gossip of movie stars and magazines. Not the watchful eye of fathers watering lawns in the light of the afternoon sun, or mothers preaching about the worst that could happen to us, arguing about whether our retribution would come because of me and Violet or because of the two of us with Bud. No one to find us. Violet whispered, "Hey girl," and Bud laughed his answer. I filled myself with their scents and laughed at us all while I told myself I wasn't really dreaming. This was really happening. I really could see bright shadows lining the walls, and trees turned rosy, their leaves fuzzy splotches of darkness against the wallpaper's own pattern of fake trees. The house welcomed evening, its timbers popping as it settled in. The smell of murky dampness mingled with body musk, with the jasmine of bath salts and aftershave. The pressure of bodies drew me into muscles that pounded, I thought, mimicking true confession magazines, too much like a heartbeat. "Girl, this is stupid," I said to myself. Then I took a deep breath.

# XII

The harsh overhead light sliced shadows without redemption. Maude blustered her way around the kitchen—seasoning a pot of beans, dicing onions, drinking wine. "Lord, it's hotter today than it was yesterday, don't you think?" I agreed, although she didn't wait for my comment. "Isn't Vi going to work today? If she don't, she'll lose that job for certain. I was telling Miz Evans . . . I say, Beulah, young folks don't know what it is to NOT have a job. That's what's wrong with Violet. She ought to learn from you, chile. You keep your head about you, you do." I grunted again and flushed out my solitaire spread by pulling a queen I'd overlooked from the discard pile. "Ain't everything in this world having a good time," Maude continued. "Got to work and got to play." She stopped for a moment to taste the beans, her face, under the cloud of steam from the pot, as dark as the varnished wood in the hallway. "Precious Lord, take my hand . . ." she half-sang and half-hummed. I reshuffled the cards for another try at solitaire. "You don't seem to be doing so well with them cards today," Maude said. I shook my head. "Mighty quiet too," she added, and peered at me real close. I smiled. She began stripping slices of bacon into a hot skillet. I laid out the cards and wondered vaguely if my mother had started supper. Both Maude and I looked up sharply as three heavy thumps echoed in the hall. "I guess Miz Queen Bee's calling you," Maude laughed. I pushed my chair away from the table. "Spect you be staying for supper too, huh?" I shrugged and gave Maude a kiss on the cheek before I left the room. She was already singing when I reached the door, and into a third chorus of "I Ain't Gonna Study War No More," by the time I reached the end of the hall. Bud was waiting in front of the open bathroom door. "Mercy," he said, as if someone would have mercy on me. As I opened the door, he said, "My love's coming down." Violet threw a clump of bath foam toward us, its bubbles bursting in the steamy hot air almost before they left her hand. "Don't let it get to you," she told him. Then she looked at me, and we both laughed. When I closed the door, it thumped along its hinges, sticking for a moment, then sliding shut. I sat on the edge of the tub and began to sponge Violet's back. We could hear Maude calling Bud, but no one answered her. Bud leaned against the wall, cleaning his nails, the sound of his nail clippers clicking like a telegraph key. Violet leaned away from me, blowing foam in little puffs of air and cooing in time with the pigeons who pranced in the rain gutters outside the bathroom window. I looked up just as one hopped onto the eave by the window pane. His fat black body almost filled one leaded glass square, and his head was cocked so that one red eye stared into the hothouse steam of the bathroom. I cocked my head at the same angle and stared back at that stupid, unblinking eye. After a while, we heard Maude singing again.

# Ma'Dear

## TERRY McMILLAN

Terry McMillan's storytelling talents extend beyond her well-known, bestselling novels. In this story, McMillan creates a vivid portrait of an elderly woman who refuses to give in to the blues. Her seventy-two-year-old widow lives a life of no regrets. Her determination to say yes to life and give the slip to misfortune and hardship marks her as a totem of strength in a world indifferent to the plight of the elderly. Voice, always a strong component of McMillan's work, is here vivid in dialect form and an important reflection of her character's need and ability to define her life on its own terms. First published in *Callaloo* in 1987, the story was reprinted in *Breaking Ice: An Anthology of Contemporary African-American Fiction*.

for Estelle Ragsdale

LAST YEAR THE COST OF LIVING crunched me and I got tired of begging from Peter to pay Paul, so I took in three roomers. Two of 'em is live-in nurses and only come around here on weekends. Even then they don't talk to me much, except when they hand me their money orders. One is from Trinidad and the other is from Jamaica. Every winter they quit their jobs, fill up two and three barrels with I don't know what, ship 'em home, and follow behind on an airplane. They come back in the spring and start all over. Then there's the little college girl, Juanita, who claims she's going for architecture. Seem like to me that was always men's work, but I don't say nothing. She grown.

I'm seventy-two. Been a widow for the past thirty-two

years. Weren't like I asked for all this solitude, just that couldn't nobody else take Jessie's place is all. He knew it. And I knew it. He fell and hit his head real bad on the tracks going to fetch us some fresh-picked corn and okra for me to make us some succotash, and never come to. I couldn't picture myself with no other man, even though I looked after a few years of being alone in this big old house, walking from room to room with nobody to talk to, cook or clean for, and not much company either.

I missed him for the longest time and thought I could find a man just like him, sincerely like him, but I couldn't. Went out for a spell with Esther Davis's ex-husband, Whimpy, but he was crazy. Drank too much bootleg and then started memorizing on World War I and how hard he fought and didn't get no respect and not a ounce of recognition for his heroic deeds. The only war Whimpy been in is with me for not keeping him around. He bragged something fearless about how he coulda been the heavyweight champion of the world. Didn't weigh but 160 pounds and shorter than me.

Chester Rutledge almost worked 'ceptin' he was boring, never had nothing on his mind worth talking about; claimed he didn't think about nothing besides me. Said his mind was always clear and visible. He just moved around like a zombie and worked hard at the cement foundry. Insisted on giving me his paychecks, which I kindly took for a while, but when I didn't want to be bothered no more, I stopped taking his money. He got on my nerves too bad, so I had to tell him I'd rather have a man with no money and a busy mind, least I'd know he's active somewheres. His feelings was hurt bad and he cussed me out, but we still friends to this very day. He in the home, you know, and I visits him regular. Takes him magazines and cuts out his horoscope and the comic strips from the newspaper and lets him read 'em in correct order.

Big Bill Ronsonville tried to convince me that I shoulda married him instead of Jessie, but he couldn't make me a believer of it. All he wanted to do was put his big rusty hands all on me without asking and smile at me with that big gold tooth sparkling and glittering in my face and tell me how lavish I was, lavish being a new word he just learnt. He kept wanting to take me for night rides way out in the country, out there by Smith Creek where ain't nothing but deep black ditches, giant mosquitoes, loud crickets, lightning bugs, and loose pigs, and turn off his motor. His breath stank like whiskey though he claimed and swore on the Bible he didn't drank no liquor. Aside from that his hands were way too heavy and hard, hurt me, sometimes left red marks on me like I been sucked on. I told him finally that I was too light for him, that I needed a smaller, more gentle man, and he said he knew exactly what I meant.

If you want to know the truth, after him I didn't think much about men the way I used to. Lost track of the ones who upped and died or the ones who couldn't do nothing if they was alive nohow. So, since nobody else seemed to be able to wear Jessie's shoes, I just stuck to myself all these years.

My life ain't so bad now 'cause I'm used to being alone and takes good care of myself. Occasionally I still has a good time. I goes to the park and sits for hours in good weather, watch folks move, and listen in on confidential conversations. I add up numbers on license plates to keep my mind alert unless they pass too fast. This gives me a clear idea of how many folks is visiting from out of town. I can about guess the color of every state now, too. Once or twice a month I go to the matinee on Wednesdays, providing ain't no long line of senior citizens 'cause they can be so slow; miss half the picture show waiting for them to count their change and get their popcorn.

Sometimes, when I'm sitting in the park, I feed the pigeons old cornbread crumbs, and I wonders what it'll be like not looking at the snow falling from the sky, not seeing the leaves form on the trees, not hearing no car engines, no sirens, no babies crying, not brushing my hair at night, drinking my Lipton tea, and not being able to go to bed early.

But right now, to tell you the truth, it don't bother me all *that* much. What is bothering me is my case worker. She supposed to pay me a visit tomorrow because my nosy neighbor, Clarabelle, saw two big trucks outside, one come right after the other, and she wondered what I was getting so new and so big that I needed trucks. My mama used to tell me that sometimes you can't see for looking. Clarabelle's had it out to do me in ever since last spring when I had the siding put on the house. I used the last of Jessie's insurance money 'cause the roof had been leaking so bad and the wood rotted and the paint chipped so much that it looked like a wicked old witch lived here. The house looked brand-new, and she couldn't stand to see an old woman's house looking better than hers. She know I been had roomers, and now all of a sudden my case worker claim she just want to visit to see how I'm doing, when really what she want to know is what I'm up to. Clarabelle work in her office.

The truth is my boiler broke, and they was here to put in a new one. We liked to froze to death in here for two days. Yeah, I had a little chump change in the bank, but when they told me it was gonna cost $2,000 to get some heat, I cried. I had $862 in the bank; $300 of it I had just spent on this couch I got on sale; it was in the other truck. After twenty years the springs finally broke, and I figured it was time to buy a new one 'cause I ain't one for living in poverty, even at my age. I figured $200 was for my church's cross-country bus trip this summer.

Jessie's sister, Willamae, took out a loan for me to get the boiler, and I don't know how long it's gonna take me to pay her back. She only charge me fifteen or twenty dollars a month, depending. I probably be dead by the time it get down to zero.

My bank wouldn't give me the loan for the boiler, but then they keep sending me letters almost every week trying to get me to refinance my house. They must think I'm senile or something. On they best stationery, they write me. They say I'm up in age and wouldn't I like to take that trip I've been putting off because of no extra money. What trip?

They tell me if I refinance my house for more than what I owe, which is about $3,000, that I could have enough money left over to go anywhere. Why would I want to refinance my house at fourteen and a half percent when I'm paying four and a half now? I ain't that stupid. They say dream about clear blue water, palm trees, and orange suns. Last night I dreamt I was doing a backstroke between big blue waves and tipped my straw hat down over my forehead and fell asleep under an umbrella. They made me think about it. And they asked me what would I do if I was to die today? They're what got me to thinking about all this dying mess in the first place. It never would've laid in my mind so heavy if they hadn't kept reminding me of it. Who would pay off your house? Wouldn't I feel bad leaving this kind of a burden on my family? What family they talking about? I don't even know where my people is no more.

I ain't gonna lie. It ain't easy being old. But I ain't complaining neither, 'cause I learned how to stretch my social security check. My roomers pay the house note and I pay the taxes. Oil is sky-high. Medicaid pays my doctor bills. I got a letter what told me to apply for food stamps. That case worker come here and checked to see if I had a real kitchen. When she saw I had a stove and sink and refrigerator, she didn't like the idea that my house was almost paid for and just knew I was lying about having roomers. "Are you certain that you reside here alone?" she asked me. "I'm certain," I said. She searched every inch of my cabinets to make sure I didn't have two of the same kinds of food, which would've been a dead giveaway. I hid it all in the basement inside the washing machine and dryer. Luckily, both of the nurses was in the islands at the time, and Juanita was visiting some boy what live in D.C.

After she come here and caused me so much eruptions, I had to make trip after trip down to that office. They had me filling out all kinds of forms and still held up my stamps. I got tired of answering the same questions over and over and finally told 'em to keep their old food stamps. I ain't got to beg nobody to eat. I know how to keep myself comfortable and clean and well fed. I manage to buy my staples

and toiletries and once in a while a few extras, like potato
chips, ice cream, and maybe a pork chop.

My mama taught me when I was young that, no matter
how poor you are, always eat nourishing food and your
body will last. Learn to conserve, she said. So I keeps all my
empty margarine containers and stores white rice, peas,
and carrots (my favorites), or my turnips from the garden
in there. I can manage a garden when my arthritis ain't
acting up. And water is the key. I drinks plenty of it like the
doctor told me, and I cheats, eats Oreo cookies and sal-
tines. They fills me right up, too. And when I feels like it,
rolls, homemade biscuits, eats them with Alga syrup if I can
find it at the store, and that sticks with me most of the day.

Long time ago, used to be I'd worry like crazy about
gaining weight and my face breaking out from too many
sweets, and about cellulite forming all over my hips and
thighs. Of course, I was trying to catch Jessie then, though I
didn't know it at the time. I was really just being cute,
flirting, trying to see if I could get attention. Just so happens I lucked up and got all of his. Caught him like he was
a spider and I was the web.

Lord, I'd be trying to look all sassy and prim. Have my
hair all did, it be curled tight in rows that I wouldn't comb
out for hours till they cooled off after Connie Curtis did it
for a dollar and a Budweiser. Would take that dollar out
my special savings, which I kept hid under the record
player in the front room. My hair used to be fine, too: long
and thick and black, past my shoulders, and mens used to
say, "Girl, you sure got a head of hair on them shoulders
there, don't it make your neck sweat?" But I didn't never
bother answering, just blushed and smiled and kept on
walking, trying hard not to switch 'cause mama told me my
behind was too big for my age and to watch out or I'd be
luring grown mens toward me. Humph! I loved it, though,
made me feel pretty, special, like I had attraction.

Ain't quite the same no more, though. I looks in the
mirror at myself and I sees wrinkles, lots of them, and my
skin look like it all be trying to run down toward my toes
but then it changed its mind and just stayed there, sagging

and lagging, laying limp against my thick bones. Shoot, mens used to say how sexy I was with these high cheeks, tell me I looked swollen, like I was pregnant, but it was just me, being all healthy and everything. My teeth was even bright white and straight in a row then. They ain't so bad now, 'cause ain't none of 'em mine. But I only been to the dentist twice in my whole life and that was 'cause on Easter Sunday I was in so much pain he didn't have time to take no X-ray and yanked it right out 'cause my mama told him to do anything he had to to shut me up. Second time was the last time, and that was 'cause the whole top row and the fat ones way in the back on the bottom ached me so bad, the dentist yanked 'em all out so I wouldn't have to be bothered no more.

Don't get me wrong, I don't miss being young. I did everything I wanted to do and then some. I loved hard. But you take Jessie's niece, Thelma. She pitiful. Only twenty-six, don't think she made it past the tenth grade, got three children by different men, no husband and on welfare. Let her tell it, ain't nothing out here but dogs. I know some of these men out here ain't worth a pot to piss in, but all of 'em ain't dogs. There's gotta be some young Jessies floating somewhere in this world. My mama always told me you gotta have something to give if you want to get something in return. Thelma got long fingernails.

Me, myself, I didn't have no kids. Not 'cause I didn't want none or couldn't have none, just that Jessie wasn't full and couldn't give me the juices I needed to make no babies. I accepted it 'cause I really wanted him all to myself, even if he couldn't give me no new bloodlines. He was satisfying enough for me, quite satisfying if you don't mind me repeating myself.

I don't understand Thelma, like a lot of these young peoples. I be watching 'em on the streets and on TV. I be hearing things they be doing to themselves when I'm under the dryer at the beauty shop. (I go to the beauty shop once a month 'cause it make me feel like thangs ain't over yet. She give me a henna so the silver have a gold tint to it.) I can't afford it, but there ain't too many luxuries I can. I let her put makeup on me, too, if it's a Saturday and I feel like doing some window shopping. I still know how to flirt and sometimes I get stares, too. It feel good to be looked at and admired at my age. I try hard to keep myself up. Every weekday morning at five-thirty I do exercises with the TV set, when it don't hurt to stretch.

But like I was saying, Thelma and these young people don't look healthy, and they spirits is always so low. I watch 'em on the streets, on the train, when I'm going to the doctor. I looks in their eyes, and they be red or brown where they supposed to be milky white and got bags deeper and heavier than mine, and I been through some thangs. I hear they be using these drugs of variety, and I can't understand why they need to use all these thangs to get from day to day. From what I do hear, it's supposed to give 'em much pleasure and make their minds disappear or make 'em not feel the thangs they supposed to be feeling anyway.

Heck, when I was young, we drank sarsaparilla and couldn't even buy no wine or any kind of liquor in no store. These youngsters ain't but eighteen and twenty and buys anything with a bite to it. I've seen 'em sit in front of the store and drank a whole bottle in one sitting. Girls, too.

We didn't have no dreams of carrying on like that, and specially on no corner. We was young ladies and young men with respect for ourselfs. And we didn't smoke none of them funny cigarettes all twisted up with no filters that smell like burning dirt. I ask myself, I say Ma'Dear, what's wrong with these kids? They can read and write and do arithmetic, finish high school, go to college, and get letters behind their names, but every day I hear the neighbors complain that one of they youngsters done dropped out.

Lord, what I wouldn'ta done to finish high school and been able to write a full sentence or even went to college. I reckon I'da been a room decorator. I know they calls it by that fancy name now, interior designer, but it boil down to the same thang. I guess it's 'cause I loves so to make my surroundings pleasant, even right pretty, so I feels like a invited guest in my own house. And I always did have a flair for color. Folks used to say, "Hazel, for somebody as poor as a church mouse, you got better taste in thangs than them Rockefellers!" Used to sew up a storm, too. Covered my mama's raggedy duffold and chairs. Made her a bedspread with matching pillowcases. Didn't mix more than two different patterns either. Make you dizzy.

Wouldn't that be just fine, being an interior designer? Learning the proper names of thangs and recognizing labels in catalogs, giving peoples my business cards and wearing a two-piece with white gloves. "Yes, I decorated the Hartleys' and Cunninghams' home. It was such a pleasant experience. And they're such lovely people, simply lovely," I'da said. Coulda told those rich folks just what they needed in their bedrooms, front rooms, and specially in the kitchen. So many of 'em still don't know what to do in there.

But like I was saying before I got all off the track, some of these young people don't appreciate what they got. And they don't know thangs like we used to. We knew about eating fresh vegetables from the garden, growing and picking 'em ourselves. What going to church was, being honest and faithful. Trusting each other. Leaving our front door open. We knew what it was like to starve and get cheated yearly when our crops didn't add up the way we figured. We suffered together, not separately. These youngsters don't know about suffering for any stretch of time. I hear 'em on the train complaining 'cause they can't afford no Club Med, no new record-playing albums, cowboy boots, or those Brooke Shields–Calvin Klein blue jeans I see on TV. They be complaining about nonsense. Do they ever read books since they been taught is what I want to know? Do they be learning things and trying to figure out what to do with it?

And these young girls with all this thick makeup caked on their faces, wearing these high heels they can't hardly walk in. Trying to be cute. I used to wear high heels, mind you, with silk stockings, but at least I could walk in 'em. Jessie had a car then. Would pick me up, and I'd walk real careful down the front steps like I just won the Miss America pageant, one step at a time, and slide into his shiny black Ford. All the neighbors peeked through the curtains 'cause I was sure enough riding in a real automobile with my legitimate boyfriend.

If Jessie was here now I'd have somebody to talk to. Somebody to touch my skin. He'd probably take his fingers and run 'em through my hair like he used to; kiss me on my nose and tickle me where it made me laugh. I just loved it when he kissed me. My mind be so light, and I felt tickled and precious. Have to sit down sometime just to get hold of myself.

If he was here, I probably woulda beat him in three games of checkers by now, and he'd be trying to get even. But since today is Thursday, I'd be standing in that window over there waiting for him to get home from work, and when I got tired or the sun be in my eyes, I'd hear the taps on his wing tips coming up the front porch. Sometime, even now, I watch for him, but I know he ain't coming back. Not that he wouldn't if he could, mind you, 'cause he always told me I made him feel lightning lighting up his heart.

Don't get me wrong, I got friends, though a heap of 'em is dead or got tubes coming out of their noses or going all through their bodies every which-a-way. Some in the old folks' home. I thank the Lord I ain't stuck in one of them places. I ain't never gonna get that old. They might as well just bury me standing up if I do. I don't want to be no nuisance to nobody, and I can't stand being around a lot of sick people for too long.

I visits Gunther and Chester when I can, and Vivian who I grew up with, but no soon as I walk through them long hallways, I get depressed. They lay there all limp and helpless, staring at the ceiling like they're really looking at something, or sitting stiff in their rocking chairs, pitiful, watching TV and don't be knowing what they watching half the time. They laugh when ain't nothing funny. They wait for it to get dark so they know it's time to go to sleep. They relatives don't hardly come visit 'em, just folks like me.

Whimpy don't understand a word I say, and it makes me grateful I ain't lost no more than I have.

Sometime we sits on the sun porch rocking like fools; don't say one word to each other for hours. But last time Gunther told me about his grandson what got accepted to Stanford University, and another one at a university in Michigan. I asked him where was Stanford and he said he didn't know. "What difference do it make?" he asked. "It's one of those uppity schools for rich smart white people," he said. "The important thang is that my black grandson won a scholarship there, which mean he don't have to pay a dime to go." I told him I know what a scholarship is. I ain't stupid. Gunther said he was gonna be there for at least four years or so, and by that time he would be a professional. "Professional what?" I asked. "Who cares, Ma'Dear, he gonna be a professional at whatever it is he learnt." Vivian started mumbling when she heard us talking, 'cause she still like to be the center of attention. When she was nineteen she was Miss Springfield Gardens. Now she can't stand the thought that she old and wrinkled. She started yakking about all the places she'd been to, even described the landscape like she was looking at a photograph. She ain't been but twenty-two miles north of here in her entire life, and that's right there in that home.

Like I said, and this is the last time I'm gonna mention it. I don't mind being old, it's just that sometime I don't need all this solitude. You can't do everything by yourself and expect to have as much fun if somebody was there doing it with you. That's why when I'm feeling jittery or melancholy for long stretches, I read the Bible, and it soothes me. I water my morning glories and amaryllis. I baby-sit for Thelma every now and then, 'cause she don't trust me with the kids for too long. She mainly call on holidays and my birthday. And she the only one who don't forget my birthday: August 19th. She tell me I'm a Leo, that I got fire in my blood. She may be right, 'cause once in a while I gets a churning desire to be smothered in Jessie's arms again.

Anyway, it's getting late, but I ain't tired. I feel pretty

good. That old case worker think she gonna get the truth out of me. She don't scare me. It ain't none of her business that I got money coming in here besides my social security check. How they 'spect a human being to live off $369 a month in this day and age is what I wanna know. Every time I walk out my front door, it cost me at least two dollars. I bet she making thousands and got credit cards galore. Probably got a summer house on the Island and goes to Florida every January. If she found out how much I was getting from my roomers, the government would make me pay back a dollar for every two I made. I best to get my tail on upstairs and clear everything off their bureaus. I can hide all the nurses' stuff in the attic; they won't be back till next month. Juanita been living out of trunks since she got here, so if the woman ask what's in 'em, I'll tell her, old sheets and pillowcases and memories.

On second thought, I think I'm gonna take me a bubble bath first, and dust my chest with talcum powder, then I'll make myself a hot cup of Lipton's and paint my fingernails clear 'cause my hands feel pretty steady. I can get up at five and do all that other mess; case worker is always late anyway. After she leave, if it ain't snowing too bad, I'll go to the museum and look at the new paintings in the left wing. By the time she get here, I'ma make out like I'm a lonely old widow stuck in a big old house just sitting here waiting to die.

# In the City of Sleep

## WANDA COLEMAN

"In caring lies responsibility" says the narrator of Wanda Coleman's story. The reference to Delmore Schwartz's poem "In Dreams Begin Responsibilities" helps to illuminate the story's revision of a proverbial theme: freedom to choose can be a terrifying one. In the case of Coleman's narrator, freedom is thrust upon her by a lover's untimely rejection. Coleman's dreamlike prose and the story's loose, ambling, meditative style also convey the narrator's probing for the center of self where traditional roles and relationships once stood. The story is included in Coleman's 1988 book *A War of Eyes and Other Stories*.

STILL I LOOK FOR LOVE. It eludes me. Still I look in this haze/night settling over me . . . ever it eludes in this City of Sleep. There's no love, no hate. Only being and being healed.

There's a war going on. There is so much of everything going on and going and going. My man is a soldier in this war, and I was waiting for him to come home so that we could be lovers again. So we could start to build a life together again. That life dismantled by the war in southeast Asia. The yellow war. The war for tungsten. The war I watched take seed after Korea, as a child in my parents' home while looking at the news on television. And at that time I wondered what the war could possibly mean to me. I was only nine years old and had no mind for men or the stuff of men. Laos was a funny word and its pronunciation eluded me.

He looked so tall and sad when we parted at the induction center. I still remember him standing there in his purple jumpsuit—that braid of gold hanging at his chest. God, he was so tall and bronze and *hey good lookin'*. And I had no idea why he was going or where. In a way I thought it was kind of nice—his going. This black man accepted into a military that had rejected my father in '42 as being "ground sick."

"What's ground sickness?"

"Hell if I know." And mother steered me discreetly aside. "They didn't like black men in the service."

And I understood. Somehow my questions to Daddy about what he did during World War II had hurt him. My curiosity had been prompted by the white chemistry teacher at school. He had told the class how he worked on top secret projects in the Army Air Corps and carried on daring correspondence with a Russian chemist. His children were very proud of him. I wanted to be proud of my dad too. Somehow I was denied and didn't understand why. Then I began to reason that perhaps it was a mistake to be proud of men who went to war and built death machines and had clandestine correspondences and killed other men. Men like my father, who didn't qualify for such activities, were superior. And my reasoning made me feel better.

Now my lover was going off to war and I was going to be alone. I feared I couldn't handle the idea that he might never come back to me. Even if he lived to return home, I knew he might not be returning to me. That knowledge made our last moments together very poignant. We both knew. It didn't stop me from babbling on about sending him "care packages" of homemade cookies, cigarettes, chocolate bars, and stuff. We kept trying to make each other feel there was some possibility. It was possible he'd return home whole; that we'd marry and have children. It was possible we'd buy a home in the suburbs on his G.I. Bill. That he'd get a loan against the home and use it to go into business. It was possible that I'd help him turn that business into a corporation. It was possible that we'd be modestly wealthy. That we'd be able to send our children to good universities. That we would retire early and live comfortably off our earnings, perhaps travel and see the world as we've both longed to see it. It was possible I could be faithful to him every single day he was overseas.

Dear Jane,

You know I don't want to hold you back. And you were such a nice young brown-skinned lady with a big future ahead of you. And I'd hate to be a stumbling block for you. I'd hate to hold you to a promise you made at a weak moment. I'm releasing you from your promise so you can get on with your life. Here is a picture of me with my Vietnamese girlfriend. We have good times together. You should see the insects here—biggest suckers I've ever seen in my life. And you can turn a corner and suddenly you're face-to-face with an elephant. And this heat—this fuckin' heat makes the Mojave feel like a deep freeze. Anyway, this is quite a trip. I just wanted you to know. You are free to be whoever you want to be. And with whoever you want to be.

Goodby. Good luck.

Whenever I am hurt, I go to the City of Sleep. It is warm and welcoming and I can be there until the pain heals. I lay in the park under the trees that sing. I sit on a couch of stones that surround and soothe me. Or I enter the hushed halls of buildings eager to salve me in solitude. Or I watch the glistening passengerless autos that flow silently along crystal avenues like fish aswim in a stream. I curl up and I go there. Adrift on and above my pain. Until it disappears and is forgotten. Then I return to the world. I wake and go on. Until the next time I'm hurt.

When I was little I always went to the City of Sleep after a spanking. I'd go there until I felt loved again and that I had learned my lesson and that it was understood that I'd never be bad or make that mistake again. I'd sleep through the afternoon or morning. And when I woke Mother always had something for me to eat. Or I could go and quietly watch television or play outside, understanding that the crisis had passed. After waking everything bad was gone. It was okay again.

I have thought about taking up permanent residence in that city. It's a wonderful, carefree place. But it's not enough to be free. Mere freedom carries with it the weight of responsibility. To be without care/responsibility/encumbrances. That is the ideal state. I've always thought of it in that way. I could always understand those who had to be free of caring about the world. Free of caring about what goes on in it. Or caring about things like skin color. In caring lies responsibility.

In my City of Sleep the days whiz by if I want them to. And to be free of care is also to be free of worry. I don't worry about what's at the end of my days, for example. I know what's at the end of my days—more sleep. Everlasting sleep. Lasting freedom from care.

When his letter came, I read it and went into shock. I was hurt to the bone. I turned on television and curled up in bed and reread his letter, over and over until the pages were damp and I was exhausted with tears. I had to be sure I had read everything—had wrenched from it all possible meaning.

*Here is a picture of me with my Vietnamese girlfriend.*

Why don't they allow women to go to war? So we can be near our men. So that they won't forget us. So that we won't lose them. So that we can watch over them. So that we can care and feel responsible for them. So that if there's a change we can understand what brought about that change a whole lot better. We don't have to be on the battlefield or get in the way. We can be on the sidelines, nursing, mitigating, observing, rooting them on. . . .

I sound silly. I tend to get silly when I enter the City of Sleep. Things get distorted. Lines are no longer sharp or clear. Colors mute, fade, run into one another. And I have to really concentrate in order to bring objects into focus. Distinctions are blurry on sleepground.

She is a very pretty woman, this new girl, the one in the photograph. Very pretty. She's tiny—a much smaller woman than I am. She has long straight hair that almost reaches her waist. She has on a "Susie Wong" dress of pink satin, and there are elaborate stitchings on it in silver thread. And he is sitting there in his camouflage uniform, holding his helmet on one arm and her on the other. There are cards and cigarettes on the table next to them, a bottle and two glasses. It looks like a hut, but it could easily be a club.

*I'd hate to hold you to a promise you made at a weak moment.*

Was that a weak moment? Was giving myself to him done out of weakness? I had never felt so strong in my life at that moment. I felt I had the power to will away war. I felt my love was so powerful, it protected him/would guide him safely through it and bring him back to me unharmed. Was that weakness? At that exact moment, when we lay naked and open to one another, I felt armored by our love. When he kissed me I felt my own strength redoubled as his flowed into me on his tongue. And I felt so strong and secure in arousing his nature. Knowing he wanted me, feeling him hard against my thighs. Was that weakness? It's so confusing. When he entered me, that incredible joy I felt as we joined—all of that a weak moment? And as we lay together in the long peace afterward, curled up and cooing in that delicious stink, clinging to each other as one. That was weakness? How could I mistake weakness for glory?

I'm missing something. What?

*I'd hate to be a stumbling block for you.*

He means love. Love is a stumbling block. Suppose he fell in love with her and wanted to marry her and bring her home. He knows I'll be here waiting. Or, suppose I met someone else and wanted to marry. I didn't realize it was possible for me to have that kind of joy with anyone else. I guess that's another way in which I'm silly. I believed all that stuff I was taught about love being eternal and unique. That once having loved it could never be the same again with anyone else. I guess I will soon find out. I will be free of caring for one man. Free of responsibility for seeing to one man's happiness. Free of one man's dreams. Our dreams.

In the City of Sleep there are no dreams. Sounds like a contradiction, but it's not. I just sleep. Dreams are full of cares and responsibilities. The City of Sleep is an alternate reality. There is nothing in that city that I don't want. No pain. No heartbreak. No people to involve myself with. Animals are decorative like shadows. They're quiet creatures —cats and birds. They ease round corners and flit from tree to tree. They enhance without creating disturbance. And that's very nice. I don't have to tend to them. They are a part of sleep.

In dreams I'm always busy doing things. My dreams are very exciting; they can be quite compelling—as compelling as reality—so compelling I often confuse the two. But when I don't enjoy the excitement, when I need a rest from them, when they turn into nightmares, I escape into the City of Sleep. The key word is excitement. There is no excitement in the City of Sleep. It is languid and tropical. The sky is forever blue. The houses are of white adobe. The sidewalks are of nephrite and marble. I waft along. I float. I'm just there. I never do anything. And nothing is done around me.

*I want to release you from your promise so you can get on with your life.*

I was getting on with my life. My life was structured around waiting for him to come back to me. I was making all these plans. He was going to be gone for two years. That's what he said—maybe three. Okay, so what was I going to do? Well, I was going to get a good job and work hard and save up as much money as I could. I was going to buy a new car. In two years, I'd have it just about paid for and it would be mine—ours. And I'd have enough money saved so that when we made the down payment on the house with his G.I. Bill, we'd be able to furnish it to our taste. And if we decided to have children within a year or two of that, the money would cushion against my being unable to work while I carried our child. It would also give him enough time to readjust to civilian life. I've always heard that soldiers coming back from war have a difficult time readjusting even under ideal circumstances. And that people who love them never understand. But I would be ready to understand him. I'd spend two years working hard towards that understanding. And while he was going through his adjustment period, I'd still keep working, and be patient and allow him all the time and space he'd need. And then, when he gave word, we'd get married. Of course, I'd set aside a portion of my wages to cover the wedding. I've always wanted a big fantasy wedding, or a traditional church wedding. Or, if he wanted, something small and intimate—it wouldn't matter. Just as long as we married.

I *was* getting on with my life. I had determined to stay so preoccupied in my planning, I wouldn't have time to miss him. Why would he say such a cruel thing in his letter. He was my life and I was getting on about him. And now it's all nothing. I certainly don't feel like getting up and going to work—ever again. I want to curl up in bed and sleep.

She's a very pretty girl. She has smooth yellow skin and bright white teeth. I've always heard that women in foreign countries have bad teeth. There's nothing wrong with her teeth. And her lips are very red and glossy. They shine. She looks as happy as I used to feel. Is it my imagination, or is that guilt I see in his eyes? His mouth is smiling. His eyes are not. They're narrowed and looking straight into the camera. He's trying to reach me.

*Yeah, she kisses as good as you kiss, Babe. She's different not better. She's here and you're not. You think I'm a sonofabitch. And yes, I know you would have waited for me no matter how many women I had as long as I didn't fall for any of them. You can get past the sex. It's the love that makes you crazy. And you think I don't understand women, don't you, Babe.*

I'm getting sleepy. I can hardly keep my eyes open.

Thinking about something too much usually makes me sleepy even when I've had a cup of coffee. But that kind of sleep always brings dreams with it. When I sleep tonight I won't have any dreams.

*You are free to be whoever you want to be.*

That's outright a lie. I'm not free to be with him in Viet Nam. I'm not free to confront him and his new girlfriend and call her a tramp and call him a dirty lowdown two-timer. I'm not free to make a scene and try and fight her for my man. I'm not free to be his wife. I'm not free to have his child. That is the who I want to be and I'm not free to be any of it.

It hurts and makes me angry—both. Because he's lying to me. This is the first time he's ever lied to me about anything. Why is he lying when this photo makes lying so unnecessary?

I'm going in circles again. It's the sleepiness.

Let's see—how many pills did I take? I can't remember. But I think I took enough. Three and I could sleep through the atomic bomb. And the best thing to do now is sleep.

I wish I could visit my City of Sleep and never return. I wish that. Because if I wake up, I'm going to have to do something. And at this moment I don't know what I'm going to do. Now that I'm free to do it. Now that he has freed me.

Upon waking I will have to take responsibility for myself. I will have to care for myself. I will have to find something to do. Damn it. I'll have to mother myself.

Can I?

I'll have to if I wake up. I'll have to.

# The Last Day of School

## MAXINE CLAIR

"The Last Day of School" is the uplifting final story of Maxine Clair's 1994 collection *Rattlebone*. The stories track the coming-of-age of Irene Wilson, a bright, precocious girl growing up in the mostly black fictitious community of Rattlebone on the hardscrabble outskirts of Kansas City. It is the mid-1950s, the era when *Brown* v. *Board of Education* made Kansas the center of the move to desegregate American public schools. In the first story of the collection Irene publicly betrays her grade school-teacher, a woman named October Brown who has been romancing her father and disrupting her parents' marriage. The act begins one of many unfolding lessons Reenie learns in and out of the classroom in *Rattlebone,* which culminate in this final tale. Reenie is now a graduating high school senior making application for college scholarship to a sorority of black women teachers headed up by none other than October Brown. As in much African American writing, life's cyclical aspect brings opportunity for redemption. Brown's forgiveness and Irene's triumphant emergence from a school and a town that literally will not be destroyed may be read as a parable of African American women's lives and writing in the contemporary period. It may more simply be read as a stunning example of the richness and beauty of short story writing by African American women.

WHEN THE TWO JET PLANES made the first pass over the north end of Kansas City, the noise jiggled the windows of our building. In our homeroom on the top floor, most of us bent low to get a look. Mr. Cox flashed one of his expressions that said we would never amount to a hill of beans if we kept this up, then went back to his reading. I collected my books, anticipating the bell that would scatter us to our first-hour classes. It was almost nine o'clock.

Before the government took over Blackwell Aviation Training, we spent many an afternoon listening to the prop planes drone like buzz saws as they went in for grandstand landings at the airfield a few miles from Douglass High. Jets, though, were another story, a new order of power, and they thrilled us.

That morning I wished for short sleeves. September nights often cooled down to the fifties, but the days could still heat up like the scorchers of August. Our windows were raised, and whiffs of honeysuckle drifted in. If I listened closely, I could hear scraps of chatter from the neighborhood women in the garden alongside the fence that encircled our stadium. They were busy rooting weeds and harvesting late collards. Again the jets' rumble approached, crescendoed overhead, and died away.

"You people try to do something, just one single thing that is productive today," Mr. Cox said. He stood up from his desk, and his lanky frame idled toward the windows. We weren't fooled. He loved to watch fighter planes go through their paces.

To show good faith in the "equal" part of "separate but equal," the state had made our school identical to Horace Mann High, right down to the last sand-colored brick. With all its sections and lawns, our building stretched a whole city block. If you looked out the west windows, you saw the manicured terrace, the wide winding steps and concrete walk that led to our sports field.

To the east, beyond the front lawns and across Emerson Street, Gethsemane Baptist Church stood facing the school and copied our beige brick as if it were an extension. Behind the church, the squat little place with the glass front and the pink neon NETTIE'S DINETTE sign lit up the neighborhood with the promise of something tender smothered in onions. Farther down the block, the Union Hall rose three stories, and that morning if I could have seen that far, I probably would have seen my father there, sitting on the steps, waiting to be called for a job.

Along with Nettie's, the Hall formed a little pocket of city life in our small-town neighborhood of two-story houses with porch swings, pear trees shading tricycles, backyards with trash drums tilting over. Douglass High School presided over this pleasant edge of Rattlebone with such stateliness that whenever out-of-town relatives came to visit, we made certain that we drove past the school on our way out to the lake, or to the real city in Missouri.

The two pilots, probably Air Force cadets, must have been determined to do it right this time. I saw them in the distance, holding formation, streaking along the horizon, wing-to-wing like two bullets across the autumn's serious blue. Then they curved in a wide arc and turned back eastward toward us.

"What were we supposed to do for Algebra II?" John Goodson whispered as he tapped my back with his pencil. I hunched my shoulders. I was not about to start again this year keeping him up on his math.

My eyes were drawn to the planes—two plus signs above the horizon, growing larger, heading in fast. They seemed locked together in their repeat maneuver, flying lower. Mr. Cox glanced out the window. John whispered, "Look at that."

The first-hour bell rang. Instead of joining the happy pandemonium in our halls, a few of us hung back, looking out the windows. In the garden outside, women stood up straight and looked into what strip of sky they could make out. Something in the way they strained to see organized everything around them. The very trees seemed tense. The rest happened in an instant.

They were coming in dangerously low, coming, coming. The pilot in one plane must have been trying to urge the other to pull up. Then the one climbed the sky in a sharp angle, exposing its silver belly to the sun. The other appeared to be locked into a steady plunge. Mr. Cox spun around and yelled, "Run!" The plane had rotated slightly, so that it seemed to be coming broadside straight for us. By the time we considered running, it was too late. The whole room exploded in a fury of glass.

Screams and cries, explosions went on forever. I remember seeing blood on my hands and my ears ringing. Mr. Cox on the floor. I became aware of the fire alarm sounding and a man's voice on the public address telling us which door to use. John and I held on to each other and bolted into a hallway jammed with other students. There seemed to be no way to get outside. Then we were a swarm in confused flight, darting down stairways, a herd of frightened cattle hurtling through the gym and out of the building.

Once outside, I realized that the school was not in flames. People were everywhere—women and men, some of them parents, mostly teachers—calming or calling out, persuading us to run down the slope to the football field. "Hurry!" "That way!" Sirens wailed. We got ourselves to the field. I remember that the ground was very wet. John, Cece, and I locked hands and sat on the grass with others who covered their heads, too stunned or too afraid to look at the fire raging just beyond our school. Suddenly I thought of my father. He might have been at Union Hall. I couldn't focus on what he had said that morning, or even if he had been home when I left the house. From the flames and the dense black smoke, I knew everything on the block, including the Hall, was gone. The three of us sat shivering for the longest time, refugees watching our homeland burn.

Then I saw him. Near the building. Running. It was definitely him. And my mother behind him, running with her arms in the air, yelling something. He reached back for her hand, and they ran down the slope toward the field. I stood up. Here was everything mother and father could ever mean, tearing through hell to get to me.

They wrapped me in their arms. With stricken faces, they said to calm down and stop crying. And no, my father had not gone to Union Hall that morning. He had tried, but he didn't get there.

"Mercy, look at your hand," my mother cried. "Let me see your legs."

My father tied his work kerchief around my hand. "I was about to go to the Hall," he said, "but Pemberton came by. Good thing he did."

"Lord, it's a wonder it didn't get your eyes," my mother mumbled, unsteady now herself. She touched my face. "We've got to take you to the hospital. You need stitches."

About that time police arrived with blankets. More fire engines from Quindaro and Armourdale. Ambulances with oxygen. Wanda and Mr. Pemberton came too, pulling Wanda's brother Puddin along by the hand. Medical people began washing and bandaging, taking us, four or five at a time, into the ambulances.

When the plane came down, it had, mercifully, missed our building by the flimsiest margin. The force of the explosion broke windows, rearranged desks, warped doors. Gethsemane lost its roof. Just yards beyond the church, where the plane finally blew apart, devastation was heaviest. One wall of Nettie's collapsed, and Union Hall burned to ashes, taking with it seven lives. Six other people died in their homes. Metal shaved whole second stories, shredded trees, and set most of the block afire.

The crash became the period at the end of the sentence about life in Rattlebone. After that, nothing was the same. In years to come, people would chronicle events using the crash as a time line. "Before the crash we used to . . ." "Ever since the crash . . ." For some, it remained a tragedy they would never get beyond. For others, it was God's way of putting things right, a new beginning.

Stories of terror and heroism covered the front pages of *The Kansan.* In the wake of the crash, the entire city seemed transformed. At first the pall of loss and grief paralyzed us. We saw the names of the dead, saw their kin at church. Strangers bearing flowers came to funerals and visited hospitals.

Then the focus switched to the survivors and rebuilding. Volunteers began right away on the houses. They put new windows in the school. Horace Mann High donated new, ornate front doors to replace the warped ones at Douglass, their "adopted" school. Every student who attended Douglass became a celebrity with a story to tell. I wore my bandages like medals. People thought, correctly, that this near miss was a miracle. A whole generation of Kansas City's black children had been spared.

At church Reverend asked all the young people who were students at Douglass to come forward and sit in the front row as testimonies of God's grace. Woolworth's on the avenue gave us a ten percent discount at the Colored Only eating counter.

Less than two weeks after the crash, businessmen—black and white—did what people said they should have done long ago. They launched a scholarship fund for the young people of Rattlebone in the name of the men who had lost their lives at Union Hall. Not to be outdone, the Mizells offered to reduce the price of their six-month training course in mortuary science.

Another token of goodwill came from one of the black sororities, the Alpha Kappa Alpha, in Missouri. During study hall one day after school had reopened, Cece and I sat at a long table in the school library and "researched" the comics in *The Kansan*. She showed me the article.

"You ought to do this, Reenie," she said.

"What?"

"Look—" and she pointed out the story.

It gave details about the sorority, explaining that they were a black "sisterhood" of teachers who were "dedicated to education for the future," and that they awarded a scholarship every year. It said that ordinarily they were active only in the state of Missouri, but now they were encouraging black girls on the Kansas side of the river to apply. Cece ran her finger down the column.

"Remember her?" she said.

My eyes followed her finger. As I read the words, my head cleared like I had suddenly inhaled something pungent and sharp. It said: *Qualified applicants should send letters of request for application to: Miss October Brown, Basileus; 4623 Claremont Avenue; Kansas City, Missouri.*

"Copy the address, why don't you," Cece said. "Who

knows, she might even remember you. You know how teachers love to take credit for brainy people, and she always thought you were smart."

I knew not to go into this any deeper; it wouldn't take much for me to feel like an eight-year-old with a lie bump on my tongue. I turned the page.

"I sure would write to her if I were you," Cece said.

I shifted the entire paper to Cece's part of the table and reached for my stack of books. I didn't need that kind of opportunity.

In the thick of the city's revitalization, my father counted his blessings. The way he told it, on the fortuitous morning of the crash, Mr. Pemberton had given him back his life. He had already left the house on his way to Union Hall when Mr. Pemberton waved him down and held him there on the corner "fumbling with facts and figures" for half an hour.

The deal was that Carl's Cleaners on Fifth Street was closing. The owner had died and the family wanted to sell the business. Mr. Pemberton wanted my father to go in with him and buy it.

"I thought he was crazy. Where would I get that kind of money?" my father said.

But Mr. Pemberton had insisted that at the very least they needed to talk it over. My father put him out of the truck and hightailed it up Seventh Street. That's when he saw the plane go down. The fires and the smoke.

He said, "Right then I felt handpicked. I knew the plane had fallen right on the spot where I would have been standing if Pemberton hadn't come by."

Many a night I listened at the vent upstairs as he sat at the kitchen table telling that story and explaining the practical side of destiny to my mother.

"Pemberton wants us to be partners," he said. "But he don't want to operate the place. He don't need the headache. If I kick in a few hundred and run the place full-time, he'll put down the rest."

My mother was leery. "What you know about running a cleaners, James?" she asked him.

"All I have to know is how to work the presses and how to count money," my father said. "The cleaning part is all by machine. You do it once, you got it."

She wasn't convinced. She brought up how, even during the good months, they could hardly see their way clear. He hinted that if she was so worried, she should get the "ironing customers" that she'd had for ten years to bring their clothes down to the cleaners. He insisted that if my mother helped him every day, they could do it all themselves. "Wouldn't have to hire nobody. We'd probably be making more."

Then my mother got to the part where I thought trouble might lie.

"Me and you living only halfway together as it is," she said. "What makes you think we can both work at the same place?"

My father didn't answer right away. My guess was that he didn't want to wake their sleeping dogs.

Then he told her, "One thing don't have nothing to do with the other. You ain't heard me make a peep, and I ain't heard you complaining either."

"Well, who's going to see to the kids?" she said.

"Don't worry about the kids. They all in school. Reenie can help. People do it all the time."

"I don't know," my mother said. But I could see my father was winning her over. Finally they agreed that they would try it for one year, and my father became part owner of Shorty's New Look Cleaners. When my mother bought the idea, she bought the whole concept, including the ridiculous name.

Those first few weeks had them fighting constantly. One day in the place, and I could see why. It had nothing to do with the cleaners itself. A delicate bell above the door announced each customer. That was fine. The chemical they used was not all that unpleasant. Admittedly, giant cones of thread did crowd the front counter a little, along with too many coffee cans crammed with buttons and pinking shears, but they only added to the feeling of easy comfort. My mother had moved her Singer from the house and it fit right in. She could have been inviting me to the YWCA for tea the way she presented the stool for me to sit on and the paper cup of cold soda pop.

However, the pleasant atmosphere evaporated the minute they both started up the pressing machines. As I watched the steam stream out and envelop my mother, I thought of the newsreels from war days, the pictures of factory women working single-mindedly, caught up in the cause. She was all rhythm and speed: lay out a sleeve, press, now the collar, press, now position the shoulder flap, now the tail. My father, on the other hand, though methodical, worked like a reluctant little boy. Even with a flat pair of pants, he would position and reposition a leg, checking it a few times before he lowered the press. Eventually, from what I could gather, they decided to divide the work, and after each of them established a domain, they stopped fighting. Junie and Bea had fits about having to stay with Wanda and Mr. Pemberton every evening until one of us came home. Except for that, we settled comfortably into our new routine.

Around the middle of November every year, the whole area geared up for American Royal Week—for the American Royal Parade in particular. Throughout the state, riding clubs outfitted themselves. Chambers of commerce, farmers, 4-H'ers, even the exclusive country clubs built lavish floats to show off prize steers, beauty queens, and enormous papier-mâché crops. Although we were barred from most of the pageantry, we were invited to the parade. In fact, each year our corps—our school band, together with the drill team, majorettes, and cheerleaders—was the only black anything in the parade. And so, in the undeclared competition of marching bands, we were bent on preserving our reputation for performing the most complicated routines with the tightest precision to the hippest marching music the city had ever heard. And above all else, we had to look good.

All the dazzle that could be drawn from the various combinations of crimson and white, and from the gold trim inside pleats, along seams, and around sleeves, was enhanced by the expertise of my father and mother and their now-excellent enterprise. That November, partly because I was a Douglass student, and partly because my father was a "new businessman," our shop was chosen to clean and repair all the uniforms. And we did it. Beautifully.

I loved our new status. You would have thought we were rich the way John and Cece teased me about the pink Cadillac my father was sure to buy. Maybe it wouldn't be a Cadillac, but my parents now had a savings account at the bank. We were sure to have a car before we got another truck.

People I had never seen before recognized me on the bus.

"You must be Shorty's daughter, I can see it in your face," they'd say. "Wilson, from the cleaners, right?"

We were fast becoming "established," and for a change nothing stood in our way. I could imagine myself waving college brochures with the best of them at school. I couldn't believe I had been so timid before, trembling over a name on a piece of paper, afraid to write the letter that could get me a scholarship. What could they do to me?

Without the least hesitation now, I sent for an application, and when it arrived, I filled it out, signed it, and sent it to Miss October Brown.

As the holidays approached, to my father's delight, business doubled. We had a good Christmas. One afternoon I walked the seven blocks in the snow to the cleaners just to take in how far we had come. Dramatic flourishes across the front window now announced my father's ownership in gold, trimmed in black. Through the glass I saw the two of them, my mother chatting while she sat on the stool and hemmed a pair of pants, my father with his back to the window, nailing up new Sheetrock on one of the back walls. He turned and said something to her. She paused in her sewing, laughed in the way she had of wagging her head, and tossed him a measuring tape. When she sat down again she noticed me. I waved and went on home.

By the time we finished dinner that same evening and I had done the dishes, they had settled at the table with the day's receipts. My mother clicked away on the adding machine while my father went over figures in their ledger.

"This right?" he said, and turned the book around for her to see.

"Yeah. Remember we said we'd change it next time?"

"Right," he said, and continued with his pencil.

"Guess what Maizy Carpenter told me," my mother said to him, and he looked up.

My mother clicked the keys a few more times and cranked the arm of the adding machine.

"She takes her drapes and slipcovers uptown and pays her weight in gold to have 'em done," she said.

"This time next year we ought to have a down payment on some new equipment," my father said.

"You reading my mind," my mother said. She raised her eyebrows and rubbed her fingers together as the sign of money to be had. "Maizy could be ours . . ."

At such times I noted that working together had changed them. They regarded each other with more good humor, casually, without defense. Yet when the night grew late, they fell back to the habitual estrangement of separate bedrooms, alone and apart. I wondered when that too would change.

At this point in my senior year of high school I understood some things. For one, what was past was past. Life for my parents was better now; they had more security. Perhaps they could also create something better between them. Something softer. Romance maybe.

From my perspective, opportunity flaunted itself every day. My father need only show a little more affection. My mother liked delicate things like the heart-shaped porcelain dish where she kept her earrings. And she had a birthday coming. I played around with the idea of suggesting to my father that he get her something with lace. It couldn't be a one-way street, either. My mother knew very well how much he liked jazz records. I could remember the times she had made lemon cake from scratch and dared us to touch it until he had had a piece. Little things, but special. This was what they needed.

The first time my father dropped my mother off without coming inside, I thought little of it. She seemed unconcerned and said he had to go back to the shop. A storm had been predicted, and when it began to snow, I expected him to be late. When it was still snowing the next morning and it was clear that he had not been home all night, I worried.

"I thought I told you," she said. "He stayed down at the shop. Wasn't no need to come home in the middle of the night just to go back this morning. I'm fixing some breakfast to take down there." Sure enough, she packed breakfast and lunch for him, and he shoveled his way to our door to pick her up.

The next evening when they came home, he stayed only to have dinner, get a change of clothes and a few things out of his toolbox, and he was off again.

"Haven't you seen the place upstairs yet?" she said. "I thought we showed it to you. It's a nice little apartment up there, but it needs plaster and a paint job."

I didn't even know they owned the upstairs. I asked if they were going to rent it out when it was finished.

"We'll see," my mother said.

This was in February. "Down in the hole of winter," my mother called it. One night in the middle of the week, she fixed us a Sunday meal—pork chops and fried apples with all the trimmings. Splurging, I figured, because winter was dull and prosperity had knocked on our door.

After the pork chops and before the hand-packed Velvet Freeze with chocolate sauce, Junie asked, "Why are we having all this?" as if we were being silly and being sensible had just occurred to him.

For the briefest of seconds, my father's eyes met my mother's and they both looked away. Something was wrong.

"Since when don't you want a little ice cream?" she said to Junie. "Some days need a little sprucin up."

Right then, I wanted to know what she meant, but we all went on eating dessert with my mother, father, and Bea making chitchat. My father finished first and got up to leave the table.

Junie said to him, "Daddy, you going back down to the cleaners tonight?"

"Yeah," my father said, and went on into the front room. I heard him throw himself down on the sofa. "But not right this minute," he yelled to Junie.

"Why? Why do you have to go back?"

Bea echoed, "Yeah, why?"

"That's enough," my mother said. "Y'all stop all the racket and finish eating."

My father came back to the kitchen doorway. "It's okay, Pearl," he said. "Ain't no need to wait no longer."

"Wait for what?" I asked.

"Let's all sit down in the front room, then," my mother said. "No need in making no big to-do at the table."

We all went to the front room. My father sat down on the sofa and rubbed his hands together. We sat down too. I knew that in the next moment some sweet part of our lives was going to turn sour.

My father looked first at my mother, then at us, then sailed right through it.

"Me and your mamma decided we'd like to live apart from now on, so I'm going to be living up over the cleaners and she's going to be staying here with y'all."

Nobody made a sound.

Then Bea hugged my mother's arm. "Nobody else's mother has to live by herself," she said.

"Well, look at Mrs. Coles," my mother said, making light.

"I knew it!" Junie said. He breathed hard, tuning up.

"Hey, June Bug," my father said. "How you think you're gonna like coming down on Friday nights and me and you going to get us some ribs?"

I could hardly believe it. I looked at them with their new united front.

"So you all are getting a divorce?" I asked them.

The look on their faces said I was right.

"We'll see," my mother said.

"What's there to see?" I croaked.

"That's enough, Irene," my mother said. "You just calm down before you get these children upset."

Because no more words could form themselves right then, I stood up and glared at them.

"Sit down, Irene," my father said.

I could hardly stand still for the torture in my chest.

"Girl, you better sit down now, this is between me and your daddy." She looked at him for support.

He said weakly, "Sit down, Reenie. Me and your mamma already worked this all out."

I could feel a big ugly sound welling in my throat, and I ran upstairs.

That evening they coaxed Junie and Bea into helping pack more of my father's things, and the four of them went to see the apartment where he would live. Just like that, our family was over.

Early in March, amid all this change, my letter of invitation arrived from the Alpha Kappa Alpha sorority. They wanted me to come for an interview a week later at Central High School in Missouri. I folded the letter. How could I back out now?

On the day of the interview, ominously enough, it began to snow a long wet snow. The ordeal of getting overtown to Missouri by bus gave me several chances to wonder why I should so blatantly tempt fate.

I waited outside the door of the office and saw a self-assured young woman leave before a Miss Boswell came out to get me. Miss Brown was one of the other three committee members who greeted me. Except for the fact that her vitiligo had spread to her neck and hands, she looked as I remembered her—a stylish and slender dark woman with a camel's prance and wild hair.

A gleaming tea service stood on a silver tray in the middle of the desk, and the women sat in chairs scattered over the office.

"Would you like some hot cocoa, Irene?" Miss Boswell asked. I declined the cocoa, but said I would like a cookie. That was a mistake. Once I took it, I had to bite it, chew it, and wipe crumbs off my face. One of the women hung my coat on the coat rack and admired my skirt. Miss Boswell told me to have a seat in the easy chair, set like an inquisitor's device in the middle of the room. They all drank cocoa. They asked me, and between swallows I told them, about my bus trip overtown.

Miss Brown didn't chat. Instead, her interest seemed fixed on my application.

"First, let me just say that this is the informal part of the process of selecting our girls every year," she said. "So relax, Irene, nobody's writing anything down." She smiled at me. "These are my sorors, Miss Cates, Mrs. Bracken, and of course Miss Boswell."

I said "How do you do" to each of them. Miss Cates began. "Talk a little bit about yourself, Irene, how you're doing in school, your hobbies, that sort of thing."

It was all there on the application, but I told them about my interests in drama and math. Miss Brown merely smiled. They asked me about my brother and Bea, and if we went to church. Nothing direct about my parents.

"Tell us, Irene, in your own words, why do you think you should have this scholarship?"

I had written what I considered an outstanding paragraph about why I wanted to go to college, but looking into their expectant faces, I couldn't remember a word of it. I only knew that I wanted some kind of future somewhere. I wasn't sure that I really answered the question, but I managed to convey that surviving the crash had made me think about my own future. That because of it, I had learned a lot about myself and other people. And that I believed I would prove myself worthy of their reward. Something like that.

They nodded approval as I spoke, and I assumed that they were not disappointed. As we chatted about what subjects I might pursue in college, I felt relief. It was not as difficult as I had feared. Miss Boswell got up to get my coat and said that I would hear from them in a few weeks, indicating that the interview was over.

"One final thing," Miss Brown said. "I'd like to ask you, Irene, if you had to name your worst flaw, what would it be?"

Miss Cates interjected, "It doesn't have to be something dreadfully wrong or ugly, Irene. Just something you'd like to work on."

I felt ambushed. Quickly I went down the mental list of the Ten Commandments. Did she want me to say *lying*? I feared God, honored my parents, I'd never kill or steal. Covetousness was the only commandment I could think of that I could break and still be a decent person.

"I guess it would be envy," I said. "Wanting what somebody else has. I guess that's what I would work on."

"Fine, fine," Miss Cates said. I sensed that anything I said would have been fine with her. Miss Brown looked amused and helped me into my coat. As she walked me to the door, she put her arm around my shoulders.

"You always were a crackerjack, Irene," she said. "You'll do well, no matter what."

On the bus, going home, I thought about her words. What did she mean when she said "no matter what"?

The hard winter held through the Easter holiday in late March. Yet more and more, a west wind softened the bitter edge of the cold. And then there were the robins. Foolish birds. Their song should really have been a complaint; they had returned to a desert of snow. Still, they managed to find an occasional spot of ground soft enough to yield a worm or two.

Perhaps I needed to know that a thaw was coming before I could finally go to visit my father. The cold evening that I walked to his place, I counted up the days. It had been more than six weeks.

I hadn't expected the place to be so nice. Nicer than our house. Nicer than the place Wanda used to have. It was a room, with an alcove bedroom and a tiny bath. It smelled like paint, and everything was so clean. So shiny! Even the wooden floor. My father was nervous, but he was excited, too. "Look at this." He had a bright blue studio couch with two pillows. The biggest thing in the whole place was his console—record player *and* radio. AM *and* FM. And he had a shelf now for all his records. "Did you see these?" All his dishes matched, and he even had highball glasses. In the little refrigerator-freezer he had one small pint of ice cream.

I could see that he was happy. I had to admit that I felt a little twinge of happiness for him. But as soon as I did, I began to wonder about my mother: perhaps he had actually abandoned her, perhaps she was protecting him, suffering in proud silence.

"And just who do you think saw to it that he got that furniture and stuff so he could move up there?" my mother said when I asked her about it. "Chile, don't you worry 'bout your mamma. She's always gonna get what she needs." A whole minute passed before she winked and added, "And we ain't goin another-further into that!"

Exactly one month after my interview, the letter arrived. Alpha Kappa Alpha. I took it immediately to my room and laid it on my bed. Not yet. I went down and opened a can of salmon to start croquettes for dinner. I chopped onions. I crushed crackers with the rolling pin. Junie and Bea came in and rifled the refrigerator. I peeled potatoes and put them on to boil. I couldn't wait. Upstairs again, I opened the letter. "Congratulations," it said.


They were juniors. All girls. They encircled us like angels shepherding the redeemed into the Promised Land. In white dresses they formed their traditional daisy chain around the graduating senior class and walked us en masse onto the football field, now set with rows of wooden folding chairs. Already the rest of the student body of Douglass High filled the stone stair-step bleachers. The promise of the feast to come wafted our way on smoke from the barbecue drums at the far end of the field.

The day wore its widest blue sky and wrapped itself in the scent of a million flowerings. From my seat in the first row with the others who would receive scholarships, I could see men finishing the roof of Gethsemane. Their hammers pumped silent blows that registered a moment later on our ears.

In my mind's eye I saw what I had seen so many times when I turned the corner where Gethsemane stood and followed the street for seven blocks to the cleaners now called Wilson's Cleaning and Tailoring: my father sorting while my mother ran the presses for the one-day-service shirts; my mother bending over him to examine a tiny moth hole that required an extra charge if she fixed it; him pouring half a Nehi orange soda pop into a cup with ice cubes and setting it on the sewing machine for her, then drinking the rest himself. Two contented people. Then at six o'clock my mother all but skipping out the door to her new worn-out '49 Ford that she drove like a bucking horse, and that she liked "better than all y'all put together," and she loved us a lot.

As I looked up at the suddenly quiet bleachers, at the faces turned toward us, the band started up. The Daisy Chain Girls began to serenade us with their version of "Thanks for the Memory." A jet plane flew over, drowning them out for a moment, but they came back strong. On the morning breeze the melody made its way throughout the whole of Rattlebone. The awards ceremony had begun.

# NOTES ON THE AUTHORS

TONI CADE BAMBARA (1939–  )
Born in New York City, Bambara took a bachelor's degree
from Queens College in 1959, the same year she published
her first short story. In 1964 she earned a master's degree
from City College of New York. In 1970 she edited *The
Black Woman: An Anthology*. In 1971 she published the anthology *Tales and Stories for Black Folks*. Her own best-
known books are the short story collections *Gorilla, My
Love* (1972); *The Sea Birds Are Still Alive* (1977); and the
novel *The Salt Eaters* (1980), which won the American
Book Award. She has also taught at Rutgers University.
Bambara presently lives in Philadelphia.

ARTHENIA BATES (MILLICAN) (1920–  )
Born in Sumter, South Carolina, Arthenia Bates received
her degree from Morris College in Sumter. After receiving
a master's degree in English from Atlanta University in
1948, she began teaching as an instructor at Southern University in Baton Rouge in 1956. She received her Ph.D. in
English from Louisiana State University in 1972. Bates was
first inspired to write by Langston Hughes, who taught at
Atlanta University while she was a student there in 1947.
Primarily a short story writer, Bates has received awards
from the National Endowment for the Arts and a Delta
Pearl award for literature. Her poetry and fiction have appeared in *Negro Digest, CLA Journal,* and the *National Poetry Anthology*. She is also the author of a novel, *The Deity
Nodded,* in which "A Ceremony of Innocence" is a chapter.
Her work has also been anthologized in books like *Black
Women's Blues*. Bates has retired from teaching and now
lives in her hometown of Sumter, where she continues to
write.

GWENDOLYN BENNETT (1902–1981)
Bennett was born in Giddings, Texas. A talented visual artist, she studied fine arts at Teachers College at Columbia University and graduated from Pratt Institute in 1924. Bennett's artwork appeared on the covers of prestigious black magazines and journals, including *Opportunity* and the *Messenger;* her writing, mostly essays and poems, appeared in a variety of publications, including *American Mercury* and *Crisis,* and she wrote her own column for *Opportunity* called "Ebony Flute." Bennett studied painting in France after receiving a scholarship and later taught watercolor and crafts at Howard University. She was one of the founders and contributors to the short-lived Harlem Renaissance journal *Fire!!,* where "Wedding Day," her only short story, appeared. Bennett returned to Harlem in the 1930s to become director of the Harlem Community Arts Center. She died in Kutztown, Pennsylvania.

BECKY BIRTHA (1948–   )
According to *Contemporary Lesbian Writers of the United States: A Bio-Bibliographical Sourcebook,* Birtha was born in Hampton, Virginia. In 1969 she left college and moved to Berkeley, California, where she witnessed the antiwar protests firsthand. She returned to school at State University of New York at Buffalo, receiving a degree in children's studies. She has since lived in Philadelphia. In addition to *For Nights Like This One: Stories of Loving Women,* Birtha has published the books *Lover's Choice* (1987) and *The Forbidden Poems* (1991). She is the recipient of a National Endowment for the Arts Creative Writing Fellowship in 1988 and a Pushcart Prize the same year.

MARITA BONNER (1899–1971)
Bonner was born in Brookline, Massachusetts. In 1922 she graduated from Radcliffe with a B.A. in English and comparative literature. She moved to Virginia, then to Washington, D.C., to teach high school. There she met Harlem Renaissance writers Langston Hughes, Countee Cullen, and Jessie Fauset, and with them frequented Georgia

Douglas Johnson's "S" Street Literary Salon. Her best-known and most important works were stories written during the 1930s, after she had moved to Chicago with her husband. The stories are collected in *Frye Street & Environs: The Collected Works of Marita Bonner* (1987). Bonner died as a result of a fire in her apartment.

HAZEL V. CAMPBELL (DATES UNAVAILABLE)
According to *Harlem Renaissance and Beyond: Literary Biographies of 100 Black Women Writers,* the only available source, Hazel Campbell published only two stories in *Opportunity* in the mid-1930s, including "Part of the Pack." The second, "The Parasites," appeared in the September 1936 issue. It describes the life of a young black couple on welfare in a decrepit urban apartment. Campbell is believed to be from New Rochelle, New York.

ALICE CHILDRESS (1920–1994)
Childress was born in Charleston, South Carolina, to a poor family. Though her early education was interrupted, she eventually attended Fisk University and won a Harvard appointment to the Radcliffe Institute. She began her career as an actor, performing and directing with the American Negro Theater in Harlem from 1940 to 1952. Her plays include *Florence, Gold Through the Trees,* and *Trouble in Mind,* which won an Obie Award in 1956. She is perhaps best known for her novel *A Hero Ain't Nothing But a Sandwich* (1973). *Like One of the Family: Conversations from a Domestic's Life* was first published in 1956 and was reprinted by Beacon Press in 1986.

MAXINE CLAIR (1939–    )
Clair was born and raised in Kansas City, the second of nine children. In college, she trained as a medical technologist and after a divorce worked as chief technologist at Children's Hospital in Washington, D.C., while raising two children. Later she earned an M.F.A. in creative writing from American University. Clair has published a book of poetry, *Coping With Gravity* (1988). Her short stories have appeared in *Antietam Review, Icarus,* and *The Kenyon Re-*

*view. Rattlebone* is her first collection of short stories. She currently teaches writing at George Washington University in Washington, D.C.

### WANDA COLEMAN (1946– )

Wanda Coleman was born and raised in Watts, Los Angeles. She participated in the Watts insurrection in 1965. Early in her career she was involved in theater and dance. She later wrote a teleplay that earned her a nomination for the NAACP Image Awards. She is the author of several books: *A War of Eyes and Other Stories* (1988), from which "In the City of Sleep" comes; *Heavy Daughter Blues: Poems & Stories 1968–1986* (1987); *African Sleeping Sickness: Stories and Poems* (1990); and *Hand Dance* (1993). All of these have been published by California's Black Sparrow Press. Her poetry brought her a National Endowment for the Arts Award for Poetry in 1981–82 and a Guggenheim Foundation Award. A recording artist as well, Coleman's most recent solo release is *Berserk on Hollywood Blvd.* (New Alliance). She also writes a regular feature for the *Los Angeles Times* on Los Angeles urban life.

### J. CALIFORNIA COOPER (193?– )

Cooper was born in Oakland, California. She has published four short story collections: *A Piece of Mine* (1984); *Homemade Love* (1986); *Some Soul to Keep* (1987); and *Some Good Friend* (1990). She was named Black Playwright of the Year for her play *Strangers* in 1978. She has also received the James Baldwin Writing Award (1988). *A Piece of Mine* was published after encouragement by Alice Walker, whose Wild Trees Press published the book. Cooper still works and resides in Oakland.

### ANITA R. CORNWELL (DATES UNAVAILABLE)

Anita Cornwell was one of the first black women to proclaim her lesbianism and to write about it. Her book *Black Lesbian in White America* (1983) contains essays on the theme of "womynhood," first published in journals like *Dyke: A Quarterly, Sinister Wisdom,* and *The Gay Alternative.* A former freelance writer and newspaperwoman,

Cornwell has also written one novel. She is a graduate of Temple University and once worked for the Pennsylvania Department of Public Welfare.

MARION VERA CUTHBERT (1896–?)

The little information available on Cuthbert has mostly been gathered up in *Harlem Renaissance and Beyond: Literary Biographies of 100 Black Women Writers 1900–1945*. The book reports that Cuthbert was born in St. Paul, Minnesota, and received her bachelor's degree from Boston University in 1920. Between 1920 and 1926 she served as a school administrator, then became dean of Talladega College from 1927 to 1930. She received her Ph.D. at Columbia, writing a dissertation entitled *Education and Marginality: A Study of the Negro Woman College Graduate*, published as a book by Garland Publishing in 1987. During the 1930s Cuthbert published a handful of essays detailing the problems of black men and women. In 1936 she published a poetry collection, *April Grasses*. "Mob Madness," published in *Crisis* in 1936, is her only recorded published story. Cuthbert worked as a professor at Brooklyn College until the 1960s. Her literary and life record since then is difficult to obtain.

RITA DOVE (1952–   )

Born in Akron, Ohio, Dove graduated from Miami University in Oxford, Ohio, attended the University of Tübingen in Germany as a Fulbright Fellow, and received an M.A. in fine art from the Writers Workshop at the University of Iowa. In addition to her short story collection *Fifth Sunday*, she has published the novel *Through the Ivory Gate* (1992) and several volumes of poetry, including the Pulitzer Prize–winning *Thomas and Beulah* (1985). She has also won numerous scholarships and awards, including the National Endowment for the Arts Fellowship and the John Simon Guggenheim Memorial Foundation Award. In 1993 she was named Poet Laureate of the United States. Dove is presently Commonwealth Professor of English at the University of Virginia and lives in Charlottesville, Virginia.

ALICE DUNBAR-NELSON (1875–1935)

Dunbar-Nelson was born in New Orleans, the city that provides the local color for her characteristic fictional portraits of Creole culture. Herself of mixed ancestry—black, white, and Native American—Dunbar-Nelson graduated from Straight College in 1892 and later studied at Cornell, Columbia, and the University of Pennsylvania. She married and took the name of the celebrated poet Paul Laurence Dunbar in 1898, a marriage that lasted just four years. Her first book, *Violets and Other Tales,* included poems, essays, and short stories. The second, *The Goodness of St. Roque* (1898), was the first collection of short stories published by an African American woman. Dunbar-Nelson was also the first African American woman elected to the Delaware Republican State Committee.

JESSIE FAUSET (1882–1961)

Born in New Jersey to an African Methodist Episcopal minister and his wife, Fauset grew up in Philadelphia in a large, stable middle-class family. In 1901 she attended Cornell, one of the first black women to do so on scholarship. She taught in high schools in Baltimore and Philadelphia before returning to school to receive her master's degree from the University of Pennsylvania in 1919. In the same year she became literary editor of *The Crisis* in New York. There she helped to "midwife" the Harlem Renaissance into being, publishing work by Countee Cullen, Jean Toomer, and Langston Hughes among others. Between 1924 and 1933 she published four novels: *There is Confusion* (1924), *Plum Bun* (1929), *Chinaberry Tree* (1931), and *Comedy: American Style* (1933). During the 1920s she also traveled to Paris and Africa. In 1926 she left *The Crisis* and resumed teaching. She married in 1929 at age 47 and died of heart failure three years after her husband's death.

JULIA FIELDS (1938–    )

Julia Fields was born in Uniontown, Alabama, in 1938, where she lived and worked on a farm until she was eighteen. A poet and short story writer, she has taught creative writing at Hampton Institute and has been a visiting poet at Miles College, East Carolina University, and North Carolina State University. Her short stories and poems have appeared in *New Negro Poets, Beyond the Blues, Massachusetts Review,* and *Negro Digest.* Her books include *East of Moonlight* (1973) and *Slow Coins* (1981). Her most recent book, *The Green Lion of Zion Street* (1988), is her first for children. She lives in Washington, D.C.

Nikki Giovanni (1943– )

Giovanni was born in Knoxville, Tennessee, and attended Fisk University in Nashville, graduating in 1967. She began her writing career in the 1960s, publishing three books of poetry early on: *Black Judgment* (1968), *Black Feeling, Black Thought* (1970), and *Re-Creation* (1970). After completing graduate work at the University of Pennsylvania School of Social Work, she became more committed to writing and teaching, earning teaching appointments at Rutgers University and Virginia Polytechnic Institute. She is the editor of *Night Comes Softly (Anthology of Black Female Voices)* and of a book of poems by Langston Hughes. Giovanni has received numerous awards, including a National Endowment for the Arts award in 1968 and a Ford Foundation grant.

Angelina Weld Grimké (1880–1958)

Born to a white mother and mulatto former slave, Grimké was raised in relative privilege and comfort in Boston, where her father was executive director of the National Association for the Advancement of Colored People. Grimké graduated from Boston Normal School for Gymnastics (now Wellesley College) and taught at Dunbar High School in Washington, D.C., the same place where Jessie Fauset worked. Most of her poems, short stories, and essays were published in *Crisis* and *Opportunity.* A play, *Rachel,* was produced in 1916. In 1991 Oxford University Press published the *Selected Works of Angelina Weld Grimké,* her only major book.

FRANCES ELLEN WATKINS HARPER (1825–1911)
Born a free slave in Maryland, Harper was educated in an academy for young blacks founded by her uncle. After schooling, she worked as a domestic beginning at age thirteen. In 1845 she privately published *Forest Leaves,* a prose volume, and in 1854 launched her literary career with *Poems on Miscellaneous Subjects.* She later married, and raised a daughter and three stepchildren after the death of her husband. During these years she worked for the abolitionist movement and was a founding member of the National Council of Negro Women. In 1892 she published her most famous work, the novel *Iola Leroy, or Shadows Uplifted,* the story of a mulatto woman who devotes her life to racial reform.

PAULINE E. HOPKINS (1859–1930)
Born the year Harper published the first African American short story, Hopkins's life extended to the very end of the Harlem Renaissance. She was born in Maine and educated in Boston, where she began her writing career with a four-act musical play about the Underground Railroad. She sang and performed with a family musical troupe when young, then took up stenography in the early 1890s. Her early short stories were published in the *Colored American Magazine,* where she became literary editor after successful publication of her first novel, *Contending Forces: A Romance Illustrative of Negro Life North and South in 1900.* She resigned as editor in 1904, when Booker T. Washington took over the magazine, in protest of his accommodationist politics. In 1916 she became editor of *New Era Magazine,* where she published her last work, the novella *Topsy Templeton.* Hopkins died from burns suffered when her dress caught fire while heating water on an oil stove at home.

ZORA NEALE HURSTON (1901–1960)
Born in the all-black community of Eatonville, Florida, where much of her fiction is set, Hurston moved north to attend school in Baltimore and later Howard University, where her first short story was published in the campus

magazine *Stylus* in 1921. She received a scholarship to enter Barnard College and graduated there with an English degree in 1928, meanwhile publishing short stories in magazines like *Opportunity* and *Crisis.* In 1925 she assisted Langston Hughes, Wallace Thurman, and Gwendolyn Bennett in founding the avant-garde journal *Fire!!.* Under the influence of anthropologist Franz Boas, Hurston began collecting southern folklore and transformed it into her major books of the 1930s: the folktale collection *Mules and Men* (1935) and the novel *Their Eyes Were Watching God* (1937). Other novels include *Jonah's Gourd Vine* (1934), *Moses Man of the Mountain* (1939), and *Seraph on the Sewanee* (1948). Hurston died poor in Florida. Her reputation has soared only since her death, boosted by her rediscovery and promotion by Alice Walker beginning in the 1970s.

GAYL JONES (1940–   )
Jones was born in Lexington, Kentucky, and received a B.A. from Connecticut College and an M.A. and D.A. from Brown University. In addition to her short story collection *White Rat* (1977), she has published the novels *Corregidora* (1976) and *Eva's Man* (1979). She has also written plays and published two volumes of poetry. Jones has taught at the University of Michigan.

NELLA LARSEN (1891–1964)
Born in Chicago to a Danish mother and West Indian father, Larsen attended school in California and later Fisk University. After receiving her nursing degree, she served as head nurse at the John A. Andrew Hospital and Nurse Training School at Tuskegee, Alabama, from 1915 to 1916. She moved to New York and became a children's librarian in Harlem from 1922 to 1929, during which time she began writing. Her 1929 novel *Quicksand* won the bronze medal from the Harmon Foundation; her 1929 novel *Passing* was her last. In 1930, the plagiarism charges surrounding "Sanctuary" (recounted in this anthology) caused her to stop writing. She worked briefly as assistant secretary for the Writers League Against Lynching, but toward the end

of her life worked mostly as a nurse in Brooklyn. Her awards include the first Guggenheim Fellowship presented to a black woman. Her travels took her to Denmark, the partial backdrop of *Quicksand.* Larsen's short, bright career ended unhappily but has been revived by recent republication of her novels and short stories.

MELISSA LINN (DATES NOT AVAILABLE)
It is possible that "All That Hair" is the only literary work Melissa Linn ever published. No existing records show any other work by her. *Negro Story* contributors' notes identify her as a resident of Columbus, Ohio. "All That Hair" won her the *Writers Digest Contest* sponsored by the magazine. Linn was born in Marietta, Ohio, and attended Ohio State University. She came out "educated up" with no place to go but the Depression. She apparently held numerous jobs during the 1930s, including working as a domestic, newspapering, and teaching adult education classes.

VICTORIA EARLE MATTHEWS (1861–1907)
Born into slavery, Matthews attended school and, like Harper, worked as a domestic when young. Her adult life was devoted to journalism and the promotion of civil and social rights for black women. She was a part-time reporter for both black newspapers such as the *Boston Advocate* and *A.M.E. Church Review,* as well as for white papers like the *New York Globe.* She also published children's stories. As an activist, Matthews was a member of the National Federation of Afro-American Women.

COLLEEN MCELROY (1935–   )
McElroy was born in St. Louis, attended the University of Maryland, and received a doctorate from the University of Washington. In addition to *Jesus and Fat Tuesday and Other Stories,* McElroy is the author of the short story collection *Driving Under the Cardboard Pines* (1990). She has received numerous awards, including a fellowship from the National Endowment for the Arts. She is presently professor of English at the University of Washington.

TERRY MCMILLAN (1951–   )

McMillan was born in Port Huron, Michigan. She received her bachelor's degree from the University of California, Berkeley, and did graduate work in film at Columbia University. She quit that program to join the Harlem Writers' Guild. McMillan has received numerous grants and fellowships. Her novels *Mama* (1987), *Disappearing Acts* (1989), and *Waiting to Exhale* (1992) have made her one of the most popular and commercially successful black writers of all time. She lives in San Francisco.

DIANE OLIVER (1943–1966)

Oliver's life and writing career were cut short by an auto accident when she was only twenty-three. Oliver was born in Charlotte, North Carolina, and graduated from the University of North Carolina at Greensboro in 1964. She later attended the University of Iowa Writers Workshop, which conferred a posthumous master's degree after her death. She published her stories in *Negro Digest, Red Clay Reader,* and *The Sewanee Review,* which published "Neighbors" in 1966. The story was selected for inclusion in *Prize Stories 1967: The O. Henry Awards.*

ANN PETRY (1912–   )

Petry was born in Old Saybrook, Connecticut. As a young woman she studied pharmacology. She worked as a pharmacist until 1938, when she went to New York and worked for both the *Amsterdam News* and *People's Voice* newspapers. Her first short story appeared in *Crisis* in 1943. "Like a Winding Sheet" was named the best American short story of 1946. She is best remembered for her 1946 novel *The Street,* which won a Literary Fellowship and sold more than one million copies. Her other books are the novels *Country Place* (1947) and *The Narrows* (1953). She has also written several children's books and was briefly professor of English at the University of Hawaii in 1974–75. She lives still in Old Saybrook.

ANN ALLEN SHOCKLEY (1927–   )

Shockley was born in Louisville, Kentucky. She graduated from Fisk University and later earned an M.S. in library science. She has worked as a librarian at several universities and is presently associate librarian for special collections and university archivist at Fisk University, where she is one of the nation's leading university archivists of black women's writing. Her book *Afro-American Women Writers 1746–1933* (1988) is one of the best and earliest comprehensive reference works on well-known and obscure black women writers. Her creative works include *Loving Her* (1974), a novel; *Say Jesus Come to Me* (1982), a nonfiction work; and her short story collection *The Black and White of It* (1980), from which "Play It, But Don't Say It" comes. She has won several major awards, including the National Short Story Award by the American Association of University Women (1962) and the Martin Luther King Award (1982) for literature.

RUTH D. TODD (1878–?)

Very little biographical information about Ruth Todd survives. Primarily a short story writer, her work appeared in *Colored American Magazine* while Hopkins was literary editor there. She is identified in a 1900 census as a black servant in a Philadelphia home. Two of her stories, including "The Taming of a Modern Shrew," are anthologized in *Short Fiction by Black Women 1900–1920*, ed. Elizabeth Ammons (New York: Oxford University Press, 1991).

GRACE W. TOMPKINS (DATES UNAVAILABLE)

Grace Tompkins's life and literary career emerge mostly from her connection to *Negro Story* magazine. Tompkins was an associate editor of the magazine starting with its second issue, July–August 1944, where her story "Justice Wears Dark Glasses" also appeared. Contributors' notes identify her as holding a B.S. in education from the University of Illinois, and as a contributor of stories and poems to *Opportunity*. She was also a music critic for the *Chicago Defender*, Chicago's leading black newspaper of the 1940s.

Tompkins regularly contributed fiction and poetry to *Negro Story* during its two-year tenure.

### ALICE WALKER (1944– )

Walker was born in Eatonton, Georgia, to sharecroppers. She attended Spelman College from 1961 to 1963, an experience that was the source of her novel *Meridian,* and graduated from Sarah Lawrence College in 1965. After college she returned to the South to work for voter registration. Her well-known short story collections are *In Love & Trouble* (1973) and *You Can't Keep a Good Woman Down* (1981). Her novels include *Meridian* (1976) and *The Color Purple* (1982), which won a Pulitzer Prize and an American Book Award. Walker has also published several volumes of poetry and books of essays, most notably *In Search of Our Mothers' Gardens* (1983). Most recently Walker has studied ritual female genital mutilation as practiced in some African countries, and written about it in the novel *Possessing the Secret of Joy* (1992).

### DOROTHY WEST (1912– )

Dorothy West, the only child of an ex-slave, grew up in Boston, where she was educated at Girls Latin High School and later Boston University. West won her first literary contest with her story "The Typewriter" at the age of eighteen. In 1927 she toured London with a stage version of *Porgy* and later visited Russia with Langston Hughes, intending to make a film about African Americans. Upon her return she became editor of *Challenge* magazine; in 1937 she founded *New Challenge* with Richard Wright as associate editor. During the Depression she joined the Federal Writers' Project of the Works Progress Administration. Her 1948 novel *The Living Is Easy* is her most memorable and important work. In 1995, West published *The Wedding,* a novel about the Negro elite in Boston. West lives on Martha's Vineyard and continues to write stories and journalism.

OCTAVIA WYNBUSH (1894–CA. 1972)
Contributor's notes in *Opportunity,* where she published at least one story and one poem, indicate that Octavia Wynbush graduated from Oberlin College. The little remaining published evidence of her life, gathered in *Harlem Renaissance and Beyond,* indicates that she received a B.A. in German from Oberlin, worked in a variety of teaching jobs throughout the 1920s, then published short stories with some regularity in *Crisis* throughout the 1930s. In 1941 she published a children's book, *The Wheel That Made Wishes Come True.* There is little publication record extant beyond that date. *Harlem Renaissance* also indicates that Wynbush married in April 1963, becoming Mrs. Lewis Strong.

## Primary Sources

Adoff, Arnold. *Brothers and Sisters: Modern Short Stories by Black Americans.* New York: Macmillan, 1970.

Ammons, Elizabeth, ed. *Short Fiction by Black Women, 1900–1920.* New York: Oxford University Press, 1991.

Anderson, Mignon Holland. *Mostly Womenfolk and a Man or Two: A Collection.* Chicago: Third World Press, 1976.

*Anglo-African Magazine,* vol. 1 (1859). New York: Arno Press and the New York Times, 1968.

Baker, Houston A., Jr., ed. *Black Literature in America.* New York: McGraw-Hill, 1971.

Bambara, Toni Cade, ed. *Tales and Stories for Black Folks.* Garden City, N.Y.: Doubleday, 1971.

Baraka, Amiri (LeRoi Jones) and Amina Baraka, eds. *Confirmation: An Anthology of African American Women.* New York: William Morrow and Co., 1983.

Barksdale, Richard, and Kenneth Kinnamon, eds. *Black Writers of America: A Comprehensive Anthology.* New York: Macmillan, 1971.

Bates, Arthenia. *Seeds Beneath the Snow.* Washington: Howard University Press, 1975.

Bell-Scott, Patricia, Beverly Guy Sheftall, et al., eds. *Double Stitch: Black Women Write About Mothers and Daughters.* Boston: Beacon Press, 1991.

Birtha, Becky. *For Nights Like This One: Stories of Loving Women.* San Francisco: Frog in the Well, 1983.

Bonner, Marita. *Frye Street & Environs: The Collected Works of Marita Bonner,* ed. Joyce Flynn. Boston: Beacon Press, 1987.

Chapman, Abraham, ed. *Black Voices: An Anthology of Afro-American Literature.* New York: New American Library, 1968.

———, ed. *New Black Voices: An Anthology of Contemporary African-American Literature.* New York: New American Library, 1972.

Childress, Alice. *Like One of the Family: Conversations from a Domestic's Life.* Boston: Beacon Press, 1986.

Clair, Maxine. *Rattlebone.* New York: Farrar Straus Giroux, 1994.

Clarke, John Henrik, ed. *A Century of The Best Black American Short Stories.* New York: Hill and Wang, 1993.

——, ed. *Harlem.* New York: New American Library, 1970.

——, ed. *Harlem USA.* Berlin: Seven Seas Books, 1964, reprint ed. New York: Collier Books, 1971.

Coleman, Wanda. *A War of Eyes and Other Stories.* Santa Rosa, Calif.: Black Sparrow Press, 1988.

——. *Heavy Daughter Blues: Poems & Stories 1968–1986.* Santa Rosa, Calif.: Black Sparrow Press, 1987.

Coombs, Orde, ed. *What We Must See: Young Black Storytellers.* New York: Dodd, Mead, & Co., 1971.

Cooper, J. California. *A Piece of Mine.* Navarro, Calif.: Wild Trees Press, 1985.

Davis, Arthur P., and Saunders Redding, eds. *Cavalcade: Negro American Writing from 1760 to the Present.* Boston: Houghton Mifflin Co., 1971.

Davis, Charles T., and Daniel Walden, eds. *On Being Black.* Greenwich, Conn.: Fawcett, 1970.

Dove, Rita. *Fifth Sunday: Stories by Rita Dove.* Lexington: University of Kentucky Press, 1985.

Dunbar-Nelson, Alice. *The Works of Alice Dunbar-Nelson.* 3 vols. ed. Gloria Hull. New York: Oxford University Press, 1988.

Elam, Julia Corene, ed. *The Afro-American Short Story: From Accommodation to Protest.* Ann Arbor, Mich.: University Microfilms, 1971.

Emanuel, James A., and Theodore Gross, eds. *Dark Symphony: Negro Literature in America.* New York: Free Press, 1968.

*Fire!! Devoted to Younger Negro Artists.* Reprint ed. Westport, Conn.: Negro University Press, 1970.

Ford, Aaron Nick, and H. L. Faggett, eds. *Best Short Stories by Afro-American Writers, 1925–1950.* Boston: Meador Publishing Co., 1950, reprint ed. Kraus Reprint Co., 1969.

Hamer, Judith A., and Martin Hamer, eds. *Centers of the Self: Short Stories by Black American Women From the Nineteenth Century to the Present.* New York: Hill and Wang, 1994.

Hill, Herbert, ed. *Soon One Morning: New Writing by American Negroes 1940–1962.* New York: Alfred A. Knopf, 1963.

Hughes, Langston, ed. *The Best Short Stories by Negro Writers.* Boston: Little Brown and Co., 1967.

Hurston, Zora Neale. *Spunk: The Selected Short Stories of Zora Neale Hurston.* Berkeley, Calif.: Turtle Island Foundation, 1985.

James, Charles L., ed. *From the Roots: Short Stories by Black Americans.* New York: Dodd, Mead & Co., 1973.

Johnson, Charles S., ed. *Ebony and Topaz: A Collecteana.* New York: Opportunity: Journal of Negro Life, National Urban League, 1927; reprinted by Freeport: Books for Libraries Press, 1971.

Jones, Gayl. *White Rat.* New York: Random House, 1977.

Jones, Leroi (Amiri Baraka), and Larry Neal, eds. *Black Fire.* New York: William Morrow, 1969.

Kanwar, Asha, ed. *The Unforgetting Heart: An Anthology of Short Stories by African American Women (1859–1993).* San Francisco: Aunt Lute Books, 1993.

King, Woodie, Jr., ed. *Black Short Story Anthology.* New York: Columbia University Press, 1972.

Knopf, Marcy, ed. *The Sleeper Wakes: Harlem Renaissance Stories by Women.* Rutgers, N.J.: Rutgers University Press, 1993.

Long, Richard, and Eugenia Collier, eds. *Afro-American Writing.* vol. 2. New York: New York University Press, 1972.

Marshall, Paule. *Reena and Other Stories.* Old Westbury, N.Y.: Feminist Press, 1983.

———. *Soul Clap Hands and Sing.* Chatham, N.J.: Chatham Bookseller, 1961.

McElroy, Colleen. *Jesus and Fat Tuesday and Other Stories.* Berkeley, Calif.: Creative Arts Book Co., 1987.

McMillan, Terry, ed. *Breaking Ice: An Anthology of African-American Fiction.* New York: Penguin, 1990.

Mirer, Martin, ed. *Modern Black Stories.* Woodbury, N.Y.: Barron's Educational Series, 1971.

Moraga, Cherríe, and Gloria Anzaldúa, eds. *This Bridge Called My Back: Writings by Radical Women of Color.* Watertown, Mass.: Persephone, 1981.

Naylor, Gloria. *The Women of Brewster Place: A Novel in Seven Stories.* New York: Viking Press, 1982.

Petry, Ann. *Miss Muriel and Other Stories.* Boston: Houghton Mifflin, 1971; reprinted Boston: Beacon Press, 1989.

Reed, Ishmael, *19 Necromancers from Now.* Garden City, N.Y.: Doubleday & Co., 1970.

Sanchez, Sonia, ed. *We Be Word Sorcerers: 25 Stories by Black Americans.* New York: Bantam Books, 1973.

Shockley, Ann Allen. *Afro-American Women Writers 1746–1933.* New York: Penguin, 1988.

———. *The Black and White of It.* Tallahassee, Fla.: Naiad Press, 1980.

Shuman, R. Baird, ed. *A Galaxy of Black Writing.* Durham, N.C.: Moore Pub. Co., 1970.

Smith, Barbara, ed. *Home Girls: A Black Feminist Anthology.* New York: Kitchen Table, Women of Color Press, 1983.

Stadler, Quandara Prettyman, ed. *Out of Our Lives: A Selection of Contemporary Black Fiction.* Washington: Howard University Press, 1978.

Turner, Darwin T., ed. *Black American Literature—Fiction.* Columbus, Ohio: Charles E. Merrill, 1969.

Walker, Alice. *In Love & Trouble: Stories of Black Women.* San Diego: Harcourt Brace Jovanovich, 1973.

———. *You Can't Keep a Good Woman Down.* San Diego: Harcourt Brace Jovanovich, 1981.

Washington, Mary Helen, ed. *Black-eyed Susans: Classic Stories by and about Black Women.* Garden City, N.Y.: Anchor Press/Doubleday, 1975.

———, ed. *Invented Lives: Narratives of Black Women 1860–1960.* New York: Doubleday, 1987.

———, ed. *Midnight Birds: Stories of Contemporary Black American Writers.* Garden City, N.Y.: Anchor Press/Doubleday, 1980.

# Secondary Sources

*Afro-American Writers from the Harlem Renaissance to 1940.* Dictionary of Literary Biography, vol. 51. Detroit: Gale Research Press, 1987.

Baker, Houston. *Workings of the Spirit: The Poetics of Afro-American Women's Writing.* Chicago: University of Chicago Press, 1991.

bell hooks. *Yearning: race, gender, and cultural politics.* Boston: South End Press, 1990.

———. *Ain't I a Woman.* Boston: South End Press, 1981.

Bell, Roseann, et al., eds. *Sturdy Black Bridges: Visions of Black Women in Literature.* Garden City, N.Y.: Anchor, 1979.

Bullock, Penelope. *The Afro-American Periodical Press 1838–1909.* Baton Rouge: Louisiana State University Press, 1981.

Carby, Hazel. *Reconstructing Womanhood.* New York: Oxford University Press, 1987.

Daniel, Walter C. *Black Journals of the United States.* Westport, Conn.: Greenwood Press, 1982.

Dann, Martin E., ed. *The Black Press 1827–1890.* New York: G.P. Putnam's Sons, 1971.

Evans, Mari, ed. *Black Women Writers (1950–1980): A Critical Evaluation.* Garden City, N.Y.: Anchor Press, 1984.

Hull, Gloria T., Patricia Bell Scott, and Barbara Smith, eds. *All the Women Are White, All the Blacks Are Men, But Some of Us Are Brave.* Old Westbury, N.Y.: Feminist Press, 1982.

Johnson, Abby Arthur, and Ronald Maberry Johnson, eds. *Propaganda and Aesthetics: The Literary Politics of Afro-American Magazines in the Twentieth Century.* Amherst: University of Massachusetts Press, 1979.

Kellner, Bruce, ed. *The Harlem Renaissance: A Historical Dictionary for the Era.* Westport, Conn.: Greenwood Press, 1984.

Perry, Margaret. *Silence to the Drums: A Survey of the Literature of the Harlem Renaissance.* Westport, Conn.: Greenwood, 1976.

Pollack, Sandra, and Denise D. Knight, eds. *Contemporary Lesbian Writers of the United States: A Bio-Bibliographical Sourcebook.* Westport, Conn.: Greenwood Press, 1993.

Pryse, Marjorie, and Hortense J. Spillers, eds. *Conjuring: Black Women, Fiction, and Literary Tradition.* Bloomington: Indiana University Press, 1985.

Roses, Lorraine Elena, and Ruth Elizabeth Randolph, eds. *Harlem Renaissance and Beyond: Literary Biographies of 100 Black Women Writers 1900–1945.* Boston: G.K. Hall, 1990.

Shockley, Ann Allen. *Afro-American Women Writers 1746–1933: An Anthology and Critical Guide.* Boston: G.K. Hall and Co., 1988.

Shockley, Ann Allen, and Sue P. Chandler, eds. *Living Black American Authors: A Biographical Dictionary.* New York: R.R. Bowker and Co., 1973.

Tate, Claudia, ed. *Black Women Writers at Work.* New York: Continuum, 1983.

Walker, Alice. *Living by the Word: Selected Writings 1973–1987.* San Diego: Harcourt Brace, 1987.

————. *In Search of Our Mothers' Gardens.* San Diego: Harcourt Brace Jovanovich, 1983.

Willis, Susan. *Specifying: Black Women Writing the American Experience.* Madison: University of Wisconsin Press, 1987.

Yancy, Preston, ed. *The Afro-American Short Story: A Comprehensive and Annotated Index with Selected Commentaries.* Westport, Conn.: Greenwood Press, 1986.